WHEN THE BOUGH BREAKS

June Considine was born in Dublin. Over twenty years, she has written extensively for children and young adults. Her published works include the acclaimed 'Luvender' fantasy series and the 'Beachwood' series for teenagers. Her short stories have been included in a number of British and American anthologies, and she was short-listed for the 2001 Hennessy Award. June has also worked extensively as a freelance journalist and editor. *When the Bough Breaks* is her first adult fiction novel. She lives with her husband in Malahide, Co Dublin.

JUNE CONSIDINE

WHEN THE
BOUGH BREAKS

**NEW
ISLAND**

Copyright © 2002 June Considine

WHEN THE BOUGH BREAKS
First published May 2002
by New Island
2 Brookside
Dundrum Road
Dublin 14

This edition published 2003

The author has asserted her moral right.

ISBN 1 902602 86 2

British Library Cataloguing in Publication Data.
A CIP catalogue record for this book is available
from the British Library.

Typeset by New Island
Cover design by Artmark/Sin É Design
Printed by Norhaven Paperback A/S

New Island received financial assistance from The Arts Council, (An
Chomhairle Ealaíon), Dublin, Ireland.

10 9 8 7 6 5 4 3 2 1

To my husband Sean
With love

Rock-a-bye baby on the tree top Rock-a-bye baby on the tree top Rock-a-bye baby on the tree top Rock-a-bye baby on the tree top Rock-

-bye bal Part One e tree top

Rock-a-b 1957–1971 n the tree

top Rock-a-bye baby on the tree top Rock-a-bye baby on the tree top Rock-a-bye baby on the tree top Rock-

-bye baby on the tree top Rock-a-bye baby on the tree top Rock-a-bye baby on the

CHAPTER ONE

Her father was a magic musician. Mr Music Man.

"Dance, Beth, dance!" he shouted. "Dance, my pretty girl." He played for Beth, tapping his big black boots off the kitchen floor. It was dark outside the window and she wanted to keep dancing on her toes … on and on and on … until the sun came up again and chased the monster away.

The monster lived upstairs in the wardrobe with the mothball smell and the old clothes Mammy did not wear any more, hiding small and mean until the light went out and Beth was all alone. He hid behind the red dress with the velvet buttons and made noise when he touched it, soft as trees whispering in her room. She knew he would carry her away in his arms as soon as she fell asleep.

"Your mother was the talk of the town when she wore that dress to the Emerald Ballroom." Her father winked when he told the story of the red dress. His words made pictures in her mind. The spotlight spinning rainbow colours in the Emerald Ballroom and the feet of the dancers crashing thunder as they danced up and down, in and out, round and round to his magic music. Her mother was a bright flame and the dancers whirled her away from the stage where Mr Music Man stood tall and handsome, playing magic tunes only for her.

"All the boys whistled at her, Beth. But I was the only one she heard." He moved his fingers up and down the keyboard and the accordion sang sweet and high. "I danced my pretty lady the whole way home and changed her name to Tyrell."

"A pity I bothered listening." Beth's mother tossed her hair and frowned. "Will you stop filling the child's head with your nonsense, Barry Tyrell. It's way past her bedtime." She took out her knitting and clicked the needles. She wrapped pale pink wool around her fingers. Beside the fire Sara lay in her Moses basket, tiny under the pink blanket. She had little fingers and a bump where her belly button should be. Her mother powdered it and shouted if Beth touched the soft place on top of her head. "Bold *bold* girl! I told you to leave the baby alone. You'll hurt her."

Beth's father put his accordion in the cubby hole under the stairs and she felt herself growing smaller, curled up tight inside when he lifted her on his shoulders and carried her up the stairs. He blew kisses with his fingers and turned out the light. The darkness sighed around her.

In the Emerald Ballroom the dancers were waiting for Mr Music Man and off he went when the van with 'Anaskeagh Ceili Band' written on the side and shamrocks for dots above the 'i' letters stopped outside the house. Her mother climbed the stairs, making shushing noises when

Sara cried, love noises that Beth could no longer hear when their bedroom door closed. She wanted to be with them, snuggled warm and cosy under the eiderdown with only the clock ticking in the dark and the baby smells.

On the road outside she heard the van. Her father was coming home to chase the monster away. He would chop the wardrobe into matchsticks. She waited for the squeaky sound he made when he whistled but the van went by the house … away … away … and the light went chasing along the wall and along the wardrobe and the monster was free. She could see his devil face. His breath tickled her cheeks. Her hair lifted when he put his claws on her head. Even when she hid under the pillow she could see his bold eyes watching.

She cried, quietly at first. But the sound kept coming up her throat and burst right out of her mouth. Her mother was sleepy-cross when she came into the room. She wore a nightdress to her toes and her hair hung over her face. "How often must I tell you? There's no monster. Stop being such a silly girl. If I hear any more of your nonsense I'll have to bring up Charlie." She pulled down Beth's pyjama bottoms and slapped her bummy … stingy pains down her legs and the door closed hard.

Charlie hung on a hook behind the kitchen door. A bamboo cane that her father called "an instrument of torture". He threatened to break it in half. He never did. Nor did he chop the wardrobe into matchsticks. Charlie hurt more than her mother's hand so Beth did not make a sound when the monster sighed and growled and crept to the wall, watching her, ready to carry her away if she fell asleep.

CHAPTER TWO

For weeks before Christmas the women came to Fatima Parade with patterns and pictures cut from magazines. In her sewing room with the door closed, Marjory Tyrell cut and tucked and stitched and spoke to her customers with her mouth full of pins. Every time Beth opened the front door and another woman entered the sewing room, begging Marjory to please *please* try and fit her in, she wanted to scream with annoyance. Her Christmas dress needed sleeves and a hem and lay forgotten on the shelf alongside the material for her new coat. If she asked when it would be ready Marjory got cross and said Christmas was not just about new dresses or presents from Santy Claus. It was the birthday of the baby Jesus and Beth should remember that *He* was born in a manger and wrapped only in swaddling clothes. He did not go on and on about green velvet dresses or demand expensive presents because he understood the meaning of money and how difficult it was to earn it.

Sara's dress was finished. So was her navy coat with the silver buttons down the front and across the shoulders. At the children's mass on Christmas Day, she would carry the baby Jesus in her arms up the aisle of the church. Whenever Beth thought about it she fell into a sulk. Usually, the girl chosen to carry the baby Jesus was older than Sara, who was only four. Uncle Tom said she was a natural born angel and Fr Breen agreed.

"That brother of yours is a right fixer," said her father when he heard the news. Beth could see he was really pleased but her mother's mouth tightened as if he had said something mean. She told him he should be proud of his youngest daughter instead of making his usual smart remarks about Tom Oliver, who was the most successful businessman in Anaskeagh.

"A successful chancer, you mean." He winked at Beth. "He may be able to pull the wool over the eyes of the world but Barry Tyrell is no man's fool when it comes to spotting a chancer. Isn't that a fact, Beth?"

He winked again but she was afraid to smile at him in case her mother saw and took down Charlie.

Uncle Tom owned a factory and a fancy furniture shop. He called his shop "his showrooms" and put red notices in the window about 'Unbeatable Bargains'. When he called to Beth's house he did not knock on the front door. "Anybody home?" he shouted, opening the door with his own key. He brought gifts, presents for Christmas and for the girls' birthdays, broken furniture from his factory and envelopes with money. When no one wanted new clothes and people no longer danced to the music of the Anaskeagh Ceili Band, he opened the kitchen press and placed the envelopes behind the milk jug.

"When are you going to get yourself a real job, Mr Music Man?" He slapped Beth's father on his back and jerked him forward. "One that supports Marjory and the children? Just say the word and I'll fix you up tomorrow. A regular wage and the delivery van to take home with you in the evenings."

"I'm well able to look after my own family, thank you very much." Barry's face turned red, a rash of anger on his cheeks. "When I want charity I'll ask for it. But you'll see me eat grass first."

After he left, Marjory always smiled and said, "Thank God for the goodness of Tom. I dread to think how we would manage without his kindness."

Barry talked about moving to Dublin where he could get proper work with a proper band in proper dance halls. There was nothing "proper" about Anaskeagh, he said. It suffocated him, its small-town gossip, with people interfering in other people's business and running to the confession box every time they put a little finger out of place. He would die rather than drive a delivery van for Tom Oliver. That was the beginning and the end of the matter. The sooner they all moved the better.

He told Beth about the wide streets in Dublin and the lights shining in shop windows, and how the women in their clicking high heels and red lipstick always met their boyfriends at the foot of Nelson's Pillar. He promised to climb to the top of the pillar with her. They would enter the clouds and touch the stars, and the world below would be so tiny she would think she was in heaven.

"Dear me, Beth, what a cross little thing you are today," said Aunty May when she called to Fatima Parade on Christmas Eve to collect her new dress.

Uncle Tom had a pet name for May. She was his "Blossom", he said, as fair as the fields of May. He kissed her on her lips when people were looking, which, said Marjory, puckering up her mouth as if she had seen something bold, was a very rude thing to do. A bad example to set in front of the children.

"Right you are then, my fine girls. We've got a turkey to pluck." After they finished dinner and Marjory had returned to her sewing room, Barry carried the turkey into the kitchen. It had been hanging in the shed since Uncle Tom gave it to them the previous Saturday. He won it playing golf. His third turkey, he said, smiling at Beth with his big teeth, and what else would he do with it except give it to his favourite sweetheart.

Barry cut off the feet and pulled the sinews so that the claws wiggled. When it seemed as if they were dancing, he chased the girls around the kitchen. Beth did not want to make any noise in case it disturbed their mother but Sara shrieked. She ran round the table with her father chasing, pretending he could not catch her. Beth's heart thumped. She knew her mother would hear and say it was her fault for not setting a good example. She imagined Charlie on her legs, the pain running hot to her toes. When Marjory came out of the sewing room she was as angry as Beth expected but she used her hand instead of Charlie.

Afterwards, she said: "Let that be a warning to you,

young madam. Next time I have to come out you'll feel the full weight of my cane on your fat backside."

"Don't be so hard on her," shouted Barry. "It's Christmas, for Christ's sake. All we're doing is having a bit of fun."

"I wish I had time for fun," she shouted back and slammed the sewing room door behind her.

He put cold water on Beth's legs and said the magic chant that made pain go away. Only the pain would not go away. She wanted him to go into the sewing room and tell her mother she had been quiet, as good as gold. Even when the horrible sharp claws scraped her cheek she had hugged the shout into herself. Sara was too excited about the baby Jesus to care, showing off with her doll in her arms and marching up and down the stairs, not helping to make the breadcrumbs for the stuffing or putting the feathers into the sack.

It was dark when Beth was called into the sewing room. The floor was covered with pieces of material and empty thread spools. Marjory pulled the dress over her head and stood behind her, staring into the long mirror. The dress was green and had a lace collar that could be taken off and washed separately. It was identical to the one she had made for Sara but it looked different on Beth, too tight at her waist where the wide white sash tied in a bow. Her ankles looked thin as sticks peering from beneath the hem.

"That will do you fine." Marjory snipped a loose thread. She sounded so relieved that Beth was afraid to say anything about her new coat. The parcel of material was still on the shelf, still tied with twine. Her mother followed her gaze and frowned. "You'll have to manage with your school coat.

It'll be fine after a good brushing." She locked the door of the sewing room and suddenly grabbed Beth's hand the way Jess did in school when she was excited about something.

"I've escaped from prison!" She laughed and swung Beth's arm up and down in the air, forgetting all about Charlie and the turkey claws until she entered the kitchen with the feathers and the breadcrumbs over the floor and the giblets leaking blood on the draining board. When she saw Beth's father sitting in front of the fire with a glass of stout in his hand she burst into tears and called him "a lazy, good-for-nothing slob".

"Oh … for Christ's sake, you're not the only one who's tired around here." He shouted and banged the glass of stout on the arm of the chair so hard that foam shot out over his hand. "Can't you get it through your head, woman, that I have to work at night?"

Beth wanted to hide from their anger and the sight of her mother's face so crumpled, her shoulders hunched as an old woman. He noticed Beth and pointed his finger at her, ordering her up to her bedroom. She ran upstairs, followed by Sara, running as fast as they could but still they could hear voices rising and a chair crashing on the kitchen floor.

Sara kept talking about Santy. She put her hands over her ears and asked if Beth had ever heard sleigh bells or saw him flying with his reindeers across the sky.

At the children's mass on Christmas Day the choir sang 'Away in a Manger' as Sara walked up the aisle carrying the baby Jesus. Beth knew the baby was only a doll but it seemed so real when her sister walked past, her face not laughing or being pulled into funny shapes, but serious, as if she was doing the most important thing ever. She laid the baby in the centre of the crib with the snow and the straw and the silver star shining overhead, and Marjory blew out her breath, as if she had been holding it in all the time her daughter was walking up the aisle.

Christmas Tea in Cherry Vale. Every year it was the same. Uncle Tom's house had big bay windows and steps up to the front door. Aunty May was wearing her new dress. It swished and changed colour when she moved. The stiff lace petticoats underneath reminded Beth of a fat pink parachute.

"Guess what *my* Santa Claus put into *my* stocking?" She giggled and flashed her arm, showing off a charm bracelet with tiny figures glinting every time they caught the light. Her lips looked bigger than they really were because she had drawn a bright red line over the top one. The angel on the Christmas tree had golden wings and blonde hair like Sara, so small and dainty, her tiny feet in poms, ready for dancing.

"Don't you dare touch anything, Beth." Marjory started fidgeting as soon as they entered the drawing room where all the precious ornaments were made of glass and china. They would break if Beth stood too close to them. "Honest to God, May, I can't take my eyes off her for a second."

"Leave the child be," said her father. "You make her nervous with all your fussing."

"And how's the accordion business, Mr Music Man?" boomed Uncle Tom as he poured whiskey into a glass.

"Excellent!" Barry smacked his lips and stared into the sparkling glass as if there were pictures inside it.

"Wait until the New Year is over and then there'll be a different story to tell," said Marjory.

Beth's heart gave a hurting little kick because she knew it was the sort of thing that made her father angry and she would hear them shouting in the night, even when she pulled the blankets over her head. Her cousins sat beneath the Christmas tree, playing with a train set laid out on tracks. Conor was ten, big for his age. Kieran was eight, Beth's age but smaller which he hated. He looked up as she approached and brought the engine to a halt.

"What did you get from Santy?" he asked.

"A book and a tennis racquet," she replied.

"You'll be able to make a racket then," said Conor. He waited for everyone to laugh. When the adults did not turn around he repeated the remark in a louder voice. Beth stuck out her tongue at him, hating him because he was always making fun of her and doing Chinese burns on her arm worse than anyone she knew.

The previous summer, the back garden of Cherry Vale had been as smooth as a carpet, marked with white lines and a net stretched across the centre.

"Lady Muck, showing off as usual," said Marjory, sounding cross when Aunty May invited them over to see the new tennis court and have tea on the lawn. Her cousins, dressed in white shorts and tops, were hitting balls at each other across the net.

"You could play with Kieran and Conor if you had your own racquet," Aunty May said.

Beth told her she was not allowed to make a racket and everyone except her mother laughed.

"Really, Marjory, does the poor child know anything?" Her aunt's thin brown eyebrows disappeared under her fringe and Uncle Tom lifted Beth high up in the air. He said she was a great one for making a racket wherever she went but she was still his favourite sweetheart.

When Christmas Tea was over, Barry played his accordion. Sara danced a reel, her hair bobbing around her face, light on her toes, and when she bowed, everyone clapped as if they were never going to stop. She would have danced again only her father said it was Beth's turn. He squeezed the accordion and the notes seemed to dance with her. In her head she could hear his voice saying, "Listen to the beat, Beth." She felt herself rising, moving into the rhythm, her legs swinging high, her arms stiff beside her green velvet dress. Her mother frowned, saying something with her hand over her mouth to Aunty May. They laughed together, a silent sound buried under the music. The accordion raced away in front of Beth, her feet no longer able to find the notes. Barry slowed down and stopped. He told her to start again, not to be nervous, she was a terrific dancer. She felt hot and cross, her cheeks heavy as if she was going to cry.

"I've got the very thing to cheer her up," said Uncle Tom. "Come with me, Beth."

The back garden was cold and dark. Beth could hardly see Anaskeagh Head, the big mountain behind Cherry Vale. Her father said it was higher than Mount Everest. Fairies lived under the rocks where they spun the magic gorse blossom and covered the mountain in a coat of gold. Uncle Tom switched on a torch. It shone on the tennis court and the high bushes that bent like crouching animals, reminding her of monsters in wardrobes, silly things she had imagined when she was only a baby.

He opened the door of the garden shed. "Look at what we have here," he said, shining the torch over Sadie. His voice made goosebumps on her skin, rustling soft as the crepe paper they used in school for the Christmas decorations. The dog lifted her head and growled but did not move. "Don't go too close," he warned. "She'll snap if you touch her babies." The pups had golden coats and floppy ears. They tugged at Sadie's belly, making thin yelping noises and swiping at each other with their paws.

"We're not supposed to go near the puppies." Uncle Tom looked cross, as if it was Beth's fault they were in the shed where it was cold and smelly from the dog smells. "Blossom will murder us if she finds out. So we must keep this our secret. Do you understand me, Beth?" He crouched down in front of her, trapping her between his knees. "If you don't tell anyone I showed you the puppies I'll give you one when it's weaned from its mammy. What do you say, Beth? Our big secret, huh? Say it now. Come on, our big secret."

"Our big secret." Her throat felt sore, as if it was closing over and she would never again be able to swallow. She wanted to go back to the drawing room with the log fire and the Christmas tree and Sara, sitting between her cousins, watching the train running fast and far away along the tracks. She made herself think about Jess O'Donovan, her very best friend in school, and she sang the song Sr Maria taught them, singing it so loudly inside her head that she could not hear anything else except the words of 'Over the Sea to Skye'. Speed bonnie boat like a bird on the wing … carry me safe to Skye.

He ran his finger inside the collar of her green Christmas dress. He untied the white sash at the back and she heard the silvery clink of the zip opening. "I didn't think little girls wore woolly vests any more." He was laughing softly, as if he had said something very funny. He pushed down the shoulders of her dress, lifting out her arms, first one and then the other. The vest her mother had knitted hurt her face when he pulled it over her head because he did not know he was supposed to open the buttons at the side. But she was afraid to cry in case he told her mother, who would sigh and say, "Honest to God, Beth, I can't bring you anywhere."

Sadie's eyes were closing. The pups were quiet, sleepy quiet. Their names were Goldie, Banjo, Lily and Pete. Uncle Tom asked her if he was her favourite uncle. She nodded her head and he said, "Then give me a kiss to prove it."

Her heart pounded as the hot red feeling opened up in her head and her uncle whispered, "Jesus … Jesus … Jesus", as if he was in the church on his knees saying his prayers.

CHAPTER THREE

Statues was a game of absolute stillness. The girl who was 'on' stood with her back to the other girls, trying to guess the exact moment to spin around and catch one of them moving. Sara was the best at the game, nimble on her feet or frozen as a statue. Beth was always caught, stumbling forward, swaying to the side, sometimes falling.

When her uncle called to Fatima Parade she stayed perfectly still and silent. Invisible, until he looked at her and smiled. "Little liar, Beth. Black spots on your soul. If your mother finds out you're a liar she'll bring you to Sergeant O'Donnell and he'll put you where he puts all the bad girls ... in jail forever." In Cherry Vale, when no one was watching, he pointed to her reflection in the big mirror above the mantelpiece, and said, "God sees your soul, Beth Tyrell. He sees the dark stains upon it and his heart bleeds because he knows you're a naughty girl, a girl who tells wicked lies."

Her eyes had been stolen from a witch, he said. His

breath was warm in her ear. Green eyes that cast a spell and
bewitched him. She did not want to be a witch with big
bold eyes. She wanted baby-blue eyes like Sara and long
blonde hair in ringlets. But her black hair never curled, no
matter how often her mother twisted it tight in rags at
night. "Forked lightning," sighed Marjory, trying to comb
it in the mornings. She cut it short with her dressmaking
scissors, traced a parting at the side, and said, "At least it's
manageable now."

Beth stared at her white witch's face in the mirror and
saw what Uncle Tom saw. Her soul was no longer small and
pure as the Eucharistic Host, but spotted like a sheet of
blotting paper, inky sins that spread and spread until all the
space was gone and she was ready to burn in everlasting
flames. How to make it pure again. At night she prayed,
her knees numb on the lino, and Sara shrieked, complaining
about her sister's cold feet, when she finally climbed into
bed.

In confession Fr Breen was silent when she told him she
had committed a grievous mortal sin. His face beyond the
grill was lost in a dark holy place. He leaned towards her.
She could see his eyes. He was searching beyond her body,
staring deep into her black soul.

"Tell me this sin, child. Don't be afraid." His stern voice
commanded the truth. She tried to find the words to describe
what happened in those hidden moments. When she sobbed
Fr Breen sighed, as if he was very tired. "Child, you must talk
to your mother. Come back and see me next week when you
have done so. Do you promise to talk to her?"

She nodded wordlessly, afraid to explain about Charlie

and jail and how hell was waiting for her because of the disgrace she would bring on her family. Little liar, Beth. Black spots on your sinful soul.

Catherine O'Donovan wore wellingtons and jeans and drove a tractor. When she was not herding cows down the lane to be milked or digging up turnips in the fields, she was reading books about the stars. Not Marilyn Monroe stars but distant planets and bright celestial bodies. She kept a telescope under her bed. On clear nights she went up to the hill field and studied the sky. Sometimes she took Jess with her, and Beth too, when she was allowed to stay overnight on the farm. Catherine pointed to Venus, traced the Milky Way, the Plough and the Great Bear. When they returned to the kitchen they toasted bread in front of the range and drank hot milk with sugar sprinkled on top. In the evening Frank O'Donovan and his sons milked the cows in the byre and sang cowboy songs. They asked Beth to sing 'How Much is that Doggie in the Window', which her father had taught her, and Frank swore her singing turned the milk into pure cream.

Beth loved the farm where the wild yellow cats dozed under the tractor and the geese marched up and down the cobbled yard, flapping wings when they were shooed away from the open kitchen door. A pot of stew simmered all day on the range. When the O'Donovan children complained of hunger Catherine waved her hand towards the pot and said, "You know where it is, my Honeybuns. God gave you hands for a reason. Help yourselves."

On the farm no one told Beth she was wicked. When she accidentally broke the cut-glass bowl used only for the

Christmas sherry trifle Catherine said it was one less dust-gatherer to worry about. She handed Beth a blouse from the laundry pile and ordered her to dry her eyes. Tears should only be shed for reasons of the heart. Beth was not sure what she meant. Maybe it was supposed to stop her heart pounding, and it did, but she knew deep down, no matter what Jess's mother said, that she was a very bad little girl.

The friends were separated in fourth class when they were discovered playing dot games on the back pages of Beth's copybook. Sheila O'Neill was moved into the bench beside her. She had chilblains on her ears and her pale blue eyes reminded Beth of a frightened rabbit. Not that Beth had ever seen a frightened rabbit. Only dead ones that the O'Donovan brothers shot. Or a fleeting glimpse of their bobbing tails disappearing into burrows on the slopes of Anaskeagh Head. When the rabbits were dead their eyes were pale as glass stones. Sheila's eyes moved all the time, darting around as if she believed people were watching her behind her back and she would catch them staring. Her three sisters in America sent her parcels of jeans and candy bars and nylon dresses with flounces on the hems. She talked about them all the time, whispering behind her hand in case their teacher, Mrs Keane, heard. Another sister called Nuala lived in London. Mrs O'Neill told everyone she worked in a fancy department store. Beth's mother smiled. Her lips were thin when she said that that was rubbish. Even the dogs in the streets knew that Nuala O'Neill had shamed her family's good name forever.

Sheila brought photographs into school. Before she

showed them to Beth, she made her cross her heart and hope to die screaming if she broke her promise.

"Nuala made the baby inside her tummy. Swear to God you won't tell?" She leaned closer, her hand cupped close to her mouth, breathless with the need to share the secret that caused her sister to disappear one day and her mother to cry whenever Sheila asked when she was coming home.

Beth studied the photographs, holding them on her knees in case Mrs Keane saw. A baby with plump cheeks in a lace christening cap and gown sitting on his mother's knee. Nuala O'Neill used to play camogie for the Anaskeagh Juniors and had danced every Saturday night in the Emerald Ballroom.

"How did she make the baby?" Beth whispered.

"Derry Mulhall put a seed from his willie inside her tummy and the baby grew from it. That's how grown-ups do it but it's a mortal sin if you don't wait until you're married. That's why Nuala had to go away."

Beth felt hot and sick, as if the air had suddenly been sucked from the classroom. Sheila's whispering hurt her head. The photographs merged into dots, black and dancing, causing her to sway forward as they fell to the floor.

"Oh God, we're done for!" hissed Sheila, scrabbling frantically to retrieve them. When she straightened up Mrs Keane was standing at the desk with her hand outstretched. The teacher studied the photographs, frowning when she recognised Nuala.

"You two! Come with me," she ordered.

Their footsteps echoed along the corridor as she escorted them to Sr Rosa's office. The photographs were spread out on the head nun's desk. Her long black habit reminded Beth

of crows flapping on the back yard wall. Sheila twisted her
fingers together as if she was playing cat's cradle without
the twine. She began to cry. Tears splashed the toes of her
heavy black shoes. Sr Rosa said she would be expelled if she
ever dared bring such sinful photographs into school again.
The rosary beads hanging from her waist rattled as she
raised her arm and slapped their hands with her leather
strap. The floor tilted in a see-saw sway when Beth walked
from her office and back into the classroom of curious,
staring girls.

That evening she tried to drown Goldie in the zinc bath
that hung on a nail in the back yard. Sadie's pup, as her
uncle had promised. Goldie had become Sara's dog, trotting
behind her wherever she went and sitting on his hind legs
when she said, "Beg!"

   Beth's head felt like a red hot fire as she pushed the
cocker spaniel under the water, ignoring the terrified,
wriggling movements until Sara came running into the
yard, fists pummelling wildly, and pushed Beth against the
wall. She lifted the dripping animal in her arms and ran
weeping into the kitchen to tell her mother. Beth welcomed
the stinging pain that followed. It was the only way to let
the badness out.

CHAPTER FOUR

Barry Tyrell was driving a van now. 'Oliver's Furniture' was engraved on the side. His accordion was silent in the cubby hole under the stairs. When Sara begged him to play music so that she could practise her Irish dancing he refused and shouted at her to stop being a nuisance. In the days of the Anaskeagh Ceile Band, he used to bring parcels of chips wrapped in newspaper from Hatty's Chipper and smuggle the girls downstairs to eat them. They would huddle around the kitchen table giggling, nervous in case Marjory woke, their fingers digging into the vinegary chips that tasted so different late at night, listening to the stories he told about the dancers in the Emerald Ballroom.

Now, there was no longer any chip smell at night, only the loud slamming of the hall door, his footsteps thudding on the floor as he passed their bedroom without stopping. Beth would waken instantly, as if an alarm had gone off inside her head, knowing he had been drinking in The Anaskeagh Arms. She would wait for the voices on the other side of the wall to rise. Smothery and hot from her sister's closeness, the prickly horsehair mattress scratching her skin, she wondered how Sara could sleep so peacefully when even the walls seemed to blister with her parent's anger.

He still talked about moving to Dublin. Beth no longer believed him and suspected he did not believe it himself. The father who had promised to climb with her to the top of Nelson's Pillar no longer existed. In his place was a small, grumpy man who told too many stories and drove a van for the person she hated most in all the world.

Beth woke one night and heard his footsteps on the landing. A suitcase bumped against the banisters as he ran down the stairs. From the cubby hole he took his accordion and slung it across his chest.

"You needn't think you'll get back into this house again," Marjory shouted, leaning over the top rail. In her long night-dress, her hair loose from the tidy bun she usually wore, she reminded Beth of a figure-head on the brow of a ship, riding furiously through a storm. "Not in a million years will you ever set foot in here again!"

"That'll be too soon for me." The crash of the front door was followed by a stark silence. She stared at Beth then looked away again, her hand moving over her stomach as if she was brushing crumbs from a tablecloth. "He's gone for good. Your precious father has dumped us."

"Where's he gone?" Beth could not grasp what her mother was saying. "Has he gone back to the band?"

"I haven't a notion where he's gone. I only hope it's to hell and that he stays there forever."

Sara woke and ran to the landing, her eyes glazed with sleep.

"Your cruel father has left us," Marjory said, soothing

her plaintive wailing. "He doesn't want us any more but that doesn't matter. Don't cry, my pet … don't cry. I'll always be here to love you. We don't need him. We never have."

Sara's tears dried as her mother comforted her, speaking soft, insistent words of hate. She brought the girls into her room where they slept for the rest of the night. The door on one side of the wardrobe was open. The space inside was empty except for a few coat-hangers. Empty space was all he had left behind.

Soon the empty spaces were filled with other things. He became a memory that only took shape when the girls heard *ceili* music on the wireless or found an old photograph that had escaped Marjory's ruthless efforts to remove his presence from the house. Once a week he sent a registered letter from Dublin. It contained money, she said. Money that would be sufficient to manage on if she was feeding a family of mice. The girls should thank their lucky stars they had an uncle who cared about their welfare or they would be sleeping on the streets.

Occasionally, Barry sent letters to his daughters. He lived near a church on a hill. Christ Church Cathedral, a very old and famous place, he wrote. The cobblestones would make a man's bones rattle. The smell of hops and yeast from Guinness's Brewery was as sweet as the nectar of the Gods. He missed his girls every ticking minute on the clock. They must visit him one of these fine days.

CHAPTER FIVE

"Beth Tyrell – thirteen years of age. Well, fancy that now!" In Hearn's grocery shop, Maggie Hearn's eyes beamed behind her glasses. She leaned her elbows on the counter. "It only seems like yesterday when your mammy was wheeling you out in your big fancy pram."

Behind her, high wooden shelves stretched to the ceiling, stacked with everything from fishing tackle to flypaper, sides of smoked bacon, bags of sugar, golden mounds of butter that Maggie sliced and wrapped in greaseproof paper.

"So? What's the plan for the big day?" she asked. "I've heard terrible stories altogether about them teenage parties."

"I'm not having a party," said Beth. "Me and Sara are going to visit Daddy in Dublin."

"Are you indeed now? Tell the old rogue I was asking for him. Many's the time and many a tune I danced to his accordion."

Beth almost laughed out loud at the idea of Maggie Hearn dancing in her wrap-around apron and cardigan, the rainbow coloured lights twirling on her bottle-top glasses. When she was leaving Maggie gave her a packet of rolos to celebrate her birthday. "You'll be running from them boyos before much longer," she chuckled. "Take Maggie's advice and make sure you pick the right one before you let him catch you."

On the morning of their departure Sara woke, sulky and hot. She puckered her forehead and refused to get out of bed.

"I don't want to see him ... you can't make me," she cried, twisting the sheet around her neck and turning her back on Beth. "He's a horrible, cruel man. Mammy says he hates me. And you're horrible too ... a big bully. You can't make me go."

She sobbed and cowered under the blankets. Beth hit her and felt her panic rising when Sara remained stubborn.

"Poor baby. What's the matter? Let Mammy make you better." Marjory crooned and Beth knew her sister would stay in bed all day, eating ice cream and drinking lemonade, even though she was only pretending to be sick.

"Make sure you behave yourself," Marjory warned when Beth was ready to leave. "There are very few girls in Anaskeagh who will ever have the opportunity of staying overnight in an expensive hotel, isn't that right, Tom?"

"It is indeed." He smiled at his niece. "But then there's very few girls in Anaskeagh as beautiful as my Beth. And it's not every day that one of them gets to be a teenager."

Barry Tyrell had grown a beard. His face was fatter, not flushed and tense any more. At first he seemed like a stranger with her father's voice and the familiar way his eyes crinkled when he smiled. Tom Oliver did not stay and talk to him. He had business in the city and would call back later for Beth.

"Well, well, well! This is good, isn't it?" Barry rubbed his hands together. He made sandwiches and cut slices of sponge cake, insisting that she eat every crumb on her plate. The house where he lived was on a terrace similar to Fatima Parade but he only had one room and his bed was a sofa. The lace curtains had holes and blue mould stains. Dead leaves were trapped under the weatherboard. He wanted to know about school and if Beth had a boyfriend yet. On the mantelpiece a black china horse reared up on its hind legs. A gas fire steamed the windows. He told her about his job, delivering planks of wood to building sites, and how at night he played in pubs. Not dance music any more but whistle tunes with a ballad group called Celtic Reign who were going places very fast.

"How much do you miss me?" she demanded, knowing he was watching the time, waiting for her uncle to collect her.

"You pull my heart to pieces every single day," he replied.

"Then why can't I live here with you?"

"Don't be daft, Beth." He glanced quickly at his watch, pretending he was pushing up the sleeve of his jumper. "You don't want to live in a slum like this."

"I don't care. I'll be with you. I can get a job and we'll move somewhere bigger."

"You're still only a child."

"I'm thirteen now."

"That's still far too young to leave home. Your mother would have my guts for garters."

"I don't care … I hate living with her. I hate – I hate …" She sobbed, unable to continue.

At the side of the sofa squashed against the wall, she saw a cardigan. A woman's cardigan, pale yellow angora with pearl buttons. Maybe, said Barry, his eyes skittering away from the cardigan when Beth pulled it free, when she was older, they would talk about it again.

He would never change his mind and even when he offered to teach her to play the tin whistle she knew he was just counting the minutes until her uncle returned.

"Still chasing rainbows, Mr Music Man?" Uncle Tom asked. How tall he seemed, standing strong in the little room, rain glistening on his oiled hair that he combed so neatly from his forehead. Her father's hair was a mess, long on the back of his neck, as frizzy as his beard.

"Get your coat, Beth" Barry nodded brusquely towards the door, his good humour disappearing. In the hall she heard him tell her uncle that what he chased was his own business.

"Ah, but it's also my concern, Tyrell. Rainbows don't help when it comes to feeding your children. That pittance you send every week to Marjory is a joke."

"It's as much as I can afford. She makes enough from the dressmaking to manage."

"If you believe that you're more of a fool than I thought. People don't want their clothes hand-made any more. Ready-made, that's the way of the future. Pick it off a rail and put it on your back. You should be ashamed of yourself, man. My sister was always too good for you but you married her and it was your duty to take care of her."

"So, what's the penance, Father? Three Hail Marys and a hair shirt … readymade?" He raised his voice. "Are you ready, Beth? Don't keep your uncle waiting. He's a very busy man."

He waved from the front door but he had closed it again by the time her uncle turned his car and drove away. She wondered how it was possible to love and hate him at the same time. Such mixed feelings confused her, so different to her feelings for the man sitting beside her. Those feelings oozed from some slimy part of her stomach, knotting it so hard it was impossible to think of anything else.

The button beside the hotel lift glowed orange when he pressed it. Far below she heard a low murmur, as if a mighty beast had been disturbed and was coming to carry her away. It grew louder, shuddering movements that stopped when it reached their feet. The gates clanged when he pushed them apart. Her stomach swooped in a ticklish thrill as the lift began to ascend.

Their footsteps were silent on the corridor leading to her room. Outside, buses were still running. She could hear them braking, the engines idling as late-night passengers crowded the platforms, hurrying to a place where they could shelter and be safe.

Such thin walls, no stronger than a sheet of paper. In the next room she heard him clearing his throat. After a while a snoring sound rose and fell away in a whistling sigh as if he was blowing air through his nose and she, behind the thin walls, was comatose … the same as the Statues game. What would he do if she lived for the rest of her life in a death-like trance? Or if she died? She imagined her family weeping around her grave as her white coffin was lowered deep into the earth. Inside, she would be pale and dead. As still as she was now. Only she would be at peace and her father would be there with the mourners, ashamed of himself because he would not let her live in his mean little room with the grimy wallpaper and the woman's yellow cardigan stuck between the sofa and the wall.

She swayed when she sat up, afraid she was going to fall from the bed. She stayed in that position, her head bent forward until it felt safe to move again. She would tell her father. The decision came suddenly, as if it had been waiting to find space in her fear. Slowly she curled her toes, bending the soles of her feet, tensing her legs. She searched for the light switch and gathered her scattered clothes, dressing silently, terrified the snoring sounds from next door would cease.

Along the hotel corridor fan-shaped lights threw a dim glow against the walls. She pressed the lift button, seeing it glow, hearing the murmuring noise from down below rushing towards her.

"What in God's name are you doing, Beth?" His red dressing gown gaped open, reaching only to his knees, showing off his hairy chest as he hurried towards her. It made him look silly, no longer important, but as he reached her the horror pushed up into her mouth and she was terrified she would throw up on the spot.

"I'm going to my daddy," she cried. "I'm going to tell on you."

"Poor child, you've had a bad dream. Come back inside now and stop making such a fuss." As the lift clattered to a halt he lifted her in his arms. Easily, as if she was only the weight of a feather, he carried her back to her bedroom. He sat her on the bed and wagged his finger in her face. "Now! You stop this hysterical nonsense at once. Do you hear me?"

He told her about her father and the woman who owned the cardigan. How she had a family, children who had become his children. Barry Tyrell no longer cared about the girls he had left behind in Anaskeagh. When Beth put her hands over her ears he pulled them away. She must listen to the truth. Then, perhaps, she would stop being a selfish and ungrateful child who was breaking her mother's heart with her tantrums.

In the Church of the Sacred Heart she stared at the crucifix above the altar. She felt the nails being thudded into the Christ figure one by one. She examined her own hands hoping to see blood pouring forth. A stigmata. A whore of Babylon, old Sam Burns shouted at young women when they walked through the town. The words seared her mind, even though Jess's mother said Sam was shell-shocked from the First World War when he had been a soldier in the trenches, and harmless behind all his ranting.

On Jess's thirteenth birthday, they climbed to the summit of Anaskeagh Head. Jess liked rituals, solemnity, the grand gesture and, on this significant occasion, she was going to bury the symbols of her childhood. In a tin biscuit box she had placed her diaries, a copy book, her favourite glass necklace, a rag doll, her First Communion prayer book, her Confirmation medal, a *Girl Friend* annual, her favourite sweets. The headland, with the crashing Atlantic ocean on one side and the town of Anaskeagh sloping away into the distance, offered her the perfect ceremonial altar to move into adulthood.

When the burial was over the friends pricked the middle fingers of their right hands with a needle. They vowed to be blood sisters for as long as they lived, sharing secrets, even the smallest, most trivial secret. This meant never lying to each other, said Jess, and told Beth she sometimes heard God's voice talking to her in the wind.

How could she share her secrets with Jess, signed in blood? How could she whisper such ugly words to her best friend, a Child of Mary who made an altar in her bedroom every May with lilac and bluebells and heard God's voice in the wind? Far below her she could see Cherry Vale and the houses beside it. How tiny they looked. So neat and orderly. The front road winding like a skein of fine grey thread into Anaskeagh. She imagined her uncle, a scurrying insect, small enough to be crushed under her foot. The sole of her shoe stamping him into a smear of blood that would be washed away forever when the rain fell.

CHAPTER SIX

Everything was simple once she decided to run away. No rush, no panic. The right moment would present itself and she would be gone, dust on her heels, churning up the road from Anaskeagh. She knew she must do it or else go mad, as loopy as old Sam Burns or Mrs McIntyre, who once ran down Fatima Parade in her nightdress waving a carving knife.

Nelson's Pillar had been blown up. When Beth heard the news she had imagined people rushing about as frantically as ants whose ant hill had been kicked apart. She felt she would be entering a different city, one whose landscape had changed dramatically. It no longer seemed such a formidable place.

One Sunday afternoon on Anaskeagh Strand she confided her plan to Jess. "I can't stick it a moment longer," she said. "I'll go nuts if I don't escape from this dump."

"Did you have another row with your mother?" Jess

asked. The rows between mother and daughter were a source of fascination to her.

"Does the Pope say the rosary?"

"What was it about this time?"

"Oh, the usual." Beth was dismissive. "She wants me to do a secretarial course after my Inter and work for my uncle."

"I'd hate to work in an office."

"Well, there's not much danger of that, is there?"

"Thank God!"

"You'll have plenty of time to do that." Beth still could not believe her friend was serious about entering a convent. At the spring retreat, Fr Ford, the mission priest who was home on holidays from Africa, had talked to the pupils of the Star of the Sea convent about the joy of becoming a beloved bride of Christ. Jess had absorbed every word. Afterwards, her face glowing with conviction, she said she finally understood The Voice. An insistent voice, no longer blowing uncertainly through the wind as it told her that the way to salvation lay in loving God above all earthly things.

"Even the Beatles?" Beth demanded.

Jess grinned. "*Especially* the Beatles."

If Jess was a 'holy Mary' like Breda Gilligan who had a crush on Sr Clare and wore a Miraculous Medal pinned to the front of her school blazer, Beth could have understood. But Jess adored Ringo Starr, hated *The Sound of Music* and collected photographs of Georgie Best. She had sneaked her mother's copy of *Lady Chatterley's Lover* from under the mattress where Catherine thought it was safely hidden from her children and read it twice before passing it on to Beth.

"It's so sexy, isn't it?" Giggling, she demanded her friend's opinion. Beth gave a wooden smile and nodded. It seemed childish to admit that she had found it disgusting, so sickening that she wanted to throw up all over the pages. The future they had planned together seemed childish now. Jobs as fashion models or air hostesses, all-night parties and strange men with beards and guitars sleeping on the floor of their flat. Only when she finally accepted that Jess was serious about her vocation did Beth realise how much she had depended on the escape route provided by such day dreams.

"What will you do in Dublin?" Jess asked.

"I'll get a flat and a job."

"It's a big city."

"I'll find my way around easy enough. I'll stay with my father until I get my own place."

"What about – you know – The Cardigan?"

"What about her? He's my father. I come first."

Jess glanced sideways at her. "Are you going to tell Sara?"

"I don't know. If I do she'll kick up an awful fuss."

"She'll go nuts if she finds out afterwards."

"Why should she? It's different for her. She gets away with bloody murder."

"I don't know what I'll do when you go." Jess put her arm around her shoulders.

"Talk to God. He'll tell you." Beth was brusque, shrugging away her friend's arm because Jess cried easily and the last thing she needed was to dent the armour she had built around herself.

"Do you think your mother's going through the Change?" Jess was struck by a sudden thought. "My mother says women get awfully crotchety at that time."

"Change! What change?" demanded Beth. "She's always been the same. Anyway, she's too young."

"It can happen at any age from thirty-five," said Jess. "Mammy's got a book about it. Madness and depression and hot flushes. Remember Mrs McIntyre?"

"Jesus!" Beth was horrified. "I hope I die first."

Hatty Beckett, who owned Hatty's Chipper on the corner of River Mall, needed someone to work from six to midnight, five evenings a week. Marjory was furious when she heard that Beth had accepted the job. Hatty had gone out with Barry Tyrell in his single days and Marjory had often accused him of going into her chip shop for more than his portion of chips.

"I'm not having my daughter serving every drunk in Anaskeagh," she declared. "If you insist on doing part-time work instead of studying for your Inter your uncle will be more than happy to give you a Saturday in his showrooms. It'll be good training for you . He's kind enough to pay for your education so the least you can do is show him some appreciation."

"I wouldn't work for that creep if he paid me a million pounds." Beth's voice was low and taunting.

"How dare you use that kind of language in my house." Marjory flushed angrily. "Apologise at once!"

"Make me. Why don't you take down Charlie and make me?"

"I'll break the cane across your back if you give me any more of your lip. I don't know what's come over you lately. Cheek! That's all I get from you. Apologise at once."

"He's a creep and he can stuff his stupid job up his arse for all I care."

For an instant Marjory was too shocked to move. Then she reached for the cane and struck Beth across her legs, lifting her arm to strike again.

Beth laughed. She was no longer afraid. Charlie was a piece of bamboo, a thin piece of cane with a hook that only came to life in her mother's hand and it was important to scream, to shout insults, to fling plates against the wall in sudden outbursts of fury so that Marjory would hurt her, hurt her so much that she would no longer feel trapped beneath her sins.

Neither of them noticed Sara entering the kitchen. The younger girl pushed between them, crying at them to stop. Too panicked to avoid the cane she took the force of the blow on her face. Her hair spilled over her hands as she clutched her cheek. Outside in the yard Goldie barked, furiously.

"This is all your fault," Marjory panted. She avoided looking at Beth as she ran a dish cloth under the cold tap and bent over Sara, gently dabbing at the welt that was deepening into an angry red blotch. "You're nothing but trouble in this house."

"It's not my fault!" Beth screamed. "You're the one holding the cane yet all you ever do is blame me for everything. *Everything*. I hate you so much it makes me sick." She spat out the words as if they were pebbles in her mouth. "I'm taking that job in Hatty's, and you'd better not try and stop me or ..." Her voice shuddered, unable to utter the words, knowing she would never be able to empty herself of them. Not that it mattered. Marjory had stopped listening. She helped Sara to her feet, trying to bring down the swelling which had already closed one of her eyes, smoothing back her blonde hair, crooning her love.

Beth battered cod and haddock and ladled chips into sheets of newspaper. The smell of fish clung to her, a pervasive scent on her clothes and her skin, no matter how often she washed herself and doused her body in Apple Blossom talcum powder. Marjory demanded half the money she earned. The rest was hidden in the dressing table drawer beneath her underwear.

When her uncle visited Fatima Parade she willed herself to think of other things. His suit had tiny, fine hairs that tickled her face when he greeted her, enveloping her in his bear-hug embrace, jovial and kind, as Marjory rushed to plump the cushions on his favourite armchair and make him tea. Beth imagined his fingers grubbing about in her mind, searching out her thoughts, the knowledge they shared visible only to each other. The bicycle he gave her for her fourteenth birthday sat shining and unused in the coal-shed, waiting. Soon, she would cycle it for the first time. It would carry her far away from Anaskeagh. Such plans, counting her money, studying the map of Dublin, checking that her bike was oiled and the tyres remained firm, gave meaning to her days. Everything else, the normal things she always did, were performed in a dream-state. As if her mind had already fled and only her body waited to follow.

Sara never stirred as her sister eased from the dip in the horsehair mattress and opened the bedroom door. It was five o'clock in the morning when Beth stepped into the kitchen. With her hand she felt along the kitchen door, lifting Charlie from the hook. In the coal shed she wheeled the bicycle through the yard where the bath still hung, gleaming palely in the gathering dawn. Goldie stayed in the shadows as Beth leaned the bicycle against the wall and hunkered beside him, feeling his withdrawal, growling low in his throat when she touched him.

"You'll never be able to forgive me, will you, you old mutt?" Her throat tightened in a spasm as the dog continued to strain away from her. She thought of Sara snuggling deeper into the mattress and then, deliberately, allowed the image to fade. Sara was not going to be her cross. She refused to carry her into her new life.

At Cherry Vale she dismounted. She lifted a large stone from the rockery and flung it towards the bay window. Glass shattered. A light was switched on upstairs. She cycled out through the gates, head down, her feet pumping to the same frantic rhythm as her heart. When she reached the Dublin Road she flung the bicycle and the cane into a ditch. "Bye bye Charlie!" she shouted, hearing it strike the leaves and sink out of sight.

Beyond the hedgerows the sky began to glow. A new day was beginning, caught in the stillness between dawn and morning. A creamery truck lumbered towards her. She lifted her hand and it slowed.

"You look like someone in search of adventure," said the driver, when she climbed aboard.

"How did you guess?" She slung her duffel bag packed tightly with her clothes on the seat between them. She did not glance back as the distance between herself and

Anaskeagh lengthened. Clouds trailed across the rising sun, mountain squiggles on a blood red painting.

CHAPTER SEVEN

The small terraced house with the yellow door was in darkness. Beth knocked twice, relieved when a light flashed on at an upstairs window. The wind gave a sudden keen and blew the rain into the wooden porch where she was trying to shelter. She heard footsteps on the stairs and a boy in his late teens opened the front door. He had pulled on a pair of jeans and was still struggling with the zip. When he saw her standing outside with the rain in her hair, her clothes sculpted to her body, his hands paused, as if frozen with embarrassment, then he gave a quick jerk and the zip slid into place.

"Does Barry Tyrell live here?" She tried to speak calmly but her teeth chattered and she swayed towards him as though she knew, with an instinctive knowledge she would later come to appreciate, that Stewart McKeever would catch her in his steady arms and set her world to rights again.

He nodded, the sleep still in his eyes and the warmth

of four safe walls behind him. "You're Beth," he said, opening the door wider and beckoning her forward without hesitation. "I've seen your photograph."

"Is he here?" she repeated. "I've been looking everywhere for him." Rain ran from her coat and formed a puddle on the hall floor. She heard footsteps crossing the landing and her father's voice on the stairs. He was wearing a pair of rumpled pyjamas. His beard was bushier than she remembered, a balladeer's beard which he chewed in mortification when he saw her. "Beth! Jesus, Mary and holy Saint Joseph! What the hell are you doing here?" he demanded.

"Don't blaspheme in my house, Barry Tyrell." The Cardigan's voice was soft but it was also firm and demanded attention. Her hair was dyed so black it shone in a hard blue sheen under the hall light. She clutched the lapels of her dressing gown across her chest and surveyed Beth. "Can't you see the poor child is half dead from exhaustion. If you'd had the decency to write her a letter and tell her where you'd moved she wouldn't be tramping the little legs off herself searching the city for you. Come into the kitchen, love, and get them wet clothes off you." She turned to her son. "Stewart, you get up them stairs fast as your legs can carry you and wake your sister. Take no nonsense from her. She's to bring down that flannelette nightdress from the hot press and make room for Beth in her bed."

Beth listened to the raised voices above her. An argument was taking place between Stewart and his sister, who was obviously furious over being woken in the middle of the night and told to share her bed with a stranger. A door banged and he reappeared with a tall, sulky girl in tow. She was older than Beth and flashed a hard look at her before sighing loudly in Barry's direction. "You want my bed and my clothes for your daughter. What next?" Dramatically, she held her wrists forward. "My blood ... go on take it. You've taken everything else."

"Shut up, Marina, and sit down. No one wants your blood but some manners would be appreciated around here." The Cardigan placed a towel over Beth's head and began to dry her hair. "Barry, bring that pot of tea over to the table and let's find out how the poor child found her way here."

No one spoke as Beth described how she had searched for the house where her father used to live only to discover it had been replaced by a building site with a hoarding around it. An old man with string on his coat waved his hands towards the hoarding and shouted insults at an invisible army of speculators who were tearing the soul out of his city. He brought her to a nearby pub where Celtic Reign played every Wednesday. The bar manager, seeing her distress, rang the singer in Celtic Reign, who gave him Barry Tyrell's new address.

"He's gone to live in the sticks," said the manager, scribbling down the address. "There's not too many buses go to Oldport but let's have a look and see." He took a timetable from behind the counter and ran his finger over a page. "If you rush you'll just catch the last one."

Beth did not mention the tears and the despair that swept through her as she tried to follow his directions to the bus-stop and how the city swamped her with its indifference. Nor did she describe her terror when the bus headed northwards, racing through grey housing estates and out into the country, brushing against overhanging branches and swerving around corners until her stomach heaved and she was afraid she was going to throw up over the seat.

Barry pushed at the sleeves of his pyjamas and glanced at The Cardigan. "Well, we'd better let her stay the night," he said, pretending he was glad to see her when it was obvious to everyone in the room that he wanted her to vanish from his life as suddenly as she had appeared.

Marina did not believe in pretence. "Your father's to blame for everything," she adamantly stated when they were alone in her bedroom. She forced a bolster down the centre of the bed to separate them. "Parasite! All we need now is his other daughter – and his wife – then we'll all have the perfect happy family."

The Cardigan's name was Connie McKeever. In the days that followed she did her utmost to make Beth feel welcome, advising her to ignore Marina, who, she sighed, had a tongue sharp enough to cut through steel. Connie was a supervisor in a local clothes factory where her son also worked.

"I'll talk to Mrs Wallace about getting you a job in Della Designs," she said. "I'm sure we'll be able to fit you in somewhere on the production line."

High green railings surrounded Della Designs. The bars across the windows reminded Beth of a squat, ugly prison. The factory was silent on the outside until the doors opened and she was swept into the clack of machinery, music booming over the loudspeaker, the smack of irons, the steaming smell of freshly pressed fabrics. Female voices rose and fell like water over her head. She was petrified by the noise and the rows of women in blue overalls who ignored her, their hands moving with such speed at their machines that she wanted to turn and run weeping back along the road she had taken.

Connie escorted her up wooden steps and into Mrs Wallace's office. Beth would go on a month's trial and train as a machinist. She laid down the rules in a rasping voice. There would be no smoking in the Ladies. Flirting with the boys in Dispatch was strictly for after hours. Punctuality was next to Godliness she said, snapping her fingers at cleanliness which was the prerogative of the individual. As for slacking off at the machines or absenteeism, she shook her head threateningly. No words of warning were necessary. She simple jerked her finger towards the exit door. The glass front wall of her office overlooked the production floor and nothing, Beth was to discover, escaped the hawkish gaze of Della Wallace.

"I'll leave her in your capable hands, Connie." She waved Beth from her office as if she was swatting a fly from her sight and picked up the telephone.

Stewart was an assistant to the production manager. He attended night classes in electronics and read technical manuals, propping them against milk bottles on the table, and staring with fierce concentration at the pages whenever Beth entered the kitchen. He blushed when he caught her eye, as if he, like Marina, hated having to speak to her. She soon realised this was shyness rather than hostility and a slow friendship began to grow between them.

"Is Marina giving you a hard time?" he demanded one day when he discovered her in tears at her machine.

Beth shook her head. "I'm just homesick," she admitted, not mentioning the letter that had arrived the previous day from her mother. Bitter and short, the words had jumped from the page, shocking her with their venom. "Since you have refused my request to return home and insist on living with your adulterous father in his whore's house I no longer recognise you as my daughter."

She had burned the letter, watching the notepaper blacken and curl the words into ash.

At night, when she tried to sleep, the bolster firmly established as a no-man's land between herself and Marina, she heard creaking noises from the bedroom next door. A rhythmical, boisterous sound that forced her head deeper into the pillow. She suspected that Marina was also awake, restlessly turning away from the evidence of her mother's lovemaking.

"If my father was alive he'd break every bone in your father's pathetic body," she muttered one night after the sounds from next door had ceased. Beth pretended to be asleep. She knew the story of Marina's father. How he drowned at sea, his body swept ashore many miles from where his fishing trawler sank. When Marina called her a culchie parasite it no longer hurt so much. She realised she was simply a target for Marina's anger, nothing more.

Oldport was different to Anaskeagh yet many things reminded Beth of home. On sunny mornings the sea had the same fierce glitter but it flowed into a calm estuary. The fields were flat, miles of fields filled with straight rows of vegetables and flowers for the markets in the city. It had once been a fishing village but the old harbour beyond the estuary was no longer in use and the remains of sunken fishing boats could be seen at low tide, arching from the water, smooth and sleek as seals. The biggest difference was the sense of space. Beth could look in all directions, unlike Anaskeagh where the headland loomed over everything.

In the evenings Connie's house was filled with noise and music. Barry practised his tin whistle, Stewart played his records and Marina giggled in a high trilling solo whenever Peter entered the room. He was Stewart's best friend, the son of Mrs Wallace, and Connie had known him since he was a baby. She called him her "almost son" and treated him the same as the rest of her family, scolding him when he teased Beth or flirted with Marina.

"Keep your eyes to yourself if you don't want them scratched out," warned Marina one night after he left. "Peter Wallace is madly in love with me. He's going to immortalise me in oils."

"Oh! So that's what it's called nowadays?" said Connie, overhearing. "In my day it was called 'getting a girl into trouble'. You concentrate on your studies, Marina McKeever and you'll be far better off."

"You should know all about trouble." Marina cast a belligerent look towards Barry who was watching television. "When's he leaving? I'm sick of putting up with strangers in my dead father's house."

"Stop your nonsense, Marina. I won't have it." Despite the firmness in her voice, Connie looked distressed.

"And I'm sick of your nonsense. You're the talk of Oldport … living with a married man when your husband's hardly cold in his grave. Don't give me any lectures about morality unless you understand what it means."

From the frying pan into the fire, Beth thought. Trouble and strife, no matter where her father laid his head. She wanted to return to Anaskeagh and climb to the top of the headland with Jess. She longed to see Sara, to snuggle against her in the dip of the horsehair mattress, to hold her warm and cosy as they drifted off to sleep. But Anaskeagh was also her dark shadow and she knew she would never return to its shade.

CHAPTER EIGHT

Beth had spent six months on her machine when she discovered that a typist had been sacked for arriving late. She approached Mrs Wallace and told her she had studied shorthand and typing for a year before leaving the Star of the Sea Convent. "If you give me a chance to show you what I can do you won't regret it," she said, forcing herself to sound brave under the astute gaze of her employer.

"A week's trial," said Della Wallace. "One mistake and you're out on your ear. Start on Monday."

The office staff ignored Beth. It was the first time anyone from the factory floor had become part of the clerical section and her sudden promotion upset the insular pecking order that existed in the company. The machinists were also suspicious of her.

"Stuck-up cow," said Marina. "She thinks she's too good for us since she moved up with the la-di-das."

Marina had been expelled from school for smoking. She did it openly during her Commerce and Bookkeeping class and blew smoke rings at her teacher. Shortly afterwards, she joined Della Designs, sulking and sewing collars on coats, only brightening up when Peter came to the factory to tease the older women and whisper in her ear. She ignored Beth, making jokes about culchies and bog accents when she walked past. Sandwiched between the factions in the factory and the office, Beth kept her head down. The sales manager's secretary had become engaged. She flashed a large solitaire and confided to her friends that she intended conceiving a baby on her honeymoon. When her job fell vacant, Beth would be ready to take it over.

At the weekly hop, called the Sweat Pit by those who packed the small parish hall, Marina jived with her friends and danced the slow sets with Peter. She confided intimate secrets to Beth across the bolster. She 'did it' regularly with him on bales of blue velvet material in the storeroom. She posed nude for him in his artist's studio when his mother was out. She was his Mona Lisa. She laughed at Beth's shocked expression and tossed her long dark hair.

"When he finishes art college he's going to become a famous artist and we're getting married. I'm going to live in Havenstone – then we'll see who's the la-di-da around here."

Havenstone, where Mrs Wallace and her son lived, was a large house set in its own grounds with a back view over the estuary. Beth imagined Marina in her miniskirt and high white boots strutting through the rooms and smiled to herself. She had a feeling that Marina's escapades mostly happened in her head. But untangling the lies from the truth was a tedious task so she stayed silent, listening to fantastic stories that ended abruptly when Peter danced the slow-sets in the Sweat Pit with a girl from Quality Control. Later, reported Marina's best friend, they were seen outside, kissing each other against the wall.

"She's a bike," Marina sneered. "Cheap peroxide slut." She was going to move to London and become a proper model on a catwalk instead of a canvas. Oldport was the tomb of the living dead.

"I have my eyes set on higher things," she said when Beth found her in the bedroom wiping mascara from her eyes. "Peter Wallace can stay down on his bended knees forever but he won't make me change my mind." She blew her nose and applied a heavy layer of pan-stick make-up, demanding to know why Beth was staring. Peter Wallace was nothing but a swollen ego and a tiny prick. She hated his guts. Beth left her weeping into the bolster. A week later Marina left, armed with her portfolio of photographs and a letter of introduction to a modelling agency from Della Wallace.

The sales manager's secretary duly became pregnant on her honeymoon and Beth moved smoothly into her place. Andy O'Toole, the sales manager, filled the office with cigar smoke and refused to allow windows to be opened because he suffered from draughts. She discovered a bottle of vodka in the filing cabinet and understood why his wife rang in so often with excuses about his ill health. His bullying became a ritual part of every day. She quickly realised that no matter how hard she worked she would never please him.

"What a diligent young lady you are," said Mrs Wallace, coming upon her one night when everyone had gone home.

"It's the third time this week you've stayed on. Don't you have time to do those invoices during the day?"

"I didn't get them until late," replied Beth. "And Mr O'Toole wants them on his desk first thing in the morning."

"Does your boyfriend mind you working such long hours?"

"I don't have a boyfriend so there's no problem."

"At your age I would see that as quite a problem."

Beth was surprised at the personal direction the conversation had taken, especially when Mrs Wallace smiled, a rare occurrence that softened the tough lines around her mouth. Not knowing how to reply, she stayed silent, knowing that her employer understood this need to work compulsively, even if she pretended otherwise.

The Wallace money came from spinning, three generations of tweeds and worsteds making the family fortunes. But Mrs Wallace's childhood had been far removed from the graciousness of Havenstone. Connie, her childhood friend and neighbour, liked to remember those humble beginnings, one room on the top floor of a tenement. A dismal block of flats in the centre of the city where the walls wept in winter and rats froze to death in the outside toilets.

"Such hard times, Beth," she would sigh, remembering, a hint of nostalgia in her voice. "But Della always vowed that one day she would wear pearls and live in a mansion higher than the highest tenement."

Mrs Wallace was fourteen when she set up her first factory, making overalls for a local businessman in a cramped back room of the same tenement block. Her second factory, a ramshackle building that was always damp and rat-infested, burned mysteriously to the ground. Beth asked if Mrs Wallace had organised the fire to collect the insurance money. This question made Connie shake her head so vehemently that Beth knew it was true. By the time they moved to a custom-built factory in Oldport, Mrs Wallace had her pearls, many strings to her bow, and Connie was still by her side, still supervising.

Bradley Wallace was sixty years old when he married the young Della. She was in debt to his textile company and wrote it off by signing her name on their marriage certificate. He gave her security and she gave him a son whom she never had time to love. Connie shook her head, sadly.

"She could have married many times before Bradley waved his cheque book in her direction but a man was only of use to Della if he could balance her books or run an efficient production line. Poor Peter, he has everything and nothing."

One evening, shortly afterwards, Beth's employer brought her to the storeroom where rolls of fabric were stacked on shelves. Mrs Wallace unrolled a thick bale of tweed that had been delivered that afternoon and asked her opinion.

"There's nothing different about it." Beth rubbed her hand over the rough texture, imagining the heathery-flecked coats being assembled piece by piece along the production line and finally, draped on the shoulders of mannequins in department stores. "It'll make up into the same coat style we've been manufacturing since I started working here."

"What's wrong with that, may I ask?" her employer demanded. "It's proved to be a very successful design for this company."

"But it's so old-fashioned. People want modern styles, not something their grannies wear to mass on Sunday."

Della Wallace seemed startled by her blunt reply. "How old are you?" she asked.

"Seventeen."

"Aren't you rather young to be so opinionated?"

"You asked my opinion so I assumed you wanted the truth."

"That's not Mr O'Toole's opinion and he's the one who brings in the orders. I haven't noticed any decline in our customer base – have you?"

"But there's no growth either. Young people don't even know the label exists."

"We're not in the business of pleasing young people. Perhaps that's just as well if they're all as outspoken as you. Are you as honest when my son asks your opinions on his paintings?"

"When people ask my opinion I always assume they want the truth," Beth replied.

She wondered if she would be fired for her outspoken views. If so, she would emigrate to London and live with Marina who wrote occasionally, boasting about her success on the catwalks and offering Beth a bed if she ever decided to leave the tomb of the living dead. She could do worse, Beth supposed. Like lying down on a bed of nails. She could endure Andy O'Toole and his small-minded meanness. When he finally took the bottle of vodka from the filing cabinet she would be ready to take over his job.

At first she had refused to visit Havenstone. The thought of entering her employer's home intimidated her. It looked so big and grand with its tree-shaded walls and high wrought-iron gates but Stewart finally persuaded her to come with him.

"You never go anywhere," he argued. "Come on. Peter's a big mouth but he won't bite you. All we ever do is listen to records."

To her surprise she had enjoyed the evening which turned out to be the first of many. Peter led them up a curving wooden staircase into his studio, a large L-shaped room, south-facing, filled with natural light. He was in his third year at art college and planned to study in Italy when he graduated. The studio was filled with what looked like rubbish; pieces of driftwood, broken glass, jagged bits of steel, all marked with 'Hands Off – Artist at Work' warnings in case his mother threw anything out. The only nude she saw was a self-portrait of Peter hanging from the moon in chains of barbed wire. He looked mortified when he realised it was among the canvases she was examining.

"It's a protest against the Apollo moon landings," he explained, quickly turning the painting to the wall. He believed that man had desecrated the moon by trespassing on its surface. She did not agree. Neil Armstrong was right. It was a giant leap for mankind. Stewart joined in the argument, insisting that technology was the new religion. Some day the world would be ruled by robots with human brains, a suggestion that triggered another discussion about the integrity of the human psyche. They listened to Jimi Hendrix and the Rolling Stones, lolling on bean bags as the music pounded around them.

"That was good, wasn't it?" Stewart said on the way home. "Aren't you glad you came?"

She nodded. A full moon reflected on the estuary. A melon moon pitted with craters, desert landscapes, a vast empty space – but all she could see was the long slim body of Peter Wallace filling it. He said she had incredible eyes. He wanted to paint them. Cat's eyes. The mirrors of the soul.

On Saturday afternoons they drank mugs of coffee, listened to loud music and argued over whether Peter should play Jimi Hendrix again or slow down the pace with Simon and Garfunkel. He talked about artists who had influenced him, Cézanne and Picasso, and his favourite artist, Paul Klee, who had painted a famous golden fish with a flower instead of an eye. He threw words like surrealism, abstraction and cubism into his conversation as he painted Beth's eyes into his Cat-astrophic Collection.

"Cat-astrophic," he would chant, breaking the words into syllables. "Cat-apult, Cat-aclysmic, Cat-walk, Cat-atonic, Cat-erpillar, Cat-holic, Cat-hedral."

She sometimes wondered if he was mad. Mad in a harmless way that translated itself into crazy paintings of cats, destructive, dangerous cats, sometimes so distorted that they resembled nothing she could recognise, apart from their eyes, familiar eyes that she saw every time she stared into the mirror.

In his first completed painting – which he called *Cat-apult* – a cat-figure with a grotesquely large head and elongated body hurtling through stars; a flaming comet hell-bent on destruction. In his *Cater-pillar* painting, he painted the bank in Oldport, recognisable by the ornate pillars at the entrance. A cat with blazing eyes arched against one of the pillars, an almost playful pose until it became obvious that the building was buckling beneath the force of the animal's fury. Beth asked if he was trying to upstage Jesus with a cat, laughing when she saw it and reminding him that the money scene in the temple had been done already. He said it was not what had been done before that mattered but how it was done by him.

"Have you ever wanted to destroy something and obliterate it from the face of the earth?" he asked when he was doing *Cat-walk*. Later, he showed her the finished canvas, a monstrous misshapen cat that looked more like a bulldozer, crouching in the centre of a green shady space that would soon become a housing estate. Her eyes were the headlights, glowing vengefully.

Afterwards, away from the studio, she was uneasy, aware that she was being manipulated. He painted such emotion into her eyes; as if they were indeed the mirror of her soul. She felt like a vessel, his voice pouring into her, opening her up with words that touched her fears, the anger she tried to suppress. The loneliness that swept over her when she allowed herself to remember. Yet she went back each Saturday, drawn by the growing intimacy between them, the sense of being part of something they were both creating. There were layers to his paintings that were not always apparent. She suspected the completed collection would contain a lot more of herself than she, or even he, realised.

At the end of each session he drove her home. His car had a low roof, a red low-slung two-seater that always attracted attention when he drove too fast through Oldport. Flared denims sat low on his hips, his sallow skin showing between the hip band and his paint-streaked T-shirt. His hair hung to his shoulders, scraggy, uncombed. A true artist at work.

"Artist, my arse!" hooted Connie, soon after the painting sessions began. "That brat couldn't whitewash a wall if I stood over him with a whip. If he touches one hair on your pretty head I'll tear his heart out. There's no need to look so shocked, Beth Tyrell. All that painting nonsense and the two of you alone up there in his bedroom for hours on end – it'll come to no good."

"It's his studio, Connie."

"Oh, so that's what he's calling it now?"

"Yes, Connie. I've never been inside his bedroom."

"Well, there's many a girl in Della Designs can't say the same thing," warned Connie. "Not to mention my poor Marina with her broken heart. Drinking, dancing and double-dating, that's all that fellow wants from life."

She wondered what Connie would say if she knew about the hash. He said it was a winding-down smoke and Beth would not be so uptight all the time if she shared an occasional joint with him. It annoyed her that he saw her like that, especially when he painted her in so many different images, none of them human, some not even animate.

"You mind what I'm saying, Beth Tyrell," Connie warned. "Peter Wallace has a tongue that would charm snakes from a basket. But easy words are soon forgotten."

Forgotten by whom, Beth wondered. She never forgot anything he said to her. Every casual compliment was branded on her mind. Words as airy as thistledown, blown carelessly in her direction, floating light, without substance.

Della Wallace also disapproved of the Saturday sessions. She usually found some excuse to enter the studio, cold with Beth for encouraging her son, sarcastic when she looked at his work. Her attempts to undermine his confidence infuriated Peter. Her presence was a constant reminder of the future she planned for him. The thought of working in the factory filled him with dread.

Beth was unsympathetic when he complained. "It's your own fault. This studio, the way you live. It's all laid on for you. Maybe you should move out and let your mother know you're serious – that's if you are serious."

"Of course I'm serious. It's all I've ever wanted to do." She had annoyed him and it pleased her that she could reach beyond the charm and confidence he displayed so effortlessly.

Her father complained of chest pains. He had difficulty breathing and could no longer play his tin whistle. When he was admitted to hospital for tests Beth wrote to her mother. Marjory replied by return of post. Barry Tyrell's problems were not her problems. She had no intention of allowing Sara to visit him.

A month later Barry was discharged from hospital. He was as fit as a fiddle, he declared. He returned to work on the building site and resumed playing with Celtic Reign.

Every Saturday afternoon Beth wrote to Jess and Sara. Only Jess bothered to reply.

Dear Jess

I was sorry to hear that you only achieved three honours in your Leaving Cert, especially as you made three novenas to St Jude. An honour per novena is an extremely poor return on your investment. If God intends making you his bride he should do a better job of looking after your interests.

And now, for my confession. Will you still be my friend if I tell you I've lost my faith? When you hear God's voice in the wind (how those words haunt me) I hear silence. But that's all right. It doesn't make me sad or anything. I'm an atheist now. I debated between becoming atheist or agnostic but I chose the former because I don't want any uncertainties in my life. It's strange, not believing in anything but it makes me feel free.

However, I still believe that our friendship is stronger than faith – or the lack of it.

Write soon with all the news.

Beth, your very best friend.

Dear Beth,

Your loss of faith saddens me but I agree – our friendship is indeed stronger than faith or, as in your case, the lack of it. With your permission I will pray for your conversion back to the one true religion. My novitiate begins in September. I'm coming to Dublin with Mammy to buy everything. You should see the list of things I need!! Glamour personified.

Latest news flash from Anaskeagh.

1. Your mother has opened a boutique on River Mall. It's called First Fashion, a most appropriate name since it's the first time fashion ever got its nose inside Anaskeagh.

2. Your uncle has become a county councillor. Big party in Cherry Vale. All the nobs went.

3. His creepy son, Conor, he of The Thousand Chinese Burns, will be going to University College Dublin to study law. God help the criminals, that's all I have to say on that subject.

4. Saw Sara on Anaskeagh Head last week taking photographs with the camera you sent her for her birthday. I asked her to reply to your letters but she told me to mind my own business. Sorry, Beth.

5. Best news last – I've persuaded Mammy to book us into the Oldport Grand when we come to Dublin on our shopping spree. I want you to spend every spare minute with me. Imagine – four years since we've seen each other. A life time ago.

Counting the minutes until I see you.

Love you forever xxxxx

Jess.

CHAPTER NINE

Catherine O'Donovan no longer had time to read books or study stars. The farm was losing money and when she took off her wellingtons in the evenings it was to change into the flat white shoes she wore on her night shift at the Anaskeagh Regional. She looked tired when she arrived in Oldport. Beth wondered if she ever felt lonely. Jess was her second child to leave home. Her oldest daughter sold second-hand clothes from a market stall in London. In Beth's opinion, bartering from a second-hand junk stall was a far more civilised existence than getting up in the small hours of the morning to chant at an non-existent God.

"Will you miss Jess when she goes into the convent?" she asked Catherine.

"Of course I will," Catherine replied. "But I'd have more chance of stopping a tornado in its tracks then making that young lady change her mind." She enjoyed being back in the hospital where she had originally trained but she had to keep on her toes to understand the changes that had taken place, particularly the drugs. She shivered just looking at the labels.

"I did my training with your Aunty May," she said. "The pair of us were great pals in those days."

"I didn't know you were friends with May." Beth was surprised.

"Not any more." Catherine smiled, ruefully. "May's been cutting a lot of old ties since she became a councillor's wife."

Beth's mouth clenched. Her pleasure in hearing about Anaskeagh was always marred by the mention of his name. Even after four years, it still had the power to terrify her.

Catherine lifted the heavy fringe from Beth's eyes. "Don't cover them up, Honeybun. They're beautiful. Tell me this and tell me no more, are you happy since you left Anaskeagh?"

"Very happy."

"The truth, Beth."

"It *is* the truth. Honest."

"Then why do you have the saddest pair of eyes I've ever seen on a young girl's face?" she asked.

She took out her photographs of Anaskeagh and handed them to Beth. The familiar farm, the O'Donovan children with their big bones and cheeky grins. Sara was included in some of the photographs. How tall and leggy she looked, playing Hamlet in the school play. She was the Blessed Virgin in the Lourdes tableaux, which was performed in the Star of the Sea assembly hall. Her eyes stared past the adoring crowd at her feet. Another photograph showed her dancing at the Anaskeagh Feis, ringlets bobbing as she did her reels and jigs. Beth handed the photographs back without a word. The older woman held her close when she began to sob.

"Come home, Honeybun. Your mother misses you." She sighed when Beth shook her head. "Young people ... why do they always hurt the ones who love them most?"

Jess laid out her new clothes on the bed. She giggled, holding up a thick pair of knickers with elasticated legs. Beth snatched them from her and waved them in the air.

"Black knickers! This looks like a serious mortal sin, Sr Holy Mary Ringo. Shame on you."

"Black everything," sighed Jess. She fitted on one of her dresses and admired herself in the mirror.

"You look more like the bride of Dracula than the bride of Christ," declared Beth. "And your boobs have disappeared." She prodded her friend's chest. "Is this a miracle of the flesh – or just bad tailor-ing?"

"Oh shut up and be serious for a minute." Jess's eyes were solemn, accusing Beth of making fun of her. "You think this is all one big joke, don't you?"

"Of course I don't, Jess." But it was difficult to understand this all-embracing need her friend described. It transcended the loneliness she must feel at leaving her family, of never falling in love or having babies of her own. A life that had become so alien to Beth she was afraid it would separate them. They would no longer be able to talk and laugh and simply be happy being together. "It's just ... oh, I don't know ... do you still hear His voice calling you?"

"Just my own voice," Jess replied, quietly. "That was all I ever heard. And it always told me the same thing. My life belongs to Christ. I can't see myself living any other way."

Beth felt like crying because her friend spoke and looked like a stranger, pale and stalky under the voluminous black folds. This was actually going to happen. She was going to become a bride of Christ. Even the words sounded crazy. She would rise at dawn to chant at a non-existent God and float through life on incense and divine grace. What would it be like to experience the kind of love Jess described? Consuming, adoring, safe.

On their final night in Oldport they went to a local pub called The Fiddler's Nest to hear Celtic Reign playing. Peter Wallace joined them, pulling his chair close to Jess and flirting with her. Her vocation was a crime against mankind, he declared. She was too earthy, too vibrant to be incarcerated behind high walls. Saints were all mystery and soul. Jess was all heart and curves. She enjoyed him, giggling into a gin and orange and getting quite tipsy. All heads turned when Marina McKeever entered. Her black hair fell to the hem of her hot pants. She was back in the tomb of the living dead for a short visit. She opened her large handbag to show everyone her photographs. She had appeared in a trade magazine for medical aids, modelling an acne face wash, a surgical shoe for fallen arches and tablets for indigestion. Her ambition was to do chocolate advertisements.

"Subliminal sexual desire," she boasted. "It's what everything's about these days, darlings." She no longer wore falsies in her bra or any bra at all, for that matter. As always, Beth felt invisible in her exuberant presence.

"Sexual liberation's the 'in' thing," she informed Jess, who was fascinated by her glamour and by the packet of pills with the days of the month marked on them, which Marina showed her in the Ladies.

"I want to understand what I'm missing," she confided in a low voice to Beth. "This is my last opportunity."

"Oh – you're such a *pseud*, darling." Marina shrieked when she heard about the *Cat* paintings. She told Peter he could show her his etchings any time he was in London. Beth hated her. She hated the way she clicked her fingers at sex, laughing and batting her false eyelashes at all the men in the pub. Beth wondered how it would feel to 'do it' on a bale of blue velvet material – or on a sighing bed in the darkness of a London flat. Her stomach heaved at the image that came into her mind. She pressed her hand against her mouth and slowly the choking feeling went away. Love was red dresses and swirling music. A rainbow of dreams.

She wanted to tell Jess about the terror of those moments when the atmosphere changed, grew quiet, expectant. The deepening breath of the young man beside her, knowing he was going to put his hands on her skin and how the horror would swoop high as a bird fluttering in her chest. It didn't matter where it happened, the back seat of a cinema, the shelter of the sand dunes, the dark shadows in the back of a car.

"You're a raving lunatic," Billy Brennan from Dispatch had yelled, after his one and only date with her. When he parked his car facing the estuary and forced his hand inside her blouse she released the handbrake. His frantic efforts to stop the car entering the water had been successful, but only just.

"You could have fucking drowned me." He was unable to stop shaking as he drove her back to Main Strand Street.

"So I could." Beth laughed her terror away. "Imagine what a loss that would be to humanity."

In the office the young women knotted nylon scarves around their necks to cover love bites, slyly showing them off to their closest friends. Over coffee breaks and lulls in typing, she listened to their conversations, hoping to find a clue, something to reassure her that her fears were normal. There had been others besides Billy Brennan. Men from Della Designs or those who slow-danced with her in the Sweat Pit. But when Stewart brought her for a ride on his new motorbike it should have been different.

Stewart had changed from the painfully shy boy she had known when she first came to Oldport. His slouching, lanky frame had filled out and his powerful hands no longer looked too big and awkward for his body. He was not handsome in an obvious way like Peter Wallace, with his honey skin and luminous eyes, but she liked how his strong square face came to life when he laughed.

"Since when did you join Hell's Angels?" she asked when he arrived home one Saturday in leather and parked a motorbike outside the house.

"Ask no questions and you'll be told no lies." His excitement was palpable as he stood beside the gleaming bike. "I've been saving for years. What do you think?"

"A Harley Davidson – it's fantastic."

"Want a ride?"

"What are we waiting for?"

He placed the helmet over her head and steadied her on the pillion seat.

She allowed herself to feel the speed, the roar of the

engine throbbing beneath her, his body shielding her from the wind that rushed past, singing in her ears. She held tightly to his waist as they left Oldport and headed towards Skerries. Black suited him, she decided, unsure whether it was the novelty of the motorbike or the image of him, dark and vaguely threatening in his biker boots and jacket, that lifted her spirits. Impulsively, she tightened her grip, hugging him closer.

"Like it?" he shouted.

"Love it," she shouted back.

He pressed her hands briefly and she felt a sudden shiver along her arms, as if his touch triggered some dormant emotion, rushing it free in the exhilaration of the moment.

The house was empty when they returned. Connie and Barry had gone to the cinema and would not be home until late. They sat on the sofa, mugs steaming on the coffee table, sharing a plate of biscuits, reminiscing about the first night they met.

"I can still picture you when you came into the house. As if you wanted to cut us in half with your eyes." He smiled, speaking so low she could hardly hear him. "God, you were terrifying, standing there with your duffel bag and that skimpy coat and the rain running out of your hair. I think that was when I fell in love with you. Or maybe it was five minutes later when you smiled and I realised you were the most beautiful girl I'd ever seen ... you must know how I feel, Beth. You *must*."

She nodded, glancing down at her hands as they began to tremble, a faint vibration which she tried to control, tightening them into fists when he leaned towards her.

He held her shoulders, his eyes warming her, drawing

her to him. When she did not push him from her a waiting space opened between them, questions asked and answered in the silence. He slid his arms around her waist. She felt the hard contour of the sofa underneath her, the ridge at the edge pressing into the back of her knees.

"I'm crazy about you." He muttered the words into her neck, his breath warm on her skin. She heard again the shyness in his voice. The effort it took to say what he needed to say. He kissed her, softly at first, then pressing more firmly, moving, searching for some response and she heard a moan deep in his throat, terrifying her with its force. Her breath shortened, catching dry.

"No! Leave me alone – leave me alone." She pushed him away and sprang to her feet. Only when she saw the scratches on his face did she realise she had torn his skin. "I'm sorry, Stewart ... I'm terribly sorry ... I can't stand it ... you mustn't ... mustn't ..." She gripped the arm of the sofa, willing the horror away.

For an instant he seemed dazed by her reaction. He tried to speak but couldn't get the words out. Abruptly, he stood up. "I thought – ah, forget it. I've been a fool." He grabbed his jacket and slung it over his shoulders. She could smell the new leather, hear the faint creak it made when he moved up the hall and out the front door.

Stewart should have been different. He was not Billy Brennan or the other faceless young men with whom she sought oblivion. Stewart was her friend. His strength should not threaten her. His hard cold strength, overwhelming, crushing her into nothing.

CHAPTER TEN

At first Celtic Reign played quietly, afraid their music would intrude too harshly into the internal world the sick man had created within himself. Crowded together in Connie's sitting room, the musicians filled their glasses with whiskey or snapped the tops off Guinness bottles. This small room with its glass ornaments and dried flowers in the window was the 'showing off room', used only when visitors arrived. Cigarettes were lit, smoke spiralling upwards. Barry coughed and muffled the sound into his fist.

The session was Connie's idea. At first he was irritable when she suggested it. He feared the musicians were humouring him. He did not want them to see him like this, an empty, dried-up shadow. She assured him they needed this time with him. They wanted to participate. She did not say, "in your dying", but the words hung in the air and Beth felt this understanding flow swift as a current between the two of them.

Before the musicians arrived, Connie eased him from

his bed, exchanging his crumpled pyjamas for a pair of jeans and a shirt with neon flowers, a gaudy pattern that only succeeded in emphasising his wasted body. She seated him in the armchair so that his friends would not notice how slowly he moved. Beth trimmed his beard. Like his hair it had grown sparse over the past months and was cut into shape with a few snips.

As the glasses emptied the tempo of the music quickened, carrying its own momentum. Soon the musicians were lost in the notes and Barry became one with them, his eyes bright as he jigged his foot. For a short while he played the spoons. His hands were skeletal, the spoons rapping off his skinny knees. The sound reminded Beth of rattling bones. He called on her to dance. She was seized by the familiar embarrassment, reverting to the panic of a small child asked to perform in front of adults. She had not danced since that Christmas at Cherry Vale. Something painful caught in her memory and was released in the same instant. A sensation so familiar she hardly noticed it.

The fiddle player, Annie Loughrey, ran the bow over her fiddle, shouting, "How about a reel, Beth? We'll go easy on you."

She took off her shoes but her feet still felt heavy, clumsy because she had not danced for so long. When the musicians yelled and stamped she was carried away by their enthusiasm. She was aware of Stewart watching her, his shoulder propped against the wall, a glass of beer in his hand. She moved to the increasing tempo, arms stiff by her side, hair flying. Her legs kicked out, her shirt swirled. His eyes told her he liked what he saw before he looked away.

Peter did not look away. When she finished dancing he swung her around and kissed her cheek.

Soon afterwards her father's shoulders slumped. The animation left his face. Connie moved swiftly towards him but he insisted on one more tune.

"Play 'Carrickfergus', Annie. No one can stroke that tune the way you can."

"It would draw tears from a stone," agreed Blake Dolan, bending his head dolefully over his bodhrán.

Annie began to play. The young girl had long delicate fingers. The notes rose, a thin quavering lament. The thoughts of each person in the room seemed to fuse, achingly aware of the wasted man sitting so still in their midst. Soon afterwards, the musicians left to play in the Fiddler's Nest, hearty in their farewells, not admitting that this was the last goodbye. Barry, equally anxious to keep up the pretence, joked them from the room.

"Cheer up, me darlin'. I've seen him looking worse on many a morning after a hard session in the Nest." At the front door, the bodhrán player joked with Beth. He patted the back of her head, as if he was already offering his condolences. Peter also said goodbye. He had a painting to finish before morning.

When Connie came downstairs after settling Barry for the night she poured a glass of whiskey and drank it neat, tilting her head back. Under the light Beth noticed grey roots fading into her black hair.

"You're going to collapse before this is over if you don't watch yourself," she warned. "Daddy should be back in hospital."

"You know how he feels about hospitals," replied

Connie. "Anyway, what can they do for him except prolong his agony. He wants to die here and as long as I can look after him I'll be with him."

"Connie … does he realise … does he talk to you about it?"

"We've talked about it, yes." Connie's voice was slightly slurred. Lipstick stained the glass, a bruised kiss clouding the rim.

"Then why won't he talk to me?" demanded Beth. Her eyes were scalded with unshed tears but her father had not given her permission to cry. He always spoke to her about cheerful things and what he would do as soon as he recovered, meaningless plans that made her ashamed when their time together was so short. "He keeps pretending he's going to get better."

"He hasn't the words to tell you what he's feeling. It's different with me. We have no history, no regrets."

Beth reached forward and squeezed her hand. "Celtic Reign coming here was a terrific idea. I hope he's carried away on a stream of music."

The older woman poured another drink, sipping it slowly this time. "Sara should be here. I can't understand why your mother's being so stubborn. She's breaking his heart."

Stewart came into the room. He took the empty glass from her and placed it on the table. "You should try and get some sleep, Ma, while you have the chance."

Connie's footsteps dragged wearily as she mounted the stairs and entered the bedroom where Barry dozed uneasily. It seemed so unfair, Beth thought, his wasted years with Marjory and a few short years with the woman he loved.

An unforgivable love in the eyes of so many people, selfish in the demands it had made on their families, yet she did not resent the brief happiness they had known.

"I'm going for a walk." Stewart took his leather jacket from a hook on the door. He glanced at the empty bottles, the overflowing ashtrays and stale sandwiches. "I need some fresh air before I tackle this lot. Want to come?"

Beth's head throbbed from the stuffy heat in the room. She linked his arm as they turned without hesitation towards the estuary road.

A light burned from one window in Havenstone. His studio. He sometimes slept on the floor when he was working and everything was flowing in the right direction. An animal in his lair, she thought, comfortable where he dropped, stretched out on an old mattress he kept propped against the wall. Moonlight touching the half-finished canvases as he drifted off to sleep.

At Pier's Point a heron, caught in the glow of moonlight, lifted its wings and glided into the darkness.

"I had a dream about flying last night," she said. "I woke up thinking that that's the way it must be when you die … flying into the sky and everything down below becoming dimmer and dimmer until you are all alone in the dark."

"Maybe you're flying through the dark to get to the light," said Stewart.

"That sounds like something Jess would say."

"How is she?"

"On her knees chanting litanies, I should imagine."

Jess still wrote every week. Serene letters brimming with

descriptions of silent meals, needlecraft, woodwork sessions, basketball practice, prayer vigils, meditation and contemplation. Sometimes, in the early hours when she was in the church praying, she felt herself lifted high on a wave of bliss, so powerful it made her tremble in case it was ever taken away from her.

"I touch the core of my being," she wrote. "And God is there waiting for me to arrive."

Beth believed this was magic mushroom stuff. Smoke some grass and see the Lord. Or a state of mind brought about by overwork. Jess's daily schedule read like the itinerary of a Siberian gulag. In her last letter Beth wrote back: "It must be wonderful to know yourself so well that when you feel the touch of happiness you can claim it as your right."

Reading over what she had written she was puzzled by the meaning in her own words but she left them there, knowing Jess would under-stand.

She touched Stewart's arm. "I don't know what to do."

"About Sara?"

"Yes. She won't come to the phone when I ring. I can't believe she'll let Daddy die without saying goodbye to him."

"I'm sure she'll change her mind. Come on home. Standing here in the cold won't solve anything. It's time you were in bed."

Reluctantly, she left the pier and turned in the direction of Main Strand Street. As they approached the house she noticed the long car parked outside.

"A Mercedes!" Stewart stopped to examine the registration plate. "Very flash." He sounded impressed. "Wonder who that belongs too?"

"I know the owner." She was surprised at the calmness in her voice. She turned the key in the front door and entered.

Tom Oliver had put on weight. She could see it on his face, under his chin. He stood in front of the fireplace, smiling. He had grown a moustache. It tickled her cheek when he hugged her. She was swamped in his warmth, the familiar scent of Old Spice and soap.

She forced herself to stand still until he released her. "What the hell are you doing here?" she demanded.

"What a way to greet your uncle, love. I'm surprised at you." Connie sounded amazed. She made an attempt to tidy bottles out of the way then stopped, embarrassed by the debris of the party.

"Well, I'm surprised too. He only comes to Dublin when he has something nasty to do. I'm just wondering what it is this time?"

"I came when Marjory told me the sad news. Poor Barry. A fragile grip on reality at the best of times." He stared at Stewart, then back at Connie. "I presume this young man is your son, Mrs McKeever?"

"He is indeed." Beth saw her mouth tremble as Tom Oliver ignored Stewart's outstretched hand. A whistle shrilled from the kitchen where the kettle boiled. She rose to her feet. "Councillor Oliver, tea or coffee?"

"Tea will be fine, Mrs McKeever."

When she left the room he took off his jacket, easing his shoulders in circular movements. "That's better. I've had a long drive. It's good to see you again, Beth, although I hoped we could have met under happier circumstances – like a visit home to your unfortunate mother."

"I asked you a question and you still haven't answered it," she replied. "What are you doing here?"

"I think it's fairly obvious why I'm here. I've booked into the Oldport Grand for the night. In the morning I've organised an ambulance to collect your father and bring him home to Anaskeagh."

Beth froze. "No fucking way!"

"Beth!" Connie, horrified, stood in the doorway, a tray in her hands. "I can't believe my ears. Shame on you."

"I'm sorry, Connie. But he can't just suddenly appear and start taking over. He wants to take Daddy away."

Connie placed the tray on the coffee table. She glanced fearfully towards the councillor and shook her head. "I'm afraid there's some mistake, Councillor. Barry has no intention of going back to Anaskeagh."

"Please, Mrs McKeever, don't make a scene." He smoothly interrupted her. "I'm only doing what is right and proper under the circumstances. This is not exactly the ideal environment for a sick man." A smile touched his lips as he surveyed the room, raising his eyebrows at the sight of an empty whiskey bottle lying on the floor.

"Daddy is not going anywhere." Beth shouted. She was aware of Stewart holding her hand, trying to calm her down.

"Mr Oliver, you can't just ignore what my mother is saying. Barry wants to stay here with us."

"Young man, I mean no disrespect to your mother." He gave a slight bow in Connie's direction and swept his gaze back to Stewart. "But I need hardly remind you that she is not Barry Tyrell's wife. As the law stands she has absolutely no rights, no say, no decision." His tone changed, became placating as he turned his attention back to Connie. "Let's look at it this way, Mrs McKeever, you must be worn out looking after a sick man. I'm relieving you of the burden of responsibility—"

"She's worn out all right but that's the way she wants it," Beth interrupted. "He made her promise to be beside him when he … goes."

Her uncle shook his head, firmly. "I'm afraid it's not that simple. Your father is coming home to Anaskeagh where he belongs. To be with the people to whom he belongs. With his wife's permission I've booked him into a private ward in the Anaskeagh Regional. He'll have the best of care and the chance to die peacefully, with dignity and surrounded by his own."

"Appearances!" Beth shrieked. "That's all you care about. Just because you're a county councillor – you don't give a tinker's curse about my father. Neither does she! She wouldn't even let Sara visit him."

"Beth – calm down. I'm not having any arguments in my house when Barry is so ill. Tomorrow when he's stronger we'll let him decide what he wants to do."

"I'm afraid not, Mrs McKeever. It is as I've stated. There will be no further arguments." Tom Oliver did not try to disguise his anger. "In the morning you will come with me, Beth. You will do what a good daughter should do and look after your father instead of allowing outsiders to do it for you. As for you, Mrs McKeever, an ambulance will be at your house at nine in the morning. I don't think you'd like to deprive a dying man of his last opportunity to see his wife and daughter. If there are farewells to be made let them be made before then. I don't want to see you or your family near Anaskeagh at any stage. Is that clearly understood?"

CHAPTER ELEVEN

Barry Tyrell took a month to die. Once he was admitted to hospital the stoicism he had shown in Oldport deserted him. He snarled and spat and suffered his way through his final weeks until even Beth dreaded spending time with him in the small ward he called "Death Row". When his lips dried into cracked sores she swabbed them with wet cotton wool. She spooned cold drinks into his mouth and wrote the letters he dictated to Connie until his mind wandered, unable to concentrate. Then she composed them herself, escaping into the fresh air for a few minutes to post them. She read Connie's replies to him, taking the letters with her when she left the hospital in case Marjory found them.

Twice his family were called to his bedside in the middle of the night and twice the doctors brought him back again. Lonely, resentful, frightened, he lingered on.

"Meddling bastards," he raged. "Why can't they let me die in peace? I'm spent, washed up. What good will it do to give me a few more days?"

Catherine O'Donovan said he was the most bad-tempered patient she had ever nursed. "I've had some lulus in my time but he takes the biscuit. Poor devil."

Every time the postman called Beth expected a letter from Mrs Wallace informing her that she was fired. Twice a week she rang Stewart from the public phone at the hospital. She looked forward to hearing his voice, reassuring her that there was another world outside Death Row and its cocooned, glass-house atmosphere.

Marjory's visits to the hospital were brief and businesslike. She talked to the ward sister and the doctor on duty. The nurses brought her cups of tea and biscuits. They wanted to know what new styles were in the boutique and she promised them a discount of ten per cent. Fr Breen, doing his hospital rounds, blessed her and called her a saint in the truest sense of the word. Beth always left the ward as soon as her mother entered, ignoring the pleading look Barry gave her, the tight, dry grip of his fingers. He wanted her with him all the time. She resented the responsibility his dependence placed on her, longing to be back in Oldport, feeling guilty at the intensity of this need, knowing she would only be released when he was laid to rest.

So many changes to be absorbed. First Fashion boutique added to the prosperous air of the town. Even Marina would be impressed, Beth decided, staring in the windows at mannequins in hot pants, long sleeveless cardigans, maxi dresses, tousled hair. A Chinese restaurant and a launderette had opened on River Mall. The old cinema, known as The Flea Circus, had been turned into a bingo hall. Maggie

Hearn had sold her grocery store and a modern supermarket with chrome shelves and pale stripes of florescent lighting stood in its place. Fresh pebbledash livened up the grey walls of the council houses on Fatima Estate. But Marjory was determined to move and had bought one of the new houses being built on the site of the Emerald Ballroom.

"The next time you decide to honour us with your presence I'll have moved as far as possible from this slum your father forced me to live in," she informed Beth soon after her arrival.

"I'm glad things worked out so well for you—" Beth attempted to soothe old wounds.

"Oh no, things didn't work out." Marjory interrupted, her voice quickening. "I made them happen. Despite everything!" She too had changed. The weight she had lost suited her, although heavy make-up gave her face a mask-like appearance. Her hair was bleached and short, bobbing sleekly on her cheekbones.

Her sewing room was now a spare bedroom where Beth slept for the duration of her visit. The wardrobe, a den where monsters once crouched and waited in the darkness of childhood fears, still had a mothball smell. Standing on carved claws, in need of a good polishing, it looked curiously alien in its new surroundings. There had been no monster. Only the shadow of her uncle, vague and threatening. She was four years old when she opened her eyes one night and saw him standing beside her bed, the wardrobe door open behind him. For an instant she thought he had been hiding inside and had jumped out to scare her. Four years of age … maybe he had come to her room before then. She had no memory. Only when she was four did she understand the meaning of fear and she had carried it as a shield in front of her ever since.

No matter how often she tried to change the subject, his name ran like a magnetic thread through her mother's conversation. Since becoming a councillor he had galvanised the county council with his energy and dedication. A new primary school was being built. He had plans for attracting big business into the town. He was the driving force behind the GAA. He was lobbying for funding to improve the town's sewage system.

"At least that should give him enough space to take a shite," sneered Beth. This remark was the end of the uneasy truce they had tried to maintain since her return home. She was relieved they did not have to pretend any longer.

"How dare you use that kind of filthy language in my house." Marjory glared at her. "You're disgusting! Working in a factory certainly hasn't improved your manners. Your uncle may be a busy man but he never forgets his family. We wouldn't have anything if it wasn't for him."

"Can we occasionally change the tune?" Beth tried to control her temper. "I'm sick hearing about St Thomas, patron saint of the needy."

"Then you can hear it again," insisted Marjory. "While your father was swanning around Dublin with his whore my brother took the time to sit down and help me draw up my business plan. He's financed my boutique, lock, stock and barrel. When Sara finishes her Leaving she's going to university, thanks to him. At least one of my daughters will be able to rise above the level of working in a factory."

"What about me? What favours did he ever do for me?" Beth leaned towards her mother. "Fuck all – that's what!"

"Stop it! Stop it … both of you." Sara, who had been sitting between them, jumped to her feet. "I'm sick listening to the two of you going on at each other." She turned furiously to Beth. " At least we have peace when you're not here. If you can't stop fighting with Mammy I don't want you to come home ever again." She ran from the room, slamming the door behind her.

"Satisfied?" demanded Marjory.

"It's strange." said Beth. "Daddy's dying and all we can do is say hurtful things to each other. I hoped it would be different when I came home but it's still exactly the same."

"And who's to blame for that, may I ask?" Marjory lit a cigarette, inhaling deeply. "It's too late for apologies, madam. Over four years too late. The only reason you're here is because your uncle insisted you do your duty." She removed a flake of ash from her lip, appraising her daughter behind a haze of smoke. "How do you think I felt? My daughter disappearing without a word and not even one visit in that time. Not even for Christmas. You certainly gave the gossips plenty of ammunition—"

"So, what did I have?" Beth interrupted. "A boy or girl – or was it twins?"

"You think it's so funny? Well, let me tell you something, Miss. If it wasn't for Sara I wouldn't let you set foot in this house again. Any more smart remarks or language and you're out on your ear so fast you won't know what hit you? Do I make myself clear?"

"Crystal clear," replied Beth. "It's great to be home."

Sara never stayed for long at the hospital. Her father's laboured breathing made her fidget and stare out the window. His presence placed a burden upon her young shoulders that she was ill-prepared to carry. She made no effort to talk to Beth and spent most of her time in her bedroom. One day, when she was at school, Beth looked inside the room they had once shared. Sara had painted the walls white. She had filled it with white veneer furniture, white curtains and a pale blue carpet. A large white bear was propped on a wicker chair, the only childish thing in this cold clinical room. Enlarged photographs hung on the walls. Shots of Fatima Parade, doorways, alleyways, open gates, starkly empty. The river running through the centre of the town had a sinister fury. It reflected the high octagonal tower with the clock face on River Mall. Sara had written 'Time Flows By' at the bottom of each photograph.

Beth was uneasy as she closed the door quietly behind her. She felt as if her presence had left a smudge on the pristine surroundings, like the twiggy footprints of a bird running over a surface of snow.

Anaskeagh Head was still a forbidding challenge. One afternoon the sisters climbed to the summit. Goldie moved stiffly, limping slightly. Arthritis, Beth guessed. She rubbed his back, noticing grey hairs in his coat, pleased when he did not pull away. Time had obviously healed his fear or brought him to terms with it. His breath grew quieter as he rolled over and offered his belly to be stroked.

They followed a passage Sara had discovered on the slopes of the headland, almost overgrown with ferns and briars that clung to their jeans. It might have been used by

sheep or maybe it had been created by the way the wind
blew into the scrub and forced it to grow naturally apart.
It lead them to Aislin's Roof, one of the biggest rocks Beth
had ever seen, almost cavernous in its width and
overhanging slant. Sara was unable to keep still. The camera
Beth had sent to her for her twelfth birthday hung from
her neck. She photographed birds in flight and a dead tree,
twisted stunted limbs outlined against the sky. The wind
blew stronger as they climbed upwards and the sun, clearing
the clouds for a few moments, struck against the granite
rock, surrounding the girls in flickering walls of mica.

"This is what I miss most," said Beth. She sat down and
waved her hand at the peaks. "Oldport is so flat. Just fields
of vegetables and flowers – although Peter says I should
enjoy it while I can. Soon it will be covered in houses."

"Tell me about him? Is he a good painter?" Sara asked.

"How should I know?" She was taken aback at the
suddenness of the question. "Personally, I don't like what he
does. I can never figure it out."

"Even when he paints you?"

"Especially when he paints me." She laughed abruptly.

"Are you in love with him?"

"I certainly am not!" She was glad her sister was not
looking at her. "He's the most self-opinionated person I've
ever met."

"What about the whore who was living with my father?
Tell me about her." She turned and stared down at Beth,
challenging her.

"You sound just like Marjory." Beth was furious.
"Connie McKeever is *not* a whore and you'd better stop
calling her one."

Her sister shrugged and aimed her camera, moving closer to Beth, focusing on different angles of her face. "Why did you run away and leave me?" she asked, suddenly.

"Stop it, will you?" Beth shielded herself with her hands.

"Why? Why? Why?" Sara clicked on each word than ceased as suddenly as she started. The camera dangled from one hand. A bemused expression settled over her face, as if she was trying to remember the question.

"You know why! All that shit with Charlie. Imagine calling a cane Charlie. When I think how terrified I used to be of it."

Sara sat down beside her and flung her hair back in a sudden jerk. "Did you break Uncle Tom's window?" she asked.

"No." Beth's heart leapt. "Which window?"

"The big bay one in the front. Someone broke it the night you went away."

"Why would I want to do a daft thing like that?"

"I don't know. I'm just asking. You're always saying horrible things about him so I thought ..."

"Well, you thought wrong. It wasn't me."

"If you say so." She giggled suddenly, nervously fisting a hand in front of her mouth. "Tell me about the whore's son. Do you fancy him too? Stewart. That's his name, isn't it?"

"Sara! Why are you behaving like this?" Beth's anger snapped. "What's wrong with you?"

The young girl drew her knees to her chin and encircled them with her arms. Her hands were hidden under the loose sleeves of her jumper. The slate-grey shade drained her face of colour. Shapeless over her jeans, it was the most unattractive thing Beth had ever seen her wear. She was a circle within herself, projecting neither thought or emotion until suddenly, without any change in her posture, she began to cry.

"Don't go back to Oldport," she sobbed. "There's no reason to go back to those people. You don't belong to them."

"Why should I stay here? I'd smother if I had to live an extra minute in this one-horse town."

"It's not so bad. We're somebody here. Mammy has her shop and we're moving to the new house soon. It'll be great, Beth. She wants you to work with her. She's afraid if she asks you'll say no."

"Are you away with the fairies, or what?" She was glad to have something to rebuff. "Why don't we bring Charlie as well. Then we could all have a jolly old reunion."

"It doesn't have to be that way, Beth, it doesn't. It was easier when you lived here – she didn't expect so much from me." Sara's voice was husky. She coughed, trying to clear mucus from her throat. "Please stay here … please, Beth."

"No!" She was trapped by Sara's closeness, the guilt her sister aroused in her. "I won't stay here and that's the end of it. Stop going on at me."

"I should have known you wouldn't listen. You don't care about anyone but yourself – and that Peter Wallace. Cat's eyes, cat's fucking stupid eyes! I've never heard of anything so stupid in all my life."

"Sara … what are you saying? I can't believe you're using such language."

"I'm not using language. I'm just telling the truth. I don't want you here – or him either. Why can't he just die and get it over with?" She began to shout, banging her fists off the grass.

"Don't worry," Beth replied, coldly. "I'm sure he'll oblige us before long. Then we'll all be out of your precious way again – only he'll be gone for good. Your precious Councillor Oliver hi-jacked him from the people who loved him and he allowed it to happen so that he could be with you."

"So? Am I supposed to fall on my knees and thank him? He was the one who left in the first place. Just the same way you did, and you're leaving me again so you can be with your precious artist. You needn't write any more of your stupid letters. I never bother reading them."

"Sara, please stop." When Beth stroked her sister's shoulder she felt the slightest of tremors, almost a reflex, a nerve impulse. "As soon as you want you can come to Oldport and live with me. You'll love it."

"Lay off, will you?" Sara whipped back from her touch. "I'm not a fucking dog. Perhaps that's just as well – you'd probably drown me if I was."

For an instant Beth was too shocked to speak. Then she realised that there was nothing she could say, or wanted to say, that could erase the cruelty of her sister's remark. They did not speak as they descended the headland. As soon as they arrived home Sara entered her bedroom and slammed the door behind her.

Barry Tyrell died in the middle of the night, suddenly and alone. By the time his family reached the hospital it was over. Sara did not want to see him. She sat outside the ward, a mug of tea untouched by her feet.

"I'll have nightmares," she said. "He's only a shell, anyway." She had knotted a bright red scarf at the neck of her jumper and nervously pulled at it, twisting it tighter. Her feet tapped rapidly against the floor, sending tremors through her legs. She seemed unaware of the tremulous movements until Beth put her hand on her knees to calm her down. The younger girl's face was white, glistening with a sheen of perspiration. She swayed and slumped forward. Beth tried to press her head between her knees but Sara fended her off, struggling to remain conscious.

"I have to get away from this place." She walked down the corridor, almost running as she neared the lifts. On the tiled corridor her boots clacked loudly, red, the same shade as her scarf. She stopped briefly to speak to Catherine O'Donovan, then hurried on again.

"Poor little Sara. She's very upset." Catherine sat down beside Beth and handed her a mug of hot tea. "No matter how well prepared you think you are it's always a shock when someone you love dies. God bless him, he's at peace at last. Have a good cry if you feel the need."

Beth leaned into the crisp white apron to be hugged. The hospital was silent. The small hours when death comes quietly. She did not feel like crying but the solid feel of the nurse's arms comforted her.

"I'll phone Jess first thing in the morning and tell her the sad news," said Catherine.

"I miss her something awful. I wish she could be here now."

"We all do." Catherine sighed. "But as long as she's happy that's what counts."

Her mother and uncle were still inside the ward, making

decisions. Beth wondered if she should try and find her sister. The effort of moving was too great. She stared dully at the opposite wall. She must feel something. There had to be certain emotions suitable for the occasion. Exhaustion. She was floating on a wave of exhaustion. His death had given her permission to be tired.

The coffin gleamed on the altar steps. Voices murmured the responses. The silence of transubstantiation was disturbed by someone coughing at the back of the church. The Eucharist bell jingled. Everyone bowed their heads except Beth who stared woodenly at the altar. At communion the congregation held back, making space for the Tyrell family to lead the procession to the altar rail. Fr Breen stood waiting, the host upheld in his hand. Marjory walked slowly towards him, sharp and dramatic in a black suit and high heels.

"Move," whispered Sara, standing up to follow Beth.

"I'm not receiving." Beth shifted her knees, allowing her sister to pass. Her uncle slid into the space vacated by Sara. "Have you no respect for your father's memory?" he asked, his voice low but commanding. "Stand up at once and go to the altar."

"No."

"Do as I say!"

"Why? God does not exist." She hissed the words into his ear. "He's a fake – just like you."

She wondered if the tabernacle would shatter. If blood would flow from the Eucharist in a tidal wave of outrage? Would the flame from the sanctuary lamp gutter and die?

Blasphemy was a sin that marked the soul of the sinner with an indelible brand, Sr Clare had warned them in First Year.

Tom Oliver's mouth opened, shocked. "May God in his mercy forgive you. You have disgraced the memory of your dead father." He bowed his head and moved past her. The congregation rose respectfully to its feet and followed him.

CHAPTER TWELVE

It was good to be back in Oldport, like coming home, thought Beth, not sure whether to feel sad or happy at this realisation. Much to her surprise Mrs Wallace informed her that she would be working directly under her. Away from cigar smoke and the grumbles of the sales manager, life was good, providing she did not think about Sara and the tears she had shed on Anaskeagh Head. Or the silent phone calls that haunted her since her return. They came late at night when she was preparing to go to bed, always around the same time. She dreaded the eerie silence as she waited for someone to speak.

She confided in Stewart one evening when he returned from a motorbike rally in Skerries. He believed they were obscene phone calls and should be reported. She disagreed. Obscenity was heavy breathing. Fear and control. Ugly suggestions and demands. This was different. An invisible presence, wraith-like, holding on, trembling at the brink of words.

"I know it's Sara."

"Why don't you go home and see her?"

"I can't ... not yet."

"You've more important things to do, I suppose." He made no effort to hide his jealousy. "Surprise me and tell me he's finally finished those paintings."

"Almost." She did not want to discuss the Saturday sessions with anyone, particularly Stewart, who always looked sceptical whenever Peter's name was mentioned. He seldom went to Havenstone any more.

"What exactly is he doing?" he asked. "Please educate me on the finer aspects of art."

She tried to explain about the *Cat-astrophic* Collection and watched his eyebrows climb.

"I'll say this for him, he's feeding you a great line in bullshit," he angrily interrupted her. "And there's only one reason you're falling for it."

"It's not like that," she protested. "You've got it all wrong."

"Have I?" He quickly turned and faced her. "What have I got wrong? The bullshit or the fact that you fancy him like mad."

"Both!" she snapped. "I'm too busy to fancy him, or anyone."

"Busy doing what?" he asked. "All you ever seem to do is work. No one expects you to run Della Designs single-handedly." He lifted his arm, as if he meant to put it around her shoulders then let it drop to his side. "Everyone falls in love sooner or later. For some of us it's sooner ..." He paused and cleared his throat. When Beth stared stonily ahead, he left the sentence unfinished.

The final painting was called *Cat-holic*.

"Sacrifice," said Peter, smiling in his know-it-all way as he stood in front of her. "No more cats. This is about martyrdom. Washed in the blood of the Lord."

"I'm an atheist," she retorted. "Shouldn't you be talking to Jess about this?"

"I'd have to carry her over the convent wall." He laughed as he raised her arms above her head and linked her fingers together. "My father was an artist. He tried to capture the ecstasy of martyrdom and failed. That's when he gave up. I saw his paintings once – a strange experience."

Her body felt as if it was suspended by chains. Her heart began to pound when he moved closer and she sensed his excitement, felt his body pressing lightly but insistently against her. She was aware of his strength and also of her vulnerability as he drew her arms higher and her breasts tautened, her hips thrusting forward involuntarily. Her face tilted upwards, their lips almost touching before he moved away and picked up a sketch pad.

"Try and hold the pose, Beth. Sublime ecstasy, that's what I want to capture. I want to lift your body into the celestial light."

"Stewart is right. You do talk a load of bullshit." Her eyes challenged him. Her arms ached with the effort of holding them aloft. He often spoke about his father, an art collector, who died when Peter was twelve, describing him as a frail religious man who read old books through a magnifying glass and rarely spoke to his son. At the back of Havenstone he had grown vines. Bottles of homemade wine were still stored in the basement, dusty and forgotten. The vines had perished in a frost soon after his death and the vineyard, which Peter showed her once, was invisible now, overtaken by wild ivy that covered the back boundary wall and coiled around the withered bark of crab apple trees.

"What's the problem, Beth? I'm trying to paint you, not rape you." He put down the sketch pad and walked towards her, lowering her arms, then resting them on his shoulders. When she tried to pull away his grip tightened. "Who are you, Beth Tyrell? What's the big mystery behind those eyes? Beautiful girl, no boyfriend. No existence outside the walls of a dead-beat factory. I can understand my mother being a workaholic, but you're too young – too gorgeous – and I want to kiss you. What have you got to say about it?"

She resisted for an instant, drawing back from the pressure of his mouth. Then, with a low sigh of surrender, she kissed him back. His hand touched her waist, sliding inside her blouse, confidently moving towards her breast. Her heart pounded, suffocating her with its fury. She felt him slipping away, vanishing in front of her eyes as the walls of the studio folded in and crushed her into darkness where nothing existed except the sound of heavy breathing and the touch of flesh stealing away her senses. She struggled, flailing wildly, dragging herself back from the edge of memory.

"Leave me alone! Don't your dare touch me …don't you dare!" Ashen-faced, almost hysterical, she stared at him, his face swimming into view again, angry, puzzled, then frightened when she began to weep violently. "I can't. I just can't!" She covered her eyes, no longer able to look at him. "I have to go … you don't understand … no one does. Leave me alone!"

She understood now why she had never been jealous

when he talked about his girlfriends. The women he loved briefly had helped her to play a waiting game. To deny her fear. To dream that when the right time came it would be different with him. She would experience the sensations that made the women in the office coy and giggly when they discussed their boyfriends. She knew the names they called her. Frigid Brigid. Arctic Knickers. She deserved the nicknames. Her skin lifting in horror, her body clenched, rejecting even him.

The following weekend, four months after her father's death, she returned to Anaskeagh to visit Sara.

CHAPTER THIRTEEN

Since leaving Dublin the rain had been falling steadily. She shouldered her rucksack and left the fuggy heat of the bus, crossing Turnabout Bridge and heading towards the town. The river was swollen, swirling high under the bridge, carrying the sheen of bogs and the dead chill of underground caverns. In the early spring old Sam Burns had died in this river. Some said it was an accident. Too much red biddy and a belief that he could walk on water. Others believed it was suicide, an old man tired of ranting.

The smell of chips made her mouth water. Through the steamy windows of the corner building on River Mall she saw Hatty, busy as ever on a Friday night. She opened the door and joined the queue.

"Would you take a look at what the cat dragged in?" Hatty waved a vinegar container at her. "And a drowned one at that. I must say you picked a strange weekend to come home considering your mother only went away last night."

Startled, Beth stared at her. "What do you mean? Where has she gone?"

"Ah now – that's a good question. There's many around here would like an answer to it." She worked fast at moving the queue along, talking non-stop over her shoulder. "She's kicking up her heels with the rest of them chancers in the Anaskeagh Chamber of Commerce. They're supposed to be at a conference in Blackpool finding out about tourism but it could be Timbuktu for all we know."

"Blackpool? Are you serious?"

"Taking that lot off on a 'fact-finding mission' is enough to make a donkey stop laughing." Hatty, as sturdy and round as a small barrel, was an insatiable gossip. Barry used to claim she could draw secrets from a corpse. She lifted a pan of sizzling chips, expertly pinching one between her fingers, then plunged them back for extra crispness. "It's not that I'd begrudge your mother the break. It was time for the poor widow to kick up her heels after the terrible time she's been through – and who is Hatty Beckett to even mention the word 'junket'?"

Where's Sara?" Beth asked.

"You'll find her at Cherry Vale."

"Did my uncle go on the trip?"

Hatty nodded, emphatically. "He organised it. He wants to bring the tourists here to enjoy our golden beaches and quaint little town. And why not? It's time to put Anaskeagh on the map and there's no better man knows how to organise a junket – sorry – fact-finding mission, than your uncle."

"Hatty Beckett would be wise not to go bandying words

like 'junket' around the place." May was not amused when Beth repeated the conversation. She was watching television and eating chocolates when her niece arrived. "How long are you staying this time, may I ask?"

"Only the weekend. I'm so busy."

"Well you're back in Anaskeagh so you can just ease your foot off the pedal. You can sleep in Kieran's room but don't touch anything. He gets very upset when he comes home from boarding school if his things are not exactly the same as he left them." May smiled her wafer-thin smile at Beth. "Why didn't you come back for your sister's show?"

"What show?"

"The nuns, for reasons best known to themselves, decided to show off her photographs. Not that I'm one of Sara's fans. I told her so, straight out. She had the nerve to make Fatima Estate look like a slum after all the great work Tom did on the houses."

Sara appeared to be asleep but she opened her eyes immediately when Beth entered the room.

"What are you doing here?" she asked, limply lifting her head before letting it fall back again on the pillow.

"I came to see you." Beth sat gingerly on the edge of the bed. "May told me about your exhibition. Congratulations. I'm really sorry I missed it."

"It wasn't anything much. Just an old school thing …" Shadows smudged the skin under her eyes. She yawned and pulled the blankets over her chin. "Go away, Beth. I'm too tired to talk to you."

"Just tell me first, are you ringing me at night and then not speaking?"

"Don't be so stupid!" she shrilled angrily and turned her

face to the wall. "I'm so busy I haven't time to think about you let alone waste my time making phone calls. Let me go to sleep."

Once during the night Beth woke, not sure what had disturbed her until she heard movements from next door. A thumping sound as if Sara was dancing or exercising which was too ridiculous because it was after three in the morning. While she lay in a half-doze the sounds assumed a dreamy sequence and she drifted back to sleep again.

By the following morning the rain had eased to a light drizzle. May applied a slash of lipstick on her mouth before driving off to Anaskeagh to have her hair set. Her statuesque figure was encased in a purple suit. A blouse frothed lace at her neck. She intended dropping Sara off at First Fashion to help in the boutique. If Beth wanted a lift into town she could come with them. Beth shook her head. She planned to visit O'Donovan's farm.

Catherine was still in her nurse's uniform when she arrived. Night duty in the casualty ward always left her exhausted. Beth made her a mug of tea and persuaded her to go to bed. She promised to feed the fowl and fetch Frank from the hill field when the vet arrived to look at a sick horse.

The day passed swiftly. Frank and his son, Bernard, arrived in at noon for dinner. The stew pot still simmered on the range and the men were joined briefly by Sheila O'Neill, who had cycled over from Anaskeagh. Sheila was engaged to Bernard. They planned to build a bungalow on the farm. She still had jittery eyes and the same compulsion to talk about her sisters who were coming home for her wedding. She took off her engagement ring and showed it to Beth, who twisted it towards her heart and made a wish.

"How's your sister Nuala?" Beth asked. "Is she coming home for the wedding as well?"

"I don't know." Sheila looked away, suddenly embarrassed. "I'd like her to come but you know my mother. Anyway, she's mad busy working in this craft place. It's some kind of co-operative that these women run in a basement. They make pots and candles, that sort of thing. Nuala sells the stuff for them."

"Did she ever get married?"

"Married!" Bernard held up his hands as if warding off an evil word. "The only man in her life is the kiddie she had after she was in the traces with Derry Mulhall. She's one of those women's libbers now. A holy terror she is when it comes to us poor men." He winked at Beth. "What about you? Are you doing a line with one of them Dublin jackeens or saving yourself for the local lads?"

"That's for me to know and you to find out?" retorted Beth, slipping easily into the familiar banter of the O'Donovan household. Sheila was working in the new supermarket. She listed the recent engagements, marriages and births that had taken place in Anaskeagh. When Beth mentioned Oldport, she checked her watch and said she had to run, bored by events that had no relevance outside the circle of her own world.

By evening time the rain had cleared and the countryside was bathed in sunshine. Goldie lay on the lawn in Cherry Vale, his head flopped between his paws, looking reproachfully at them through the open French doors. May fluttered anxiously around the table, her bare arms quivering as she ladled mashed potatoes, carrots and peas. Two slices of roast beef glistened on the side of each plate. She talked throughout the meal. She had always been a talker but Beth was surprised at how aimless her conversation had become; rambling monologues that relayed the minutiae of her daily routine and the demands that were made on a busy councillor's wife. Her nieces were not expected to participate in the conversation, only to nod at appropriate intervals.

Sara moved her food around, chewing continuously on a piece of meat, as if the effort of swallowing was too great. Her aunt leaned across the table and coyly tapped her knuckles with a fork.

"I heard about your latest conquest, you sly puss boots?"

The young girl looked up from her plate, puzzled. "What do you mean, Aunty May?"

"Ben Layden!" She glanced over towards Beth. "His family own the new supermarket. I was talking to his mother last week and she spilled the beans."

"Baked, were they?" asked Beth.

May ignored her. "He fancies our little Sara but she gives him the cold shoulder, don't you, you heartless vixen? It won't do, my dear. It won't do at all. You can't dazzle the poor boy with your wiles and then pretend not to notice him."

"I don't pretend—"

"Every boy needs a little push to get him moving in the right direction. And he's a shy one, God bless him." May's eyebrows arched, coy slivers of brown pencil. "I'll have to arrange a little tête-à-tête to get the two of you together. More carrots, Beth?"

"No thank you, May."

"Eat up now and none of your nonsense." She ignored Beth's protesting hand, ladling another helping of vegetables onto her plate. "You're far too scrawny for your age. A man likes a girl he can cuddle and there's little to cuddle on a broomstick."

"I saw Conor at a dance in Dublin a while back," said Beth, staring at her aunt's flushed face. "When did he start drinking so heavily?"

May's smile disappeared. "What do you mean? Conor has never broken his Confirmation pledge."

"Oh! Then maybe it was drugs. This fellow came up and asked me to dance. He vomited over my shoes. Suede. Such a waste. I had to throw them away. I was sure it was Conor – but under such circumstances it was hard to be certain."

"I'm quite sure it wasn't my son." May replied, grimly. "Conor is a student of law. I don't imagine he's in the habit of frequenting the same dance halls as common factory girls."

"She's unbelievable. Yap, yap, yap," Beth muttered when their aunt went into the hall to answer the phone. "She never shuts up for a minute."

"She's lonesome with the boys gone all the time," said Sara. "And Uncle Tom's so busy he's never here—" She swayed, slumping forward. Sweat broke out on her upper lip.

"What's wrong?" Beth half-stood but Sara lifted her hand and pushed her back. An action that was surprisingly strong, considering her crumpled position. "I've got a stomach cramp," she gasped. "I think I've picked up a bug."

"Were you sick during the night?"

Sara nodded. She rose unsteadily to her feet, holding the edge of the table for support. For an instant, as she bent forward, she was silhouetted against the evening sun. It shone through the fabric of her dress, pale blue chambray, soft creased pleats, a maxi style falling loose to her ankles. Her stomach, high and swollen, stretched tight. Her small full breasts rested on the curve.

It was so obvious. Beth wanted to fling the reality far back into the cold reaches of her mind. Her eyes, seeking relief, stared down at the linen table cloth and almost immediately came back to Sara. Dust motes danced in the shaft of light, shimmering energy. It had to be her imagination. Sara had just turned fourteen, a school girl who played with her dog and took strange photographs of empty lanes and time running away.

Beth tried to speak. Her throat was too raw for words. Her breath wheezed, carried on a wild sob. The young girl moved from the light, oblivious of what had been revealed, moving heavily, her hand reaching instinctively to touch the small of her back. She opened the door and disappeared from view.

The telephone call ended and May was back, annoyed at people's lack of consideration, ringing at meal time when they knew her husband was away and would not be able to deal with their problems.

"Sara's gone upstairs to lie down for a while," she said. "Poor child, it's probably her monthlies. I used to be cursed with them myself when I was her age. You really are a bold little scut, Beth, teasing me about Conor."

"I'll go and check if she's all right." Beth ran up the stairs, her heart pounding at the thought of confronting her sister. The bedroom was empty. When she ran downstairs May was standing in the hall, her jacket slung over her shoulders. "Is she all right? Does she want me to bring her up a hot water bottle before I leave?"

"No, she's sleeping."

"That'll do her good. I'm off to play bridge with the ladies. I should be back about midnight."

As the puzzle pieces slotted into place one by one Beth realised she was not surprised. The signs had been obvious yet she had deliberately ignored them. No, surely not deliberately. How could she have guessed what was incomprehensible? Sara had put on weight, a fine layer of puppy fat softening her face. Her strange behaviour, sudden outbursts. Hormones. Moody teen blues. An explanation for everything except the truth. Sara crying on Anaskeagh Head because there was no one to tell. Sara on the phone, panicked, desperate, silent. She had dismissed her suspicions, refused to give them any credence because she wanted to be with Peter Wallace, playing word games, stupid, stupid word games with no meaning. Images on canvas; the mirror of the soul.

CHAPTER FOURTEEN

Goldie had disappeared from his position outside the French windows. The gate at the foot of the back garden swung open. A narrow road ran at the back of Cherry Vale with hedgerows on either side. At one end it swept around to join the main road leading into Anaskeagh. The other path led to the headland. Beth followed the curve until it ended on the bottom slopes in a boundary of ash and willow. It was easy to find an opening through the thicket. Soon she was walking over clumps of stubby grass that squelched under her feet. Boggy moisture seeped into the thin soles of her runners and the bottom of her jeans.

This was a spent area that had been flattened and dug, leaving trenches of bog water and scaly steps hacked into the earth. She strained her ears, hoping that Goldie would bark. The moon became visible, a pale disc that lit the trail, but once she moved from this path the dense shadows of rock and gorse were almost impossible to penetrate. She switched on the torch she had grabbed from the garage before leaving Cherry Vale. Slate-grey clouds banked behind Anaskeagh Head. The peaks, the rocks, the black jagged trees rising above her were fleeting impressions, a nightmare glimpsed through a swirl of descending mist.

Sara crouched under Aislin's Roof. She was kneeling, her stomach thrust forward, the pale blue dress rucked around her waist. Goldie lay beside her. He whimpered, licking her ankles, shivering. This was the picture Beth absorbed when she finally stumbled upon them, illuminated in the glow of a torch. A tableaux that was to imprint itself forever on her mind.

"I'm here, Sara." Beth collapsed on the grass. Her heart hammered with panic and exertion.

Her sister did not look up. She seemed incapable of focusing on anything other than the pressure that fused her body into the downwards contraction and tore a shuddering gasp from her. Her hands gripped the edge of the rock. When the moment passed and her body relaxed she began to sway backwards and forwards. The sound she made, a humming monotone, seemed to rise through the roof of her mouth, almost inaudible.

"Are you having the baby ... tell me what's happening to you?" Beth put her arms around her. She sobbed with terror because she did not know what to do. She lifted Sara's hair, pushed it back from her face, wiped her hand across her sister's cold, damp forehead. The swaying movements ceased. Sara stared at her. No recognition flickered in her eyes as she pushed Beth away. She crawled into the shelter of the overhanging rock and crouched in the darkness.

"No one can see me." She ground the words between

her teeth. "No one can see me … no one … no one can see me."

"Are you having the baby now?" Beth repeated, trying to follow her. She shone the torch under the slant of rock. Framed in the glow Sara hunkered against the sloping wall, cornered. Her body was in spasm, her breathing heavy and fast. Goldie barked, responding to her panic. Mindlessly she touched his head, shushing him. He pawed the earth, scattering damp muddy clay. Beth noticed he was digging in a hole that was already partly dug.

"Sara, I'm here with you … it's Beth. I've found you … everything's going to be all right … come out from there and let me help you—"

"Get away … get away! Don't come in here … get away," Sara hissed. She pressed her face into her knees and waved her hands outwards as if she was pushing against an invading force.

As Beth accepted and came to terms with the unfolding tragedy she realised that Sara had not just fallen into the earth to give birth. Aislin's Roof had been carefully chosen. The rock, embedded on a flat shelf of earth, offered shelter and protection. But Sara was restricted by the low level of the ceiling and the tight space into which she had wedged herself. If Beth was to help her sister she must concentrate only on what was about to happen, not on what had happened. Softly, she coaxed Sara forward.

"You should be out here. Sara … it's safe out here. No one can see you … it's the best place to be." She reached out one hand, continuing to talk softly, concentrating the beam of the torch on the ground in front of her, using it to beckon the young girl forward.

Clouds parted. The moon shone on Sara's upturned face. She leaned back into the rough grass. Her elbows supported her weight. She drew her knees forward, tensed her feet, arched her body like a bow then sank again into the earth. Beth knelt in front of her, spontaneous actions, intuitive knowledge. When she reached into the dark space between Sara's legs her hands felt something moist, solid.

"Sara. I've touched the baby's head, push again, it's coming – coming – push, you have to push harder, Sara, push!" The young girl looked outwards, unseeing, her eyes opaque with terror. Beth sensed her travelling beyond the moment, her mind moving away even as her body pulsed and prepared to give life. A sundering cry was forced from her. A hard cry of denial. Beth placed her hands over the emerging head and drew her sister's child into the moonlight. Still kneeling, she held the baby in her arms. She ran her hands over the tiny frame, hair slicked smooth with blood and mucus. She touched the smooth incision between the baby's thighs. A thin wriggling body that could slide so easily to the ground.

"It's a girl, Sara," she whispered.

"Give it to me," Sara's voice was hoarse. She lay still, her legs splayed, milky white in the angled glow of the torch. Blindly, refusing to look, she allowed Beth to lay the child on her stomach. She shuddered at the contact. Her movements were slow, trance-like. "Cut the cord," she cried. "Cut it quick. In there – under the rock. The bag, get the bag."

Under the gap of rock Beth discovered a white plastic bag. Inside it she found a towel, cotton wool, pieces of ribbon and sanitary towels. Her chest knotted when she saw

Marjory's dressmaking scissors. It clanged against the handle of a small shovel from the bronze companion set her mother kept beside the fireplace. When she cut the cord, instinctively using the ribbons to clamp it at either end, her sister's head flopped sideways, as if someone had released her from the pull of an invisible string.

The placenta came away. A rippling, muscular tremor passing through her hands when she placed them on Sara's abdomen. A fusion of smells rose around her, blood, excrement, perspiration, bodily emissions that had swept this tiny life into existence. She needed water. She had seen it in films, steaming cauldrons of boiling water. She needed to clean Sara and to stem the flow of blood. She needed blankets. It was cold on Anaskeagh Head and the wind was rising. Sara appeared to be drifting in and out of consciousness. Her body was flat, as if it was being absorbed into the grass. The baby, wrapped in the towel, lay in her arms. Each time she cried, Sara started awake and gazed with blank eyes at the tiny bundle. When her sister tried to take the baby, she kicked out with such ferocity that Beth froze, afraid a wrong word or movement would send her over the edge and out of reach.

"We have to leave here, Sara. Can you try and sit up?"

Dully, Sara pulled herself upright. The movement disturbed the child whose mouth puckered as she turned her face inwards towards the young girl's chest.

"Monster ... monster." She screamed suddenly. Her free hand scrabbled in the darkness.

"Stay easy." Beth tried to hold her but Sara drew back from her and, in the instant before the blow was struck, Beth saw her upraised hand, the stone clenched in her fist.

"No! Sara, no don't." She flung herself across her sister's knees, knocking her hand sideways. The blow lost its force and scraped against the side of the child's forehead. The startled wail, a shrill, outraged cry, reminded Beth of Goldie, scrabbling frantically up the side of the bath.

"Leave me alone … I have to destroy the monster." Sara sobbed, flailing out. "Kill the monster – kill it."

"Listen to me." She forced Sara's hand backwards until it was twisted behind her back. The stone fell with a soft thud. "I'm here. I'll help you. It's your baby girl, Sara. You can't harm her. Calm down! I'll take care of the two of you." The baby continued to cry. Beth was terrified in case she fell from Sara's arm or was flung against the rock. "Give her to me, Sara. You must rest … sleep."

"Fucking monster!" She began the familiar rocking movements, still squeezing the child.

"She's a beautiful baby, Sara. They'll find her if you bury her here. Look at Goldie. Tomorrow the dogs will come and dig her up. Everyone will know you killed your baby. Mammy will know and Uncle Tom—"

"Oh, Jesus." She rocked faster. Her face twisted in a grimace, distorted. "You left me here … for him. Bitch! Get away from me."

"Sara, listen! I'll hide the monster. I'll hide it in a place where no one will ever find it. Give the monster to me, Sara. This is our secret." Her voice lulled, controlling as she lifted the baby into her arms. She stood up, her legs cramping, pins and needles causing her to stumble when she tried to walk.

"I'll be back soon … stop crying, Sara. Everything's going to be all right."

It was almost eleven o'clock, only an hour since she found Sara. She tried to imagine the terror that had sent her sister crawling like an animal under a rock to give birth and then to try and take it away. The baby made a snuffling noise as if she was having breathing difficulties. Beth pressed the corner of the towel against the wound. She shone the torch on the tiny face, the withered blue flesh. Panicking, she wondered if she should baptise her because she would surely be dead by the time she was discovered. It seemed hypocritical to chant words she did not believe. If she was wrong and there was a merciful God waiting to receive this child then a meaningless ritual should not hinder her progress into the light.

If she had allowed Sara to kill her, a swift merciful blow that would have crushed the fragile scull, their secret would be resting under Aislin's Roof, slowly decomposing into the earth. How many babies born in the same secret desperation were mouldering in fields and ditches and rivers, alive only in the mind of those who had shared their brief existence? Yes, Sara would have suffered, remorse ebbing and flowing through her life. But there would have been an ending; a secret in the shade of Aislin's Roof. Instead, Beth was unleashing a story that was going to have so many consequences. The police could come to their house and arrest Sara, arrest them both. And if the baby died they would stand in the dock accused of murder; their lives over before they had even got used to living them. Yet, she also knew that this frail child had to live or they would never be able to move forward from this terrible night.

Her legs juddered as she pushed her way through the narrow trail, treacherous with unseen briars and moss. The path reached a fork, dividing sharply to the left. This was a little-used trail, leading away from the boggy slopes and onto firmer ground. A trail she had travelled many times with Jess when they used to take a short cut to the farm. She beamed the torch, keeping it low in case it was noticed. Not that she expected to see anyone. Anaskeagh Head was too rough and formidable to attract young couples seeking privacy.

At first, her concern had been to escape from Sara and her rage. The decision to go to O'Donovan's farm only crystallised when she reached the dividing fork. A light shone in the front porch. Early risers, the family usually went to bed around ten o'clock except for Catherine who was on night duty.

In the barn Beth pulled an empty sack loose from the bundle on the floor. Next door in the stable she heard the sick horse coughing. It seemed incredible that on this same day she had fed chickens and walked to the hill farm to call Frank O'Donovan when the vet arrived. She removed the towel and wrapped the baby loosely in the coarse sacking. She laid the bundle in the centre of the porch and knocked hard on the front door. When an upstairs light was switched on she slipped silently back down the lane.

She heard the door opening, voices raised. Her chest ached where the baby had rested. She blended into the night, murmuring. Goodbye … goodbye … goodbye.

CHAPTER FIFTEEN

Sara was slumped against the rock when she returned. Her hands were covered in clay. Her eyes stared beyond Beth. She did not speak as she was coaxed and supported to her feet. They descended slowly, Beth half-carrying her, their feet slipping, thorns tearing their clothes, not noticing until they reached the back garden of Cherry Vale. The knowledge that her aunt's car would soon be pulling into the driveway filled Beth with terror as she helped Sara into bed. She lifted her dress over her head, noticing with growing horror the seeping blood stains. She sponged her, crooning words without meaning.

"Why are you always following me around?" Sara spoke for the first time since they left the headland. Her voice shook, gaining strength. She flung her head from side to side. "Leave me alone – do you hear me? Leave me alone."

Beth slumped on the edge of the bed. "Sara, I have to tell you—"

"No!" The young girl began to tremble. Her eyes slanted

upwards until only the whites were visible. "I buried it ...
deep in the clay ... dead in the clay." She fell back against
the pillow, holding Beth's arm in a vice-like grip.

"Sara, that's not true. Talk to me. We have to talk about
this."

"Our secret." Her grip tightened. "Promise. Don't tell.
We'll forget ... don't tell ... don't! It's done. Swear to God
you won't tell. *Swear*."

"I swear." Beth began to sob, her body swaying in terror.
She stayed by her sister's side throughout the night. The
hall door closed. She listened to May's heavy tread on the
stairs. The luminous hands on the alarm clock moved into
the small hours. Sara never stirred. Her breathing was so
shallow that Beth suspended her own breathing until she
made out the faint rise and fall of her chest.

Towards morning her temperature began to rise. When
she tossed the bedclothes from her shoulders the metallic
smell of blood was so strong that Beth recoiled. She sponged
her down again, horrified by the amount of blood she was
losing. When May left for mass she washed the dress and
put the sheets into the washing machine. The sound of
footsteps crossing the landing alerted her. Towels lay on the
floor of the bathroom, covered in blood stains. Sara had
returned to the bedroom and was on her knees, frantically
rubbing the mattress with a face cloth.

"Leave it, Sara. I'll turn the mattress. It's going to be all
right."

"No one must know." Frantically, she kept rubbing,
beating Beth's hand away.

"Stop it!" Beth screamed. "You're driving me crazy."

Desperately, she lifted her sister off her knees and half-dragged her back into bed. Sara moaned softly but did not move. Her arms felt rigid; skin, bone, sinew and muscle rejecting any form of comfort. They heard footsteps on the stairs, the bathroom door opening, the startled exclamation.

May, finding the bedroom door locked, rapped loudly. "Sara, open the door immediately. What's going on? What happened to my towels?"

"It's all right, May," Beth shouted. "She's trying to sleep. I'll be out in a minute."

"Open the door immediately. Do you hear me?" She knocked a second time, louder, prolonged. "This is my house, remember? I don't allow locked doors."

Beth tried to ease herself from Sara's grip but her sister held her, entreating her to stay silent.

"We can't hide it any longer." Beth prised her hands free and stood up, protecting Sara from her aunt's shocked gaze.

May still had her hat and jacket on. "Sweet Heart of Jesus!" She gasped, looking at the mattress. "What's going on here? Speak up, will you? What's wrong with you, Sara?"

"She's sick … she's haemorrhaging … we have to call the doctor."

Sara shook her head from side to side, whimpering. She stared dully at May. Her eyes glittered, the flush of fever on her cheeks.

"How long has this been going on?" May demanded.

"Since last night …" Beth bowed her head.

"Last night?" May pressed her hand against her chest, then pointed towards the door, shouting at Beth. "You get out and wait downstairs. I'll deal with you later."

An hour passed before she came downstairs. "Who else knows about this?" she demanded.

Shakily, Beth got to her feet. "No one."

"Marjory? She must surely know?"

Beth shook her head. "No one but us. Is Sara going to die?" she sobbed.

"It's a heavy bleed and an infection. She'll recover. I remember enough from my nursing days." Hard-faced she stared at Beth. "The whole town's talking. Jesus Christ! How could she have allowed this to happen in my house? And you – didn't you think about me? That I had a right to know?"

"I didn't know myself until last night."

"I don't believe you. You were always a liar, Beth Tyrell. If it was you I wouldn't be surprised. But Sara—" Perspiration shone on her forehead. She dabbed her skin with a tissue, touching her lips, smudging lipstick, hardly aware of what she was doing. "I don't want to know the whys and wherefores of what your sister's been getting up to but it's obvious she was doing more than taking photographs in her spare time."

"What about the baby?"

"As dead as makes no difference."

"Dead!"

"With a fractured skull it probably is by now. And just as well too. What luck would it have coming into the world the way it did?"

"Why are you blaming Sara?"

"Because it always takes two to tango and Sara has landed us in a fine mess. Any shame on your family reflects on mine. That baby is probably in the morgue by now and Councillor Oliver's name could be dragged into this sorry mess. Dear Jesus! You Tyrells have bad blood in you and that's a fact. Between yourself and your father you've caused enough tongues to wag in Anaskeagh and now this—"

"He's to blame ... Tom ... ask him ..." She was unaware that she had sobbed his name out loud until she saw the shock in her aunt's eyes.

May sat down suddenly. Her face sank, grew old. "You disgusting little slut! How dare you use my husband's name in that vile way. Has your sister been making those accusations?"

Beth shook her head. "She doesn't have to. I know."

"You know nothing." May's bosom heaved.

Beth stepped backwards from her fury. "I know everything." She was unable to control her tears. "That's why I ran away. He's to blame ... he is ... he is ..."

"Get out of my house," May's voice rasped with fury.

"I won't leave Sara."

"I'll take care of your sister because, and *only* because, she's my niece. If you dare utter one word – one word – that could damage my husband's good name I'll drag you through every court in the land for slander. Do you hear me, Beth Tyrell?"

"I'm not leaving her with you ... and him."

"Get out! Get out! Get out!" Unable to restrain herself any longer May ran from the room, her breath wheezing as she climbed the stairs. She flung Beth's clothes into the rucksack then walked past her as if she did not exist. The hall door was flung open with such force that it slammed back against the wall. A crack appeared in the frosted glass. A hairline fracture running through fragile bone.

"I have to see Sara before I go." Beth gasped. "Please let me say goodbye."

"Get out … get out." May continued to chant the words. Saliva had dried on the corners of her lips. The rucksack was flung into the garden. Then Beth felt herself gripped by the shoulders and shoved forward. "Get out of my sight and don't ever darken my door again."

Rain whipped her face as she struggled towards Aislin's Roof. Last night when she returned from O'Donovan's farm she had been unaware of anything except getting Sara back to Cherry Vale. Now she saw that the hole had been filled in, the loose clay already flattened into mud. She picked up a twig and loosened the mound, finding what she had expected to find. Quickly she scrabbled the clay back over the placenta. She allowed the tears to flow down her cheeks. They rolled into the corners of her lips, hot, salty.

The rain continued to fall as she turned her back on the headland. It seeped into gorges and ancient fissures where streams murmured and roared, splashing white over rocks or free falling into space, seeking hidden ravines to shape their journey through the centre of Anaskeagh. The earth was being cleansed, baptised.

Part Two

1971–1998

CHAPTER SIXTEEN

Everyone's story has a beginning. An instant when the earth moves. When ovum and sperm collide, collude, create. Biological facts are difficult to dispute. But afterwards, after the downwards swim into light, what then? As Eva clawed the air, as she uttered her first mucous cry, was she held briefly in a stranger's arms? Or did she lie abandoned, welcomed into the world with a stone?

On her forehead there was a dent, so slight it was difficult to see, covered by purple skin, almost transparent. A shiny purple coin. A fairy kiss that was, according to her father, bestowed on her the instant she was born. When she was older, she demanded a more rational explanation and sensible Liz provided it. A fall from the high steps at the back of the house when she was waltzing around in her baby walker. Her hair was heavy, a curly weight over her forehead. A birthmark was easy to ignore. She never paid attention to it until the night her grandmother confided harsh secrets into her ear and Eva finally understood.

It seemed cruel to demand the truth from a dying woman but Eva wanted a beginning to her story and Brigid Loughrey, high on morphine and the adrenaline of approaching death, held her hands tightly and ordered her to have courage. Eva did not feel courageous. Nor did she feel angry. Twenty-seven was too old to have an identity crisis. She kissed her grandmother's withered lips and sat silently beside her until the elderly woman drifted into sleep.

When she returned from the hospital Eva studied her scar, her fairy kiss. She touched it tentatively, wondering what violent memories echoed within this fragile membrane? She forced her mind away from the question, but it slid back again insidiously. In medieval times they buried their dead with stone pillows at their heads. Their bones had been uncovered on corroding sandy headlands, skulls resting peacefully on smooth oval stones, strong teeth smiling. But those stone pillows were laid down in rituals of respect, a loving finite gesture to bring them comfort in the next life. Eva shuddered, imagining a raised hand, a vengeful cry, a stranger's face distorted in a rictus of hate.

CHAPTER SEVENTEEN

She was six months old when she came to Ashton, a soft blanket replacing sackcloth and the unyielding earth.

"A cocoon of love," said Liz.

"A fairy princess," said Steve.

They had been trying for a long time to conceive a child, vigorously at first, then with grim and timely discipline. Month had followed disappointing month, and the arrival of this frail miracle child into their lives was a cause for rowdy celebration. Her parents had deep roots in Ashton and their families, the Frawleys and the Loughreys, arrived in droves to raise their glasses and welcome Eva into their lives. Steve sang 'When I'm Sixty-Four' and Liz's sister, Annie Loughrey, played her fiddle until Liz, mindful of early morning feeds and mysterious milk formulas, swept the revellers from her doorstep in the small hours.

Ashton was a small Wicklow backwater, and those who lived in its shade of spruce and beech prayed it would remain so.

Steve's garden centre was a familiar landmark with a reputation that brought customers from the hinterland and beyond. Next door, Liz ran the guest house, Wind Fall, catering to commercial travellers and hill walkers. While the garden centre budded and blossomed with the demands of the seasons, the ordered serenity of Wind Fall never varied. Eva woke each morning to the sound of her mother's footsteps passing her bedroom door as Liz went downstairs to prepare breakfast for the overnight guests.

Liz made no secret of her daughter's adoption, fearing traumatic disclosures in school playgrounds or in the hot-house environment of family parties if elderly relatives drank too much sherry. At night, Steve sat by her bed and uttered the magical words that began her story. *Eva's Journey to Happiness* was a fairy story of thwarted puppy love and family feuding; a vicious vendetta that forced a young girl and boy to give their love-child to a convent of kindly nuns, who passed her on as a gift to her parents. Eva imagined herself as a parcel, wrapped in birthday paper and streamers. Her body tingled with sympathy for the puppy lovers and their desperate attempts to be together. But she remained untouched by any emotional reality, settling down to sleep afterwards with the same sense of exhausted contentment that followed the telling of *Rapunzel* or *The Sleeping Beauty*.

Maria, her cousin, suffered regular crises of identity, and confessed to Eva that she harboured deep suspicions that she too was adopted. It would explain everything. A swan in a nest of ugly ducklings. But that was during the teenage years, the war years when all Maria wanted from life was to muck out stables and vow eternal devotion to horses.

For Eva, horses served only one function: bearers of dung

for her father's precious plants. Maria hated the smell of roses
and walked unheedingly over seedling beds until Steve barred
her from entering the garden centre. Eva and her cousin were
the same age, best friends, incompatible and inseparable.
When Maria grew tired feeding sugar lumps to her favourite
horses and mucking out stables at the Ashton Equestrian
Centre, and Eva was not needed in the garden centre, they
played in the long meadow grass or swam on summer
evenings in Murtagh's River. Soft sloshing mud between
their toes, snapping rushes on their bare skin, the flow of
water, boggy and brown, rippling over their shoulders.
Sensations that belonged to a small space in summer yet,
later, looking back to those days, they seemed to span the
whole of Eva's childhood.

One evening, they saw Maria's older sister, Lorrie,
walking hand in hand with Brendan Fitzsimon through the
Murtagh's Meadow. In a hollow overhung with whitethorn,
they lay down and failed to notice the girls hiding in the
long grass. Lorrie lifted her slender knees and moved them
urgently apart as Brendan sank between them. A spasm of
shock swooped through Eva. She flattened her body deeper
into the earth and when she looked across at her cousin,
the glazed brightness of Maria's eyes and the flushed bloom
on her cheeks reflected her own feelings. They began to
giggle, convulsively, hands clasping mouths, as they crawled
away, terrified a snapped twig or the waving ferns would
betray their presence.

Out of earshot they flung themselves on the ground,
rolling wildly over the grass. "Disgusting, oh my God, it's
so disgusting." They gasped, breathless and giggling, vowing
they would never ever allow any man to do such awful

things to them. As their blood cooled they became thoughtful. Maria wondered if her parents did it.

"You bet your life they do," Eva replied. Maria's brother was six months old so it seemed a safe enough assumption to make, even if it was impossible to imagine her fragile Aunt Claire squashed beneath Uncle Jack, who auctioned cattle and had a voice as loud as a drum being played too fast. Her parents did not need to do it because they had adopted her. She felt proud of Liz and Steve. It set them apart from everyone else, gave them a dignity that removed them from damp river banks, trampled grass and noises that still sang inside her head.

Soon afterwards, she asked her mother how long she had stayed with the puppy lovers before she was sent to the convent. She wanted Liz's practical answers rather than the gentle rambling stories Steve would offer.

"Six months," Liz said. "You were a delicate child." Suddenly, her words had a hollow ring, an echo Eva could not penetrate. For the first time the full significance of *Eva's Journey to Happiness* dawned on her, and she understood how she, and not the rebellious Maria, became the swan in the nest of the clamorous Frawley and Loughrey clans. But this realisation did not fill her with curiosity about her past. She loved her parents and questions as to why, when, where and how she came to share their lives were irrelevant.

CHAPTER EIGHTEEN

When Eva completed her Leaving she decided to study horticulture. Steve was suspicious of his daughter's need for diplomas and degrees. "Haven't I taught you everything you need to know?" he demanded, shaking his head when Eva outlined her plans for the future. "You don't need a fancy piece of parchment to tend a sick rose. A diploma won't heal an ailing hydrangea if you can't give it the loving touch."

Her father's ability to personalise his plants and shrubs was an endearing trait but, on the subject of parchment, Eva was adamant. She wanted to become a garden designer and host her own television series, with Frawleys of Ashton providing the perfect backdrop. Steve shuddered away from such ambitions, imagining bossy television producers ordering him around his beloved rose arbour and cameramen trampling his geraniums. He was a simple son of the soil, content to live his life selling his bedding plants, fruit orchards and weeping willows.

When Eva emerged from horticultural college, waving her fancy piece of parchment, she decided the time had come to modernise and expand his business. A computer was installed which reduced Steve to palpitations every time he laid his hands on the keyboard. She drew up a three-year marketing programme, forcing him to watch graphics and spreadsheets flicking across the screen. She submitted a proposal to RTE for her television series and waited in vain for a reply. When she suggested buying the field next to the centre and turning it into a landscaped show-garden with her design service and a coffee shop attached, he shook his head, firmly.

"People want to dig their own gardens," he argued. "It's therapy, fresh air, good exercise." His voice held more than a hint of suspicion that Eva was undermining his authority.

She told him about the time pressure young couples were under, how they were too busy to feel the soil under their fingernails. They had parking bays and gravel lawns and terracotta pots on patios. Those with gardens wanted water features and Zen lay-outs and lakes of exotic fish swimming under delicate water lilies.

"Not my customers." He shook his head, decisively. "They want to pot and plant, to see the familiar flowers unfold with the seasons. It's the best therapy they can get."

Her grandmother advised her to strike out on her own. As the owner of the Biddy's Bits & Pieces chain of souvenir shops, Brigid Loughrey was a shrewd business woman who had made a fortune selling garish tri-colour mugs, shamrocks and shillelaghs. She had no problem tackling the intricacies of the World Wide Web and blocked her ears when anyone dared mention retirement.

"You'll never be able to move your father," she told Eva. "Steve runs his garden centre the way he wants it and forcing his arm will do neither of you any good. There's no sense burying your ambitions in Ashton, especially when you've so many excellent ideas."

"What good are my ideas when I've no money to put them into practice?" Eva asked.

"Then borrow," replied Brigid. "How do you think I started my first shop? By emptying my piggy bank?"

Eva was still contemplating her future when Frank O'Donovan, a distant relation to her father, died. Eva had never heard of him until Steve read the death notice in the *Irish Independent* and decided to attend his funeral. Her parents left Ashton the following morning and Eva, busy throughout the day in the garden centre, was shocked when a phone call from Anaskeagh Regional Hospital informed her that her parents had been injured in a car accident. The nurse quickly reassured her there was no need to worry. It was a minor accident; Liz would be discharged in the morning and Steve transferred to a Dublin hospital within the next few days. Eva left immediately, driving westwards, obsessively repeating the nurse's words, but unable to find a crumb of comfort in her crisp, clinical reassurances.

On the approach road to Anaskeagh, a tractor in front of Steve had stalled suddenly and, although her father managed to brake in time, the driver following behind had skidded on the wet surface and ploughed into the back of his car.

It was late when she arrived in the small country town. Liz was sitting by Steve's bed. She would be discharged in the morning, but his arm was broken and X-rays had revealed a number of cracked ribs. Arrangements were being made to transfer him to St Vincent's Hospital in Dublin. Eva stared at the intravenous drip feeding into his arm and the closed screens surrounding his bed.

"I was so scared … don't you ever dare do anything like that to me again." She began to weep, scolding them hysterically. Steve winced from her fierce embrace, his body still in shock from the impact of the collision.

"It's not the end of the world, pet. I'll be right as rain in a day or so." He offered her a tissue with his free hand and stroked her head. "Sure, isn't it hard to kill a bad thing?"

She was blowing her nose when she became aware that someone had entered the ward and was watching her from the foot of the bed. She noticed his eyes first, a penetrating blue stare, and though she experienced an instant rush of recognition, she was unable to remember where they could possibly have met.

"Good heavens, Greg! It's so late." Liz rose to her feet and warmly greeted the stranger. "I didn't expect to see you back here again tonight."

"I wanted to make sure everything was OK before I returned to the hotel." As he spoke his eyes swept over Eva and he gave a slight nod of acknowledgement when Liz introduced him as the driver who had been behind them when the crash occurred. He had been discharged earlier and, apart from a bandage around his left hand, he seemed unscathed.

"It's been a most unfortunate day for all of us," sighed Liz. "But Greg's done everything he can to help us through it."

"If there's anything else I can do—" He glanced

enquiringly at Steve, who shook his head, his body in spasm when he tried to cough.

"For starters, you could try practising the rules of the road," Eva snapped, hearing the painful rasp of her father's breath. Recalling her terror on the long drive to Anaskeagh, her voice shook with anger. "I hope you're satisfied with your day's work. You could have killed my parents with your careless driving."

"I've already made my apologies to them and I'm glad to have an opportunity to apologise to you in person." He made no effort to defend himself. "I'm sorry you had to hear such frightening news over the telephone. I can only imagine the shock you got—"

"You're right, it was a shock," she interrupted, suspecting that such an abject apology was simply a ruse to diffuse her anger. "Hopefully, you'll remember that the next time you drive too close to the car in front."

"There's no need to be so upset, Eva." Liz's grave voice calmed her down. "Greg has accepted full responsibility for the accident and we've sorted everything out between us. All that matters is that we're alive to tell the tale."

"If there's any way I can make amends ..." His voice trailed away as he shoved his hands into his pockets, the shock of the accident visible for an instant on his face. After he said goodbye to her parents she rose and followed him outside to the corridor.

"Thanks for stopping by to see them," she spoke quietly. "I'm sorry for sounding off in there. I'm not usually so rude when I meet people for the first time."

"Then, perhaps, when all this is over, you'll have a chance to prove it." His steady blue eyes unnerved her, but when he smiled he no longer seemed so intimidating, just intriguingly familiar with his long, intense face and finely boned cheeks.

"Have we met before? You look vaguely familiar yet I can't remember where or when …"

He shook his head emphatically. "We've never met before. If we had, I'd remember you." He made no effort to hide his meaning and she felt herself responding, her eyes linking into his gaze for too long, and she was suddenly excited by the unmistakable signals passing between them.

"Then why do I feel as if I know you?" She was the first to look away.

"You've probably seen me on television." He sounded embarrassed by this admission of celebrity, self-consciously pushing his fingers through his thick brown hair. "I work on a current affairs programme."

"Of course – 'Elucidate'. You're Greg Enright! I can't *believe* I didn't recognise you."

"It happens all the time." He laughed, ruefully. "I'm not instantly recognisable, just *vaguely* familiar. People usually suspect I'm their child's teacher or their window cleaner. It's not good for the ego but I'm used to it."

"I suspect very few politicians would agree with you." She smiled for the first time since receiving the phone call from the hospital. "No wonder Liz forgave you so readily. 'Elucidate' is her favourite programme. She enjoys seeing politicians shrunk to size and drenched in acid. What takes you to Anaskeagh?"

"A documentary on a day in the life of a rural TD, boring but occasionally necessary if we're to avoid accusations of Dublin 4 bias." He shook her hand, grinning as a nurse passed and ordered him from the hospital. Visiting hours had ended an hour ago. "Is there any possibility you might recognise me the next time we meet?" he asked when the nurse had returned to her station. He still held Eva's hand. "I'll recognise you, Eva Frawley. But not vaguely, believe me – not vaguely."

The following morning Liz insisted she was well enough to attend the funeral. Frank O'Donovan was a local farmer and the church in the centre of Anaskeagh was crowded. The O'Donovan family filled the top pews, a large clan gathered to unite in mourning. Towards the end of the service a middle-aged woman stood on the altar to give the eulogy. She wore a navy dress with a plain navy cardigan and her voice was filled with emotion as she spoke about her father. A nun, murmured Liz, working in a health centre in Malawi and home for the funeral. Another sister had returned from London and a brother had made the journey from Australia for the first time in twenty-four years. They reminded Eva of her own family, an Irish Diaspora scattering and uniting to grieve or to celebrate as the occasion demanded.

Frank O'Donovan was buried in a country graveyard at the foot of a high headland. The lush slopes gradually rose upwards into a formidable rocky outcrop that loomed above the small town, clearly visible on this fresh windy day. But Eva could imagine it cloudy and shrouded in mist, a hovering presence dominating the lives of the population.

Later, in a local hotel, the mourners gathered to shake off the chill of the graveyard, enjoying sandwiches and steaming whiskey toddies. Catherine O'Donovan, the recently widowed wife, sat in her family circle, flanked by the nun and a middle-aged man. The prodigal son from Australia, Eva guessed.

"Would you like to meet the O'Donovans?" Liz asked. She seemed subdued, uneasy in the presence of so many strangers and anxious to be back with Steve in the hospital. When Eva shook her head, reluctant to partake in the ritual of condolence when she did not know the family, Liz made no effort to dissuade her. "Then I'll say goodbye to Catherine and we'll be on our way. Steve must be wondering what's keeping us."

The arrival of the 'Elucidate' television crew created a sudden silence in the bar. Unperturbed, Greg Enright led the way to a cordoned-off area which had been reserved.. He shook hands with an elderly man whose thick mane of white hair gleamed under the lights. Obviously the local politician, Eva thought. She had noticed him shaking hands at the graveside, his expression concerned as he placed his arm around Catherine O'Donovan and escorted her back to the limousine. He was equally at ease in front of the camera, joking with the camerawoman, ordering her to focus only on his good profile. Greg was in deep conversation with him as she passed and did not notice her. Judge Dread in action. The erring politician's nightmare.

The following Saturday, in the rose arbour uprooting bushes, Eva heard footsteps and knew, without turning, that he was behind her. When she faced him, aware that she was flushed and wind-blown, he stretched out his hand and removed leaves from her hair.

"Recognise me, Ms Frawley?" he asked, raising his

eyebrows in a gesture that usually signified sardonic disbelief when seen on television.

"Vaguely." She smiled as he tossed the leaves away. "What took you so long?"

"I left Anaskeagh four hours ago," he admitted. "The journey usually takes five."

"Still driving too fast, Mr Enright?"

"Not any more," he replied. "I've arrived at my destination."

That night they dined in Ashton's only restaurant. He talked about his career, his future plans, his reputation. His admirers called him righteous and rigorous, a committed journalist who stopped at nothing to expose the truth. Those who disliked him claimed he was an opinionated, self-serving muck-raker. He was twenty-eight years old and his only responsibilities were to his fish aquarium, which he managed with meticulous devotion, and to his mother, an independent widow who tolerated his fortnightly visits as long as they did not clash with her bridge evenings or the 'Late Late Show'. He lived alone in his small apartment in the old Liberties, with Christchurch Cathedral behind him and the downward sweep to the Liffey in front. He had his music, his books, his workstation, a futon and a stream-lined kitchen in which he loved to cook. His future with 'Elucidate' was clearly traced on an upwardly mobile graph.

Eva teased him, calling him a bloodhound who sniffed in the footprints of other people's sins, and they laughed together, at ease in each other's company.

"Tell me how it feels to have the power to destroy people?" she asked.

"People can only be destroyed if they have something to

hide." Greg was suddenly serious. As an investigative journalist his job was to lift the stones and let the worms wriggle where they would. If, after an 'Elucidate' exposé, a marriage fell apart, a career was destroyed, a nervous breakdown or heart attack occurred, that was not his concern. If that was wielding power, then so be it. He accepted it without being moved, intimidated or suppressed by its responsibility.

"That's why I always tell the truth," he said. "And why you must believe me when I tell you I've fallen in love for the first time in my life."

How easily the words settled between them. How easily they were reciprocated. She watched him watching her and felt the same anticipation reaching her in waves, as if simply being close to each other released something unguarded, dangerous, thrilling. They returned to Wind Fall where Liz, protective of her only daughter, subjected him to the same grilling he gave his 'Elucidate' interviewees. He commented on the resemblance between them. "You'll never be able to disown each other," he said.

"We'd never want to disown each other," Eva replied. She placed her arms around her mother, demanding that Liz share her happiness. She felt as if she was falling from a safe ledge. This urge to fly was the most exhilarating emotion she had ever experienced.

Afterwards, she told Greg that she was adopted. "People are always commenting on the resemblance between us. Some tell me I'm the image of my aunts, that I'm a real Loughrey."

"Then they must be the most beautiful women in the world," he replied.

The Loughrey sisters were indeed a handsome trio.

Annie was a musician, a fiddle player, never at home. Claire lived close to Wind Fall and managed Biddy's Bits & Pieces with her mother. When people told Eva she was made in their image she had every reason to feel proud. Except that she did not resemble them. An expression, imitative gestures, a head of blonde shaggy hair that broke combs and drew tears to her eyes when she tried to separate the strands. Superficial resemblances, but they satisfied her in those sparkling early days when nothing mattered except being with Greg and the slow tender happiness building between them.

Only later, after Faye had touched the roots of her past, did Eva discard forever her neatly packaged history and sanitised puppy-love parents.

When Maria heard that her cousin was making wedding plans, she demanded to know if Eva was crazy or pregnant. Otherwise, why marry a guy who was probably a member of the Inquisition in a former life? She called into the garden centre one lunch hour to remonstrate.

"What's this nonsense about you and Judge Dread getting hitched?" she demanded, perching on an upturned terracotta pot. She clicked her fingers in Eva's face and ordered her to get a grip. So what if he had a terrific dick, she demanded. Terrific dicks were ten a penny if one looked in the right places. It was a dismal excuse for marriage. Eva was rapidly regretting the indiscreet secrets she had confided in her friend's willing ear.

"Greg Enright is not the marrying kind," Maria stated. This was a loaded comment, backed by insider information. Eva concentrated on the clematis plants she was staking and ordered her to dish the dirt. Maria prevaricated for a while before throwing the name Carol Wynne at her. Eva tossed it back, growing angry. But being angry with Maria was a lost cause. She simply ignored it, waiting until the emotion was exhausted before returning to her original point.

Eva knew about Carol Wynne. She had seen her for the first time in Anaskeagh, a camerawoman with cropped, vermilion hair and razor eyes, nifty on her feet when she filmed door-stepping interviews, sharing Greg's excitement, the thrill of the chase. Her relationship with Greg never had a shape, easy to take up and put down again. No demands.

"She's dead wood," said Eva.

Maria groaned, demanding to be spared the horticultural metaphors. Her childhood devotion to horses had never wavered and she now ran the Ashton Equestrian Centre. Carol Wynne was one of her pupils. If Eva was going to be metaphorical then she should know that the lady in question had a tight grip once she got a horse between her knees.

Eva hauled her to her feet and ordered her off the premises. Maria would be her bridesmaid. A vision in lilac.

Shortly before the wedding Annie Loughrey arrived back in Ireland at the end of a European tour. Eva adored her aunt, who was incapable of sitting still for longer than ten minutes without exhorting everyone around her to sing and dance. Yet she always had time to listen to her nieces and nephews, who inevitably confided their problems and secrets to her whenever she came to Ashton.

"So, a marriage made in heaven," she said when Eva asked her to play at the wedding. "No rows? No dramatic break-ups and passionate make-ups?"

"None." Eva shook her head, laughing. Then, without realising the thought had even existed, she said, "I wonder if my birth mother senses what's about to happen in my life?"

"This is the first time I've heard you mention her." Annie looked surprised. "Have you discussed this with Liz?"

"No. And I don't want to. It's not important," Eva retorted, and brought the conversation back to the wedding, allowing the sudden unexpected yearning to fade away.

Annie Loughrey played the fiddle as Eva walked up the aisle on the arm of her father. Steve grew quite emotional when he handed her over to her future husband. Although Eva had objections to this age-old ritual of being passed from one male to the other, she loved Steve too much to deprive him of the pleasure of giving her away. At least, on this occasion, she had some control over who played pass the parcel. She suspected he was secretly relieved she would no longer be around the garden centre to bully him, but his eyes were touchingly moist when they danced together to the strains of 'Daddy's Little Girl'.

CHAPTER NINETEEN

Eva intended establishing her own garden centre. While she searched for a suitable site, she worked with a company called Planting Thoughts. The company was owned by a friend from her college days, Gina Davies, who ran a garden design service as well as supplying unusual and flamboyant floral arrangements for special events. Business was expanding and she asked Eva if she would be interested in managing the floral contracts. Eva agreed and was soon roaming the city in a Planting Thoughts van, decorating hotels and exhibition centres with exotic orchids and plants, turning dull rooms into vibrant jungles and tiger lily sanctuaries.

Eva's possessions over-spilled Greg's apartment. His sense of order, his meticulous need to have a place for everything, was impossible to maintain. She seemed incapable of moving without jogging her elbows off his stereo or tripping over the low sprawling armchairs. In the kitchen she eyed his presses of exotic cooking oils and spices with trepidation, unable to imagine herself feeling comfortable in a place where a stray orange peel on the counter or scattered breadcrumbs marred the perfect symmetry. Only in the bedroom did she feel at ease. At night, in the shadowed slant of light through the blinds, they made love on the tumbled futon. In such moments, when the terse control he exercised over his life was abandoned, she believed nothing could ever invade their happiness.

They invited his friends from 'Elucidate' to dinner. She served lamb with a rosemary crust but they were mainly vegetarians and concentrated on the salads. They filled the apartment with smoke and hot air. Carol Wynne touched the furniture with familiar hands.

"I believe you arrange flowers," she said. "Such an interesting hobby." A remark not exactly designed to inspire love. She asked Eva's advice about her yucca plant in case she felt excluded from the conversations about political manoeuvrings and who was sleeping with whom on the coalition benches.

The conversation turned to Michael Hannon, the leader of Democracy in Action. As the new, informed face of a minority right-wing party, his profile had risen considerably in recent months. He was a dignified politician who did not rant or make emotive statements. Nor did he invade family planning clinics carrying posters of dead foetuses. Instead, he spoke in measured tones about the rights of the unborn, the dispossessed by divorce, the assault on the traditional values of family life. He believed it was only a matter of time before his party, small yet with a powerful voice, would enter coalition.

But a rumour, too vague to be taken seriously yet floating among journalists for years, hinted that after the cut and thrust of politics, the blood letting and vigorous debate, frustration needed an outlet. When Rachel Hannon appeared by her husband's side, her social smile never wavered. If she was a battered wife she was not the type to seek barring orders or display her bruises as evidence to sympathetic judges. Her bruises, if they existed, were hidden behind designer suits and impeccable shoulder pads. Nothing had ever been proven. Journalists who dabbled with the story found themselves facing a wall of denial from anyone they contacted. Editors, imagining libel suits and early retirement without pensions, refused to touch it. Even the producer of 'Elucidate' was adamant. If Greg presented her with broken bones she would give them full disclosure. Anything less, forget it. 'Elucidate' sailed close to the wind but was not in the business of self-destruction. Michael Hannon remained beyond his grasp and Greg, patient and ruthless, was willing to wait.

Eva thought of wolves circling, her husband heading the pack. She listened to them talking, sharing in-jokes as they cheerfully dismantled the lives of the pompous and the powerful. She wanted them out of their apartment but it wasn't really their apartment. It belonged to Greg, whose ordered existence had ended as soon as she stepped into his life.

She saw the site advertised in the window of an estate agency in Oldport. "Where's Grahamstown?" she asked Judith Hansen, a florist who regularly supplied Planting Thoughts with dramatically sculpted reed and wild grass arrangements. "Is it worth checking out as a location for a garden centre?"

"Could be," Judith replied, helping to carry her arrangements to the van. She owned a small flower shop called Woodstock in the centre of Oldport village and had been a regular guest lecturer during Eva's college years. "It's set for development now that work on the motorway has started. Talk to Carrie Davern. She's the estate agent looking after the site."

"I saw Tork busking last Saturday," Eva said as she was leaving. "He was very impressive."

"Impressive!" The florist sighed. "Tork is an incendiary device. I'm trying to persuade him there are easier ways of earning a living than belching fire but he's not listening."

The florist's son was a melancholic youth with dreadlocks who performed his dramatic flame-swallowing routine every Saturday on Grafton Street. He occasionally helped out in Woodstock, making floral deliveries for his mother, and had once confided in Eva that he hoped to become an organic farmer. She had tried and failed to understand how he would combine busking and farming but, looking at his earnest face, had resisted asking him if a scorched earth policy would be a more appropriate career move. She saw him walking towards her as she crossed the road. His face brightened when he noticed her but she was in a hurry and lifted her hand in a farewell gesture as she entered the estate agent's office.

Carrie Davern was a shrill-voiced, persuasive woman with a firm handshake and, Eva suspected, the jargon to make a cat's basket sound like luxurious living. She showed

Eva the development plans for Grahamstown and gave her directions to the site. It sounded exactly right.

The following afternoon Eva and Greg drove northwards from the city, over the Liffey and past the Four Courts, through Drumcondra, Swords, Oldport and on to Grahamstown. February was a mild month with a promise of spring in the air. Early daffodils splashed gold along the central verge of the carriageway and the bare hedgerows tossed in a warm southerly breeze. Greg grew silent, irritably asking every now and then if they had much further to go.

When the road narrowed, he viewed the fields and solitary roadside pubs with increasing nervousness, staring in amazement when she braked outside a small cottage set behind a rusting gate. A corrugated iron roof was almost hidden beneath tufts of grass and ivy. The windows had fallen in. The door had also disappeared and there was ample evidence that cattle regularly sought shelter within its crumbling walls. But Carrie Davern had made Eva see beyond the obvious and she had no problem with vision and ambition, standing positive in front of her husband, who clung to the gate for support. It squeaked as he pushed it open and entered an overgrown, dilapidated wilderness.

He demanded to know if this was a joke, hoping against hope that she would laugh and take his arm and say, "Fooled you, didn't I?" She did laugh. His expression demanded some response. She took his arm and led him forward, striding purposefully towards thick hedging. Eva had a fine stride, long and decisive, shoulders back. The ankles of a colt, said Maria, which may have lacked refinement as a compliment but her friend was precise in her observations and Eva's legs were her finest asset. They walked through a field at the back of the cottage.

"This is what it's all about, Greg." She pointed to the knee-high grass and nettles where plastic bags of rubbish had been dumped and torn apart by dogs. She saw her cottage rising from the rubble, restored, the roof thatched, secure. There would be a front garden with cottage flowers spilling perfume into the air. Her office would have long windows with a back view over her garden centre as it sloped towards a small lake where, even as she watched, two swans emerged from the rushes and glided across the water.

She held his hand, wanting him to share her excitement. He was thinking about leaving 'Elucidate' and returning to print journalism where he had originally begun his career. Eva saw this as the ideal opportunity to move from the city. Technology knew no boundaries. With his work station installed, he could write his stories from home. Corruption could just as effectively be exposed in the company of swans and hanging baskets of begonias.

"Can you think of anywhere nicer to live?" she asked.

"Yes, I could," he said. "How about hell – for starters."

She pressed her fingers to his lips. Work had started on the motorway and Grahamstown would eventually have direct access to it. She told him about the new housing estates that were being built, a new population seeking their dream gardens. The estate agent had recommended a builder. Matt Morgan was an artist when it came to restoring old cottages. The more Eva enthused the more Greg's eyes glazed. He said it was too far out from work. He waved his hands towards the ruins, as if his frantic gesture would make them disappear. If she wanted to live in the company of swans why had she left Ashton? Why had she married him? In years to come maybe, when they had time to consider a family, perhaps then – but not now. Not when his career was carefully mapped within earshot of city bells.

Occasionally since their marriage she had sensed a slight air of pomposity about this man she had chosen to love; a self-righteous, hectoring note in his voice when she did not agree with his opinions. Now, as they stood angrily apart, she realised that they each had completely different visions of their future life together.

"I'm suffocating in the city," she cried. "This place is perfect for my needs."

They waded through dead ragwort, arguing bitterly. Their anger frightened them. The realisation that this was their first serious row silenced them, Adding to their tension as they tried to find their way forward. Below them, the swans streaked across the lake in a flapping rush of wings, then rose with ungainly energy into the air. When Greg reached towards her, she walked without hesitation into his arms and the man she loved, the man who loved her with a raw and sensuous passion, swept her into the shelter of the ruined cottage.

"We'll work it out," he said, kissing her urgently. They made love against the rough stone wall, finding an illicit pleasure in the discomfort of their surroundings. Beneath layers of heavy clothing they sought each other, laughing at the horror of being discovered even as they moaned with passion and came together, breathless.

When they left this hidden place the swans had disappeared. Perhaps there was a nest in the rushes. When they came back again there would be cygnets trailing in their wake. Eva believed it was only a matter of time before her husband believed in her dream as fervently as she did.

They conceived a child beside the lake. Having a child was not part of their plan, rather a decision they would make in time when they had the space to consider another person in their lives. Weeks passed and she was unaware of tiny cells relentlessly multiplying. Every time she mentioned the cottage Greg looked blank, suddenly busy on the phone or rushing to keep an important appointment, dodging and feinting. Her dreams were overwhelming him, demanding time and energy he was unable or unwilling to give. Not that it mattered. She needed money but her ambitious plans did not impress the financial establishment. An interesting project but high risk, she was told time and again by bank managers. Every week she rang the estate agent to see if the site was sold. Luck stayed on her side. No one else sensed the potential in the land and it remained fallow.

The city air choked her lungs. When she grew pale and wilted with tiredness she suspected it was due to the pressure of traffic and working indoors. As she stabbed flowers into an oasis one morning, and nausea rose in her throat she was forced to a standstill, calculating backwards.

Greg's dismay was palpable when she told him. Too soon, he said. How could she be pregnant when they practised safe sex? She reminded him about a lake of swans and an exploding, lustful few moments against the back wall of her dream cottage. He grappled with this truth, suddenly terrified at the thought of another intrusion into his busy, ordered life. "It's the last thing we need at the moment," he said. "I can't believe this has happened to us."

She saw his face and was unable to believe she had ever loved this man. She felt something else, vibrations of fear as this new life clung grimly to the walls of its dark protective cavity. She began to weep. He knelt before her and pressed his head against her stomach. He apologised for his unthinking words. That night when he held her, their passion was tender, a quiet loving shared with this new life they had created so unheedingly.

Their daughter was born on a silver morning in October. Greg was beside Eva throughout. She was swept high on a wave of pain, the mask flung aside because she wanted to know … to feel this moment. No epidural. The nurse told her to inhale deeply; she felt light-headed relief, voices floating above her. Fingers invading, another needle jab, pethidine. Her gynaecologist was on his way. She began to pray even though she had not prayed since she was fifteen, meeting Maria and the boys by Murtagh's River instead of going to evening mass … Hail Mary full of grace … blessed is the fruit of thy womb … sweet fruit, my apple, my love.

The gynaecologist told her to push. She was hurting, tearing, bearing her body downwards as Greg called out, such joy in his voice as their daughter was placed on her stomach. Tiny fingers pressed against Eva's flesh. A closed, wrinkled old woman's face at the end of a long journey. Faye, a fairy child. So beautiful. So ephemeral.

CHAPTER TWENTY

Faye was three months old when the information about Michael Hannon finally landed on Greg's desk. The anonymous note contained a date and an address. In a plush hotel on the crest of a Portuguese mountain, Michael Hannon – whose anthem was 'God Save Our Gracious Family' – planned to engage in a discreet indiscretion with a female companion of long standing.

Greg was confident he knew the identity of the sender. Political destruction as compensation for domestic brutality. If the politician could not be nailed on a wife-beating accusation this would be just as effective. He showed the letter to Sue Lovett, his producer, who looked at it for a moment before ordering him to pack his sun-screen lotion. She was booking him on a flight to Portugal. Carol Wynne would accompany him.

"Don't worry, you can't not go," said Eva, assuring him they would be fine on their own. Apart from the necessity of following the Hannon story to its conclusion, she suspected he would be relieved to escape for a short while from the domestic reality of a small baby. Night feeds, nappy changes, colic, windy smiles. Enchantment, chaos.

"Marital bliss," murmured Carol Wynne when she joined them at the airport. "Who would be without it? Just wait till you're a daddy of ten." She hitched her camera over her shoulder and they marched side by side through the departure gate.

Breakfast, he would later tell Eva, had been decided as the appropriate time for a door-stepping exposure. Who could dispute the evidence of a pot of marmalade on the table?

In a quiet hotel on the summit of the Serra do Caramulo, Michael Hannon and his companion dined on chilled fruit and cheeses, cold meats and crusty bread rolls. Below them, emerging from the morning mist, a grove of lemon trees edged the terraced fields like black serrated knives. The woman was the first to notice Greg. She stretched out a hand to warn the politician but it hung, motionless, between them.

"Is this your definition of family values, Mr Hannon?" Greg, like the politician, had been known to milk a platitude or two when under duress. Lime-flavoured marmalade, he noted, as he thrust his micro-phone forward to catch a muffled curse, the crash of an overturned chair. It was over in minutes.

As he drove down the winding mountain roads and the countryside fell away into forests of olive trees and eucalyptus, he wondered if his heart was large enough to entertain pity for the shattered ambitions of Michael Hannon. He wanted to believe it did. He knew it did not.

His mobile phone rang as he checked into Oporto airport. Eva's voice, calm with the numbness of grief, called him home.

CHAPTER TWENTY-ONE

Faye's death was an inexplicable mystery. Three months old, her downy skin frozen when Eva leaned over the carry-cot to lift her for her morning feed.

She touched her baby's hands before they took her away, stroked the delicate skin between her fingers. She studied the veins on her eyelids, her spiky black eyelashes, the sweet curve of her mouth.

Greg wept bitter tears at the graveside. He begged Eva's forgiveness, crying into her shoulder as they lay sleepless in bed. She said there was nothing to forgive. It was not his fault. Or hers. No one was to blame. A cot death was an act of God. They still had each other, a future. Her words trailed into silence as they stared at each other across their daughter's empty space.

For a fortnight after the funeral they stayed at Wind Fall. Greg brought Faye's possessions back to his wife. She gave them to the crèche in Ashton, keeping just a few mementoes which she wrapped in tissue paper. Days passed but she had no idea where time went. Liz made futile conversation, insisting that time would heal, insisting on understanding her pain.

"How can you understand?" Eva asked, refusing to allow her mother to condense such grief into a platitude. "A failed sperm bottle experiment is not exactly the same as a dead baby." She was amazed at her cruelty. Liz hated her in that instant. She saw it reflected in her eyes and, as her mother struggled to forgive, Eva loved her more intensely than ever. But she was caught in a bleak place and forgiveness could only come when she allowed herself to be absolved. She knew she would always remain her judge and jury, condemned.

If only she had woken on time to feed her child. But she was tired. She slept on. If only the traffic had not been so heavy when the ambulance drove through the bottlenecks, its siren scattering cars too late. Her thoughts moved in a tight, unforgiving circle. It could have been different. It should have been different.

The tests came back from the hospital. All negative. A cot death was a riddle, the everlasting question. If only … if only … if only …

The paediatrician was willing to give them time. He seemed to believe they would draw comfort from knowledge. But what knowledge could be drawn from a mystery? Greg asked intelligent questions, as he always did in an interview situation. She could sense the paediatrician's surprise and growing admiration. No doubt he was used to parents collapsing in a muddle of grief and incomprehension.

When they were leaving, he told Greg how much he

admired him on 'Elucidate', how important it was to have people of his fine calibre who were courageous enough to expose the ugly underbelly of life. Eva imagined rotting vegetation being raked over, translucent maggots scrabbling for cover before her husband pinned them to the ground with his piercing questions. Her head was full of hideous images. The paediatrician said it was a natural reaction and would fade away when her hormone balance settled back to normal. She asked him to define "normal". Greg frowned and held her arm as they walked away.

Liz, gazing at the bereft faces of her daughter and son-in-law, suggested they take a short holiday. "You need time to find each other again," she said as she waved them off. She was right. They had many things to discuss.

Greg's big opportunity had arrived. Since the Michael Hannon exposé his star had risen. Politicians, it seemed, erred everywhere, especially in New York, and the producer of 'Stateside Review', a prestigious US current affairs programme, was headhunting him. A two-year contract was offered, linked to a salary which drew a whistle of astonishment from him.

He tried to discuss this new opportunity with Eva. It was a chance to begin their marriage anew in a ghost-free environment. But she found it impossible to visualise a future when the past held her captive and the present was a time that had to be endured.

They drove to Dingle on a rainy afternoon. Annie Loughrey had offered them her cottage while she was touring with her band. Loughrey's Crew was a seasoned group of musicians who lived in Dingle but was equally at home in the clubs and Irish bars of New York.

The peninsula was quiet. The hedgerows, usually bowed with the weight of wild fuchsia, had not yet begun to green. They walked by the harbour and drove through the Connor Pass. They ate in candle-lit restaurants and drank Guinness in pubs where a few locals gave them a cursory glance before ignoring them. At night they made love with a rough, unthinking haste, as if the anonymity of a strange cottage gave them a freedom they no longer possessed in places where Faye once rested her head.

Loughrey's Crew arrived back at the end of the week. The band was playing in one of the local pubs and Annie persuaded them to come along. Her fiddle trilled in welcome when they entered. As giddy as a poodle on speed, that was how Liz described her youngest sister; single, care-free, in love with the music and the young men who played it with her. After she finished the set she came down and embraced them.

"Stay on," she urged. "We're having a session after hours. That's when the fun really begins."

Greg listened to the musicians, his face growing more clenched as the night wore on. Usually he was a cautious drinker, too self-contained to enter the realms of the indiscreet, and Eva grew nervous as he continued to drink with grim concentration.

When the session was over they left the smoky pub and walked along the harbour. In the grey Atlantic swell a friendly dolphin rested his bones, waiting for the summer when he would begin his high-diving performances, pursued by sonar boats and screaming children.

Greg's voice was slurred when he pressed his face into her neck. He sobbed and asked her to forgive him.

"You heard the doctor. There was nothing either of us could have done." She stroked his face. His skin was cold, his high cheekbones raw and red from the wind. "You have to stop tormenting yourself."

"I could have phoned you – if I'd rung you'd have woken and realised something was wrong with Faye. It might not have been too late – but I couldn't ring you … not then …"

For the first time since their child's death she heard a deeper resonance in the words he uttered. His repentance was not just the grief of a stricken father. It demanded a greater absolution.

"What stopped you ringing me?" she asked.

"Guilt …"

Guilt was tearing at the heart of his marriage. The truth shivered and broke between them. Many miles away on a mountain in Portugal, a world apart from her grief, her husband triumphantly brought a politician to his knees – and betrayed her.

Why do men insist on confession? Later, in the numbed aftermath of everything, Eva would ask herself this question. She had no desire to be the wife who was the last to know. She did not want to know at all. Indiscretions could be absolved by time and silence. Guilt, on the other hand, was a heavier burden. Those who were not strong in their resolve to keep their secrets had a need to share this guilt, to cast it off through the seeking of absolution. In a previous era Greg would have breathed his sins into the ear of a weary priest. He would have received a rosary as penance, recited slowly and with feeling. Eva would have received flowers and attention, perhaps even a fur coat, depending on the nature of the indiscretion, and worn it proudly because in the good old days it was not considered necessary to empathise with the suffering of skinned animals. Instead, she – wife, priest, psychologist, deceived – she got the truth.

Aerobics on a mattress. That was his description. Unexpected yet inevitable from the moment Carol came into his room with a bottle of vodka and they began to talk about old times. Nights when they had bunkered down on the edge of breaking a story, the intimacy of sharing anonymous hotel rooms in cities where they were strangers, walking free. Laden memories, stirring an unexpected, responsive desire as he pulled her close, her mouth opening, seeking him, their excitement heightened by the knowledge that Michael Hannon was enjoying the same swamping passion on the floor above them, unaware that retribution was at hand.

While they were in Dingle, Eva's grandmother had been admitted to the Blackrock Clinic for tests. "I've nothing left to do," she said to Eva who visited the hospital as soon as she returned, "except to follow the fairy child."

When a problem was insurmountable, Brigid Loughrey never wasted energy trying to solve it. She died a week later.

After her will was read it turned out that Brigid had more than bits and pieces. Adding up the stocks and shares, the properties and insurance policies, it came to a mighty sum, even when divided amongst her loved ones. Eva no longer needed to grovel to bank managers who waved her from their offices with regretful smiles. Thanks to her grandmother's generosity she had become a woman of means.

When she discovered that the Grahamstown site was still on the estate agent's books she informed Greg she would not be accompanying him to New York.

He refused to believe her. "This is your way of punishing me. How can I make amends? Tell me and I'll do it – and do it again and again."

Eva imagined him and Carol Wynne lying together in the white dawn light of the Serra do Caramulo and felt nothing. It was unnatural. Even though she did not want to experience again the scalding hurt that followed his confession, some emotion was essential. "My decision has nothing to do with your infidelities," she said. "You made a decision to offload your guilt and you've no right to blame me for refusing to accept it."

"Eva, you're breaking my heart." He caught her arms and shook her, trying to arouse her emotions. "We can't destroy our marriage over one mistake."

His voice came to her from a great distance. Nothing could be resolved by running away, she told him. There was no ghost-free environment. The past was always present.

CHAPTER TWENTY-TWO

They spoke little on their way to the airport. The early morning traffic heaved and shuddered forward in a monotonous crawl. The taxi driver used the brake aggressively. He recognised Greg and called him "a rottweiler without a heart", in a tone that suggested admiration for his ability to draw blood during the interviewing process. Greg smiled grimly, acknowledging the compliment. Or perhaps he was remembering another occasion, another canine metaphor, a bloodhound sniffing in the scent of other people's sins. Dizzy, giddy days when everything was possible and a silent drive to Dublin Airport was not even in their range of vision. The forecast said rain but the sun was shining, hard and bright as a newly minted coin.

Two years of marriage. Such a short time, said Liz, awash with tears when they told her. It was too soon to give up. They must not make decisions when grief and guilt and loss were confused in their minds. Love, Liz believed, is elastic, expanding to the demands which are placed upon it. Eva reminded her that elastic also contracts. It shrivels, sags and no longer binds securely.

The departure hall was crowded with early morning commuters on tight business schedules. The holiday makers in their colourful parkas moved at a more leisurely pace. Eva saw everything and absorbed nothing. If this was a nightmare she would awaken now, forcing herself from a troubled sleep into grateful awareness. But this was no dream filtering through a busy morning. Beside her, not touching, not speaking, Greg loaded his luggage onto a trolley and they headed towards the check-in desk.

A woman in a red suit stood purposefully before them in the queue, speaking loudly into a mobile phone. She tapped her acrylic nails on the counter, annoyed to discover that the seats in the first row of business class were already allocated. The ground hostess assured her that even if she was seated in the last row of business class she would still arrive in New York at the same time as the rest of the passengers. It seemed a reasonable argument but this woman needed to be first off the plane, not to stand in line while passengers blocked the aisle, fumbling with hand baggage and sides of smoked salmon. If there were any blips to her business schedule she would hold the airline personally responsible. Having fired this parting salvo she shouldered her laptop, gripped her monogrammed briefcase, snapped open her mobile phone and moved briskly out of their lives.

Not so long ago, they would have exchanged glances, controlling their laughter until they were alone and had an opportunity to mimic this woman's inflated sense of importance. Now, she simply offered them relief from having to focus on the future.

At the departure gate they faced each other. He pushed her hair back from her forehead, as if he needed to see her face unadorned before he said goodbye. He promised to ring as soon as he arrived in New York. She wondered if he remembered Faye's grip on his finger the last time they stood together in the same place, a family huddle, embracing. Was he picturing her startled eyes, her tiny mouth puckered as the sudden announcement of an impending flight boomed around them. She shuddered away from the memory and from his tense embrace.

"I'll always love you." His voice was bleak. "No matter what we decide to do, that will never change."

"I love you too," she replied. Her voice trembled. "What a pity it isn't enough."

The viewing gallery was empty. Why should it be otherwise, she thought, walking towards it. What was so exciting about flying to distant destinations when the world was becoming a global village? Down below her, the transfer corridor was wheeled away. Ground staff walked towards the terminal building. She wanted the plane to lift swiftly and cleanly into the air, yet it remained immobile, stretching the tension inside her as she waited.

In the crush of passengers at the departure gate, Greg had turned to stare back at her, as if he was unable to believe there were no words they could utter, no gesture that would bring them back together. She had avoided his challenging gaze and when she looked again he had disappeared. In that waiting instant it would have been so easy to wish time away, to forfeit even the brief, unforgettable joy Faye had brought into their lives, if only they could dally in the past.

Her nose began to sting, a certain prelude to tears. She blinked them firmly away. Decisions had been made and enough tears had been shed in their making. She accepted that her feelings were not dead. They had simply been replaced by more demanding preoccupations. She would reserve her grief for Faye and build a new life on her own.

Finally, the plane lumbered into position and taxied down the runway, the grace of speed transforming it almost imperceptibly from a clumsy travel capsule into a sleek graceful bird winging into the distance.

CHAPTER TWENTY-THREE

Brigid Loughrey did more than leave beloved memories and a substantial inheritance behind her. She had cast light on a dark journey that began on a rock-strewn headland twenty-seven years earlier. Eva's scar appeared different when she stared at it in the mirror. It felt more sensitive when she touched it. It had become a question demanding answers.

In the National Library she sought her roots. The moment was not planned, nor did she realise that the subconscious is such a treacherous force, at its most subversive when it appears to be lying down, quiescent. She was early for an appointment to discuss the purchase of the Grahamstown site with her solicitor. She could have passed her time drinking coffee in the Shelbourne Hotel or window shopped on Grafton Street. There was no reason to stride through the black wrought-iron gates, to stride without hesitation through the hushed hall where fat-bellied angels on the ceiling stared impassively down on the rows of silent people scanning microfilm and old books.

The young man seated at the reading table had brown hair tied in a pony-tail. Eva thought he was a woman until she noticed his chin. Long and narrow, with a ridged bone jutting it forward, dark stubble. He reminded her of Greg. When he glanced up at her, Eva's expression terrified him back into the fixed study of some ancient volume. An older women sat next to him, writing feverishly with a silver pen. Porters in uniforms loitered by the main information desk, chatting quietly.

She steadied the viewfinder and focused on headlines. Her past did not take long to swim into view. 'Gardaí Plea to Mother of Anaskeagh Baby.' 'Anaskeagh Baby Off Critical List.' 'Anaskeagh Baby in Care.' 'Still No Sign of Mother of Anaskeagh Baby.'

She wondered how many people had sat in this building, outwardly calm, while their past was enlarged on microfilm before their eyes? Did they, like her, want to scatter headlines in front of the absorbed hushed readers. To shout, "Look – look – that's me!" To breathe slowly until the trembling ceased.

Was it Andy Warhol who said that everyone has fifteen minutes of fame, she wondered. Eva had more than her average, being two weeks old before she was out of the public gaze. Not that she always snatched the main headline. Sometimes she was just a side column, or sandwiched between the violence in Northern Ireland, the bombings of North Vietnam and the posturings of dear old Tricky Dicky. Her birth was a minuscule incident compared to these earth-shattering events, yet journalists had a field day, accusing the Irish nation of collective guilt. Old chestnuts pulled from the fire, still roasting. The irresponsibility of men who shagged and shied away from the consequences. The boat to England, aborted babies, the dual standards of religion and hypocrisy. Even the clergy were in on the act, writing about the need for charity, for soft hearts and open minds. Adopted women spoke about their mother searches and psychologists shaped the mind frame of this woman, writing knowledgeably about her desperation, her pain.

The unfortunate inhabitants of Anaskeagh bolted their doors. They drew up the drawbridge, refusing to comment on the reasons why their lack of charity and understanding had resulted in such a heinous act taking place on their doorstep. As Anaskeagh Head was a mile from the town and jutted out into a raucous Atlantic, it seemed an unfair accusation, but then the whole country seemed convulsed by her mother's anguish. Somehow, Eva was lost in this forest of comment and opinion. She was simply 'The Anaskeagh Baby'. The catalyst. Then it all stopped. No more intriguing glimpses into her life. No sudden mother–daughter reunion. The blood of Northern Ireland buried its roots in the Irish psyche but who remembered abandoned babies?

She sat back and flexed her shoulders. She switched off the machine and left this monument to tall tales and forgotten history. Did she hate this faceless woman who had given birth to her? If she did, it was a hatred without passion. Did she understand this stranger's desperation as she struggled to hide her shame from a closed righteous society, waiting to condemn? Eva's mother grew up in an era of Pill freedom and feminist power. A condom train came over the border and jubilant women thumbed their noses at Church and State alike. There were argumentative 'Late Late Shows' and a nation no longer willing to dance at the crossroads. Yet, she was wrapped in a sack and left on the doorstep of a hill farmer? No, she did not understand. Neither did she hate or pity or condemn. She felt nothing but growing awareness, questions answered, questions still to be asked.

Her heels rapped sharply on the path as she walked through the gardens of Merrion Square. She rang the doorbell of her solicitor's office and was smoothly ushered inside.

Nowadays, when she returned to Ashton, her village seemed caught in the time frame of a nostalgic postcard. She drove past the old-fashioned post office, the church spire glimpsed through dark spruce and Murtagh's River glinting amber in the sun. Liz was stacking the dishwasher when Eva entered Wind Fall. Loaves of freshly baked brown bread cooled on a wire rack.

"What is it, Eva? What's wrong?" She moved quickly towards her daughter and guided her to a chair.

"I went to the National Library. I read the papers. Some puppy lovers …" Eva's voice rose, cracked. She fell silent, staring at her mother. "What else do I need to know?"

The dishwasher hummed softly in the background as Liz talked about the young nun, Jess O'Donovan, still in her novitiate, who had interceded with her community of nuns on Eva's parents' behalf. Eva was six months old before she left the convent. The nun had called her Eva, the meaning of life.

Liz sighed. "No one ever discovered the identity of your mother. Poor soul."

"Poor soul!" Eva stood up, almost knocking the chair over. "Spare me the tears, Liz. I'm grieving for my baby who died for no reason. Faye is a statistic on a report sheet yet I managed to kick my way into life because someone disturbed my mother before she could smash open my skull."

"Stop it, Eva!" Liz spoke firmly. "Try to imagine what it was like for her. The desperation she was feeling ..."

Eva imagined a raised hand. A stone glancing off her forehead. She thought of Faye. A pale lost face, so cold. As cold as her heart.

Only in Murtagh's Meadow, watching the relentless rippling motion of the river, did she feel calm. She never tired watching the water, listening to its soothing murmur as it flowed past. She knew her parents would welcome her home. But she had moved on from the certainties of their secure world.

In her old bedroom a poster of Frankie Goes to Hollywood was pinned to the wall. A collection of gonks crouched balefully on the dressing table. Cindy dolls and toy furniture were packed in boxes at the top of the wardrobe. Everywhere she looked she uncovered the trappings of childhood and teenage years. Yet the room seemed curiously alien, as if the child who had handled such things had disappeared and Eva, an impostor, was trying too hard to fit into these once-familiar surroundings.

"Why won't you let us take care of you?" her mother demanded when Eva announced that Greg's apartment had been rented for a year and she was moving to Grahamstown while work on the garden centre and the cottage was underway.

"Why can't you stay with us until everything is finished, or at least drive back here in the evenings?"

"I can't. I have so much to do. I don't want to waste time travelling. If I can move the caravan on-site I'll be able to supervise everything."

The caravan in the garden of Wind Fall was used occasionally by her parents when the guest house overflowed. Liz was horrified. It was too dangerous for Eva to live alone at the side of a remote country road. What protection would she have if she was attacked? She invented horror scenarios of murder and mayhem but her daughter remained adamant. She needed to move on to the next stage of her life.

Greg rang regularly from New York. He sounded purposeful and excited. He had moved into an apartment in Greenwich Village. A ghost-free zone. He told her he missed her. His voice stammered, as if he found it difficult to say the words. She wondered how he had time for such lost emotions? He was part of the new Irish wave who drank in trendy bars and attended poetry readings. No armchair politicians this lot, mourning Ireland's oppression and vowing eternal vengeance on the Brits. They assimilated and earned big bucks.

On 'Stateside Review' he had a certain novelty appeal. Viewers were impressed by his opinions. A new slant, an objective eye. He sneered at American-pie politicians. He called them the control freaks of the world. He was a thorn in the side of right-wing Republicans. A blight on the vision of capitalism. A fly in the ointment of liberalism. How happy he must be, Eva thought, pleasing no one.

She wondered how he would react if she told him the real story was here. The big exclusive, insider knowledge. She imagined him in action, lifting stones, letting the worms free. He would take her story from her and give it back to the world. Twenty-seven years on, the Anaskeagh Baby searches for her roots.

Those roots had been set deep in Ashton, a gentle place that nurtured her childhood, as if making recompense for the hard unyielding landscape into which she had been cast. But she felt them loosening, their tentacles twining in new directions, linking her to a family of strangers: bound to them by blood and tears, by an ancestral history, and a secret that belonged to the foreboding headland she had last seen looming over the small town of Anaskeagh.

Part Three

1997–1998

CHAPTER TWENTY-FOUR

It was an ordinary day turned extraordinary. Afterwards, that was all Beth could remember, a routine Monday filled with routine chores and nagging anxieties. She had not achieved the title "obsessive neurotic" from her eldest daughter without earning her stripes. Uptight, upright mother of four, her life absorbed through the prism of her children's needs and achievements. All she wanted was to keep then safe from harm. Such a simple wish, so impossible to achieve. This need had consumed her from the moment they were born and she felt their clinging dependence. In time, Robert, Paul and Gail, would go their own ways, make their own mistakes and forge their futures from such experiences. For the moment they were safe in her care – but Lindsey was another matter.

She sat on the edge of her daughter's bed and dangled a bra from her fingers, gazing into the contents of a wardrobe that was mainly confined to the floor. A warehouse of drugs could remain undetected beneath the clutter of magazines, strewn clothes and the mould-infested crockery that looked capable of forming its own life force and crawling towards her – if it could find the space to do so. Lindsey was a teenager with attitude and angst, who demanded the right to live in squalor. This attic bedroom with its slanting ceiling and posters of rap stars glowering from the walls, was her private domain. Organised chaos, she called it, and pinned defiant 'Keep Out' notices to the door whenever Beth uttered fumigation threats. If her mother did not approve of what she saw then all she had to do was close her eyes and get a life.

The diary was hidden in a jumble of T-shirts at the back of the wardrobe. Beth began to read it, scanning the pages for one name. Lindsey was meeting Tork Hansen in the derelict privacy of Base Road, a lonely place since work began on the new motorway. The previous night she had spotted them together when she was driving home from the village, recognising his distinctive dreadlocks in the car headlights. Lindsey's shabby army jacket with its epaulets and hand-painted graffiti was also impossible to mistake and Beth had resisted her immediate urge to drag them apart, to slap him smartly across his wide toothy mouth and bundle her daughter into the car. Nothing would be solved by confrontation. That much she had learned from her many arguments with Lindsey – but any ideals she still cherished about rights of privacy were strictly laid aside when she entered the attic bedroom.

She searched methodically for scraps of tin foil, scorched spoons and burned matches, the scent of hash, strawberry stamps, mood enhancers; the modern mother's dread list. The lack of anything remotely resembling abusive substances did nothing to allay her suspicions and, when it was time to collect the two younger children from school, she closed the door behind her and retreated downstairs. She had gleaned little information from the diary entries which were mostly confined to appointments with friends, study arrangements, a drawing of a red heart with Tork's name in the centre, and occasional references to Sara.

Judith Hansen was picking flowers from one of the buckets outside her shop when Beth drove past. Lindsey had worked in Woodstock during her school holidays. The romance with the florist's son must have started then. A summer romance making its way through autumn. Not a romance. Nowadays it was called a relationship. Beth winced away from the expression. Romance was about lingering glances and slow burning passion, a tender courtship, the blush of expectation and anticipation. Relationships were about sex. Even the word had a sundering quality and Lindsey was too young, not yet seventeen, definitely too young to lurk in a deserted cottage gateway, swamped in the arms of a glass-eating, grass-smoking busker. Her mind shied away from images of rubber bands and wasted veins, Lindsey huddled and broken beneath his threatening figure. Easy on the paranoia, Beth, she warned herself as the afternoon gathered its own momentum.

At four o'clock Robert rang the doorbell in successive blasts in case she had developed chronic deafness since he left for school that morning. He treated her to an obligatory grunt when she enquired about his day. A routine question, a routine response. Since his twelfth birthday, this grunt was capable of expressing either joy or anguish and, after two years of communicating with him in this fashion, Beth interpreted this one as meaning he was not in danger of imminent expulsion. He was followed soon afterwards by Lindsey who headed straight for the press, piling a plate with crackers and peanut butter.

"I don't want any dinner," she announced. "I'm going to Melanie's house to work on my French project. Her mother is making *Coq au Vin*."

"You can forget about *Coq au Vin*," Beth warned. "You promised to baby sit. I told you I was bringing Granny Mac to the theatre for her birthday."

"*Baby sit*." Lindsey was outraged. "They're seven and ten – some *babies*. Anyway, I never promised. You just assumed I'd do it without even asking if I'd other plans. You *never* remember *anything* I tell you."

Beth sighed. "Despite your best efforts, Lindsey, I haven't started suffering from senile dementia, *yet*. You made a promise. I expect you to keep it."

"All I'm trying to do is get an honour in my French. Is that a crime? Ring Melanie's mother if you don't believe me. Go on! Let the world know you don't want me to pass my Leaving. Why can't Robert look after the *babies*?"

"I don't mind at all." Robert shrugged.

Five syllables in one day from Robert was a record-breaking achievement and convinced Beth that money had changed hands between her two older children. She rang Joanna Murray who assured her that six young people were indeed descending on her house in thirty minutes. She was up to her elbows in garlic, chicken and wine. She sounded supremely in control, amused by Beth's obvious anxiety.

"OK. You can go," Beth replaced the receiver. "I'll collect you on my way home from the theatre."

"We've arranged to walk back together and I have to be wheeled home like a baby in a pram." Lindsey waved her hands despairingly in the air. "Why do I always have to be different?"

"All right! All right! But I want you in here by ten-thirty. Is that understood?" The beginnings of a headache tightened across her forehead. She tried to remember when she had last walked out of her front door without a thought or care. Lindsey clattered up the stairs and returned shortly afterwards in baggy camouflage trousers and the military jacket which looked as if it had been scavenged from the body of a dead soldier. The front door slammed and peace of a certain kind settled over the house. In warfare, she had a staying power Beth no longer possessed. Such rows exhausted her but Lindsey seemed to gather energy from them, forcing Beth into roles she had no desire to play, prying, suspicious, nagging.

Was this motherhood? she wondered, this obsessive anxiety that clung like a dank paw to her shoulder. Get a life, Mother. Get a life. Lindsey's familiar refrain mocked her. Sara had a life. A career as a photographer. A fine old house Beth had once coveted. A husband she had once cherished. Bad old days, Beth, she warned herself, checking her watch. Five minutes fast as usual.

A bird was singing a shrill unrelenting note outside the kitchen window, and voices on the radio were arguing about the latest crisis in Northern Ireland – implacable old hatreds churning up the airwaves – when Peter rang. She stiffened when she recognised his voice, a reflex action, like the faint but unmistakable quickening of her heartbeat. He was in Germany on a business trip with her husband and for an instant, unable to think of any reason why he should call her, she wondered if something had happened to Stewart.

"He's fine, living for tomorrow," Peter quickly reassured her. They had flown out on Sunday on a two-day trip to visit a computer plant and would return tomorrow.

"Has Sara been in touch with you today?" he asked. "I've been trying to contact her on her mobile phone for hours. I've left messages on her answering machine but she hasn't rung back. I wondered if you'd heard from her?"

"Of course not." Beth was surprised by the question. "She never talks to any of us when she's at Elmfield. You know the routine — peace and perfect harmony all ye who enter here." She laughed. "She probably had her mobile confiscated on arrival and the reception isn't putting your calls through to her room."

The health spa in West Cork was her sister's twice-yearly retreat: five days of yoga, meditation, hill walks in the rain, mixed lettuce leaves, and no contact whatsoever from radio, television or intrusive spouses.

"Elmfield may have the regime of a concentration camp but they don't imprison their inmates. She phoned them yesterday and cancelled her visit." Peter sounded angry rather than surprised and she imagined him running his hand through his dark hair in frustration at the antics of his elusive wife.

"Have you rung Havenstone?"

"This morning and this afternoon. I'm getting the answering machine there as well."

"She probably headed off to photograph something or

other that caught her fancy." Beth shrugged and ruffled Gail's hair when her daughter entered the kitchen, her math's copybook in hand, and an expression that demanded instant attention. "You know Sara's moods. She'll be in touch when she feels like it."

"We had a few words before I left. Nothing too serious …" He hesitated, as if reluctant to discuss his marital problems with her, and she waited for him to continue. "To tell the truth, Beth, it was serious enough. She went off the deep end over some crazy notion she'd got into her head and we haven't spoken since Friday. I spent the weekend in the Oldport Grand. I suppose Lindsey told you what happened?"

"No, Lindsey never mentioned anything about it. Why was Sara so upset?"

"Oh … it's not worth discussing." He sounded off-hand but she knew by the slight inflection in his voice that he lied and it annoyed her that she was still so attuned to his emotions. "Would you mind driving over to the house and check if she's still there?" he asked. " I know she's avoiding me but I need to speak to her."

Instant action and no questions asked, just like his mother. The days when she would jump to the persuasive lilt of his voice had long gone. She told him she was busy. Dinner to make, homework to correct before she collected Connie for the theatre. Busy, busy, boring him. She heard it in his sharp intake of breath. Not that she blamed him. She was boring herself and this awareness sharpened her tone. "For Christ's sake, Peter, I haven't time to sort out your domestic squabbles. Buy her some flowers when you come home – book a restaurant."

"I appreciate how busy you are." He ignored her irritation. "But it won't take long if you leave now. You know where to find the spare key. Please, Beth. There's no one else I can ask."

She promised to call into Havenstone on the way to the theatre and ring him back if Sara was not at home. As she lifted the evening meal from the oven she debated how long it would take to get to Havenstone. During the day she could drive there in ten minutes but at peak hour the village would be congested with traffic. Sara could be anywhere. On a derelict building site or in a dingy back lane photographing winos huddled around a bottle. Misery only became real when she framed and captured it. She would focus her camera on their wizened hands, the hopeless droop of old shoulders, the bleak urine stains on the wall behind them. Or, perhaps not. Perhaps, she was in a luxury hotel enjoying the attentions of a lover. Champagne in an ice bucket, fluted glasses, curtains drawn against the intrusive evening. Sara's lifestyle had always remained a mystery, vaguely exotic, filled with foreign travel and photographic exhibitions where sophisticated strangers shook Beth's hand and moved a step backwards when she confessed to being a housewife and mother.

"Oh yuk! " moaned Paul, entering the kitchen to inspect the dish of cannelloni. "Dog's vomit for dinner again."

As a lifestyle decision, Beth was not going to moralise about her sister's choices.

The traffic was heavy as it bottlenecked through Oldport, snarling in from the city and off the motorway. She became part of the slow moving tailback, edging its way towards the village. The setting sun flung a blood-red streak across the estuary and she thought of sailors, red sky tonight, her father used to say, a sailor's delight.

Havenstone had once blended into its country landscape but now it sat arrogantly above the newer housing estates, an anachronism in a village gripped by suburban bliss and blight. The march of progress. But who was she to complain? Ten years previously, when she and Stewart moved back from London, they had set up house in that mushrooming belt; third right, first left after the tasteful granite slab carved with the letters, Estuary View Heights.

An evening mist hung over the grass as she drove through the open gates and up the avenue of Havenstone. Rooks, disturbed by the car, whirled above the old trees, raucously calling down the night. The blinds were drawn on the windows and the chiming doorbell had an echo that belonged to empty spaces. The spare key was under a terracotta plant holder at the back of the house. She debated searching for it but Connie, a punctual woman, was waiting and Beth was already twenty minutes late. She rang Peter from her mobile phone and told him his wife was not at home.

There should have been something to alert her. A banshee wailing through her long wild hair: omens, portends, the shudder of approaching chaos. But she drove away without a backward glance, unaware that her life was already sliced cleanly in two – and she had become the custodian of the past.

*   *   *

Sixteen years ago Peter Wallace carried his wife over the threshold of Havenstone. She stood in the centre of the hall and gazed around her, touching the walls, the curved wooden banisters, the white roses on the antique table, as if she was returning home to a familiar and much-loved place. Sunlight fell through the open door and dazzled his eyes, suffusing her in its radiance as she walked into his arms, and murmured, "I want to melt into your love … forever."

Did he dream that moment? How many times had Peter asked himself that question? To melt was to reveal, to be absorbed. Sara Wallace was ice, untouched by fire. He loved her. He hated her. How could two such strong emotions co-exist without breaking his heart?

She could have Havenstone. The house meant nothing to him. It was impregnated with her presence. Not with children, most definitely not with children. He had been down that road too many times to indulge the fantasy. The glossy hardwood floors, the cold marble fireplaces, a beautiful, treacherous staircase where he had fallen as a child, the scar still faintly visible on his right cheek, that was Havenstone, his inheritance. She was welcome to it.

His anger had carried him through the weekend and he had resisted ringing her before he left for Germany, still furious but clear in his mind about his intentions. A clean break, a snapped thread. This time he would see it through. His resolve remained firm throughout Monday as he inspected computerised systems with Stewart and tried to look interested during interminable technical demonstrations, and an over-long lunch with an eager sales executive, anxious for Peter's signature on the dotted line.

After dining with Stewart, they entered the hotel bar for a late-night drink. A young woman sat at a white piano playing a medley of love songs. Her voice had the late night rasp of too many cigarettes, a husky decadence oddly at variance with her long blonde hair and fresh complexion. When the music ended, she eased her body into the stool beside him and touched his hand, demanding a light for her cigarette. A tired cliché to which he responded in kind, glad he did not have to play any new games.

"Emma from Essen," she said, and so he remembered her name. She wore a low-necked glitter top and rings on all her fingers. If she was in the mood she chatted up tired businessmen and drank champagne from the mini bars in their hotel rooms. She carried a packet of condoms in the back pocket of her black leather trousers, a precaution she had taken since she was sixteen.

"The same packet?" he asked, already bored with their conversation.

"What do you think, silly man?" She laughed deep in her throat.

Young women like Emma confused him, so much confidence, so little charm. Yet her laughter reminded him of Sara, as seductive as the midnight music she had played on the white piano, and he was tempted to kiss her glossy lips, to sate a momentary passion that flared when she moved closer, willing him to breathe in the subtle promise of her youth.

Stewart disapproved of Emma from Essen. The production manager disliked the challenge of strange cities, the edginess of new experiences, hating the time he was forced to spend away from his family. When Peter insisted on ordering one more round of drinks, he tucked his mouth into a grim smile and shook his head. He retreated to his bedroom with a curt goodnight. No doubt he expected to find Emma at the breakfast table the following morning but he made no comment when Peter came down alone. A moral victory, Peter was forced to admit, that was based on lethargy rather than virtue. At least he could be thankful for small mercies. He was faithful to his wife in death, if not in life.

Mirrors glinted on the walls when he opened her bedroom door. He felt a rush of air, as if her spirit had risen and finally flown free. She had listened to music as she counted down the hours. An obscure Russian recording of choral singing which she must have picked up on one of her trips abroad. The stereo, set on the repeat button, was playing low beside her bed, the powerful voice of the female singer almost hypnotic in a repetitive, lamenting chant. Wax stalactites hung from silver sconces, the remains of perfumed candles that had burned slowly through the night and still released a faint scent of mimosa. Her slender fingers were bruised to a purple hue. Her skin was alabaster, frozen.

Sara … Sara. Did he call out her name? Or breathe it as a soft accusation? He had no memory of doing either. There was no note. No explanation. As in life, the death of Sara Wallace would remain a private business.

CHAPTER TWENTY-FIVE

Marjory Tyrell arrived in Oldport the following day. Her mouth was a wrinkled wound, her eyes dazed. As always, she stayed in Havenstone. She wanted her daughter's body buried in consecrated grounds. How could she pray to a mound of ash? Tom Oliver argued for her, softly persuasive, gently threatening, unsuccessful. Peter remained adamant.

"Sara discussed this with me once. She was very specific about a cremation ceremony. She wanted her ashes scattered into the sea off Pier's Point and that's what I intend to do."

"It's not right, Peter. It's barbaric." The older man shook his head. "Marjory needs a place where she can mourn her daughter in peace. For God's sake, man, is it too much to give the poor woman a grave she can tend with flowers and pray over, preferably in Anaskeagh?"

Peter did not seem to hear him. "Pier's Point is where we first met and that is where I will say my final goodbye. I'm determined to honour my wife's wishes." He sat with his head bowed but Beth knew by the hard lines around his mouth that he would have his way.

"What a pity you didn't honour her when she was alive." Her uncle slapped his fist off the table, his face flushed with annoyance. For an instant the smooth mask of the politician was removed but, when Beth was leaving, he placed his arm around her shoulders and murmured words of condolence. "A sad time for us all. Be kind to your poor mother. Her heart is broken."

How easily the platitudes slid from his lips. His hair was white, as thick as she remembered, still brushed back in the same glossy sweep. Age had distinguished him, giving him a stately air of assurance, a man who understood power, how to acquire and use it. She moved away from him and made no reply.

When she returned home she entered the bathroom and turned on the shower. The urge to stand still, paralysed by the force of water, came over her. What if she never moved again, if she dissolved into the enveloping steam. No dragging backwards, no reaching forwards. A moment of nothingness absorbing her into an infinity where she would cease to exist. Was that how Sara felt? Was that the force that drove her into her bedroom of mirrors and the darkness beyond? There was no answer to the question and, knowing she would never be able to ask it, Beth wept quietly into the cascading water.

*   *   *

In the small cremation chapel the priest stared at Lindsey. He had pale bleached skin and eyes that reached into her heart, shaming her. If he knew what she had done he would refuse to give her absolution. Why she was worrying about absolution was a mystery. Since she was thirteen years old she had not entered a confession box, despite Granny Mac's assurances that secret sins were best laid on the broad shoulders of a merciful God.

Her Tyrell grandmother sat stiffly beside her. The only movement she made was when Sara's coffin rolled out of sight behind the red velvet curtains. Then she fluttered her dead-leaf hands towards the vacant space and rested her head on the old man's shoulder.

Lindsey found it impossible to like her Tyrell grandmother, who insisted on being called "Marjory" because she did not want to be associated with grandmotherly labels. But seeing the old woman's face so crumpled with grief, she felt as if a rock had fallen on her chest and crushed it. Her father wrapped her in his arms. He brought her outside and stayed with her until she could breathe freely again.

Afterwards they went to the Oldport Grand for lunch. The old man bought drinks for the mourners and shook hands with everyone. He had white hair, worn long on the back of his neck. It made him look cool, unlike someone from the sticks. He sounded posh, as if he was used to speaking in public, which, of course, was what he did for a living. She knew that politicians were crooks, corrupt and full of crap, so it was kind of weird to be related to one. When he spoke to Beth, she stared over his head, as if talking to old men at funerals was a chore that had to be endured.

After she returned from the hotel Lindsey tidied her bedroom. She dumped black plastic sacks in the back garden. She folded her clothes and put them neatly into drawers. She washed the floor. But still the smell remained. Mimosa, her mother said. Sara lit candles scented with mimosa and breathed in the sweet fragrance before she died. It was in Lindsey's nostrils. Every time she drew a deep breath she could smell it, clinging – a secret smell that only she inhaled.

"You sly devious babe," Tork had said, when she told him she knew where to find a key to an empty house. On that night, that awful Monday night, the guilt had lifted clear off her shoulders as soon she saw him waiting for her at the back of the supermarket. The French project was a lie. So was the stomach upset that had fooled Melanie's mother. All that mattered were the wonderful hours stretching in front of them, safe from prying eyes in Havenstone.

If her mother had known she was meeting him it would have been curfew and curtains without a doubt. After reading about his suspended sentence in the *Evening Herald* she never let up. Anyone who wore dreadlocks and ate glass for a living was bound to become a drug addict sooner rather than later, she insisted. Lindsey had tried explaining the difference between soft and hard drugs. She might as well have been talking to the wall.

Tork did not do hard drugs. He did not eat glass. He was a fire eater. Fire and glass were two different things when it came to swallowing. Yet, her mother seemed incapable of understanding such obvious distinctions. As for the drugs – all he was doing was smoking hash and drinking cans with his friends when the Gardaí raided the rocks by the estuary. But Beth had carried on as if he was shooting up in the middle of Main Strand Street every single hour of the day.

In Havenstone, he had undressed her slowly and she had done the same to him. It was the first time they had seen each other completely naked. He kissed every part of her body, stoking up a fire inside her until she felt as if she was weeping down there, whimpering when she felt him sliding hard into her. She wanted to lie forever in his arms, her lips bruised from his kisses, his heart thumping against her breast, the sweat on his chest damp and warm.

Her mother drove right up to the front door and rang the bell. *Twice*. They saw her car when they looked out the window. The shock froze them to the spot. Suddenly everything was different and Lindsey knew she would never again be able to enter this lovely old drawing room without thinking about what they had done.

They ran from Havenstone and left Sara behind. They had not heard the music from her bedroom and only when they reached the hall did they catch the faint scent of mimosa. But it did not make them pause or wonder and the following evening, when her mother returned from the hospital, walking bent as if someone had beaten her, all Lindsey wanted to do was lie down on the floor and die too.

Such a cruel and deliberate thing to do, to take drugs and leave everyone without warning. But Sara was not cruel. She was Lindsey's ideal mother, her sister and best friend, her confidante. Now she was gone and it was impossible to forget how death stayed silent in the upstairs room while, down below, she lay in Tork's arms, his ragged breathing loud in her ears, and the blood rushing fast through her veins.

Tork was past tense now. She never wanted to see him again. He said they must not tell anyone. He was in trouble already and knowing he broke into a dead woman's house would do his mother's head in. He held her arms tightly and made her swear, never ever, to say anything. If she did there would be trouble. A charge of breaking and entering. What would a judge say? Or her uncle ... her parents ... her teachers? What would Sara say?

At night, Lindsey cried until her throat felt scratchy as sandpaper. Somewhere, hidden behind a press, lost in the post and still to arrive, there had to be a note. Sara loved her. How many times had she told her? Millions. How could she go without a word, a sign, anything?

CHAPTER TWENTY-SIX

Life slowly reverted to normal in the McKeever household. The children, relieved that their mother showed no sign of deteriorating under the shock of their aunt's sudden death, stopped tiptoeing anxiously around her. Lindsey's free time was spent in her bedroom; her miraculously tidy room with its aggressive rap music – a rhythm with an incessant beat that vibrated inside Beth's head until she banged on the door and ordered her to lower the volume. This, at least, was familiar territory for both of them. Without replying Lindsey lowered the sound, gradually increasing it again when her mother had gone downstairs.

"You must cry," Stewart advised her. As if tears were on tap, made-to-order lachrymation. In the two months since Sara's death they had not made love. He knew her body intimately and sensed her resistance when he put his arms around her. It was important to go through the grieving process, he said. The Grieving Process. The words had a safe sound. A clearly defined rite of passage which psychologists had marked in stages. Denial, disbelief, rage, loneliness, a silent shriving of the soul. She would sink in and out of depression and finally, bleached of all negative emotions, into acceptance.

But there were no stages of grief, only an intense and tearless anger that showed no sign of abating as it carried her through October. She tried to understand her feelings. Shamed, ambiguous emotions. A sense of release now that Sara had gone. She drew back in horror from this realisation but she knew that through Sara's death she was freed from a burden she had carried for too many years. She had not believed in vengeance. No vendettas. The past was the past, a shadow in time that would gather importance if she held it in hock. She had banished her childhood – suppressing memories of crystal stars seen from the hill field, the steamy comfort of O'Donovan's kitchen, the thrill of riding high on her father's shoulders, stories and music and dancing, blood sisters with Jess, giggling with Sara in the dip of a horsehair mattress. Unable to separate the good times from the bad, she was afraid those silent moments would gain strength if she shaped them with words, gave them a name. She had moved forward, reinventing herself until only phantoms remained, vaguely threatening yet distant; as if they belonged to the nightmares of someone else. She called it selective amnesia. Except that amnesia was a blank space; an erosion of time. Her memories were never erased, only vanquished until she could no longer pretend. Then she had returned to Oldport and to Sara, whose secret was a wound that refused to heal.

In Havenstone, Peter stared bleakly at her when she

apologised for not entering the house that night. She was rushing, late for Connie, worried about Lindsey, stressed. Her voice faltered as she realised the futility of what she was saying. In the studio where he had once painted the *Cat* pictures, and which Sara had taken over and used until her death, he showed her a folder of old photographs of Anaskeagh he had discovered. Beth's name was written on the front of the folder and also on the cover of an old chocolate box containing letters.

"She must have wanted you to have these," he said. "You'd better take them with you now. In fact, take whatever you want. I'm clearing everything out soon."

"The only thing you should clear out is the whiskey bottle," she replied. "It's not going to solve anything, Peter."

"You'll have to allow me to be the judge of that," he said and she nodded, unwilling to enter into an argument with him.

"I want to understand," he said, when she was leaving. "Sixteen years of marriage! She owed me an explanation."

"What explanation could she give? And would it really have made any difference?"

"She didn't have to die to escape from me."

"You had nothing to do with it, Peter. Sara died to escape from herself."

How simple she made it sound. Yet such sentiments brought them no nearer to understanding. She left soon afterwards. It was a long time since they had had anything important to say to each other.

When she returned home she untied the faded ribbon on the chocolate box. She opened the brittle pages, yellow with age, much folded. She had forgotten how often she wrote to Sara, as if, in those far-off days when she first came to Oldport, she was making amends for leaving her sister behind. She wrote about the village, the raucous women in the factory, their jokes and turbulent love lives. The snobbish, gossiping women in the office. Through these letters Sara came to know the tough and bossy Della Wallace and the maternal Connie McKeever, who had loved their father in sickness and in health. She knew about the boys Beth dated, the rows with Marina, the heady rides on the back of Stewart's motorbike, and Peter with his paint-streaked jeans and honey skin, he filled the pages with his deeds. She wrote about Havenstone and the light-filled studio where he immortalised her eyes in oils. In these letters there was no mention of home sickness and loneliness – and how she cried at night, remembering. She created a fantasy world and Sara came to Oldport to claim it. A young woman of twenty-three, armed with her beauty and her cameras. Models danced on Pier's Point. The sun melted into the sea. The battle was over before it began.

*   *   *

At night Peter watched old films and educational programmes on *The Learning Zone*. He read newspapers and remembered nothing, drew up business plans which he shredded before morning. He had joined the world of the insomniac. His visits to the factory were becoming more irregular. When he did make an appearance he found it difficult to concentrate on what people were saying to him.

Jon Davern, the company accountant, treated him as carefully as a convalescing invalid, insisting that everything was under control. When Peter, suspicious of such forbearance, demanded to know exactly what was under control, he shied away from the rapid-fire delivery of information and spread sheets the accountant placed on his desk. Stewart was also crowding his elbow, insisting on a meeting with the shareholders about the new investment programme, the reason for the German trip. Peter sensed their impatience but was indifferent to it. Everything seemed suspended, hanging in an air of unreality, as if he was waiting for a signal to awaken and take control of his life again.

Two women from a charity shop in the village came to Havenstone and removed Sara's clothes. He donated her photographic equipment to his old art college, his alma mater of lost ambitions. But when it came to removing the photographic files that filled her studio the task defeated him. The image of her at work was so bleakly etched on his mind that he stacked them into boxes and carried them up to the attic. In her dark room, prints from the last roll of film she had developed lay on the work bench – moody shots of rocks and a configuration of slabs that reminded him of a dolmen. She had taken the photographs at night and the moon, shining above the looming boulders, added a surreal, almost pagan quality to the scene.

It was a time of closure. The McKeever family were waiting for him on Pier's Point. Marjory had refused to come. She had written a curt note. A pagan ceremony in which God was not included was of no interest to her.

Beth huddled into the collar of her coat, her short dark hair fluttering around her face, her eyes dull with grief, wonderful slanting eyes that had once captivated and charmed him. She gripped the rail of the jetty as he scattered his wife's ashes on the water, eddies of fine grey dust moving away from them. This was a deep place no matter how the tide ran, bathed in an early morning stillness, pewter sky and sea merging. Seagulls ran across the shallows, leaving twiggy prints in the estuary mud. A dog raced behind them, barking in outrage when they swirled from its reach in a dismissive sweep of wings.

On the shore, a woman glanced curiously towards them. The wind gusted suddenly. She lifted her hand to push back her long blonde hair and, in that gesture, Sara came to his mind with such piercing clarity that he was forced to look away.

It seemed appropriate to pray but no prayer was appropriate. Beth was an atheist who refused to contemplate a god, merciful or otherwise. He drifted by on indifference. Lindsey read a poem she had written, simple words that reduced her to tears before she finished. She tore the paper and flung the pieces into the water. Lapping rhythms soothed them as Connie McKeever fell back on the way of old rituals, reciting tried and tested decades of the rosary, forcing them into long-forgotten responses.

He walked back to Havenstone, refusing Beth's invitation to join them for breakfast. At Base Road he took the shortcut through the undergrowth at the back of his house. Already, he could see the outlines of the new industrial estate spreading across the fields. The arms of high yellow cranes bent protectively over iron girders and shell buildings. His feet sank in dead clover, purple heads turning brown. Shrivelled nettles no longer able to sting.

Dead brambles. Dead leaves. Everything reminded him of her.

Is that how it's going to be, Sara? He raged into the emptiness of the morning. Did you spare a thought for what I would find when I entered your crazy bedroom of mirrors? I won't have it. Do you hear me, Sara? Leave me alone. Corrosive bitch. Can you hear me? Leave me alone.

CHAPTER TWENTY-SEVEN

Three mornings a week, before the family woke, Beth drove to the Oldport Leisure Centre. The village shops were still shuttered, except for the newsagents, and Woodstock, where Judith Hansen, back from the airport with boxes of fresh irises and chrysanthemums, was unloading flowers from her van. At the start of the summer Beth had joined the swimming group, hoping to tone up and lose weight but mainly to steal some precious time for herself before the day began. Her motives had changed since then. In the painful cramp of muscle, the shudder of breath in her lungs, she was able to snatch a short respite from the clamour of old memories.

Carrie Davern set the pace during these early morning sessions, her arms pumping energetically, focused on laps and time. She was a competitive swimmer, an ambitious, finely-toned woman, whom Beth avoided whenever possible. She disliked Carrie's crisp manner and thinly disguised curiosity which always revealed itself when she spoke about Sara. Their husbands worked in Della Designs and this tenuous link was the only interest the two women had in common.

One morning, when Beth finished swimming and entered the changing room, Carrie was already showered and shampooed, limbering up for a busy day in her estate agency. She tilted her head towards the hairdryer, finger-combing her red hair into shape, and waved at Beth.

"Poor Beth, you look exhausted." She switched off the dryer and sat beside her on the slatted bench. "How are you coping?"

"I'm fine, thank you."

"We must invite you and Stewart to dinner soon." She patted Beth's hand, comfortingly. "Take your mind off things. Maybe Peter too ... if he's in a fit condition to come." Her pause was eloquent. "I'm worried about him. I suppose you know he's drinking heavily and—"

"Don't worry about Peter." Beth interrupted. "The factory has been through so many ups and downs and it's still going strong."

"I wish I could be so positive. I sympathise with Peter, I really do, but there's far more than his own feelings at stake which is why it's so upsetting for Jon, as I'm sure it must be for Stewart. He has a business to run and he's out of the factory more often than he's in. If anything happens he only has himself to blame."

Her vibrant energy drained Beth. She wanted to stand up and walk away but Carrie's forceful voice only increased her inertia. Her shoulders slumped as she allowed the words to drift beyond her. Women, already dressed, slung sports bags over their shoulders and shouted goodbye.

"Have you seen the state of Havenstone?" Carrie demanded. "So sad. I believe he's going to put it on the market. I've told him I'm interested and he's promised to notify me as soon as he makes up his mind. The sooner the better. Sara must be turning in her grave – oh dear, how insensitive of me! I forgot about the cremation." She smiled apologetically and pressed her fingers to her lips. "Forgive me, Beth, such an unfinished kind of ceremony I always think. I've told Jon I want a jazz band at my graveside and everyone singing along because life has to go on—"

"Stop it, Carrie!" She stood up, curtly silencing the younger woman. "I've no intention of discussing such a private and personal matter with you now, or ever. As regards dinner, forget it. Stewart and I are busy for the foreseeable future." She forced herself to walk calmly towards the shower.

Carrie stood outside the plastic curtain and spoke firmly, a woman unable to leave without the last word. "I understand that our husbands could be out of work if Peter Wallace doesn't get his act together soon. That's a fact, Beth. Not coffee morning gossip which is something I never have time to indulge in. *Goodbye.*"

*   *   *

Havenstone looked so desolate beyond the bare trees. Even passing it on her way to school made Lindsey shiver. Her uncle's flash Jaguar snaked out of the gate. He stopped when he saw her. He looked gaunt and hungover, as if he had slept in his clothes and forgotten to shave. He offered her a lift. His eyes were sad when she shook her head and said she always preferred to walk.

*   *   *

Outside the factory he sat motionless. The ugliness of the stark grey building bore down on him. He had not bothered with breakfast and the iced water he drank before leaving the house sat heavy as lead on his stomach. He was about to switch off the car radio when he heard the politician being interviewed. As usual, Tom Oliver had much to say and most of it, Peter decided as he switched off the sound, was instantly forgettable.

He had never understood his wife's respect for the old fraud, who always treated her with a patronising tenderness when they visited Anaskeagh. Her manner towards him had been deferential, as if she was still his indebted niece.

"When my father abandoned us we would have been destitute only for his kindness." Her voice had risen defensively whenever Peter criticised him. On such occasions she sounded like Marjory, unable to mention Barry Tyrell's name without biting deep into an old festering sore.

Peter understood what it was like to be indebted to the politician. Ten years previously, when Della Designs was on the brink of liquidation, Tom had invested heavily in the company.

"You're my family," he said. "I always look after my own." He never allowed Peter to forget that his money was responsible for the profitability that followed but his interest in the company remained a secret. He had no desire to publicise his financial affairs and two businessmen from Anaskeagh were officially listed as shareholders. Jon Davern and Conor Oliver, the politician's son, who also acted as his solicitor, had handled the paperwork.

He regretted accepting the politician's money. Far better to have walked away and flung the keys into his mother's grave. Ghosts did not have the power to rise from the dead and reproach him, or so he believed in rational moments. He wondered how Della would react if she knew he now only owned fifty-one per cent of Della Designs.

"She'd turn somersaults in her grave." Connie McKeever was still the factory supervisor during that troubled period. "It's not the first time you've had to make tough decisions." She cast her experienced eyes over the figures he showed her and shook her head. "But on the last occasion you had Beth to help you. You lost a good business head when you let her go."

"I never let her go," he protested. "She resigned without notice and married your son. She never even —"

"You let her go," repeated Connie in a voice that could instantly quell a factory of boisterous woman. "And I'll say no more than that on the subject."

With this major cash injection Peter had persuaded the McKeevers to return from London, and Stewart had taken over as production manager of the factory.

He was pacing the factory floor when Peter entered. "You're late," he said, hurrying towards him. "The shareholders are already waiting." His eyes narrowed accusingly as he took in Peter's appearance. "Jesus Christ, Peter. Are you too broke to buy a fucking razor? In case it has escaped your attention, this is a crucial meeting."

"Then why are we wasting time?" He walked rapidly up

the stairs to his office and entered, sensing the shareholders' annoyance at being kept waiting. Brusquely, he checked the agenda and opened the meeting, wondering why his accountant, a plump, humourless man who dressed impeccably in grey, always insisted on wearing brightly coloured cartoon ties when he was intent on conveying bad news.

The discussion was acrimonious from the beginning. Stewart and Jon Davern had always pulled in different directions and the tension between the two men immediately came to the surface. Stewart wanted to move the factory forward with an investment in new state-of-the-art machinery. Jon Davern simply wanted to move the factory. He had established useful contacts in the Far East where governments were stretching out beckoning hands to manufacturers. Massive grants, low wages, high technology, no union problems. An unbeatable combination, especially as Della Designs' costs continued to spiral and the union was determined to negotiate a new pay deal.

The need for another drink cramped Peter's stomach. He wanted to return to Havenstone and sink into its silence again. "We'll postpone any decision on investment until after we've had talks with the union." He forced authority into his voice. "If the workers are going to make unrealistic wage demands we have to look at any future decisions in that light." As the major shareholder he was the stumbling block to his accountant's cut-back policies but he suspected it was only a matter of time before Jon Davern had his way.

Stewart stayed behind after the others left. "I thought the purpose of the German trip was to buy new equipment," he said, flinging his report on the desk. "You know as well as I do that we need to modernise to stay in business." He rapped his knuckles hard against the folder and leaned forward. "Davern has been making too many cutbacks since he joined the company. We're not making a quality product any more and it's beginning to be noticed. One bad season and we're down, two and we're out."

"So?" Peter shrugged. "You're the production manager. You know that cost and quality have to be finely balanced. If it isn't working then it's time to look at new strategies, as Davern has suggested." The rain beat against the office window, adding to the dreariness of the morning. He was detached from his own words, as if his opinion floated on a string that could be pulled in to argue an opposite point of view with equal conviction. "You needn't worry about your job. Your position with the company is safe, no matter what changes we make."

"A global sweatshop! Is that what you want me to run?" Stewart demanded. "If you think I'm going to spend my time in some God forsaken hole on the edge of the world then think again." His voice was quiet but determined. "I've no intention of being separated from my family now or in the future."

Peter swallowed hard, fighting his way through nausea. This was proving to be the mother and father of a hangover. He wanted to smash his fist into his production manager's self-righteous face. A tight curling excitement tensed his stomach, as if his fist was already reaching across the desk and Stewart McKeever was reeling backwards in shock.

Abruptly, he stood up and lifted his coat from the rack. "I'm through for the day. As I said at the meeting, I can't make decisions until the union shows its hand. Don't worry. You'll be fully informed if I decide to make any changes."

Outside the factory he braced his body against the wind and walked towards his car. It was only eleven o'clock in the morning. The day stretched endlessly before him. His heart started to palpitate. Pain tightened across his shoulders. He breathed rapidly, bending his head over the steering wheel until the faintness passed.

In Havenstone he poured a neat whiskey and felt his stomach expand in a warm glow. The fury he had felt in the office astonished him. Sara's lies were holding him in thrall. On their last night together she had looked through him, beyond him, to a place he could not reach, then left him without answers. Such a bitter lie, she told him, her laughter as sharp as splinters in his skin. Stewart McKeever was his childhood companion. The brother he always wanted. His trusted friend. How could he know a man all his life and then discover he was a stranger? How could this quiet man be a keeper of secrets – a custodian of lost love and past mistakes?

He heard her laughter still. He imagined her moving in empty rooms, her shadow flitting by, her cool breath on his cheeks. In the mirror above the mantelpiece, he saw her phantom smile and cracked the glass with his fist. Alcohol was not the solution but he had yet to find a better way to pass the time.

*   *   *

Her uncle sounded drunk on the phone. Or maybe he had been crying. Lindsey hardly recognised his voice when he asked her to come to Havenstone and choose a piece of

Sara's jewellery before he placed the collection of precious stones in a bank vault.

"No … I don't want anything," she said but he kept going on about keepsakes. How she must take something special to always cherish and remind her of Sara.

"I don't want anything to remind me of her." She hung up before he could reply. Her hand trembled when she replaced the receiver. She wondered if he ever thought about the row. They never made up. What a terrible thing to die with anger unresolved. But how much more terrible to live with its memory.

Sara had understood the importance of secrets. She had believed there was a time to confide and a time for silence. When Lindsey was small she told her a story about a princess with a secret who, when she could no longer carry it inside her head or in her heart, knelt on the edge of a bottomless hole and screamed it into the void.

"Sometimes silence is more important then honesty," she said, closing the book of fairy stories and smiling down at the little girl. "Sometimes it's necessary to carry secrets inside us so that those we love don't suffer our pain." Lindsey was only seven at the time and had no idea what the story meant. But now she understood.

She had no intention of screaming her feelings about Tork into the void. She had wanted to shout his name from the rooftops, but with her mother chanting "Soft drugs lead to hard drugs lead to death" as if she had just discovered the secret of the universe, there was not much opportunity to toss his name into casual conversation.

On that last weekend in Havenstone, she had intended confiding in Sara. But the atmosphere in the house was so weird she hugged her secret to herself, hoping the right moment would come. It never did.

The tension was not that obvious in the beginning. Her uncle came home from his factory on Friday evening looking fed-up – but he was polite to Lindsey for a change and did not try to be funny by calling her a "suburban guerrilla" simply because she chose to wear combats. During dinner he sighed as if a bellows was pumping air from his chest. He drank too much wine too quickly and Sara advised him to take it easy.

"Whatever you say, my darling one." He held up his glass as if he was toasting her but Lindsey heard the undercurrent in his voice, the "get off my case" warning, and Sara heard it too. She smiled, smooth and calm, then left the room to make coffee.

He gave Lindsey one of his brooding stares and asked if she had considered his suggestion that she study fashion design and work in his factory. He made it sound like some sort of initiation rite carried out by members of the McKeever family. His voice went soft when he mentioned Beth, as if he was remembering something really special. Lindsey remained silent. The good old days should stay where they belonged. In the far distant past. She had no intention of designing hick clothes for women with too much money and a brain deficiency in style.

When Sara returned, carrying a coffee percolator and a plate of ginger biscuits curled like fine wood shavings, she was smiling. "I imagine Lindsey has more ambitious plans than standing on a production line sewing buttons," she said. The biscuit she picked up snapped in her fingers and scattered crumbs on the plate. "I'm sure she would prefer to talk about something more interesting. In fact, she might even tell us who's the latest love interest in her life? Come on, young lady, you're blushing. Tell all."

It would have been the perfect time to confide her secret but her uncle sat there, as surly as a bear with migraine, tapping the table with his nails, playing tunes on the polished wood – and Lindsey could not think beyond the sound. He refilled his glass, slopping a pool of red wine on the table. His voice grew loud again. He was so used to shouting above the machinery in the factory he had forgotten the decibels necessary for normal conversation. Yet her father spent even more time on the factory floor and Beth complained she could not hear him behind a raised newspaper.

Later, in the bedroom Sara had decorated especially for Lindsey's week-end visits, she heard them fighting. Their anger jerked her upright. Her scalp tingled with embarrassment. It was awful, being alone in the dark listening to the ugly words they shouted at each other. To make out what they were saying was difficult but that did not matter. The sound was everything and in its incoherent fury she heard her name. It was repeated again. A loud denying cry from her uncle. Sara's laughter rang in her ears.

She was the reason for the row. He resented her hanging around his house. He made it obvious in lots of little ways. Sara always insisted that was just his manner, brusque, his mind on other things such as work and whether he should close down his factory and get a life before he went over the edge with a heart attack. But he had shouted Lindsey's name as if he hated it. Even when everything was quiet she was aware of her uncle in one room and Sara on the other side of her, their anger seeping through the walls, clinging like a miasma to the silent bitter night.

The following morning his flash car was missing from the driveway. Sara was in the garden cutting roses when Lindsey came down for breakfast. A straw hat with a drooping brim shaded her eyes. It was impossible to tell if she had been crying. In the kitchen she threw her hat on the counter and began to arrange the roses. She looked so young and pretty in her dark-blue sweater and faded jeans, her hair tied in a pony tail. No shadows under her eyes, no tears ravaging her face. She certainly did not look like a forty-year-old woman with an angry husband and Lindsey wondered if she had dreamed the whole crazy scene.

Often on Saturday mornings they worked together in Sara's studio, not talking or bothering each other until it was time for lunch. Lindsey had brought her portfolio with her and, when she asked Sara to look at her latest paintings, her aunt barely glanced at them. Usually, she was full of praise and encouragement, but on this tension-filled morning she was impatient and closed the portfolio before she came to the end of it. She called the paintings "cute" and went upstairs to the studio, making it clear she wanted to work alone.

"I'm way behind schedule," she said, as if Lindsey's presence was an extra hassle she had to endure. She had been in Africa for two weeks on a photographic assignment – so Lindsey could understand why she was pressed for time. But it was Sara who had phoned and invited her to Havenstone, not the other way around. Downstairs, she killed time reading a magazine and growing more restless by the minute. She could have done some sketching in the

garden. It was a sunny day and the flowers were still in full
bloom but she stayed indoors, bored and resentful of Sara's
indifference. She was tired visiting Havenstone. There were
so many other more interesting things to do, like being with
Tork or joining the garage gang. Melanie said they had a
brilliant time hanging out together on Base Road. Lindsey
vowed that the next time Sara rang and said, "Doing
anything this weekend?" she would make excuses about the
looming date of the Leaving Cert, which was approaching
with the speed of an express train.

At lunch time she made soup and sandwiches, and
carried the tray upstairs. Sara had laid out her African
photographs on the floor of her studio, as she always did
when she wanted to examine her newly developed prints.
Lindsey stared at the prints, at children tumbling in the
dust, laughing out at her with toothy grins, and the women
with their dark, fathomless eyes, were smiling, proud to be
photographed with their babies. There were other
photographs of people in fields, carrying parcels on their
heads, working on looms, baking bread, school children
singing and dancing, happy faces, sad faces, and the hard
sun-baked face of her mother's best friend, Jess O'Donovan.

Sara emerged from the darkroom and blinked when she
noticed Lindsey, as if forcing herself from some imaginary
landscape. Her eyes swept over the tray and away again.
"You shouldn't have bothered," she said. Her impatience
was obvious. "I'm not hungry."

"You have to eat something."

"Please Lindsey …" She pressed her fingers to her
forehead. "Can't you see I'm working to a deadline? I'm very
busy right now."

"I'm sorry. I just wanted—"

"I'll make dinner when I come down. We'll talk then but for the time being I can do without any interruptions."

Lindsey wanted to ask about the row. She wanted to know why her name had been shouted. But she was afraid of losing Sara. Not physically, but in a way that only those who loved Sara noticed, as if she was seeing everyone from a long distance away.

CHAPTER TWENTY-EIGHT

Marjory was spending Christmas in New York with her brother. She phoned to inform Beth of her decision. "I wanted to let you know that Tom is taking care of everything, just in case you had any absurd notion of inviting me to stay with you." Her thin quavering voice was like a nail on Beth's skin. "I swear to God, I don't know where I'd be without him these days. If Peter invites me to visit him I'll have to refuse. Havenstone will be a shell without my darling child."

Peter had forgotten her existence. What sense was there in telling her that Havenstone was indeed a shell, stripped of his wife's possessions, just as Marjory had once banished all traces of her own husband from her life. It would be cruel to add to her hurt so Beth remained silent.

Kieran Oliver had invited Marjory to stay in his handsome brownstone house. She would mingle with Irish emigrants who gathered there each year to celebrate an Irish Christmas. At least one problem was solved. Beth heaved a sigh of relief. She had been worrying about how her mother would cope on this first Christmas without Sara. To invite her to Estuary View Heights would have been impossible. Connie always spent the day with her son's family and the thought of the two women meeting under the same roof was as unthinkable now as it was thirty years ago.

Kieran Oliver was a successful stockbroker, a Wall Street dandy with his spotted bow ties and finely plucked eyebrows. He would treat Marjory with kindly condescension and she, impressed by his wealth, would bask in his attention.

Every Christmas, he sent Beth a personalised greeting card, a photograph of his family smiling their strong white American smiles, accompanied by an impersonal computerised letter outlining their many achievements throughout the year. But the letter he wrote after Sara's death was for her eyes only. It rambled nostalgically through the past. Sunshine days in Anaskeagh and endless games of tennis in the back garden of Cherry Vale. So be it. Everyone was entitled to their own reality.

*   *   *

Lindsey wondered how she would endure Christmas. It would be so different this year. No morning visit to Havenstone with its silver winter-wonderland decorations and open log fire. Nobody mentioned this fact but, as far as she was concerned, the silence made it even worse. Her crazy aunt had phoned from London to say she was coming home for a week. Granny Mac wrung her hands when she heard. But shriek-a-minute Marina with her orange hair and crazy clothes would make a difference. She would get drunk on gin and repeat the same outrageous stories about her days as a catwalk model when she almost became The Face of the Seventies.

The tales she told Lindsey about the high life were wild: drugs, booze, rock and roll, all night discos. She even had an affair with a rock star, great tabloid fodder for a while. Lindsey saw him on television one night – old hound-dog face and limp hair thinning on top, reminiscing on a Seventies how-great-we-were retrospective programme. Why the elder lemons of rock believed they had anything relevant to say in this era of boy bands and slush music was a mystery, but her aunt was also locked into the same time warp.

Lindsey wondered about time warps. Did people walk unawares into them, allowing them to settle like aspic around them so that the present and the future was always about looking back at the past? The past was the past, as far as Lindsey was concerned. She hung up when Tork phoned and shrugged past him when he waited for her outside the school gates. He was hanging Christmas wreathes in front of Woodstock one evening and blocked her way when she tried to walk by him. He warned her about the garage gang.

"If you say so, O Wise One." She glanced at the rows of potted plants behind him. "What strain of cannabis are you growing in there?"

He refused to laugh. "I mean it, Lindsey. Don't hang around with that crowd, especially Kev Dalton. He's poison." He looked menacingly jealous and, for a moment, she felt the familiar tapping fingers dancing in her chest.

"Why don't we get together sometime?" he suggested. "We could talk … about everything."

"Forget it, Tork. I've an extremely busy social life these days." She crossed the road, aware that he was still watching her, annoyed that he had found out about the gang. They were an exclusive secret club, or so she had believed. It felt good to be part of something again. The garage gang was her salvation, the one good part of a sick, mixed-up world. The double standards imposed by adults drove her crazy. By all means drink beer and throw up over the pavement. Multi-coloured puke was learning about life. By all means buy drugs from a pharmacist in a white coat and overdose without leaving a note – that was learning about death.

On Friday nights her mother believed she had joined a study group with Melanie. She never bothered checking any more, which was perfectly fine by Lindsey. Base Road was past its sell-by date, living on borrowed time. All the old cottages were deserted, waiting to be demolished, along with the garage.

When it was a proper garage her father used to have his motorbike serviced there. After her parents moved back to Oldport, he had wheeled it from the shed at the bottom of Granny Mac's garden – where she had kept it safe for him – and took it apart, polishing and oiling and revving the engine. He even started wearing leather and swanking around at rallies with all the other bike freaks. Sometimes, Lindsey went with him, riding pillion as he raced all over Wicklow, through the Sally Gap, along the old military road or on to Glendalough, and when they returned home, covered in mud and unable to stop laughing over all the adventures that had happened to them, Beth would shake her head at the state of their clothes.

"You crazy pair of Hell's Angels," she would sigh, pretending to be cross because she had to wash everything. "Just as well you have your own personal whiter-than-white Brand X slave. This time I want *double* pay for my services – at least."

"More than *double*, my wonderful sex slave." He would slap her bottom and hurry her up the stairs, not caring that Lindsey thought they were total twats. But it had made her feel good when her parents behaved that way, giggly and bold, as if they were teenagers again, remembering.

Soon the diggers and cranes would move into action and work on the slip road would begin. Her mother said it was a disgrace that a local amenity should be destroyed in the name of progress and lots of people had agreed. They mounted a campaign and carried banners with 'Swans or Road Rage – Your Choice' printed on them. Sara had mounted an exhibition of her estuary photographs in the community centre. Brilliant images of birds skimming the water at dawn and swans swimming down the centre of Base Road when it flooded during the high spring tides. It was impossible not to imagine them supplanted by cars and fumes and noise. It made no difference in the end. Traffic cones were already in place but, for the moment, it was the perfect hideaway for the garage gang.

Kev had set up the sound system and got the electricity working. He was going to be a disc jockey in Ibiza when he got the right break. The windows were covered with black cardboard so that the light did not shine across the estuary, and it was cool dancing with the candles and the cobwebs. He knew how to get E and that was no big deal either. Ecstasy was not addictive, unlike heroine or coke. It was a buzz drug, recreational, the happy drug. Everyone was entitled to happiness.

*   *   *

Sara's dress rippled through Peter's fingers as he pressed the soft folds to his face and breathed in the scent of her. Or perhaps that was only his imagination, the stored memory of a subtle perfume which she had always exuded when she entered a room. He had found her dress at the back of the wardrobe, overlooked by the women from the Oxfam shop. She had worn it to Della Design's fiftieth anniversary party – difficult to believe it was over ten years ago – yet the picture of how she looked that evening came vividly to mind. Under the chandeliers in the ballroom of the Oldport Grand the dress had gleamed with the richness of a fine burgundy wine. Her creamy shoulders were bare, her hair upswept, held in place by a glinting bronze comb. She was the most beautiful woman present. His opinion was objective. He was used to the company of elegant women. The fashion industry prostituted itself on such elegance and made its profits from the wish fulfilment it created.

She had mingled with the guests, moving from one group to the next, remembering names, personal details, making the right enquiries about families and careers, attentive as she listened to Jon Davern expressing his views on property prices, then easing tactfully away to speak to Stewart, whose bulky figure looked surprisingly imposing in an evening suit.

The McKeevers had returned to Oldport some months

previously and Beth, if she experienced any nostalgia for the past, had disguised it quite effectively. She was a mother of two by then and the same commitment she had shown when working for his mother, and later, for him, had been effortlessly transferred to her family.

"Why won't you come back to us?" he had asked, sitting next to her during the meal. He nodded towards the guests surrounding them: factory and office staff, suppliers and buyers; people she had known and befriended during her years with Della Designs.

"I've no interest in working outside my home," she said, her voice so quiet he had to bend towards her. "I came back for Sara's sake. You know, and I know, that that's the only reason I persuaded Stewart to accept your offer."

She was so different to Sara and yet he had loved them both. With Beth his passion had been strengthened by years of friendship whereas Sara had overpowered his senses the instant he met her.

Later, after the models gyrated down the catwalk in a fashion presentation spanning five decades, the dancing began. Sara moved lightly to the music, her uncle's hand splayed across her back as he guided her around the floor. She danced with others, important business contacts, knowing the right people to flatter and tease, or engage in serious conversation. How long had it taken him to realise she was playing a role, the perfect response for all occasions? Sam O'Grady, the owner of the First Lady chain stores, and one of Della Designs' biggest customers, was captivated by her attention. Poor deluded fool. He probably rang her afterwards, convinced that her interest in his opinions must carry a hint of sexual intrigue, and she would have treated him with an icy politeness that stayed his words before they were uttered. But what did Peter know about anything? Maybe they shared a brief affair, amusing and stimulating her while it lasted. She would have cut him adrift as soon as he began to demand more from her, and he would have demanded more, striving to reach the deeper promise lurking behind her laughter.

Afterwards, when she returned to Havenstone, the mask had fallen from her face. The anger that had remained hidden throughout the night surfaced as she asked questions about the factory, demanding to know why it had been necessary for her uncle to make such a heavy investment. Peter had been surprised by the depth of her knowledge. She seldom showed any interest in Della Designs and he had felt no inclination to discuss Tom Oliver's financial venture with her, especially as the politician had insisted on secrecy.

"I felt such a fool in front of him," she said. "He assumed I knew everything about his investment. Why didn't you tell me he was keeping your business afloat?"

"Why are you so upset?" he asked. "It's a safe investment. He'll be well rewarded."

"That's not the point. I'm your wife. I have a right to know about your business dealings when they involve my family."

The row that followed was bitter. He had never found a way to prevent such rows. They happened when he least expected them and lasted for days, sometimes weeks, her earlier anger replaced either by a dull apathy or a heightened energy that kept her working late each night in her studio, avoiding him.

In her bedroom of mirrors Peter allowed the dress to slip from his fingers and watched it coil like a question mark on the white lace counterpane. He felt her presence moving like a current of air around him, as elusive in death as she had been in life. The lights of Oldport village spread below him, a Milky Way, flickering over the invisible lives of invisible people. He thought about black holes in space – burned out stars drawing everything inwards until all the energy was gone – and all the broken, glittering fragments were as dense and dark as the loneliness she had left behind.

*   *   *

Lindsey saw her everywhere. A flick of blonde hair, a smile, a gesture, so many reminders. Passing Woodstock one day, she glanced through the window and saw her ghost standing beside the freesias. Her arms were filled with dried reeds. When the ghost threw back her head, laughing at something Judith said, Lindsey's skin lifted in goose bumps. The sound of her laughter carried out through the open door. It was loud and free, unlike the laughter of a ghost which would surely be a thin, terrifying sound.

The woman had a baby in a sling and Judith kept making coo-che-coo noises. 'Planting Thoughts' was printed on a van parked outside. The laughter was still on the woman's face when she left the shop. Up close, she no longer resembled Sara. Younger, her shoulders too broad, her hair wild and yellow, the colour of grapefruit, rippling down her back.

CHAPTER TWENTY-NINE

Christmas morning in Estuary View Heights was filled with enforced gaiety, endured for the children's sake, especially Gail, their youngest child, whose belief in Santa was ferociously indulged by everyone. Preparing the dinner was Stewart's prerogative, a tradition that started the first year they were married. His family arrived at noon, bringing the excitement to a higher pitch as parcels were unwrapped and discarded. In her full-length fake fur coat, her fur hat and jungle-print tights, Marina McKeever was as exuberant as ever.

"Help has arrived, Big Brother," she announced, invading the kitchen where Stewart was basting the turkey. She cast a wary eye over the preparations and edged away. "I'll be out to do my shift as soon as I sink my first gin and tonic. Call me when you need me. Cheers, darlings."

"Thank God for the gin bottle." Stewart grinned at his wife. "At least it will keep her out of my hair for the rest of the day."

Peter was equally loud and jovial when he called.

Everyone seemed determined to defeat the atmosphere with noise. He dispensed his presents, Christmas cheques for the children, boxes of chocolates for Connie and Marina. Beth received perfume, gift-wrapped, expensive, impersonal. It was obvious he had been drinking. His cheek was swollen in a purple bruise that bagged the skin under his eyes and emphasised his pallor. Gail cried out in terror when he lifted her high in the air, bewildered by his exuberance. He shook his head when Beth repeated her invitation to dine with them.

"Oh, please do, Peter. You can't be alone on a day like today. *Please*." Marina linked his arm and flashed her long eyelashes.

"I'd be a killjoy," he said. "Maybe you'll all come over for a meal after Christmas. I'll give you a ring and arrange it early next week." He looked across at Beth. They both knew it was an empty promise.

She wanted to strike him and retreated to the end of the room, shaking with the force of her anger, no longer knowing where to direct it. His grief was so tarnished, tardy and self-pitying, his handsome face raddled under its force.

"I can't believe you drove over here in this condition," she said when he followed her, an empty glass in hand.

He stared beyond her, as if trying to position himself into some time frame or location. She drew back, repelled when he lurched forward and kissed her cheek. "My sweet sensible Beth. My sister-in-law of mercy." Every few minutes he stared at his watch, holding his arm stiffly in front of him to inspect its face. He began to hum, a hoarse off-key chorus. "Goodbye lady, goodbye love. Goodbye lady. We hate to see you go."

"Stop it, Peter." She stayed calm, unable to bear the thought of a scene.

"Sorry … sorry," he muttered. "It was a long night. Give me a drink, whiskey will do." He placed the glass on the bookcase table and took her hand. "I need a drink, Beth, not a lecture."

She poured a measure of whiskey, lacing it heavily with water. "I can't believe you're doing this to yourself. You must know Sara wouldn't want to see you drinking so heavily."

"Don't use platitudes on me, Beth. None of us ever had the slightest idea what Sara wanted." His voice was barely audible as he drained the glass.

She picked up her car keys, ignoring his protests. "I'm driving you home. You can come back here tomorrow to collect your car."

The state of the house depressed her. The drawing room, always the most elegant room and Sara's favourite, was overlaid with dust. The large mirror above the fireplace with its carved gilt frame was cracked, a jagged line angling across the glass. Old newspapers were scattered on the floor, along with empty bottles and unwashed dishes. She lit a fire and prepared food, an omelette with mushrooms. She buttered some stale brown bread she found at the back of the fridge. Not exactly a feast but starvation on Christmas Day went against the dictates of tradition.

"Beth, the dynamic home-maker," he muttered when she placed the dishes on an occasional table and ordered him to eat. "When did you first begin to disappear?"

"Take a look in the mirror, Peter, and try answering the question yourself." She stood beside him and gazed at his distorted reflection. His eyes met hers in the glass but made no connection.

"Can you hear it?" he asked.

"What?"

"Her laughter. I hear it sometimes at night." He shuddered. "I can't sleep, Beth. I'm going crazy from lack of sleep."

"See a doctor. A counsellor, if need be. Do something about it, Peter."

"Is that the best you can suggest, my sweet sister-in-law of mercy? You were never inclined to clichés, Beth. Don't start now." He touched the bruise on his cheek and peered closer into the mirror. "I fell coming down from the attic last night. I found the *Cat* paintings up there. Remember them?"

She nodded, surprised. "I thought you'd burned them years ago. That's what you were going to do."

"But I didn't. I took your advice and kept them for posterity." He laughed harshly. "Can you enlighten me as to what the hell I was doing?"

"You were good, Peter."

"Sara could show more emotion in one photograph than I brought to that whole collection of pretentious shit." He held her gaze in the glass, his eyes suddenly alert, searching. "I married the wrong sister, you know that … don't you? That's what she told me the last night we were together." His voice strengthened, as if his words had succeeded in briefly sobering him. "She deliberately set out to split us up."

"And she succeeded because you wanted her to succeed. Don't blame Sara for decisions you made yourself."

"She was laughing when she told me. I wanted ... I think I would have killed her if she hadn't stopped laughing. She said something about Lindsey ... if I thought for one minute it was true—"

"I don't want to hear any more," she cried, spinning on her heel and walking away from him.

"Please, Beth, listen! I need you to listen to me." He moved to stand in front of her when she tried to leave the room and gripped her arms. She thought he was going to shake her. The belief was so strong that her head lolled forward as if the strength had gone from her spine.

"I don't want to hear about you and Sara. Do you understand?" She struck his chest with her fist and he moved back, startled by the force of her fury. "I didn't want to know at the time and I certainly don't want to know now."

"What about my rights? You know what she told me? Tell me if it's true?"

"You heard me, Peter. I'm not going to discuss this with you, now or ever. We've nothing to say to each other. Not since you made your decision and I made mine. So leave me alone. Whatever torments Sara had ..." Her voice broke and she closed her eyes. "Let them rest in peace with her. Please Peter, for all our sakes."

"Rest in peace!" He raged at her. "How can I let her rest in peace when she's tearing my mind to shreds?"

"Leave me alone, Peter," she repeated. "I don't want you interfering in my marriage. Not now, not ever."

She drove away, leaving him with his own stale memories that had nowhere to escape.

Stewart was still in the kitchen when she returned. She

always found it difficult to tell when he was angry, to notice the little signs, his mouth tightening, a grimace, almost imagined. On this occasion his annoyance was immediately apparent.

"Dinner's been ready for ages," he said. "What the hell were you doing?"

"You saw what he was like. He was in no condition to drive."

"You're not his nursemaid, Beth. I could have driven him home if you'd asked."

"It's Christmas, Stewart. It's bound to be difficult for him."

"It's difficult for all of us. But he's holed up in that mausoleum with his whiskey and his self-pity and he doesn't give a tinker's curse about anyone's problems but his own."

"That's not fair—"

"Don't give me fair, Beth. No one ever said life was supposed to be fair. We do the best we can and get on with it."

"I haven't been gone that long, Stewart. I'm quite sure the turkey hasn't been complaining."

"Not funny, Beth." He rested the platter on the palm of his hand, composed his face in a smile and made his grand entrance into the dining room.

Gail clapped her hands when she saw his high chef's hat. Excitement spilled from her eyes as he carved the turkey and ceremoniously served her first. Beth wondered what would be left of Christmas when their youngest child lost her belief in magic. No more wish lists winging their way to the North Pole, no more home-made Christmas cards, tinsel and spice smells, sudden sightings of reindeer on rooftops.

Throughout her married life she had worked hard at creating enchantment for innocent minds to savour, building memories that would carry her children into the years ahead. No one ever suspected how much she hated the season with its synthesized hymns and unrelenting commercialism. Or the relief she experienced the following morning when she woke and realised it was over for another year.

After dinner, if the weather stayed dry, they would go for a walk along the estuary shore. The traditional Christmas walk. When the sky darkened they would return home to play *Trivial Pursuits*, eat chocolates and argue over poker hands. The younger children would dress up and perform their concert. Tradition. A demanding tyrant; or a reassuring thread holding the years together?

CHAPTER THIRTY

Marina McKeever had gazed speculatively into his eyes on Christmas Day and suggested they meet on his next trip abroad. Twice since then she had phoned to find out when she could expect him. In London, mending bridges with customers, Peter rang and invited her out for a meal.

The restaurant she booked was her favourite. It reminded him of a space station designed by a demented plumber but Marina glanced approvingly around the glittering chrome and glass décor, the towering ceiling with its utilitarian system of pipes, and assured him it was the latest in-place. The place to be noticed. He believed her.

Her career as a model had been short-lived and excessive. Nowadays, she worked on a cosmetic counter in a department store, warring against free radicals and wrinkles. Efficient in a white coat, she used the language of science to sell the vision of youth. He always anticipated her company, forgetting each time that he no longer enjoyed it.

The heat in the restaurant was overpowering, the food tasteless but arranged on plates with the skill of an artist from the school of minimalism. Sweat trickled under his arms, clogged arteries, sluggish blood flow, this business was killing him and he was only forty-seven. Under the table he felt her knee nudging him with practised ease. She smiled across the wine glasses at him. A languid temptress remembering old times as only Marina remembered them.

"Did Beth stay with you when she came to London?" he asked.

She seemed startled by his abrupt question. "She usually stays with me when she comes over for a visit. Why?"

"I mean then – after she left Della Designs? You know what I'm talking about?"

She gazed impassively back at him. "I'm afraid I don't. Elaborate, please?"

"Marina, I'm not a fool. Answer me."

"Is that why you asked me out?" She placed her cutlery across her plate and rested her elbows on the table.

"Of course not. I wanted to see you but—"

"But you thought we'd take a little trip down memory lane, is that it?" She curtly interrupted him and signalled to a passing waiter for the bill. "I don't know what you hope to find out but I'm not the one to ask. Do you mind if we call it a day? I've an early start in the morning."

"I wasn't trying to upset you." He touched her arm, running his fingers along her tanned skin. She drew away from him, deliberately allowing his fingers to rest on the tablecloth. "From where I'm sitting, there's only one person at this table who's upset – and it's not me."

"I'm simply trying to find out the truth about that time."

"I'm paying for this." She did not appear to hear him as she glanced down at the bill and removed a credit card from her handbag. Insistently, she pushed it towards the waiter, refusing to listen when Peter protested. Her voice grew louder, attracting the attention of nearby diners. He fell silent, knowing her ability to create a scene and wallow in the attention she would receive.

In the foyer they waited for her taxi to arrive. "Single fare," she said. "I've got a headache."

"Why are you so annoyed with me?" he asked. "All I did was ask a simple question."

"Indeed, that's all you did." Her smile, smooth as her complexion, told him nothing. "And all I did was refuse to answer it."

His business trip was equally unsuccessful. Appointments were cancelled at short notice and the buyers he met gave him a blunt warning. The quality of merchandise leaving the factory had deteriorated. Orders would not be repeated unless Della Designs improved its design and production.

Before returning home he attended a trade fair at Earl's Court. The crowd flowed past him into the huge exhibition hall. A fashion show was underway. Music boomed, models gyrated on a catwalk, dancing in and out of billowing clouds of dry ice. The pain rose suddenly in his chest. It spread across his shoulders. He gasped, reaching towards a nearby exhibition stand to steady himself and pitched forward into blackness. A sea of concerned faces surrounded him when he opened his eyes.

"I'm all right ... honestly, I'm fine." He tried to rise but an efficient woman in a tan trouser suit and pearls spoke sharply to him.

"An ambulance is on its way. Please don't move until it arrives, sir." She bossed him into obedience, her determined jaw reminding him of his mother. His mind tried to recover the lost moments and failed. He heard the drumming beat of his heart as he was lifted on to a stretcher and carried ignominiously down the steps of the exhibition centre.

"Stress is a killer, Mr Wallace." The Indian doctor had an accent that would put the royal family to shame. His nails were manicured to a rosy pink. "Don't ever underestimate its effects," he warned. "Our tests are negative. Your heart is as sound as a bell. We will send the full results of our investigation to your doctor." He smiled, glancing down at Peter's chart. "The cure is in your own hands. Apart from boycotting all exhibitions that are not absolutely vital to your survival I suggest you take a serious look at your lifestyle and see how it can be improved." The doctor shook his hand. "It's your life, Mr Wallace. Take good care of it."

Sleep was impossible. His heart began to race, palpitations, dizziness sweeping over him. The Indian doctor's clipped accent broke into his thoughts, mocking him. His life was on a slope and there was no way to stop the headlong hurtle. He rose from bed and went downstairs to the drawing room. It was still dark outside. Tomorrow he had a meeting with Jane O'Donnell, the union official. He felt weary just thinking about the confrontation that was sure to erupt as soon as they came face-to-face. He poured a drink and sipped it slowly. The solitude of his house bore down on him and he shivered, remembering other nights when he had sat alone in this room, knowing his wife had locked herself away from him in her studio, free in her world of images. Her reflections of a modern society – always reflecting the lives of others.

From the first time he saw her work, her photography had evoked strong emotions with him. He had often wondered if his own lost ambition had been part of this fascination. If, through her ruthless dedication, he glimpsed the heart of himself, of what he had once hoped to achieve.

He finished his drink but felt no inclination to pour another one. He climbed the stairs and entered the studio. The canvases he had carried down from the attic at Christmas were stacked against the walls. The strong lights shone mercilessly on the paintings with their vivid colours and grotesque imagery. He winced away from the pretentious symbolism, wondering at the thought process that had linked the paintings into such a cohesive theme. Beth's eyes dominated each one. Such emotion in her green gaze, an indefinable sadness that had intrigued him from the first time they met; a runaway child in search of a runaway father.

He remembered the coy accusations from the office staff that she was a snob, a workaholic, a man-hating lesbian. He had been introduced to her friend, Jess O'Donovan, shortly before she entered a convent, and had flirted with her, enjoying her humour and shy charm. In the flashing assessing glances she gave him, he had sensed a sexuality that even the longest and ugliest black robe would never hide. Yet Beth Tyrell, who had the freedom to love whomever she chose, shrank back in fear when he moved too close. Her disgust when he kissed her for the first time in the studio had astonished him – yet he had sensed the reverberations of passion buried under her anger. Her incoherent sobbing embarrassed him. He was not in love with her, not then. He needed uncomplicated women in his life and she had depths he was not prepared to plumb.

One of the paintings was startlingly different from the others – the cat image replaced by the figure of a young woman draped in a transparent white robe, her arms above her head, as if hanging by invisible chains. He smiled ruefully as he examined it. No wonder Beth had fled from him in fury when he kissed her, suspecting, quite rightly, that he had been aroused by the compliant nature of her pose. Even now, so many years later, he was moved by the vulnerability he had painted into the woman's gaze, her submissive body moulded by his desire yet sexually alive, aware of her own power, her freedom to move beyond her chains and dominate him with an equal passion.

Beth never returned to his studio and he had painted the image from the rough sketches he had made. He had waited impatiently for her to come back from Anaskeagh but when they met again he was not even in her field of vision and he, too, soon became preoccupied with new challenges. Not that it mattered in the end. His ambition was eventually buried under the force of his mother's will. As far as Della Wallace was concerned, there was little sense rising from a city-centre slum without leaving a legacy behind.

"If you want to be an artist then start living like one." His mother had constantly harried him, demanding to know when he was going to give up his "foolish notions" and stop living off her generosity. His first exhibition was a failure, bad reviews and few sales.

"I want you in my factory but if you have other plans then I suggest you find your own garret and starve in it." She finally laid down the gauntlet. "I've worked too hard to subsidise a life of idleness."

When he moved out of Havenstone her disappointment, if any, was hidden behind the stern lines of her face. He sold his car, rented a room overlooking the Grand Canal and waited tables in an Italian restaurant. The few words of Italian he picked up served him well when he went to Italy for the summer. He was a pavement artist on the streets of Rome when Della suffered a stroke, collapsing suddenly in her office where Beth found her slumped over her desk. She was still alive when he arrived home, still insistent that he should take over her factory. She died early the following year.

He could have sold the business but fear held him captive. Della had been his safety net. When he no longer needed to rebel against her iron will, he realised his talent was a mediocre thing, lacking passion and pain. He wanted to experience some deep sense of satisfaction when he laid the final brush stroke on a canvas instead of a growing disillusionment. Letting go of a dream he had cherished since he was a child had been difficult but there was also a sense of relief that he no longer had to aspire to his father's flawless standards.

He was twelve years old when his father died and he often wondered if Bradley Wallace's love of art would have carved a different path for him. Peter had never thought of him as anything other than old and insubstantial, with his wispy white hair and reticent manner. But his knowledge of the great painters had dominated his son's early years. When the young Peter brought his drawings to him, seeking praise, he quietly pointed out the flaws, pained by his son's lack of perfection.

"This is the essence of art, Peter." He pointed to the paintings on the walls of Havenstone. "If you want to be an artist this is the standard to which you must aspire. I struggled hard in my youth to achieve excellence but when I realised such genius was beyond my reach I became an art collector instead."

Peter's parents had separate bedrooms and his father's room remained a mystery behind a locked door. On the night of his funeral Peter entered it for the first time and drew back in shock when he saw the paintings hanging on the walls. This was a different collection to the one downstairs. He stared in amazement and growing fascination at the images of young women whipping their bodies, or being mauled by demons, hanging from chains, tortured, twisted, torn. Some were semi-naked except for wispy pieces of fabric draped over their breasts and hips, others were dressed in white clinging robes that strained against their bodies, as if they were trying to break free and fly into the radiant light streaming around them.

The full collection of paintings was auctioned off soon afterwards. New machinery was needed for the factory and fine art was not high on his mother's list of priorities. The walls were bare when Peter entered his father's bedroom again. But these paintings remained a vivid memory – the taut, ecstatic expression on the faces of the women, as if their skin had been sculpted down to bare bone and illuminated from within. What kind of man would hang such pictures on his walls?

When he had woken on a few occasions from feverish teenage wet dreams in which these women played a significant role, he broached the subject with his mother. Della looked puzzled then began to laugh. He was horrified to discover they were religious scenes his father had painted when he was a young art student. Tortured martyrs dying for a glorious ideal – saints hooked on ecstatic trances and self-flagellation to bring themselves nearer to the glory of God. Only then did Peter remember seeing the small kneeling pew in the bedroom and the glowing red light of the Sacred Heart lamp.

"Bradley should have been a Renaissance man," Della said, smiling fondly. "Or a monk. I was never able to make up my mind."

With this revelation his father no longer seemed so decadent, or even particularly interesting. Peter shivered, remembering. As the chill of the studio seeped into his bones, his grief for all he did not understand, and all he had lost, surfaced with such ferocity that he groaned out loud. He had failed his wife. His love for her, the powerful, domineering love he had felt when they lay together, had not been strong enough to touch her emotions, or awaken her cold, translucent flesh to pleasure.

His paintings belonged to the past. An arrogant youthful

past. Ashes to ashes … dust to dust. When it grew bright outside he carried them down to the copse at the back of the grounds, heaping them roughly on top of each other. Before he could change his mind he poured a can of petrol over them. Smoke billowed. He watched the paint shrivel and blacken, Beth's luminous eyes combusting into flame, and wondered if forgotten dreams could possibly rise and fly high like a phoenix from the ashes.

CHAPTER THIRTY-ONE

Peter called to the house one evening when her parents were out. Much to Lindsey's annoyance he invited himself in and she was forced to make him three cups of coffee. He asked about her portfolio, if he could look at the work she had done so far. She did not want his cold eyes passing judgement but he was silent as he turned the pages.

"Landscapes … that's where your talent lies," he said, as if he had every right to intrude on her time and make personal comments about her work. He refused to go home, even when she yawned and dropped hints about her study timetable. He asked if she knew the paintings of Paul Klee.

"*The Golden Fish*," she replied. "Flowers for eyes."

He nodded, looking pleased, then told her about eyes and inspiration and how he had tried to capture the energy of destruction and passion in his own paintings – using her *own* mother's eyes. It sounded so sick Lindsey was relieved to hear he had burned them.

"Just as well you weren't inspired by Van Gogh," she said. "Or you'd have been obsessing about her ears."

He laughed, throwing back his head as if she had said something hilarious. It was impossible to believe he had been an artist before he became a suit. Almost as impossible as imagining her mother having inspirational eyes. So weird, the olden days. When her parents finally came home her mind was in a jam trying to think of things to say to him. After he left she asked Beth what it was like to pose for him. Did she do it naked … lying on a bear-skin rug, excuse the pun … *ha ha ha*. Her mother actually blushed and ordered her to stop talking nonsense. It was just a phase Peter was going through before real life took over.

Study plans for her Leaving were pinned to the wall above Lindsey's desk. A neat detailed plan, the corners already curling. She needed to study yet she was unable to concentrate. In the garage no one worried about the Leaving. They were too busy dancing and having a good time. All that studying and trauma for what? A future filled with uncertainty, strikes and closures. She planned to go to art college in the autumn, a decision that displeased her mother who wanted her to do marketing or computers.

"Be serious," she said. "How can you possibly make a living as an artist? We're talking real life, Lindsey, not fantasy."

She sounded just like Peter Wallace, shoulder to the wheel. No wonder the workers were talking about strike action. But at least, he had not called her paintings "cute" which was a devastating word, a code for everything that was mediocre and pathetic and naff. Lindsey could not understand why Sara had used that word to describe them.

Lately, she was unable to stop thinking about little things Sara used to say. And she figured they were not so little, not really.

She was seven years old when her parents moved from London to Oldport. Her father had promised her new friends, a long garden with a swing and grass, not concrete, like the playground outside their flat. They would have a big house where she would not hear the next door neighbours shouting, even if they were the same as the Binghams, who had a row every Saturday night and smashed plates.

Lindsey hated Oldport with its cold wind blowing off the estuary and shrieking seagulls swooping over the garden. There was no grass, no swing, only mountains of mud and men on scaffolding, who whistled at her mother. The smell of paint sickened her. When she ran in front of a bulldozer Beth cried out and hit her. Then she burst into tears and hugged Lindsey so tight it hurt.

Her aunt came that evening and scooped her away from the mud. "You are such a beautiful little princess," she said.

It was the first time anyone called her beautiful. Sara knew all about being beautiful. She had golden hair and silver spirals in her ears. She smelled of flowers. She brought Lindsey to Havenstone where there were new dresses and toys waiting. They played pretend games and explored the garden at the back of the house, hiding in the crab apple orchard and wild bushes. In bed, with the old trees bending creaky into the night, she told Lindsey the story about the secretive princess, sitting on the bed beside her, fluffy pillows propped behind them.

Then Marjory came to visit and everything changed. Hate at first sight. Even at seven, Lindsey knew her relationship with this grandmother was different. Loving Granny Mac was as effortless as breathing, but this tall thin woman with her glittery eyes and long fingers that pinched Lindsey's shoulders, was different. Every time she made noise Marjory pressed her hands to her forehead. Lindsey was spoiled and demanding, she said. Even if her father came swanning back to Oldport as the production manager of Della Designs, it was only because of Peter's generosity and family links.

She was just as nasty to Beth, going on and on about bad blood and how she had rubbed salt into her mother's wounds by marrying a McKeever. They were bred from generations of poor, ignorant fishermen and now she was carrying their seed and breed into another generation. Her voice was so sharp it made Lindsey sink deep into the cushions of the sofa, wishing she could disappear and not have to listen to grown-ups fighting like the Binghams.

Sara begged them to stop. "Let bygones be bygones," she cried. "Why drag up the past every time you meet each other?"

After they returned to the new house her mother said Marjory was just being jealous and to pay no attention. Lindsey understood jealousy. When Robert was born she was so jealous she had hoped he would be carried up to heaven by an angel. But she also knew the difference between jealousy and cruelty. Marjory had said a cruel thing. Granny Mac's husband drowned when his fishing trawler sank to the bottom of the ocean. A year afterwards, she met Lindsey's other grandfather and fell in love with him.

It was weird to think that both her grandmothers had lived with the same man. Granny Mac was the only one who really loved him. His photograph was in a silver frame on a little table in her parlour. His eyes twinkled out at Lindsey. She could just imagine him being a charmer. A magic musician. She wanted to know about the old days but Granny Mac said it was all a long time ago. A long foolish time ago. She was as bad as Beth when it came to talking about the past.

The old photographs her mother took from Havenstone had offered Lindsey her first glimpse of Anaskeagh. The river running through the centre of the town writhed like a snake and the small houses hunched together had dark narrow lanes running behind them.

"I played in those lanes," Beth said. "Hopscotch and skipping and Statues." She put her arm around Lindsey's shoulders and drew her close as they stared at the photographs together. The shapes behind the houses could have been children playing. It was hard to be certain because they seemed different each time Lindsey looked.

In one group of photographs her mother looked really young and pretty with her flowing black hair, her Cleopatra eyes, and her long skinny legs in skin-tight jeans. She was sitting in long grass and her hand was outstretched, as if she wanted to snatch the camera from Sara. Her face grew angrier in each shot. Big leaning rocks surrounded her. Lindsey asked where it was and her mother replied, "Hell on earth."

"Why was it hell on earth?" She was disturbed by the passion in Beth's voice.

"Places are not hell," she replied. "It's people who turn them into hell."

So much for childhood memories. No wonder she never wanted to talk about Anaskeagh. Lindsey figured her memories were horrible. She did cruel things to Sara and now she was riddled with guilt. She forced Goldie, a lovely little cocker spaniel, under water and tried to drown him. Lindsey saw him in the photographs, curled up beside a high rock. The sun on his coat turning him into a blob of melting butter.

When Sara told her the story about her pet dog, Lindsey had cried. She could not believe that anyone, but especially her mother, could do such a cruel thing.

In her house there was a quiet tension, as if her parents had gone deep into themselves. She overheard them talking about the factory and the problems her father would have to endure if things changed and he started travelling all the time.

"We should never have come back from England. It was a bad mistake." He sounded angry but Beth said they needed the money and what was the sense in raking over old coals.

His hair was thinning in the front and there were furrows on his forehead. Lindsey wanted to smooth them away, especially when he talked about having to work in some God-forsaken hole on the edge of the world. She knew how much he hated being away from home and she hated it even more. She was furious with Peter Wallace for making his life a misery.

During dinner one evening, he told a really sick story about a manufacturer he knew who manufactured shirts in Taiwan. When one of the machines in the factory went out of control it severed three fingers from a worker's hand. The manufacturer said an abattoir would have been easier to clean up, blood all over the sleeves, and the next batch of fabric had been a slightly different shade of cream. All the shirts had to be dumped. Lost profits but it still worked out cheaper than having them made in Ireland.

Her father had asked the manufacturer about the fingers. Had they been stitched back on, dumped, buried, burned, minced with spices, perhaps? The manufacturer ordered him not to do the bleeding-heart scenario. The only way to make money these days was to produce in the cheap economies and the workers were happy as long as they got their few yuan in compensation.

"That's a finger lickin' good story, Dad," said Paul, the family comedian. No one laughed louder at his jokes than he did and Lindsey thought he would have a convulsion in front of them when he rocked back in his chair.

"Power to the workers," shouted Robert, the anarchist. "Death by automatic fire to the capitalist swine."

Gail wanted to know what happened to dead fingers. Were they burned in a fire like Aunty Sara? Her bottom lip quivered and, before Beth could reach her, she had dissolved into tears.

"Look what you've done," she snapped at Stewart, not caring that he soon would have to travel thousands of miles away from his family. "Now she'll have nightmares and I'll be up all night trying to calm her down."

When her parents quarrelled it made her nervous. She had never heard them arguing in the past and, when her mother raised her voice, or sighed loudly in exasperation, it reminded Lindsey of Sara's anger shuddering through the night – and the question it had left in its wake.

*   *   *

Jon Davern wanted to close down the factory. The shareholders were complaining about rising costs and union demands. Sam O'Grady had cancelled the First Lady contract, dismissing an eighteen-year business relationship with a few acerbic comments when Peter rang to try and organise a meeting.

The First Lady contract was Beth's first big achievement after his mother's death. Peter's mind steadied, focusing on those years when they worked together, heady, challenging years, gone to seed but not forgotten, never forgotten. He phoned her to discuss the loss of the contract but she sounded uninterested, resentful that he was laying his problems on her shoulders. He wanted to leave her alone but Sara's words continued to torment him: breeding suspicion where none had ever existed, destroying friendship and renewing memories of lost love.

"Marry Beth Tyrell," Della had advised him before she died. "She'll drag you up by the bootlaces and you'll spend the rest of your life thanking her." Her advice fell on deaf ears, as he pulled once again against her wishes, resisting the future she visualised for him and was determined to achieve.

Della had recognised her own youthful energy and ambition in the young Beth Tyrell and had trained her willing protégé in every aspect of the business. When Andy O'Toole, the sales manager, was fired, Beth slid effortlessly into his job and, in the years that followed, moved into general management until she was running the company as efficiently as his mother.

The months following Della's death had been difficult. His relationship with Beth was strained, confined to rushed management meetings and chance encounters. He ignored her advice and warnings, resentful when she made suggestions, undermined by her knowledge and experience. Their roles had reversed in a subtle but unmistakable way and the young girl who had come to his studio – awed by her surroundings and, he suspected, infatuated with him – had become a self-assured woman, whose patience as she tried to explain the intricacies of running the factory only increased the tension between them.

One evening she came into his office and insisted he listen to what she had to say. "I know what your mother wanted for us both." She came straight to the point. "Forget her, Peter. I've no intention of marrying anyone. She's dead … and so is this company if you and I don't start working together."

She outlined her plans. They needed a new label, a new image. A new marketing strategy that would put the name of their designs on the lips of fashion journalists and customers alike. The collection would be called *Allure*. She placed a glossy brochure in front of him.

"Recognise anyone?"

"Marina McKeever. My God!" He laughed. "She really did it."

Beth smiled, flicking pages. "When the new collection is ready we should get her to model it. I'll ask my sister to do the photography. Sara's done some fashion shoots in London. They're excellent. But that's way down the road.

We've a lot to do before we reach that stage. I believe it can be done. The rest is up to you, Peter. Support me in this and I'll turn the company around. Pull against me and I'm leaving."

In the months that followed, they had worked long hours, snatched short breaks, argued, panicked and planned each stage of the *Allure* collection with meticulous attention to detail. They began to know each other again but in a different way. One that had never seemed possible when they were teenagers, playing word games in his studio.

She approached the chain store and convinced them that Della Designs had the skills to produce what they needed. They celebrated the signing of the First Lady contract in a small restaurant in Howth. Flashes in time ... and afterwards ... how she had responded to his touch, learning to release her fear, the same fear he would later sense at the core of his wife's self-hatred. Remembering that night and the nights that followed, he wondered where such memories lay buried. In what crevice of the mind did they hide and then escape with such exquisite clarity?

CHAPTER THIRTY-TWO

On Grafton Street outside Brown Thomas a busker was blowing flames from his mouth. A group of mesmerised children watched him, terrified when he blasted flames above their heads. Lindsey recognised Tork Hansen, dressed as a dragon to promote a newly opened Mexican restaurant. She thought he called her name and imagined it floating towards her on a ball of fire. She ran, merging quickly into the crowd, not stopping until she reached Stephen's Green where she had arranged to meet Kev Dalton.

The ducks were nose-diving into the water when Kev sat down beside her. They smoked cigarettes and he told her about a new band he had heard the previous night. He carried a B2 bag and was doing a passable imitation of a designer-gear sandwich board. She had no intention of allowing her body to become a walking logo for some hotshot rich designer. She bought second-hand in Temple Bar and loved the authentic smell of mothballs.

Kev was excited over his first proper, fully paid-up gig.

The garage gang would have to do without him on Friday night. He slipped the plastic bag with the seal-tight into her palm, casually holding her hand for a while longer in case anyone was watching. She was conscious of the packet in the zipped pocket of her jacket as she hurried down Kildare Street, avoiding Grafton Street in case she saw Tork again.

Outside Dáil Eireann her great-uncle was being interviewed. His white hair was still the same length as it was at the funeral and the word "poser" sprang to mind. She knew she was right when she saw the way he faced the television camera, as relaxed as an actor turning confidently to his audience. He wore black leather gloves and had pulled his coat collar up around his ears.

She was about to walk away when the filming ended. The group surrounding him parted and he was looking directly at her. For an instant his face was blank then he slapped his side and boomed, "Little Lindsey McKeever. How are you, my dear child?"

The interviewer stared dismissively through her. She could not think of his name. He did a mind-bending and boring programme which her mother loved to watch. It was called 'Elaborate' … or something like that. Her great-uncle shook her hand and said it was nice to see her again. He was so old and important looking with the television crew still hanging around him, even though no one was filming. He asked her to join him for a cup of coffee.

"You mean … in there?" She nodded towards the tall building beyond the gates. The thought of drinking coffee with politicians was horrifying.

"You choose where to go." He chuckled, amused at her expression. "I'm finished for the day and would enjoy relaxing for a little while before returning to my apartment. A big city can be lonely when you don't belong in it."

They went to Bewleys on Westmoreland Street and queued at the counter. Some of the older people recognised him and stared quite rudely. What would he do if he knew she was carrying illegal drugs. She repeated the words. They had a terrifying force which excited her. Imagine the scandal – 'Politician in Drug Exposé.'

She wondered if Tork ever took E. He never mentioned doing so, just hash when he could get his hands on some. They used to tell each other everything. She did not want to think about him. She wanted to forget the way they loved each other and how his skinny shoulders once blocked out the rest of the world. It was hard to remember a time when her heart was not giving little skips of anxiety. The sense of panic, of being on the verge of discovery, was such a high, an overdose of adrenaline.

The old man told her about his home in Anaskeagh, how much he missed it when he was in Dublin on Dáil business. He enjoyed deep sea fishing with his friends and climbing to the top of Anaskeagh Head where the view was magnificent. He made it sound like the centre of the world.

"My mother hated Anaskeagh." She gulped the coffee, scalding her mouth. "She said it was hell on earth."

He stroked his chin, as if he was remembering way back. "Perhaps it was to a child like Beth. She took after her father who had itchy feet. The faraway hills were always greener and Anaskeagh was a quiet place in those days. Not any more, though. My son's children are around your age and have no desire to leave home."

"How many grandchildren do you have?"

"Six." He looked proud, counting out their names on his fingers. "Kieran's three live in New York so I only see them occasionally. But I'm blessed with Conor's family. They live in my old house. It's too big and empty since my dear wife passed on, God rest her soul."

"Have you photographs of your grandchildren?" Lindsey asked, hoping to banish the sadness clouding his eyes when he mentioned his dead wife.

"I'll bring them with me next time I come to Dublin." His deep rolling voice grew pensive when she asked if he had any idea why Sara wanted to die. "No one knows what goes on in another person's mind," he said. "We only think we know but that knowledge is based on the depth of our own feelings. The kindest thing we can do is to let her soul rest in peace."

It sounded profound, the sort of thing a politician would say. It did nothing to help her understand. He glanced at his watch and said time had wings when he was in such good company.

"Come to our house for dinner some evening," she said, impulsively. "My mother would love to see you."

A shadow crossed his face. "Your dear mother and I didn't always agree on certain things when she was younger. We'd best leave well enough alone. But I'll bring the photographs with me when I come to Dublin again and we can meet when I'm not so busy. Or are *you* too busy to spend time with a lonely old man?" He nodded, pleased when she shook her head. "Young people are always in such a rush these days, they never have time for those who have lived a little while longer. That's all it is that separates the generations, my dear. A few short years."

She thought this was quaint and sentimental, even ludicrous. Old age was a yawning gap. She could never imagine stepping over it.

*   *   *

The mirrors captured his reflection in a flashing mosaic when Peter entered Sara's bedroom. So many shapes and sizes glinting on the walls: oval, round, square, star-shaped, half-moons, bevelled, one studded with red stones, and a tiny mirror sunk in crystal. They looked mysterious, slightly decadent, promising much, and he smiled at the irony, at the juxtaposition: a bedroom of mirrors, a frigid wife.

Sara had collected them on her trips abroad, her firm voice haggling with traders in oriental marketplaces. Along the cobbled side streets of European cities she had browsed in antique shops before sitting down to drink coffee under the awning of an open-air café. She had bought the tiny crystal mirror in Germany when she accompanied him on a business trip. The season of Lent was due to start that week and the city of Cologne was full of raucous marching bands and people in fancy dress, many of them disguised as clowns. In the ancient Gothic cathedral on the banks of the Rhine, the hushed medieval atmosphere was broken by the low voices of tourists inspecting the elaborate golden sarcophagus and shrines. Sara knelt before a small statue covered with pearl necklaces and jewellery, left there by long-ago penitents.

"A fair exchange for the release of guilt," she said, rising from her knees and following him into the festive atmosphere outside. The street trader's dark eyes lit with pleasure when she haggled with him over the price he demanded for the lump of crystal into which the tiny mirror had been set. "The mirror of the soul," she said, smiling, showing it to Peter – such a small lost soul.

Peter's thoughts were interrupted when the front doorbell rang three times, a shrill summons that he was unable to ignore.

"About bloody time, man. It's brass monkey weather out here." Tom Oliver stamped his feet on the doorstep. His breath hazed in the hall light as he entered. "I've been ringing loud enough to wake the dead."

"I saw you on 'Elucidate' this evening, Tom. Shooting straight from the hip as usual." Peter led the politician into the drawing room.

Tom accepted a glass of whiskey and raised it in salute. "Cheers, man. My heart's scalded with journalists demanding interviews. They know a straight talker when they hear one and they can always rely on Tom Oliver to speak his mind. How are you coping, man? Life's a rough stage, God knows it is, and Christmas can't have been easy." The fluid sincerity in his voice set Peter's teeth on edge. He refrained from pouring a drink for himself, hoping to shorten his visit.

"It's nearly a year since my dear Blossom passed away." The politician settled himself into an armchair. "God rest her sweet soul in peace. Never an hour passes without her being in my thoughts."

What did the man want? A heart-to-heart on the widower experience? Peter decided he needed a drink after all. He had attended May Oliver's funeral, an impressive gathering that filled the church in Anaskeagh. The politician had been the centrepiece of the occasion. His long eulogy delivered from the altar was an exercise in rhetoric and nostalgia. Sara had sat attentively throughout but Peter's mind wandered after the first few minutes. His memory of May Oliver did not relate to the eloquent words pouring from the mouth of her husband. He remembered her as an overweight, flustered woman who worked throughout her married life as his unpaid secretary, receiving neither appreciation nor acknowledgement until she was safely encased in her coffin.

"I see you're not one of those new men we hear so much about these days." He flashed a white twinkling smile at Peter who, for the first time, saw the drawing room through the older man's eyes. The stale smell of neglected, airless space. The shabby tracksuit he had pulled on when he returned from the factory suddenly embarrassed him. He rubbed his chin, his hand scratching rough stubble, and realised it was three days since he had shaved.

"Things are bad with the union, I believe." The politician abruptly changed the subject. "How serious is this threatened strike? According to Jon Davern it will force the closure of the factory if it takes place."

"We do have negotiating skills, Tom. You needn't worry, your investment is quite safe."

"I'm relieved to hear it. A lot of people are depending on you, including my niece, Beth."

"I've never known Beth to be in need of anyone's help, especially yours."

"She's an independent woman, that's for sure. But Sara's death was a hard cross for everyone and the last thing she needs is to have any uncertainties in her life." He rose to leave. "God give you strength at this difficult time. Your dear wife is sadly missed by those who loved her."

Peter's hand was grasped in a warm, comforting clasp. A well-used hand, skilled at pressing the flesh and the heads of babies.

CHAPTER THIRTY-THREE

In the early stages the strikers were good-natured, as if they had been granted an unexpected holiday. Jokes and banter on the picket line initially disguised the grim reality. Even the heckling of office staff as they passed the picket was relatively low key and carrier trucks, arriving to collect consignments for shipping abroad, were asked, rather than ordered, to support the workers.

The mood began to change when unexpected flurries of snow fell and melted as soon as it hit the ground, adding to the discomfort of the strikers on picket duty. Fires were lit in braziers; hot soup, tea and sandwiches were ferried by supporters. Peter appeared on 'Elucidate' to explain the company position and was pitted against the union representative, Jane O'Donnell, who accused him of being a "profiteer", spitting out the word as if it burned her mouth. Sixty loyal workers were simply demanding their right to a fair salary. Sweat shop conditions belonged to an inglorious past. Her words grated in his ears. The journalist controlling the interview listened, a supercilious tilt to his eyebrows, as they verbally hammered each other into a circle.

Greg Enright was as tenacious as he was aggressive. Peter suspected his sympathy was with the strikers and felt his irritation rise. He was trapped in the small hot studio, aware that his discomfort was probably being beamed into homes across the country. A glance at the monitor reassured him. He looked deceptively calm as he argued his point. His beard gave him a revolutionary image, radical chic. It had grown without forethought and now he could hardly remember his face without it.

On the third week of the strike Jon Davern handed in his notice. He had accepted a new position with a property development company and advised Peter to close down the factory before the decision was forced upon him. The shareholders would make no further investment in Della Designs. He paused, to let the significance of this statement sink in. "There's only one way this factory is going, Peter. Throwing bad money after good is not going to stop its liquidation. But it's sitting on a prime site. If you want my advice you should consider selling the land. I've business contacts who have expressed an interest in building apartments in this area and there's a strong possibility the land can be rezoned for residential purposes. This is the perfect time to sell."

Tom Oliver was unavailable when Peter rang his clinic. His constituency secretary promised to pass on his message but Mr Oliver was a busy man. She could not guarantee when he would return the call. The solicitor, Conor Oliver, was equally vague. His father had made a decision based on sound financial advice and was unwilling to risk any further losses. He advised Peter to discuss the situation with his accountant.

Twenty years since he took over the reins of Della Designs. Twenty years blurring, undistinguished, wasted from his life. The following day he informed Stewart he was selling the factory.

Beth had anticipated the closure as soon as the strike was called but the suddenness with which it happened surprised her. Since then she had hardly seen Stewart. He was busy working with Peter, negotiating redundancy settlements with the union and disposing of the machinery. The clothing industry was crying out for skilled workers and the staff would have little difficulty finding new employment. Yet Connie, although she was retired, wept when she heard the news and the women from the factory complained vociferously to a journalist from the *Irish Times* that Peter had betrayed them.

Stewart was approached by a number of clothing companies anxious to employ him but he refused to commit himself to a decision. She noticed an unfamiliar hardness in his expression when she asked what he intended to do.

"I'm not interested in repeating the mistakes of the past," he replied. "We need to get away from here."

She never realised how much he hated working for Peter – or perhaps she had never allowed herself to notice – but it was becoming apparent in lots of little ways. When he arrived home in the evenings he talked about making a fresh start, moving from Oldport and setting up his own manufacturing plant. In the past he had often mentioned this possibility, short-lived schemes that inevitably fizzled out. This time he was determined. He had met Sam O'Grady and the head buyer with First Lady. They were prepared to back him with a major contract. He wanted Beth to work with him as an equal partner. This was an opportunity for them both, he believed.

"Remember how you turned Della Designs around when Peter was incapable of thinking straight after his mother died? Imagine what we could do together, the ideas you'd bring to the business."

Her life then and now. She was unable to make any connection. The excitement of showing a new range, travelling to New York, London, Paris. Bargaining with hawk-eyed buyers in black suits and flashing jewellery. Boundless energy, her mind closed to everything but her career and her future with Peter. Twenty-seven years old. In Love. Loved.

"You're living in the past, Stewart. I was a different person then."

"That's not true." He shook his head emphatically. "Your life has changed since then but you haven't changed. The big fashion chains still need small manufacturers on their doorstep who can respond to the immediate trends. There are excellent grant incentives available if we move outside Dublin." Stewart was a methodical man who never began an argument without having considered the counter-argument and she suspected that this plan had been in his mind long before Peter closed the factory.

"I'd no idea you wanted to move from Oldport. You never said anything about it."

"I've spoken about it many times, Beth. But I never had the feeling you were listening."

"I'm listening now. This is a big decision, Stewart. We're not talking about changing the colour of the wallpaper. This is lifestyle stuff, our future, the children. What if it doesn't work? What then? What security have we to fall back on?"

"Trust me, Beth. It's a wonderful opportunity for both of us." She listened to the enthusiasm in his voice and realised it was a sound she had not heard for a long time. He reached across the table and clasped her hand, pulling her towards him and a new beginning they could share together. "I know it will work if you're with me – and First Lady is just as convinced that we can pull it off."

She wanted to say something reassuring, to share his excitement as he described his meetings with the management of the chain, but she was unable to think beyond the busy routine that filled her day. This feeling of running her life on automatic pilot had increased since Sara's death and, at night, when she finally sat down, she was unable to remember where the hours had gone, or what she had done with them. Stewart deserved better and her throat tightened, as it always did, when she thought about his strength, how it had saved her when she believed her world would never come right again.

"Has it been very difficult working with him? I know how much you love Lindsey – what she means to you."

He sat very still, measuring the words he needed to say in his deliberate way. "Lindsey is an extension of my love for you and that has never had any boundaries. It's as simple and as complicated as that. As far as Peter's concerned, he's simply my employer. I had a family to support and, once we decided to come home, I refused to let personal feelings get in the way."

"And hate?" she asked, softly. "Do you hate him still?"

"Hate?" He savoured the word then shook his head. "That's too strong. I despise him. All his life he's had everything handed to him on a plate. Someone else has always carried his responsibilities. You came back from London for his sake."

"No … for Sara's sake."

"Was it?" He challenged her. "All those phone calls from him? That had nothing to do with changing your mind about returning?"

"He was worried about Sara. He believed I could talk to her, help her …" Her voice broke. "It seemed possible at the time."

"Stop tormenting yourself, Beth. No one could have done more to help Sara. She had everything going for her, *everything*. I can't understand. I simply can't get my head around it." She sensed his frustration, his anger over the hurt that had been inflicted on his family through Sara's suicide.

Occasionally, relaxing after she made love with Stewart, or sharing a bottle of wine when their children were in bed, they had discussed their childhoods. She had talked about her parents, their rows and lack of money, and how Tom Oliver had humiliated her father with his benevolence and mockery. Stewart had no difficulty understanding her refusal to invite her uncle to their house. He, too, had harsh memories about the separation between his mother and

Barry Tyrell in the dying weeks of his life. Nor did he wonder at Beth's reluctance to visit Anaskeagh, knowing the bitterness Marjory still harboured about her daughter's marriage to him. But she had never told him the truth. Even now, so many years later – when women talked openly in the media about traumatic childhood experiences, and crimes of the past were exposed in unflinching documentaries – Beth still found it impossible to confide in anyone. The blood and tears, the sighing terror, the smell of earth and the moon casting its light on the birthing stones of Aislin's Roof – and, later, back in Cherry Vale, the disgust on her aunt's face as she stared down at the young Sara – these were scenes which Beth could only endure through silence.

With Sara, it might have been possible to reach into the past. But the clumsy efforts she made were always met with resistance, defeated by the frozen stillness of her sister's face, her suspended breath whenever that lost night was mentioned. Then Beth too would fall silent, fearing Sara would collapse under the leaden atmosphere her words had created.

Stewart was at a late-night meeting when Peter called to Estuary View Heights shortly afterwards. Beth had never imagined him with a beard. His chin too strong, his mouth too defined. Like his dark hair, it was lightly streaked with grey.

He followed her into the living room, shaking his head when she offered him a drink. He sat down and crossed his legs as if he intended settling into the armchair for the night. He was still trim and moved with the same grace that had first attracted her to him.

"Your decision was a long time coming, Peter," she said.

"Twenty years too long," he replied.

"I never believed you'd take over the factory after Della died, let alone stay with it."

"It was difficult to do so – especially when you and Stewart left."

She nodded without comment, shying away, as she always did, when he tried to introduce a personal note into their conversation.

"Stewart says you're considering moving from Oldport. Is it true?" he asked.

"We'll see. It's early days yet." Her voice was casual as she poured a glass of wine and sat down opposite him.

"At least I'll be prepared this time. Not like the last occasion. I often wondered why you left so suddenly. No word, nothing."

"It was a long time ago, Peter. There's no sense going over old ground."

"Or opening old wounds? I suspect that's what you really mean, Beth."

"If there were wounds they healed a long time ago," she replied. "I've no intention of opening them again."

"Why not?" She was unnerved by the sudden tremor in his voice and stayed silent, waiting for him to speak first. The silence lengthened, adding to the growing tension between them.

"Where's Lindsey?" he asked, tearing his gaze from her and glancing around the room as if he expected her daughter to materialise from the ether. "I've seen so little of her lately. Has she submitted her art portfolio to the colleges for assessment yet?"

"She's still working on it. But Stewart is hoping she'll change her mind and study computers. She takes after him in so many ways. I often envy their close relationship, the love they have for each other."

"Why won't you tell me the truth, Beth?" The question hung like an accusation between them.

"What truth, Peter? What are you asking me to say? I don't know what Sara said to you before she died – and I don't ever want to know, *ever*. My marriage is the most important thing in my life and I will not allow you to destroy it. Do you understand me?"

He raised his fingers to his forehead as if he wanted to ward off her questions, his face flushed as he rose to his feet. "Perfectly. Tell Stewart I'll talk to him tomorrow."

She waited until the sound of the car engine faded before she closed the hall door. Her legs trembled so much, she was forced to sit on the bottom step of the stairs.

"Are you sick, Mammy?" Gail's sleepy voice sounded from the landing. The child clutched her teddy bear under her arm and held the end of her nightdress in her other hand. Her blonde hair was tousled and the sleepy expression on her heart-shaped face reminded Beth so much of the young Sara that she felt the years falling away as she hugged her daughter and carried her safely back to bed.

*   *   *

"Lindsey is your daughter. Isn't it time you opened your eyes, you blind fool?" He kept repeating Sara's words, as if repetition would weaken their force.

Connie McKeever had been his surrogate mother. She gave him the love his own mother never had time to bestow.

Did her son lift Peter's child with the same tenderness and cradle her? He would know his own daughter. His blood would rush with recognition if she appeared before him. His heart would bond with hers the instant they met. Lindsey McKeever was seven years old when her parents returned from England. Stewart's child. He had never doubted it for an instant. He searched for the truth in Beth's eyes – but in her unflinching gaze he saw no bridge to link him to the past.

CHAPTER THIRTY-FOUR

Her great-uncle's apartment had a view over Dublin city, fancy and flash. He said she must call him "Tom". It seemed weird to be on first name terms with such an important old man but after a while it sounded fine. He was on the radio all the time – at least, that was how it seemed – but Lindsey figured she had just not noticed him in the past. His voice was full of authority, boasting about all the things he did for the black spots of unemployment in rural Ireland.

He was cute in a 'has-been generation' sort of way, calling her "my dear child", but not patronising, just protective, and able to listen without letting on he knew best. He heaved his shoulders wearily when he mentioned his constituency clinic. It was so crowded with people who believed he was next to God in importance and could move mountains on their behalf. Listening to him, she could understand why they thought that way. He knew everything. He knew about the strike before it happened, and that Peter would close down the factory in case he went over the edge with a heart attack. She supposed that was what being a politician was all about. The shakers and movers of the world. He had advised her father to look after his own interests.

"Seeing to the future of his family," he said, happy that he was able to help. He shuffled his photographs together like a deck of cards and laid them one by one on the table. She saw her mother's cousins for the first time. Conor and Kieran with their children. So many relations, and they were all strangers to her. He had some old photographs too. Carnival time in Anaskeagh with the swing boats in the background and the big wheel flashing lights. Sara carried a white bear she had won on the Wheel of Fortune. Tom's hair was dark then, and shorter. He had his arm around Sara's shoulders. His wife stood on the other side of him, a small fat woman in ruffles. Mrs Smug. Marjory was there too, smiling into the camera, unlike the cranky old woman with the pursed up mouth who never had a nice word to say about anyone.

Tom smiled and poured tea from a china teapot. She told him about her paintings. He said a creative talent should be carefully nurtured and asked about her style. His questions challenged her, exciting her because he made her see her future so clearly.

"I'm not surprised that you've turned out to be such a talented young lady," he said, patting her hand. "I knew from the moment you were born you'd make your parents proud. You were such a bonnie, bouncing baby."

"Not me," she laughed. "You're mixing me up with Robert. I was the titch in the family."

"Oh?" He looked confused.

"Premature," she explained. "I scared the life out of my parents."

"Is that a fact?" His smile was a question, fixed strangely on his face. He nodded. "Like I said, blood will out, and you'll make your mark on the world, I've no doubt about it."

He called a taxi to bring her home. It was far too dangerous to walk alone along the docks. Men driving past might get the wrong idea and what would she do then? He kissed her cheek as she was leaving. He said it was a pleasure to entertain such an intelligent, creative young woman.

When she stepped into the lift and it began to descend, she stared at her reflection in the mirror and saw herself as he described, confident, talented, on the edge of life and all it had to offer. But as the lift gently halted and the doors slid noiselessly across, she wondered what he meant by "blood will out" when no one in her family understood the thoughts that crowded her mind and only found expression after she released them on canvas.

"Why don't you invite your uncle to visit us?" Lindsey asked during dinner. "He spends lots of time alone in Dublin and gets awfully lonely."

Beth sat perfectly still. Then her fists clenched on the table as if she was preparing to lift herself into the air. "When did you meet that man?" she demanded.

"When I was in town today. What's the big deal? It was my half-day from school."

"Tom Oliver is not welcome in this house and you are

not to have anything to do with him." Her mother spoke slowly, as if Lindsey was incapable of understanding.

"Why? He's really nice. I asked him to dinner but he said you wouldn't make him welcome. It's obvious he was spot on."

"Do you hear what I'm saying, Lindsey?"

"Yes. But you're not giving me a reason."

"I don't have to give a reason." She stared at Lindsey as if she was a stranger with a bad smell who had wandered into her house. "As long as you live here with us you obey the rules."

"What rules? Thou *shalt* not talk to lonely old men. Which section of the rule book will I find that in?"

"Lindsey! That's enough," her father snapped. "If your mother tells you to do something she obviously has a very good reason for doing so."

This only spurred her on. "That's what I want. Just a *reason*. And what do I get? Behave yourself Lindsey! Do as you're told! Don't ask questions! Obey the rules or we'll kick you out!"

She was unable to stop, even when Beth rose to her feet and left the room. Lindsey realised she was shivering and, it was only later in her bedroom with the music filling her, that she allowed herself to wonder at the inexplicable hurt in her mother's eyes.

*   *   *

"Do you still hate him as much as ever?" Stewart asked when the children were in bed.

"As much as ever," she replied.

He reached for the remote control and lowered the

television. "You've a hard memory, Beth. Sometimes, it's wiser to move on instead of living in the past."

"Is that what you think I'm doing?"

"To tell the truth, I don't know what you're doing any more. Lindsey was only making a suggestion. She didn't deserve to have her head bitten off."

"You know how I feel about him. I don't want him in our house."

"Fine … fine. I'm not saying you should. I've no liking for him either. But maybe it's time to bury the hatchet. You've all suffered so much since Sara died. Life's short, Beth, too short to carry hatred."

"How can you forget the way he behaved when my father was dying? How much he hurt Connie?"

"That was a long time ago." He quickly interrupted her. "Why don't you tell me what's really bothering you?"

"Talking about Sara won't bring her back."

"But it will help you to come to terms with it. And it will help us—"

"Us?"

"Yes, us. Your family. You know what I'm saying. This wall …" He sighed, a quiet man who usually relied on Beth to instigate conversations. "You've been erecting this wall around yourself, pretending everything is normal but you're not seeing us. You're not with us at all, Beth, and it's seriously beginning to bother me. I can't stand pretence. I'm trying to make important decisions and I need to know you hear me when I talk to you."

"I hear you. Of course I hear you. Are you saying I'm not allowed to grieve in my own way because it upsets you and the children?"

She was impatient at his clumsy attempts to comfort her and sat stiffly against him when he moved to the sofa and put his arm around her.

"That's not what I said at all." He sounded weary. "I do appreciate what you're going through. All I want you to do is share it with me."

*   *   *

Lindsey was sitting cross-legged on the floor when her mother entered her bedroom and pulled the plug on the stereo, creating an instant ear-popping silence. She hunkered down beside her and pointed to the sketches on the floor.

"Can I see them?" she asked.

"Leave them alone. I'm just messing." Lindsey bent protectively over her sketch pad. She hated sounding defensive but she could hear the whine rising in her voice.

"Shouldn't you be studying instead of messing?" Her mother glanced at the drawings and placed them back on the floor as if they annoyed her. "I told you what your teachers said at the parent teacher meeting last week."

"Six times you did. But who's counting?"

"Your grades have dropped, Lindsey. They've more than dropped, they've plummeted. I know how much you miss Sara, but you have to pull yourself together. Is there anything I need to know? About Tork Hansen, perhaps? I know you were meeting him ..."

Lindsey sat perfectly still without replying.

"Trust me, Lindsey. You can tell me."

"I don't see him now. Not since – not for ages. And I've

no intention of going out with him again, if that's what's worrying you. Why do you hate him so much?"

"I don't hate him. But he has a reputation—"

"*Not* Tork. Your uncle. Why do you never talk about your life in Anaskeagh? It's part of me, too, you know. I've never met any of my relations except for Marjory. You've never even taken me to Anaskeagh on a holiday."

"I had a difficult childhood, Lindsey. It's not something I want to talk about."

"Sara said you were always causing trouble, fighting and breaking things and giving cheek. You ran away without saying a word to her, not even a note. But I guess when it came to leaving notes she got even in the end, huh?"

"Why are you being so deliberately cruel, Lindsey?"

"*Cruel?* It was cruel trying to drown Sara's dog." Lindsey lifted the sketches and put them into her portfolio case. "What made you do such a horrible thing?" She had not intended asking the question, it just blurted out of her mouth, and her mother gasped as if she had been punched hard in the stomach.

"What did Sara tell you?" She sighed, as if she was suddenly very tired.

"Just that. Was she telling me the truth?"

"Yes, you're right. I did a very cruel thing. I'm ashamed that you should know about it." Her voice was so low Lindsey could hardly hear.

"But why try and drown a little dog? There must have been a reason?"

"He kept licking my hands and clawing at me. He slept between us. I couldn't stand it any more." She looked down at her hands and shivered. "I really don't want to remember that time, Lindsey. Let's just change the subject, shall we?"

For an instant, Lindsey thought her mother was going to cry. She wanted her to cry so badly. She had not seen her shed a tear since Sara died. Not once. Lindsey wanted those tears to overflow like a waterfall and then she could lean into her mother's chest and cry her own tears, tell secrets, spill them into their sorrow, so many secrets. She wanted to tell her about the row in Havenstone, the shouting voices that were growing louder in her head. The words that jumbled together like a crossword puzzle, a cryptic clue that would not go away. And how Friday night was becoming so important she longed for it all through the week.

CHAPTER THIRTY-FIVE

Silent Songs from an African Village was launched in March. A sombre occasion. No one spoke or laughed too loudly, as befitting a book launch that posthumously honoured the author. But this was a collaboration and Jess O'Donovan gave meaning to the occasion. She had written the text for the book, a diary of daily happenings in the small rural village where she lived and worked.

Little remained of the young girl who had left for her novitiate at the age of eighteen, her suitcase packed with black dresses and voluminous knickers; her child's face, puppy soft and innocent. Now her skin was leathery, too much sun, too little care. Her steadfast brown eyes were the only youthful thing about her. It saddened Beth, seeing this premature ageing, but she knew that Jess would dismiss her concerns as too frivolous to even warrant discussion.

In famine camps in Ethiopia and the Sudan she had served out her mission. She had written regularly to Beth, describing numbed feelings, fears that she would never again experience emotions of grief and pain. She now lived a quieter life in Malawi, working in the health centre she had helped to establish. But the years had taken their toll and she had returned to Ireland for an indefinite period of rest and recovery.

"Burn-out," she had earlier confided to Beth, a culmination of years living on the hard edge of survival. Before visiting her family in Anaskeagh, she was staying in Oldport for a week, sleeping late in the mornings and going for long slow walks with Beth along the estuary shore. Their life paths had moved in different directions but the spontaneous friendship they had shared as children remained the same.

A television crew arrived at the hotel to film the book launch and the camera focused on her. During her stay in Ireland she intended fund-raising for the medical centre and *Silent Songs from an African Village* was her launch pad. A tall young man with imperious eyebrows conducted the interview. Greg Enright from 'Elucidate'. He was responsible for the Michael Hannon exposé and the media frenzy that followed. Beth's curiosity as to why 'Elucidate' would turn up at such an event was laid to rest when Tom Oliver arrived.

A smile settled on his face as soon as he noticed the camera. After delivering a soundbite into the microphone, he launched the book and spoke movingly about his niece. Sara Wallace's dedication and talent would live on as a tribute to her memory. When the speech ended he came through the crowd towards Beth.

"How's my dear niece? Looking as beautiful as ever, I

see." He kissed her on the lips before she had time to turn away. "When are we going to see you in Anaskeagh?"

"When hell freezes over," she replied and walked to the other side of the room. A young woman was selling copies of *Silent Songs from an African Village* to the invited guests and the books were stacked on a table beside a cash register. Beth bought a copy and as she turned the pages she was moved, as always, by her sister's stark, powerful images.

For the duration of her photographic assignment, Sara had stayed with Jess at the small mission house. She had called to Estuary View Heights on her way home from the airport, arriving unexpectedly when Beth was preparing dinner. The younger children were noisy, hungry, demanding their mother's attention with homework questions and petty arguments that inevitably broke out between them at that time of evening. Sara had refused an invitation to eat with them and sat quietly at the kitchen table while Beth busied herself chopping vegetables and attending to constant demands from Gail to check her spellings. The little girl was in a fretful mood, refusing to sit on her aunt's knee and tugging repeatedly at Beth's hand whenever the sisters tried to talk.

Sara looked exhausted from the long flight and a stopover in London. She seemed more edgy than usual, her nervous energy almost vibrating from her as she described the village and the people she had photographed. These people now stared back at Beth from the pages of the book but she was unable to recall anything Sara had told her about them. Instead, she remembered how her sister had suddenly stood up, gripping the edge of the table as if she was going to lose her balance, and said, "Come back to Havenstone with me, Beth. We need to talk. It's impossible here. Let Lindsey look after the little ones. Please, Beth, we *have* to talk."

Her tension had stretched across the kitchen and caused Beth's heart to tremble with apprehension. But that moment, whatever it was meant to hold – understanding, acceptance, a memory released – was lost forever when Paul's prolonged shriek from upstairs startled them. Beth's youngest son did not believe in silent songs or suffering and had accidently slammed the bathroom door on his fingers. By the time he was consoled and his bruised fingers soothed with arnica ointment, Sara had left and Beth, too immersed in the demands of her children, promised herself she would call to Havenstone later that night. When they were in bed and the house was finally silent she was too tired to move, and Sara's nervousness, her anxiety as she fought for Beth's attention, began to blur – to become just another scene from a fraught and tiring day.

After the book launch they returned to the house and Stewart went to bed early, knowing the friends would talk until the small hours. Beth uncorked a bottle of wine and Jess turned the pages of the book, introducing her friends from the village, their children, and the young people who worked with her in the medical centre.

When she came to the last page she closed the book, staring for a moment at the photograph on the back cover, then began to talk, hesitantly at first, about Sara's trip to her village. Beth pictured her sister's slim, unobtrusive figure blending into the dusty landscape, knowing the precise moment to capture an instant, a gesture, an unforgettable image.

At the end of her visit, she had sat on the veranda of the mission house with Jess and wept as if she was releasing a terrible wrenching sorrow from deep inside herself. She had travelled through time and across continents for this moment of confession and, in the shade of an African night, she had opened a seal on the past.

"She told me everything." Jess gazed at her friend, her eyes luminous. "She told me about the headland and how you helped give birth to her child. Such a heart-breaking story, and you, my closest friend … all those years of silence. How you both must have suffered." She pressed her fingers together, as if in prayer, and rested her chin against them. "I never thought she could have been the mother. Never. Sara had always seemed so … so unsullied by life."

"Unsullied." Beth repeated the word then nodded slowly. Jess was right. Unsullied children, sullied forever by shame and fear.

"She spent her life yearning for a child whom she believed she had no right to seek or to love." Jess began to speak faster, as if she needed to release Sara's story into the open. "She was never able to move on from the terror that gripped her when she was pregnant and overwhelmed her on that tragic night. How could she love what she had been determined to destroy? How could she recover from such an experience when there was no one to understand, or help her to understand?"

"I tried …" Beth's voice broke but she forced herself to continue. "I wrote letters but she never replied. She was attending boarding school for six months before I even found out she had left Anaskeagh. And when she went to London I only traced her when Marina told me Sara was doing fashion photography for a magazine. When we did meet again it was as if that night never happened. Whenever I tried to bring it up she froze me out – you've no idea how powerful her silence could be."

"She was determined to talk to you when she returned home," said Jess. She lifted a glass of wine from the small table beside her then laid it back, untouched. "I guess the struggle was too great for her in the end. I wish I'd told her …" Her voice trailed away and she sat silently for an instant, her head bowed, as if she had removed herself from Beth and the comfortable suburban surroundings and was back again on a veranda in the slumbering village – listening to the hesitant, broken words that Sara was finally able to utter aloud.

"If only I'd told her I was involved in her baby's adoption," she said, reaching out to Beth when she saw her friend's shocked expression. "I needed permission before I could release any information … and now it's too late."

Too late. How final it is when time runs out, Beth thought. A moment shapes itself and then is lost forever. She remembered that moment on Anaskeagh Head when she had hesitated at a fork in the path and decided to make the journey to the farm, knowing instinctively, even in the midst of her terror, that she could trust the O'Donovans. Now, so many years later, it seemed right that the young nun should have played such an important role in the life of the child, who had been thrust so arbitrarily on the doorstep of her family. And when it came to the final scene, it was Jess who listened – while Beth, in her cosy citadel where meals needed to be served on time and the dictates of family life dominated her days – had refused to heed the signs. Her sister had walked away, as alone then as she had been on Anaskeagh Head when darkness closed in on her childhood.

The friends sat talking late into the night. Beth asked questions about the baby but Jess was reticent, revealing only that she was married and had had a happy, secure upbringing.

"Does she know Sara is dead?"

Jess shook her head. "She has never asked to meet her natural mother or shown any interest in her past, at least outwardly. According to her adoptive mother, she believed her parents were too young to care for her and gave her up for adoption only after being put under tremendous pressure from their families. But lately ..." She paused, then asked the question Beth had been dreading. "Who fathered the child? Sara was frightened when I enquired and I didn't like to pursue the matter any further. But there was gossip about my own brothers and other young men in the area. It was a difficult time, so much media attention, and the guards asking questions. Do you know his name?"

She wanted to shout out his name, fling it into the light, but even as her mind rushed towards this release, she imagined Marjory's shock, her uncle's denials – his powerful control reducing her once again to the small, frightened child he had once terrorised.

"She never told me." Suddenly, without warning, she began to cry. "I can't bear it, Jess. I can't go on remembering."

"But neither can you let this destroy you." Jess drew her

against her strong hard shoulders. "You were always the strong one, Beth. You must find the courage to keep going."

"I know … I know … keep moving on. It's my theme song. No wonder Sara hated me. You've no idea how much she hated me."

"Not hated – envied," Jess replied. "She envied the safe place you found for yourself. No matter where you went you made your life secure but she remained the child who could do no wrong. Sainthood is not an easy occupation, especially when you hate yourself."

"I'm inside her head, Jess. I don't want to be there but I can't escape."

"My poor Beth." The nun sighed. "I wish I could find the right words to comfort you."

"There was a time you would have told me to put my faith in God."

"Faith." Jess savoured the word than dismissed it. "It's a long time since I afforded myself such a luxury."

"No more voices?"

"No more voices." Jess replied. "I don't need them now."

Tomorrow, she would address students in Trinity College. They would ask her questions about her work in Malawi. Some would accuse her of white imperialism, imposing Western solutions on African culture, proselytising, patronising. She was used to such accusations, immune to the views of radicals and reactionaries alike. She had exchanged the rolling hills of an Irish farm for the baked dust of an African village and was only resting briefly on her green shore before returning to her real world.

CHAPTER THIRTY-SIX

Carrie Davern would handle the sale of Havenstone. Peter was surprised at the high price she quoted. "It's boom time, Peter," she said. "The millionaire cubs of the Celtic Tiger are roaring." He gritted his teeth, cringing at the cliché which he hated and which glibly slid from her lips at every opportunity. But his house would be safe in her hands. She examined the rooms, her professional manner unable to hide her curiosity. She fluttered her eyelashes in disapproval when he refused to unlock Sara's room.

"I need to see everything," she insisted.

"No, you don't," he replied. "If you handle this sale you do so on my terms."

"Then I suggest you get your house in order," she tartly replied. "It will need to look a lot more presentable before I show anyone around, if we're to get the maximum price. Where are you planning to live after the sale?"

"I want a small house on Howth Head with a view, preferably a sea view. Something with character and good light." He would paint in the mornings and walk the cliffs in the evenings. Simple needs. Carrie purred with enthusiasm. She knew exactly what he required.

He hired contract cleaners to organise the house and the young lad from Woodstock to tidy the grounds. Judith's son was a gangly youth with dreadlocks and a reputation for playing with fire. He stammered when Peter addressed him but he looked over the grounds with knowledgeable eyes.

Black plastic bags accumulated in a skip outside the house. Bottles were smashed at the local bottle bank. The door to Sara's bedroom remained locked. When the time was right he would take care of it. He bought paints, turpentine, an easel, linseed oil, sketch pads – all the paraphernalia of an artist – and climbed the stairs to the studio. At the door he hesitated. Tomorrow he would try again, maybe.

*   *   *

His enthusiasm was infectious. Beth could feel her resistance breaking down, her anger towards him abating. The younger children did not see anything unusual in his regular appearances but Lindsey's resentment was palpable. When Carrie Davern insisted she had found the perfect location in Howth, he asked Beth to view the house with him. It was a one-storey building slouching under thick creeper: old walls, good studio light, an excellent view from the Red Rock cliffs. But it proved to be a disappointment, too large for his needs, too many extensions.

Afterwards, they explored the hilly side streets of Howth, wending lanes that protected the privacy of the wealthy whose houses sank discreetly beyond sloping, leafy driveways. He suggested they find somewhere to eat and they sought out Luigi's, amazed to discover the restaurant was still in business. The dim interior, the fluttering candles, the smell of ripe tomatoes and garlic instantly lifted them into the past.

"We were in a more celebratory mood the last time we were here." He looked up from the menu and smiled at her.

"We'd just got the First Lady contract," she agreed.

"*You'd* just got the First Lady contract. It was your idea from start to finish." He paused, reflecting. "Who else was with us that night, apart from Stewart?"

"Louise Clifford. She designed the collection."

"That's right … I remember." He slapped the table. "She was some sexy singer. I've never forgotten that night."

She glanced down at the menu. "I'll have the salmon. It looks good."

"You never drop your guard, Beth, do you?"

"It's habit forming," she replied. "And also known as survival."

He leaned over and touched her fingers. It seemed so natural, an easy gesture, and she knew that he, too, was remembering how, in his arms, she had discovered the freedom to soar beyond her fear.

*   *   *

Lindsey's uncle looked different, not like a suit any more. He had stopp-ed drinking. It was obvious from his eyes. She disliked his beard. It was cool but it made him look older, as if he was hiding secrets behind it.

"I reckon he's getting his own back for all the time I

spent in Havenstone," she said one evening after he left. "I'm sick of him coming to the house so often when my father's not here. I don't like it."

"And do you think I liked you being at Havenstone every chance you got?" Beth asked, standing up to clear coffee mugs from the table.

"But you were always so busy with the children." It surprised Lindsey to think her mother would have been jealous over her closeness to Sara. "She was just doing you a favour."

"Was she?" Beth asked. It was more of a challenge than a question and Lindsey did not want to talk about it any more.

No one in her house wanted to talk about anything.

"Wait and see," her father said whenever she asked what he was going to do now that the factory was sold.

"Will you have to go away?" she asked and he smiled, shaking his head.

"Don't worry, sweetheart. Everything's going to be all right."

She loved him but he could be so short-sighted at times. His mouth went tight and hurt when she told him about Peter hanging around the house and asking her mother's opinion on things. Until he closed down his factory he was running it like a dictator so why did he need her advice about buying a new house. They drove to Howth and she gave him five hours of advice. *Five* hours! Then he brought her home and kissed her at the front door. Lindsey saw them through the frosted glass and Beth was smiling like a cat with cream when he left, pretending he had just been saying goodbye. She laughed and said, "Since when did the boot go on the other foot, Frosty-face?" when Lindsey demanded to know what she had been doing all that time.

"What do you think your husband would say if he knew you were running around with strange men?" It was a perfectly straight-forward question and her mother laughed again, but not so heartily this time.

"Is that what Peter is, Lindsey? A stranger?"

"Well, he's obviously not a stranger to you," she replied. "Sara told me you used to fancy him something crazy."

"Sara told you a lot of things, it seems." All the happiness had gone from her face. "I think it's time we changed the subject, don't you?"

He never had time to change the subject with Sara. They never forgave each other for hurtful words. They did not even say goodbye. He forgot all about her until he came home from Germany and found her lying all alone. Lindsey wondered how that made him feel. Was that what he was hiding behind his beard?

She was glad he was selling Havenstone. A photograph hung in the window of Carrie Davern's estate agency, fancy and posh. She felt sad and nostalgic, yet relieved in a shameful kind of way because if new people moved in they would change everything. They could knock it down and build a new house, maybe a ranch or a villa and she would no longer have to think about Sara every time she passed it by.

Beth woke at midnight from a strange dream. She was a young girl again, the wind blowing in her hair, free as air and riding a bicycle up the driveway of Havenstone. White roses were wound in a wreath on the front door and she shouted wildly as she approached, the sound rushing up and leaping free as she crashed through the door and into the hall where snow was falling, an avalanche of snow and ice burying her. Peter lifted her free, heat melting the ice, the same heat radiating between them, intense sexual heat that touched her, making her throb with desire, her body suffused with need as she curled against Stewart. Her hand reached down, stirring him from sleep, and he pulled her close, aroused as always by her touch.

Aware of his heavy breathing as he entered her, the familiar contours of his body and the hazy sensuous images from the dream, her excitement spiralled into an almost painful orgasm. She whispered Peter's name, unaware that she had uttered it aloud until Stewart froze. Slowly, he pulled away from her. He switched on the bedside lamp and angled it towards her face. The pain in his eyes shamed her.

"Look at me, Beth," he said. "This is my face – my body. If you are still confused then this marriage has been a travesty. I never believed that was possible until recently."

She tried to hold him, knowing it would be useless to defend herself. Stewart seldom lost his temper. When it happened it was a quiet fury which nothing could quell but his own decision to put it behind him. He rose and left her, sleeping downstairs on the sofa where Lindsey discovered him the following morning. Across the breakfast table she fixed angry, accusing eyes on her mother.

Stewart left for work without saying goodbye. Words were inadequate to ease his hurt and when he returned that evening he silenced her stammered excuses, reluctant to discuss the matter any further. He moved back into their bedroom three nights later but they lay apart from each other, the space between them growing wider as the weeks passed.

In the heat of passion she had betrayed him. Infidelity of the mind, Beth realised, was just as unforgivable. A name spoken aloud and the years closed in around them. Old passions resurrecting. He was tired playing second fiddle to a lost love.

CHAPTER THIRTY-SEVEN

Eighteen years, so long ago, so vividly remembered – four young people celebrating their first contract with First Lady. They sat around a circular table in Luigi's Bistro and toasted Beth. They praised her and told her she was indispensable. Later, they drove to Havenstone and opened champagne. Louise began to sing. 'Killing Me Softly With His Song'. Poignant words, aching. She closed her eyes, her head thrown back, smoke spiralling lazily through her fingers, then passed the joint to Peter who inhaled deeply.

"Relax and live," he murmured, bending down and offering it to Beth. "Life is not a sweat shop, no matter how much you insist on making it one." His fingers reached under her hair and stroked her throat. "This is our time, Beth Tyrell. We've earned it." Flickering pain in her stomach, swooping on the verge of pleasure. She sat on the floor, her back resting against his knees. He placed the joint between her fingers, wet where his lips had touched it. Smoking hash belonged to his student days, lazy sessions in his studio, the *Cat* pictures. It seemed so long ago, daft afternoons. Her hands shook when the smoke hit her lungs. Stewart was watching her, his expression grim as he refused the joint, and it annoyed her, this sense that he was waiting and hoping, always hoping.

When Peter rolled a second joint, his movements slow and deliberate, as if he was enjoying a pleasurable ritual, she could only smile, so relaxed she was expanding outwards instead of inwards, the air around her sweet, languorous, heavy. Louise's voice would go on forever, so deep and haunting, she wanted to cry out, her body demanding some release as the music moved inside her. How she used to rise to the notes on her father's accordion, his music lifting her, and it was the same sensation when Peter's hand touched her shoulder. A light pressure that begged her to stay when it was time for the others to leave.

Stewart had been reluctant to go. His hurt eyes pleaded with her until Louise propelled him firmly towards her car.

"He's one jealous man." Peter stood beside her at the drawing room window. "We're breaking his heart."

She did not want to talk about Stewart. She did not want to do anything except watch the coral dawn spreading across the sky and wait for him to make the next move.

"Look at you, trembling like a leaf and I haven't even kissed you yet." With his fingers he traced her lips, a crushed flower opening. She stood perfectly still while he stroked the warmth within her. Every move he made was exploratory, waiting for her unspoken permission before he kissed her. This time there was no monster in the wardrobe, no whimpering of new born pups, and when Beth floated, falling far far down beneath him, her body feather light, she knew there was nothing to stop the moment.

She held him tightly, allowing him to lead her beyond her fear and into the pleasure she saw reflected in his eyes. A slow pleasure building, the path of old dreams unfolding, and there was so much more to give forever and forever. Desire running along her spine, along the crevice of her passion. His voice murmured, caressed her. She opened to the touch of his fingers, ready to receive him, and cried out when he moved inside her, hard and strong, whispering her name, and when he thrust deep, deeper, she welcomed him. Surging, touching stars as her body soared upwards towards the moment of fulfilment.

"Open your eyes and look at me, Beth," he whispered. No reason for shame, for false modesty. This was pleasure of the mind, of the body. Her eyes drowning in pleasure. Lost. Stoned on pot. Stoned on love.

They were older now, middle-aged and immune to spent passions, some would say. In Luigi's Bistro he had stared into her eyes and sought the past, yearned for it.

"Lindsey?" he asked. "Tell me if it's true?"

"Lindsey is my child," she said. "Stewart's and mine. It's too late, Peter. It was always too late."

*   *   *

On the last Saturday night that Lindsey spent in Havenstone, Sara chopped mushrooms, onions and tomatoes, simmered pasta, and filled the kitchen with her laughter. She kissed Lindsey and apologised for being so offhand in the studio. She explained about the pressure of deadlines. The African trip had been exhausting and she had had to go away again on business almost as soon as she returned. But work on the book was finished and tomorrow, when she reached Elmfield, there would be time to unwind. Everything seemed perfect again and Lindsey could not imagine ever wanting to be anywhere else.

A place was set at the table for Peter but he never showed and they laughed, imagining him sulking somewhere, probably in the Oldport Grand, afraid to come home and face the music. After the meal they sat in the drawing room with the curtains open and the village lights winking back at them. Sara spoke about her days as a professional photographer. She had photographed models in all sorts of exotic locations but the fashion industry was so trite, so shallow. She shrugged aside that time in her life. Her work, her real photography, was noticed by important people.

Tom gave her the money to mount her first exhibition. He was always there for her, she said, her smile soft, remembering. The subject was Irish emigrants, homeless people sick with the need to return to their families. The exhibition was well reviewed but most Irish people hated it because it was so grim, all those sleazy rooms and weary, lined faces. They only wanted to know about the successful emigrants like her cousin, Kieran, who was hell bent on becoming a rich stockbroker in New York.

Sara poured brandy into a goblet. She swirled it around, staring into the liquid as it splashed from one side of the glass to the other. When Beth phoned her in London she had been surprised. Her sister had paid little attention to her since she ran away from Anaskeagh but then, out of the blue, she commissioned Sara to do the photo shoot.

She showed Lindsey the fashion brochure she did for Della Designs. How old-fashioned the clothes looked: Eighties gear, glitzy jump suits and power shoulder pads, but the leather was nice, sleek and dangerous. Lindsey recognised Pier's Point, the high tide lapping the jetty. Such extraordinary photographs. The models looked as if they were suspended on sun beams, as vaporous as spray. Her crazy aunt Marina was the main model, her face white as a vampire bride, skinny as a stick.

How glamorous Beth looked in those days, Sara said, as confident as if she owned the world, always laughing, flicking back her long black hair, teasing Peter with her flashing eyes, tormenting Stewart, giving orders, ignoring Sara who was just the hired photographer, nothing more.

Sara's voice was so low she could have been talking to herself and Lindsey imagined her mother looking glamorous and in control, always laughing. But why was she laughing? A sick fluttery feeling started in her chest. She did not want to hear about her mother and Peter being in love – but Sara kept going on and on about those days and she did not know how to stop her.

At first, Sara said, she thought the feeling between them was mutual. But things changed. Peter began to stare at her instead of Beth. She found it difficult to breathe when he stood too close. The air around them was electric. Sparking. She laughed and swirled the brandy faster before drinking it down in one swallow. She made a face and shuddered, laughing louder. Poor old Beth. She never had a clue about what was going on right under her nose.

Her laugher made Lindsey uncomfortable. She was unable to see the joke. She sensed an echo in her aunt's words, as if she wanted to harm Beth. It seemed wrong to talk about her mother in this intimate way, as if these disclosures stripped away her privacy, laid bare her painful love.

As soon as the shoot was over, Sara returned to London. A week later she opened the door of her apartment and he was standing outside. She married him soon afterwards because, she said, when a force wind blows you either get out of the way or you blow with it.

Beth went to London and Sara came to Oldport – two sisters moving in opposite directions. Lindsey was suddenly angry with her aunt when she thought of Beth in those days, living with crazy Marina, so miserable and sad, while Sara stole Peter away with her charms and settled into Havenstone. Queen of the palace.

How edgy Sara looked when she finished her story. She approached the mirror above the mantelpiece and twisted her hair into a tight knot at the top of her head, clamping it into place with a clip comb. It showed off her long neck, so taut, as if the skin was stretched too tight. There were lines on her cheeks, still faint, but Lindsey saw them clearly, and knew how her aunt would look in years to come. Sara crossed the floor to the drinks cabinet and poured another glass of brandy, her movements too fast, and when she replaced the bottle Lindsey thought it would break under the force she used. As if aware of her niece's thoughts, she left the room without saying a word, walking light, as if egg shells were cracking under her feet, and climbed the stairs to her bedroom. Lindsey heard her moving across the floor and then there was silence.

Lindsey switched on the television, flicked channels and

turned it off again, unable to ignore her nervousness. When half an hour had passed, she went upstairs to see if everything was all right. The mirrors on the bedroom walls glittered. They reminded her of hard staring eyes, and her reflection was duplicated many times as she entered the room. Sara was sitting in front of her dressing table. The glass of brandy was on the floor by her feet, lying on one side, empty. She did not seem to notice Lindsey standing behind her, even though their eyes locked in the dressing table mirror, and Lindsey was smiling at her.

Rings sparkled on her fingers when she raised her hand to her face. Her cheeks were marked by angry red weals, as if she had slapped or scratched her pale skin. Her fingers trembled as she touched the marks but her expression remained blank, so empty of any emotion that Lindsey reached out and stroked her shoulder in an instinctive gesture of comfort. Sara continued to stare through the mirror at her and, just when Lindsey felt she could no longer stand the tension, her aunt's eyelids flickered rapidly. Her gaze sharpened, as if she was coming back to a familiar place, and she shrugged her shoulder, shaking off Lindsey's hand, as if her touch was suddenly repugnant. Her eyes had the cold blue sheen of a winter sky.

"The sins of the mother visited on the child." She spoke softly but distinctly at Lindsey's reflection. "How dare you enter my room without permission. Get out of my sight this instant – you crazy bitch!"

For an instant Lindsey was unable to move. She knew she was looking at a stranger – and that she had become a stranger to Sara. On the mirrored walls she saw her face, pale and shocked as she turned from the dressing table.

Sara's slender neck was bowed – and their reflections fragmented until it seemed as if they had been cut into many pieces.

Downstairs, in the drawing room, Lindsey slumped on the sofa, weeping, bewildered that she could be the source of such fury. Why had Sara not locked the bedroom door if she wanted to be alone? That was what she usually did when she was in one of her moods, staying there for days or working in her studio all night.

Yes, Lindsey understood about those "reflective moods". That was what Sara called them. She had confided in Lindsey, spoken about her need to be alone, and how difficult it was to convince Peter she was not shutting him out of her life. Lindsey knew he phoned her mother at such times and asked her to come to Havenstone. Beth usually looked exhausted when she returned home, pretending nothing was wrong, but talking low to Stewart, falling silent when anyone entered the room. Lindsey had overheard them one night discussing depression and mood swings, and wanted to tell her mother she was wrong, so very wrong, because when Lindsey was in Havenstone, it was impossible to believe such words could ever be applied to anyone as wonderful as Sara.

Sara had put on make-up and perfume when she came downstairs. "I'm sorry, my darling." She took Lindsey in her arms and dried her tears. "Forgive me, please. I drank too much brandy. A bad mistake. Say you forgive me, please." She touched Lindsey's hair, ruffling it, and smiled in a dreamy off-focus way. "You could have been my child. I would have loved a daughter like you. Now, all I can do is borrow you for weekends."

Lindsey wanted to go home. She made excuses and left. She could not remember if they said goodbye. All she remembered were Sara's eyes. The hate shining. And how Havenstone, with its cold empty rooms, would soon be a deserted house where she and Tork could be together, safe.

Back at home, with the familiar sounds around her, she realised that this was where she belonged. Not in Havenstone with its high gates, blocking everything out. The story Sara told her was as cloying as a cobweb, clinging to her skin. She realised she always saw her mother in a lesser light when she compared her to Sara. Remarks her aunt made, nothing unkind or horrible, just remarks that made the feeling grow until Lindsey wanted to belong only to her. Then everything would be perfect, so effortless and elegant.

Her father followed Beth to London. Their wedding photo hung in the sitting room and Stewart, standing with his arm around her, looked so puffed up with happiness it made Lindsey smile every time she saw it. Until Sara told her story – and then it just looked like a sham.

CHAPTER THIRTY-EIGHT

Peter understood the how of loving Sara. But not the why. The how could be defined in certain words – obsessive, compulsive, demanding. But why? Why the need to possess, to dominate, to force her to love him as passionately as he loved her? How she sparkled in his company, such vitality in those early days, her voice a sultry whisper when she leaned towards him. To look back on those heady times filled him with incredulity. How could he have been so duped?

She had remained beyond his reach before their marriage, teasing him with phone calls in the middle of the night, her laughter beckoning, her voice softly provocative. In his arms she was pliable, a promise waiting to be fulfilled. He contented himself with kisses, long and passionate, excited by the yearning this created, the slow building desire that would be satisfied on their wedding night.

They married in Rome, a quiet ceremony with Marjory and Tom as their witnesses. That night she came to him in a sheer white robe, the colour of chastity. Her eyes seemed enormous as she lay beneath him. Two bruises. He ravished her. Ravish sounded softer than rape and there was nothing in her demeanour to suggest she did not welcome his mouth, his hands, his deep plunging need. Exquisite pleasure, staring down at her, devouring her with his eyes, ravishing her with his body. Shame set in as pleasure died. He had given her so little. She smiled, sleepy satisfaction, as if the spasms that had racked him had also sated her. She stretched back against the pillows, her young firm breasts jutting beneath the sheet, her gaze already reaching beyond him.

"I will love you until the day I die," he promised. "And in whatever eternity comes afterwards. All I want is for you to love me the same way."

"You make me sound like an addiction." She laughed softly.

"If that's the case," he warned. "Don't ever try to rehabilitate me."

In their early years of marriage, she pretended to feel pleasure in his touch. He wanted a wife with blood in her veins and fever in her body, and the awareness that her desire was simulated dawned slowly on him. When she realised he knew she stopped pretending.

At the mention of children her eyes, fathomless, blocked any further discussion. She was busy, successful, constantly travelling, reminding him that her career left no space for a family. He had been an only child. He longed to fill Havenstone with young voices but she was adamant, firmly dismissing his needs, threatening to leave him if he persisted.

Sometimes, the energy drained from her. She lay in bed for days without speaking, turning from him when he tried to comfort her, shaking her head vehemently if he suggested a psychologist, a psychiatrist, anyone who could help. Her tablets were hidden from him but he found a prescription once and realised she was on anti-depressants. She refused to discuss it with him. Somehow, drawing strength from deep within herself, she would recover her equilibrium and grow strong again, absorbing herself in her work, taking over his studio, claiming it as her own, and he cleared his paintings to the attic, knowing he would never use it again.

He attacked her once in the middle of a row, her mockery snapping his control in a sudden lunging violence. Its force took them both by surprise. He could not recall the words that acted as a catalyst and, afterwards, he knew it was not her words but years of frustration that placed his fingers on her throat. Her shocked gasp brought him to his senses. He heard it faintly through the mist of rage and slumped away from her, his hands tingling. Then she was gentle with him, forgiving. That night they made love. She bit into his flesh, her nails raking his back, her gasping cries driving him to a frenzy.

Afterwards, he lay awake, filled with self-loathing. Such violence, this need to maim and dominate, was so far removed from the love he still felt towards her, yet it stemmed from the same root. He was in the grip of an addiction, torn by the need to touch the fire he sensed beneath the ice. The following day he moved his possessions into the bedroom where his father once slept alone, watched over by the eyes of tortured mystics.

She did not have to die to escape from him. Sara Wallace

was no domestic slave held in thrall to her husband's wage packet. She could have left him. He could have left her. There had been other women, brief affairs that gave him brief satisfaction, but forced him to accept the abnormality of his relationship with his wife. For this reason such affairs ended cleanly, without regret. His marriage had nowhere to go yet he kept believing that his love for her would eventually triumph. How many times did he try? How many times did he fail? When did it cease to matter?

CHAPTER THIRTY-NINE

Bombshells, Beth realised, should be carefully introduced into conversations. Yet by their nature, bombshells, no matter how carefully they were handled, exploded lives which, moments before, had been seamlessly held together by habit and routine. Stewart's briefcase looked bulky and incongruous in the middle of the kitchen table. Like a fat squatting toad, she thought, it's bottom lip hanging down, disgorging information she did not want to hear. She glanced down at the brochure he handed her, daunted by statistical information she would once have absorbed at a glance. 'Action on Creative Indigenous Industry' was embossed on the front cover. He pointed to a photograph of a small factory in a semi-circle of eight similar buildings; a modern, compact business centre.

"This is a strong possibility," he said, tracing the route on the map, his finger moving westwards towards a brown headland dominating a small town. "There's a small clothing factory available here. The previous owner moved her production base to Morocco and it's a done deal, if we're interested."

"But it's in Anaskeagh – are you crazy?"

"Outside the town, where your uncle used to have his furniture factory. It was turned into an business centre some years ago. It's ideal for our needs, and the ACII want an immediate occupancy. The closure of any business has an impact on the town and, from our point of view, we'd have fully skilled workers ready and willing to begin work." He stopped short, seeing her expression. "Don't block me at the first fence, Beth. It could be the perfect solution."

She was aware that her responses were too slow, the conversation running ahead of her.

"What has Tom Oliver got to do with this?" she demanded.

His voice quickened, as if he already sensed her resistance. "He contacted me before the strike began and offered to help. At first I wasn't sure but he persuaded me to go down and look at what was available. He's got clout with the ACII and has offered to cut through the red tape. The town is thriving, well worth thinking about as a place to live. I wanted to see it for myself before I told you. Honestly, Beth, he really has been invaluable with advice and support."

"How could you even talk to him?" She struggled to understand what he was suggesting. "How could you? I can't believe what I'm hearing!"

"He's only trying to help us. I'd never have considered Anaskeagh if he hadn't told me about the centre. Now that I've seen it I believe it would be perfect for our needs."

"So, now you're handing me a *fait accompli*, is that it? Why didn't you discuss this with me at the early stages?"

"I didn't want your emotional responses stopping me before I'd fully investigated the possibilities."

"There are no possibilities, Stewart." Disbelief was giving way to anger. "I've no intention of moving to Anaskeagh. Not now, not in a million years. Never! Never! Do you understand? I won't be involved in this – I'm not even prepared to discuss it."

"Why? What's so dreadful about the town? I've never understood why you hate it so much."

"I don't want to live there. Can't you understand plain English?"

"I understand all right and I don't like what I'm hearing. You've no intention of moving from Oldport." His voice was harsh. "I don't need Lindsey's hints to know what's going on between you and Peter. He's even sharing our bed, now."

"Don't be ridiculous. How often do you want me to apologise for that night? I was half-asleep, dreaming—" She stopped abruptly, knowing she would only dig a deeper hole with her explanation. "Peter has nothing to do with this. I spent my childhood taking charity from my uncle and now you want me to do the same again."

"Charity! This has nothing to do with charity." She had never seen him so angry. "You've no idea of the work I've put into this project. Anaskeagh needs employment and I can provide it. Sam O'Grady needs a supplier and I can give him what he wants. I'm willing to beg and borrow and work all the hours God sends to support my family – and you have the gall to call that *charity!*"

"I won't return to Anaskeagh, Stewart. Don't make me."

"I've never made you do anything you didn't want to

do. But this is important to me, Beth, to us. I want to know the real reason why you're not interested. You still love him, don't you?" He held her face between his hands and forced her to look at him. "I know the signs. I had a long apprenticeship on the sidelines, remember?"

He tried to hold her but she pushed him aside and ran upstairs. She locked the bedroom door and flung herself onto the bed. She lay there, aching with the need for tears and release, aware of Stewart at the door pleading with her to let him in.

All she could see was a slumbering country road. An old pub with a half-door and milk churns in the yard. She remembered her father's strong arms when he lifted her up on the counter one warm autumn afternoon, and how he played his accordion until it was time to collect the furniture that stood in the nearby building with the corrugated iron roof.

She heard the men sawing and hammering and the sawdust swirling like a snowstorm, making her sneeze and catch her breath when she tried to speak.

"Gold dust," said her uncle. He laughed and tossed the sawdust in the air. Her father leaned against the van. He smoked a cigarette and chatted to the woman who did the wages.

It was musty in the big storeroom where chairs and tables waited for collection. She was eleven years old, hiding. He found her, as he always did, and afterwards, there was new furniture in her mother's kitchen, a table with a leg that was too short and had to be evened up with a folded cigarette box.

She would never return. She shuddered, sobbing deep

within herself until she grew calm again. When she opened the door she said, "Go if you must. I'm staying here. The decision is yours."

*   *   *

If anyone had asked Lindsey to describe her parent's marriage she would have said, "Boringly contented." As far as she was concerned, the two emotions were compatible. 'Boring' summed up the reality of two people living together and doing the same things year after year. Yet her parents seemed to accept this low-level existence with a certain degree of contentment. Or so she thought until the tension between them hit the high wires and everything changed.

Her mother kept denying there was a split. She just needed time to think things through. Her false smiles and denials were not reassuring. Her father had a look in his eyes that worried her. Determined. He took his motorbike from the garage and dusted if off. When his new factory opened, it would gleam in the reception area, along with the hanging plants and bimbo receptionist. Most of the time he was off doing deals about machines and fabrics. When he came home at weekends the high tension wires hummed every time he opened his mouth about Anaskeagh.

He wanted her to move – she wanted to stay. Stalemate followed by compromise. He would run his factory in Anaskeagh and come home at weekends. After six months they would open negotiations again. Lindsey had a feeling the solution was going to be as difficult to sew together, excuse the pun … ha ha ha, as the Northern Ireland Peace

Process. It made neither of them happy but compromise seldom did. Sara had never compromised. She did what she wanted to do and when she'd had enough of doing that she bowed out. No note, no nothing, not even a grave with flowers, only her laughter rising, mocking Lindsey. Just thinking about it made her shake with anger.

Her brother thought it would be brilliant to move to the sticks. Robert wanted to get off the world by steeping himself in Celtic mist and local dirge music. Granny Mac had given him an accordion and he was going to take his grandfather's music back to Anaskeagh. The sooner the better, Lindsey thought. The wailing sound coming from his bedroom was doing her head in. When she tried to make him see that there was trouble on the domestic front he told her she was mental. Her problem was an over-active imagination, brought about by an over-indulgence of E at weekends.

"You're dead for real if the folks find out." He knew what was going on from the school grapevine.

"Everyone's doing it," she replied.

"I'm not." He could look really smug at times. "You shouldn't mess around with that stuff. It does funny things to the brain."

She trusted him not to tell her parents about Friday nights. They shared too many secrets to break ranks. Not that anyone would have cared. When she remembered the fuss her mother used to make about her social activities, always checking out the scene before she gave permission for Lindsey to go anywhere. Now all she did was invent excuses for not moving – schools and buses and Gail's ballet class – when it was obvious that all she wanted to do was dine in Howth by candlelight and make cat's eyes at Peter Wallace.

She tackled her father about the future. She would leave the wellies and the sheep and the slurry to her parents but she had no intention of being transplanted to the edge of nowhere. He suggested that if the family moved to Anaskeagh she could live with Granny Mac and visit at weekends. Granny Mac hugged her tight and said she would love the company.

Her dictator uncle had other ideas. When he phoned to congratulate her on being accepted into art college he told her about the new house he intended buying. There would be a room waiting for Lindsey if her family disappeared into the nether regions.

"You'll need space to work and to store your art materials," he said, even offering to share space in his new studio. She would be a free spirit, able to come and go as she pleased. He frowned when she informed him that she intended moving in with her grandmother.

"Connie is an elderly lady," he said. "She will find it tiring having a young person around her house all the time." He made her sound like Methuselah's granny.

"My grandmother has never found me tiring," she replied. "Why should she start now?" He made her nervous, trying to be so friendly all the time. She preferred it when she had been an invisible blot on his horizon. To think of her mother once being in his arms was sickening.

*   *   *

Della Designs was razed to the ground. Peter stood among the crowd who gathered to watch its destruction. A swing from the arm of a crane. A blow in its solar plexus from a swaying demolition ball. An instant of indecision, as if brick and mortar could withstand the forces ranged against it. Then the old factory buckled, bowed almost gracefully before collapsing with a dull whoosh. A mushroom cloud of dust and debris rose in its wake.

He felt nothing, no emotion or quiver of nostalgia to mark its passing. When the dust cleared a new vista opened before him. Rows of houses, swatches of green, the estuary flowing under the arches. A heap of stone to mark the passing of Della Designs. His legacy, now dead.

Tom Oliver had been handsomely paid for his investment, the transaction smoothly conducted by his son, Conor. The politician's generosity had been a heavy burden and when the papers were signed, Peter felt as if a weight had been lifted from his shoulders.

Base Road was desolate. He avoided the warning signs forbidding entry for cars, and parked in front of the estuary. The air was damp on his skin when he walked by the shore. He smelled the sea, the whiff of seaweed sweeping in on the low tide, a heron standing on one spindle leg, observing. He watched children fishing off Pier's Point, just as he had fished with Stewart when they were young, searching for crabs among the rocks, building dams and channels in the soft mud. The new motorway would destroy old ways. As the suburbs edged closer to the city, Oldport was becoming another satellite town, but the pursuits of children would always remain the same.

*   *   *

Sara's ghost appeared again. This time the manifestation

took place outside Carrie Davern's estate agency. On this occasion she was not carrying her baby in a sling, which was just as well, because she walked straight into Lindsey and almost knocked her to the ground.

"I'm so sorry. Are you all right?" She grabbed Lindsey's arm, steadying her, a strong solid ghost with a firm grasp. She looked thin and tense but the same wide smile lit her face.

"You remind me very much of someone," Lindsey said as they waited for the traffic to stop before crossing the road.

"I hope she's a nice person." The woman stepped off the pavement before the lights changed and jumped back when a driver blasted his horn at her.

"She was lovely," Lindsey replied. "Are you going to buy a house in Oldport?"

"Not a house. I'm opening a garden centre in Grahamstown."

"No one lives in Grahamstown except cows."

"Well, I guess the cows are going to have to move over once the motorway starts rolling."

Judith Hanson was on the pavement stacking potted plants on stands when she saw them. "Eva, come in and have some tea. Tell me how everything is going." She sounded motherly and concerned but the woman looked at her watch and said she had to fly. Off she drove in a small van, only this time there was no name printed on the side. Lindsey also made excuses and fled in case Tork was lurking around.

She felt as if she knew the woman from a long way back. Not just because she reminded her of Sara, that was only superficial, but something stronger than time or memory.

Sara would have understood what she meant. She would have called it "a meeting of dreams".

CHAPTER FORTY

Beth no longer swam in the mornings, waking heavy-headed, longing to sink back into the pillows and stay there for the rest of the day. She stared at her reflection and saw a faded woman with lacklustre eyes gazing back at her. A stranger whom she had no interest in knowing. A woman who belonged nowhere.

Stewart was staying at the O'Donovan farm. On Saturday afternoons when he returned home he brought her news from the town, titbits to try and arouse her interest. Sheila O'Donovan – who was once Sheila O'Neill, smuggler of forbidden baby photographs – had offered to mind their two younger children if Beth decided to move. Her sister, Nuala O'Neill, had returned from London and was running an arts and crafts gallery in Anaskeagh. Nuala's baby, whom Beth remembered in white ribbons and lace, was now an architect, speaking fluent Japanese and stamping his signature on skyscrapers. Hatty Beckett sent her love. The corner building that once housed her famous chip shop had become a shopping centre and she was running the coffee shop in Nuala's gallery.

He asked her opinion on machinery, fabrics, business deals he was negotiating with First Lady. He intended calling the factory, TrendLines. What did Beth think of the name? A bungalow near the farm was for sale. It had a view of the sea, wonderful cliff walks, a fifteen minute drive from the town, no traffic jams. They could move in immediately.

Marjory had closed down her boutique and was drifting aimlessly through each day. Stewart had invited her out for a meal but his efforts to make peace were curtly rejected. What did he expect? Beth wondered. Forgiveness for the past?

She dreamt about Fatima Terrace, a child's memory shaped into an adult nightmare. The faded cabbage rose wallpaper, the lights from passing cars throwing shapes across the ceiling of her bedroom. The creak of a wardrobe door. A red dress swaying from a coat hanger. Her heart thumped as she curled into the empty space where Stewart's body had once warmed her. She turned restlessly, and woke, wondering if he was also lying awake thinking about her, unable to understand why, so suddenly and so determinedly, she had turned from him.

She eased from the bed and entered the children's bedrooms. Each room was a silent pool of darkness and quiet breathing. She did not enter the attic bedroom. Tonight, Lindsey was staying at Melanie's house, celebrating her friend's eighteenth birthday. The Leaving was beginning soon and the strain was showing on her face, tense, distracted, turning resolutely away from Beth when she asked quest-ions.

She returned to her bed and listened to the night sounds: the creaks and sighs of seasoned wood, a distant house alarm activated, a sudden blast of music and laughter, probably a party somewhere near by. Familiar comforting sounds which she gathered around her and drifted back to sleep.

*   *   *

Noise, light, energy. Lindsey could never remember feeling so happy. She was a kaleidoscope, high and spinning. Water flowed down her throat. It ran through her hair, cold on her skin, drowning her. She rose above the torrent, flailing towards freedom where there was space to dance into infinity. The floor shuddered. The walls opened outwards. She reached towards Melanie and Karen, her friends. One mind, one sensation, one body.

When they tried to slow her down she waved them away. She ignored the water and moved beyond the lights. She shivered, someone stepping on her grave, and danced harder. Tonight she would forget everything. She would banish the old man and his hard metal button eyes sinking deep under hooded eyelids. The E was brilliant, and the other stuff Kev supplied, it was giving her such a buzz. Melanie said she was taking risks but living was a high-risk occupation – and each day brought its own dangers.

Her great-uncle had touched her arm, gentle kitten strokes. When she asked the question he had smiled as if he had known that sooner or later she would come to him. Tom knew everything. No matter how she tried to forget it, the question had refused to go away, even in the garage with the music mix thudding inside her head, it was there, demanding an answer.

Last week, in his apartment, she had stood determined before him and asked, "Why did you say I was a bonnie baby?"

"That's how I always imagined you," he replied. "A strong, healthy child – not a little titch."

"Not premature, you mean? ..." Lindsey was unable to continue. She knew when she asked the question that nothing would ever be the same again. But leaving it unanswered was not an option she was prepared to take any longer.

"What are you asking me?" He leaned towards her and stared deep into her eyes.

"I want to know about my mother. Before I was born ... and my father." She fell silent when he clasped her fingers between his warm comforting hands.

"But you know the truth already, don't you, my poor, hurting child?" He spoke gently and she nodded, tears rushing into her eyes.

He drew her nearer, his voice gentle and understanding. "Lindsey, I know how painful the truth can be. But not to know ourselves is the greatest pain of all. Your mother was a young and foolish woman in love with the wrong man. Do not punish her for a mistake that turned into such joy." His eyes shone with knowledge. "Cherish what you have, my dear. Stewart gave you as much love as any father could bestow on his natural child."

She felt no surprise, just an overwhelming tiredness, as if she had come to the end of long journey that began in

Havenstone on the night she listened to Sara's angry voice rising upwards. He stroked her hair. His fingers nestled in the nape of her neck moving in a slow circular movement as his voice comforted her. She did not want him touching her hair. He had been drinking when she arrived and in his eyes she had seen something, a flicker, a gleam of satisfaction. He had wanted her to ask the question. Sara was right about secrets. There was a time when silence was more important than honesty. He had released her secret and she hated him for it.

"Let me go." She struggled from his embrace.

He held her for an instant longer, his grip hard as steel. "Can't you see his face when you look in the mirror? The sins of the mother visited on the child. The truth is everything but she refused to listen ... wicked girl ..." His voice broke as if glass had caught in his throat. His eyes seemed to be dissolving into tears.

She walked towards the door, terrified he would try to touch her again. His words followed her. She did not want to hear. He stood in his doorway, watching as she ran down the long corridor to the lift. When it glided to a halt and the doors slid noiselessly across, he still stood staring until she was safe in the mirrored space, gliding downwards towards freedom.

She walked for a long time. The lights of the city melted into glass walls. The sound of traffic was loud in her ears. People moved too fast, jostling against her. Everything looked the same as before – yet nothing would ever be the same again.

In the garage she could dance into the past. Dazzling lights spun her towards the ceiling and away again. She was outside her body, her feet skimming the earth, until darkness came like a plunging star and carried her away.

*   *   *

The telephone rang at two in the morning. The nurse on the phone made no sense. How could Lindsey be unconscious in hospital when she was staying overnight with Melanie. Unconscious. Beth kept whispering the word as she pulled on her jeans, fumbled in the wardrobe for a jacket. She woke Robert and told him to look after the younger children. In the midst of her terror, she realised that although he was shocked he was not surprised.

"What do you know about this?" She shook him fiercely and he sobbed, terrified by the look of dread on her face.

"She messed around with some stuff. – nothing heavy. Some E."

"E! You mean *Ecstasy*? Jesus Christ! Why didn't you tell me?"

"I didn't want to upset you. You were so worried about everything – Dad and all."

"She's unconscious, Robert. She could die. How am I going to feel then … when it's too late to be upset?"

"I'm going to ring Dad," he shouted. He ran to the phone, his back turned to her as he dialled. "I want him here. You should never have sent him away."

She needed him too. His calm solid presence, comforting her. "I'll do it," she said. "I'll ring him from the mobile on the way to the hospital." She hugged her son, inhaling the musky sleep smell on his skin. "She's going to be all right. I know she is. Phone Uncle Peter. Tell them to meet me in the emergency ward."

She had to stop for petrol and by the time she arrived Peter was waiting, sitting grimly between Lindsey's two friends. From his expression it was obvious that words had been exchanged. The Gardaí had already been called and names taken. Melanie was crying into a tissue, her shoulders heaving. The second girl stared blankly at the opposite wall. Peter rose to his feet and came quickly towards Beth.

"If anything happens … it's all my fault." She sobbed. "I believed she was staying in Melanie's house. Why didn't I check? I used to always check …"

The young doctor who spoke to Beth looked exhausted, gritty eyes, his white coat as rumpled as his hair. Lindsey had become dehydrated and collapsed at a rave. Her body had been wrapped in a 'space wrap', a tin foil blanket, he explained, seeing her terrified expression, to prevent further dehydration. As her friends were unsure if she had taken any substances other than E, Lindsey's stomach had been pumped with charcoal fluid and blood samples taken. Her heart was being monitored until the results of the blood tests came back and her medical team could determine if any of her vital organs had been damaged. Beth shuddered away from the information so casually offered. Her legs trembled as she followed the doctor towards a curtained cubicle.

"Can I see her?" Peter joined them as they were about to enter.

"Are you her father?" the doctor asked.

Beth did not turn her head when he replied, "Just a close family member."

*   *   *

Peter stared down at his daughter as she drifted in and out of sleep. Her face was stripped of personality, energy, expression. Only the vital elements showed. In her wide firm mouth and long chin he recognised his mother.

"Lindsey, what are you trying to do to us?" he whispered.

Her eyes flickered, staring at him without comprehension. She tried to speak.

"Can you remember anything?" Beth asked, moving to the other side of the bed. "You collapsed at Melanie's birthday party."

They leaned closer to hear her rasping reply. No party. A rave in the disused garage on Base Road. The music mix, the lights circling too fast and a pain, as if her heart was forcing its way from her chest. Then nothing, no warning – she stared at the ceiling lights and at the screens surrounding the bed. She wanted to die. "Please dear God make me die," she sobbed. Her stomach cramped. Waves of blackness came and went but she was unable to throw up.

"When will Dad be here?" she muttered. "I want him with me."

"He'll be here soon," Beth promised, her eyes locked on her child, both of them excluding him.

A young nurse entered the cubicle. "Your husband is on the phone, Mrs McKeever." She glanced at Peter. "I'm afraid I'll have to ask you to leave, sir. Only close family members are allowed."

Peter hesitated. When he touched Lindsey's hair she pulled the sheet over her eyes.

"I want him to go." She sobbed louder. "Make him go away, Nurse. He has no right to be here."

Without another word he left.

Lindsey slept and woke again. She shook her head from side to side then lifted her hands, staring at her long tapering fingers, as if she was seeing them for the first time. "I want Dad here. Will he be here soon?"

"As soon as he can," Beth promised.

"He'll kill me?" Her mouth trembled.

The young doctor re-entered the cubicle. "Why should your father do that when you can do the job just as easily yourself?" He stood at the foot of her bed and checked her chart "Feeling better?" he asked. He did not sound sympathetic or even interested in her reply. He shone a torch into her eyes and felt her pulse. "Do you often make such serious attempts to kill yourself?"

"It wasn't like that …" She sunk her chin into the sheet, too embarrassed to continue.

"Is Tork Hansen involved in this?" Beth spoke sharply when they were alone again.

"No." Lindsey was emphatic. "Tork is all right. He warned me to take it easy. I didn't want to know." She touched her flushed throat, raw where the tube had rubbed against it. "I took some stuff, tabs. I didn't care." She spoke so softly that Beth had to bend forward to hear. "He told me the truth." Tears trickled from under her closed eyelids. "I went to his apartment a few times."

Beth tried to speak but her lips seemed frozen, her mouth so dry she was unable to swallow. "Tom Oliver." She forced herself to utter his name. "Are you talking about my uncle?"

"I thought he was lonely. He told me about Anaskeagh and about Sara when she was a little girl, and all the relations I've never met. He seemed so kind. But the last time, it seemed as if hated me for something. He said— " She stopped suddenly and lay silent, her eyes fixed on the ceiling.

"What happened? Tell me, Lindsey. You have to tell me everything. Did he harm you in any way?"

"He told me about my father. My *real* father."

Beth saw a tremor pass over her child's face and accepted that the moment she had dreaded but anticipated since Lindsey's birth had arrived. She had rehearsed what she would say many times but explanations seemed futile, so hollow when measured against the loss she saw in her daughter's eyes.

"Why wasn't I told?" Lindsey cried. "Didn't I have a right to know?"

"To know what, Lindsey? "She gripped her hands, relieved when her daughter did not pull away. "To know that you wouldn't have had a loving father if it wasn't for Stewart. He was with me when you were born. Such happiness in his eyes when he held you, his daughter, his beloved child – our beloved child." She sighed. "I can't turn back the clock, my darling. No one can. You were always surrounded by love. You've no idea the difference that makes."

Lindsey suddenly leaned over the side of the bed, retching violently. Beth grabbed a sick tray and held it under her chin, wiping her face with a damp towel. She tried to make her understand, old secrets, bare bones, breaking hearts. How could she explain dead passion to a young woman who faced the truth of her existence and found it wanting?

Peter had asked for forgiveness when he told her about Sara. She despised his platitudes, his appeals for understanding – as if the love he felt for Sara was beyond his control. He asked for her friendship, standing abjectly before her, and she knew then that there was only one way to move on with her life. She boarded the mail boat at Dun Laoghaire in the early, uncertain days of her pregnancy. A debt had been paid in full and the guilt that had haunted her since the night on Anaskeagh Head fell from her shoulders. She loved Peter Wallace. She carried his child. Stewart carried her. She opened the door of Marina's flat soon after her arrival in London and he was standing outside.

Lindsey was two weeks overdue, normal enough for a first baby, the gynaecologist had reassured them, and she came into the world with a lusty cry and a strong confident kick.

"My daughter," said Stewart, staring in wonder when her tiny fingers gripped his thumb and held him tightly. Watching them, Beth vowed that this was the reality she and Stewart would create together. Their own reality. She wrote to Peter and Sara soon afterwards. A premature baby, she told them, growing stronger but still in an incubator. Soon she will be discharged from hospital. Stewart is living for the moment when we can hold our daughter in our arms.

Lindsey's eyelids closed over bruised cheeks. Her voice was still hoarse, sore where the tube had rubbed against her throat. "He told Sara as well … I think that's why she hated me that night … she knew the truth."

Beth gently laid her daughter's arms under the sheet and sat by her bed, watching over her. She listened to the night sounds from the accident and emergency ward. Raucous voices, screams, arguments, tears; quiet noises compared to the clamour in her head. She had spent her life running from a monster, never realising he was always two steps ahead of her. He remained her nightmare and now he had entered the dreams of her child. He had dominated her sister's will and sought to do the same to her.

Stewart would arrive soon. He would demand to know everything. His fury would make any contact with the politician impossible, his fledgling business destroyed by the truth. As if sensing her thoughts, Lindsey stirred and grasped Beth's hand. "Is Dad here yet?" she murmured, drifting in a half-asleep.

"Not yet … but soon. He's going to be very angry, Lindsey. He trusted Tom Oliver … just like you did."

Lindsey struggled to stay awake. Her mouth quivered as if the enormity of her thoughts could no longer be borne. "Make everything all right again, Mum." It was a childish whisper, repeated once again before her eyelashes drooped over her cheeks.

"Don't worry, I'll protect you." Beth promised.

The desire for revenge, determined in those lost years of her child-hood when she stood with Jess on Anaskeagh Head, was as strong as ever.

"I will destroy you, Tom Oliver." She whispered the words fiercely to herself, as she had never whispered them when her sister was alive. "I will destroy you utterly." An insect, crushed under her feet. The sole of her shoe stamping him into a smear of blood that would be washed away forever in the rain.

Stewart rang once again. "I'll be with you soon," he said. "I'm driving as fast as I can."

"We're waiting for you, my love," she replied. "Hurry."

*   *   *

Peter was in the garden of Havenstone when Beth came to say goodbye, not just to Oldport, but to a past they could have shared. And also, he suspected, to a tentative future that had briefly beckoned them, filled with the reverberations of old passions. Around them the branches of trees tossed in the breeze. When love and desire withered they would still be there, oak and poplar, chestnut and yew, ancient roots enduring.

He listened in disbelief to her unfolding story. She told him about the headland and the leaning rocks that had briefly cradled his wife's child. He visualised Aislin's Roof – the slanting rocks that Sara had photographed and left in her studio – remembering how he had removed them to the attic without ever pausing to wonder at their meaning.

He ached with the need to see Sara again and talk as they had never talked when she was alive. Analysing, understanding, forgiving each other. She had lost a daughter, just as he had lost Lindsey. But unlike him, she had carried the knowledge inside her while he, unaware, uncaring, came to the knowledge too late.

He was on a business trip when she returned from Africa, travelling to and fro, both of them always moving in different directions. The light was on in her studio when he came home late from the factory one night. He knocked and entered, knowing as soon as he saw her, that she was in the grip of a manic energy which always excluded him. He walked away, weary, knowing her anger had moved inwards until he no longer existed. Until it seemed as if he had assumed another identity and it was easy for her to hate him. The following night she told him about Lindsey. Her laughter had been a dark pain. He understood that now. But knowledge could not erase the sound and only an echo remained of the anger that had driven him away.

"I've lost everything I've ever wanted," he said to Beth, before she left. "My life is over."

"No," she replied. "It's moving on. That's all we can do, Peter."

But time had not moved on for Sara. It had etched her future in a dark cavity between the rocks and the unyielding earth – and when she could no longer endure, she had willed her ashes to merge with the cold tide lapping the pilings on Pier's Point.

"Do you know who fathered her child?" he asked.

Beth nodded her head. "He's dead," she replied. Her face was as emotionless as her voice.

He entered the studio and started to paint. Familiar smells, the heartbeat of anticipation. He did not stop to eat or drink. When darkness fell he was still painting, stretching beyond hunger and pain and loss until there was only the sense of movement fused on canvas. This painting was alive. Leaning rocks mossy and dank, sentinels guarding some ancient site, the play of light and shadow on a jagged landscape. Dangerous clouds darkening the moon, haphazard and chaotic; a world ending and beginning. He continued to paint until the night closed in and he was able to lay his wife to rest.

Part Four

1998–1999

CHAPTER FORTY-ONE

Eva watched from the window of Mrs Casey's guest house as the early morning mist cleared from the headland. As birth locations went Anaskeagh Head looked starkly picturesque. But as a secure cradle for a new-born baby it could only have been advantageous if she had been a mountain goat or one of those statuesque sheep with their long black faces.

"Fair weather, that's for sure once that mist blows away," predicted Mrs Casey whose guest house lay at the foot of the headland. "We're in for a hot summer, from all accounts."

The previous night when Eva arrived they had talked about Wind Fall, exchanging horror stories about guests who refused to leave by the allotted hour and stole the towels.

"You'll have a right hunger on you when you reach the top of Anaskeagh Head," she said, handing Eva a packed lunch when she was leaving. Eva had a sudden desire to ask if she remembered the Anaskeagh baby but quickly allowed the thought to die away.

As she approached the headland the road divided into a V. She drove towards a group of houses screened beyond long driveways of maple trees, cherry blossom and pampas grass. This was a narrow road with an insular sense of its own importance. Notices on the gates warned of dangerous dogs and retribution if anyone dared trespass upon the spacious gardens. The road was obviously only used for residential purposes and ended in a barrier of holly and ash lashed with ivy, too thick to penetrate, and reinforced with strong mesh wire. She returned to her car, reversing with difficulty and heading back to the junction, following the sign for *Trá*.

Ice cream kiosks on the approach to the beach were opening for business. Flags slapped against poles, proclaiming the fact that this was a clean beach, minus radioactive fish and an outflow of sewage. The sand looked white and fine but it was gritty, crunching underfoot. The rock face of the headland protruded outwards over the strand. Further along the beach she found the path she needed. It zigzagged easily across the headland, offering safe footholds and regular plateau for climbers to pull themselves upwards.

A shaft of sunshine struck the walls of distant houses, the red roofs of barns and outhouses on the foothills. Eva wondered which farmhouse belonged to the O'Donovan family. The sons had been questioned by the Gardaí in case an abandoned girlfriend had sought revenge. Sowers of wild oats, guilty until proven innocent. She wanted to find the farm but she knew the search must wait for another day. One step at a time into the past.

In the late afternoon she drove back from Anaskeagh Head and strolled around the town. The streets were easy to navigate, a main street leading into side streets. Some looked as if they had recently been refurbished. A small restaurant, a sandwich bar, a book shop and an elegant gallery were lined beside each other along one street. She entered the gallery, moving from the fine-art section towards the craft gallery where tapestries, stained glass lampshades and pottery were displayed. A far cry from Biddy's Bits & Pieces, thought Eva, checking the outrageous price tags. She followed the smell of freshly baked scones wafting from the coffee shop attached to the gallery. Women relaxed after shopping, drinking coffee and buttering scones. Some looked curiously in her direction, nodding politely as they summed her up, a stranger in town. One elderly woman with stooped shoulders met her eyes in a startled, devouring gaze before glancing fiercely down at the table.

Paintings were also on view in the coffee shop. These ones had an amateurish touch and the price tags were cheaper than the ones in the main gallery. Eva moved closer to look at one of them, a pier with moored boats and the headland in the background. She stopped before another painting which carried the same initials. This was a town scene, the clock tower on River Mall, its face lit by moonlight. These paintings did not interest Eva. She suspected they had been painted by a young hand. They lacked dangerous memories.

The elderly woman rose from her chair and joined her.

"A strange class of a painting, wouldn't you agree?" she said, nodding to the moonlight scene.

Eva muttered something inconsequential and polite, wondering if she was a proud relation, or a sales agent, but the woman volunteered no further information. She moved closer, a clinging whiff of expensive perfume and smoke on her skin. She asked Eva's opinion of Anaskeagh. Eva told her what she wanted to hear. Yes, it was indeed a pretty town.

"Can I buy you a coffee before you leave?" The jacket of the woman's crumpled trouser suit was stained. Her heavily made-up face had the same slack appearance and her scalp showed through dyed blonde hair. The image was too hard for a woman of her years, keeping time at bay with too many rings on her fingers and pearls, the size of small eggs, around her neck. Her old hands remained by her sides, hanging listlessly. There was something so pathetic about those loose limp hands with their garish rings, too heavy for frail fingers, that Eva heard herself agreeing.

The woman sat down and clicked her fingers imperiously in the direction of the counter. "Another coffee and scone, Hatty. Put in on my bill – and make sure the coffee is hot this time." A small woman with a mop of startling red hair emerged from behind the coffee urn to glower across at them.

"Keep your castanets to yourself, madam," she snapped. "You'll be served when I'm good and ready."

"Staff nowadays – impossible." Eva's companion sighed. She made small talk until the coffee was served, shaking her head in disapproval when she heard that Eva had moved from Wicklow to Dublin.

"An atrocious accent," she said. "I'm glad to hear you

haven't acquired it. My grandchildren could be talking a different language for all the sense I get out of them." She dismissed her grandchildren with a snap of her hard mouth.

Eva thought of Brigid Loughrey who had listened when her grandchildren spoke, hearing their words, not their accents. This elderly woman did not have the attributes of a true grandmother. No soft flesh or hidden treats in large handbags. She ignored her coffee, the butter melting into the scone as she talked about a boutique she once owned, designer brands only. She listed designer names, looking at Eva for reaction, her sharp eyes summing up her jacket and jeans; cheap labels, dismissed. She had sold her boutique, too many chain stores and shopping centres to compete against. Too many housewives in leisure suits, no style these days. A reproachful glance was cast towards a woman in a shapeless sweatshirt and baggy trousers. Eva discreetly checked her watch, regretting her impulse to linger. The woman pushed aside her cup and lit a cigarette.

"Do you have relations in Anaskeagh?" she asked.

"No." Eva did not know whether or not she lied.

"Are you a photographer?" She glanced at the camera lying on the table.

"Purely amateur. I wanted to take some shots of the headland."

The woman waved away a plume of smoke and stubbed her half-smoked cigarette in an ashtray. As the evening light flooded through the window her frailness was thrown into sharp relief. She remained silent when Eva rose to her feet. They shook hands. Eva turned back at the door but the woman was lighting another cigarette and did not look in her direction.

She drove past the brightly lit shopping centre with its arches and multi-storey car park. Apartments and town houses with colourful doorways had a fresh, recently built appearance. The flags of many nationalities fluttered from the courtyard of the Anaskeagh Arms. She crossed the bridge where spotlights reflected on the river and the tall clock face marked time.

*   *   *

Beth climbed the narrow stairs and walked to the end of the corridor where a sign on the door of the waiting room told her to enter and take a seat. Tom Oliver's reassuring face beamed down on her from election campaign posters, advising the population of Anaskeagh to cast their number one vote in his direction.

The old furniture showrooms had seemed so large when she was a child. Fancy glass doors, the smell of leather and wood, the hum of florescent lights beating mercilessly down on the cheap furniture he sold on credit to the women of Anaskeagh. How far removed from their poverty May had been, sitting behind the glass panels of her high desk, accepting their weekly repayments and snapping at children for putting their feet on the armchairs. The first floor had now become the politician's home and constituency clinic, reached through a side entrance. The ground floor had been converted into offices with a brass plaque on the outside wall engraved with the words, 'Conor Oliver. Solicitor'.

Moving back to Anaskeagh had been as difficult as she anticipated. Yet, under the revulsion she felt at living in such close proximity to her uncle, she was aware of an invigorating energy that had been missing for so long from her life. Sometimes, standing on the production floor of TrendLines with its rows of sewing machines and long cutting tables, immune to the cacophony of machinery and music, it seemed as if the intervening years had never happened and she was a young woman again, decisive, determined. At home and in the factory she was busier than ever, constantly on call to solve one problem after another. She had no title, insisting she did not want to be burdened with one. All aspects of TrendLines interested her. She needed to be accessible to everyone. It was an extension of motherhood, she thought on more than one occasion, laughing out loud at the absurdity and the truth of it.

The queue in the waiting room moved swiftly. Tom Oliver was an efficient administrator. However long his constituents wanted to gripe about their social welfare benefits, EU subsidies or difficult neighbours, they were smoothly ushered in and out with the minimum of delay. When she entered he rose from behind his desk and came towards her.

"Well, what do you know? Beth, my dear girl. Home at last."

"Yes, Tom, back at last – for better or worse."

"A wise move, my dear. Your husband was a lost man without you. A stressful time starting up a new company but when domestic problems are added it makes everything so much more difficult, don't you agree?"

"I do indeed, Tom. But it was necessary to be sure this was the right move for my family to make."

"No question about it." He gestured her towards a chair in front of his desk and sat back down, his legs crossed, one leg casually swinging backwards and forwards. "Dublin is such a rat-race these days. A sad reflection of our so-called progressive times. If you have any difficulties with schools please don't hesitate—"

"Everything is under control, thank you." She smoothly interrupted him. "Lindsey is staying with her grandmother in Oldport but she will visit us on a regular basis."

"The dear child … how is she? Recovered, I hope?"

She leaned towards him, lowering her voice. "I think it's important that we understand each other at this stage. Lindsey has told me everything – I repeat – everything. I came here tonight for one reason only, to tell you that if I see you within breathing distance of any of my children I will have no hesitation in destroying you." She rose to her feet, relieved to find the floor still steady beneath her. "Do I need to elaborate any further?"

"Dear Beth, you never change. Always the cruel word." His arrogance, his instant control of the situation was as forceful as ever. "Your daughter is a talented young lady but a mite unstable, wouldn't you agree? Drugs are the curse of our young people and it seems highly irresponsible to leave her in the care of that old woman instead of overseeing a proper rehabilitation programme for her. I'm aware that on this occasion the Gardaí took a lenient view of the whole sorry affair and organised meetings with a Juvenile Liaison Officer. Just as well we have an understanding police force. A criminal record at her age would be most unfortunate. However, she may not be so lucky the next time."

This was a game of power that could only be played if she stayed calm. "I've nothing further to say to you, except

to repeat my warning. Believe me, this is not an idle threat."
She turned and walked towards the door.

He called her name. When she turned he was behind
her, so close she could almost feel his presence forcing her
backwards against the wood. He bent forward until their
faces were level, making no attempt to touch her. "Where
is your gratitude, Mrs McKeever? The least I expected from
you was an appreciation of everything I have done for your
husband."

"Why should I thank you? Everything Stewart achieved
was done under his own steam. It had nothing to do with
you."

"Then tell him not to be so impatient. He's making a
nuisance of himself, phoning the ACII office and accusing
them of delaying his grants package. I've been informed that
he's being unnecessarily belligerent and the staff at ACII
have more to do than listen to a constant flow of
unwarranted complaints." His breath blew faintly cold on
her cheeks. He lowered his voice until the sound became
an intimate whisper. "But we are family, after all, Beth. It
would be wise to remember that the right word in the right
ear is a marvellous lubricant when it comes to oiling the
wheels of bureaucracy."

He moved away from her. For such a heavily built man
he was light on his feet. A dignified walk back to his desk,
his features arranged in his poster smile, ready to greet his
next constituent.

Tom Oliver owned Anaskeagh, a finger in every dubious
pie. She had watched him in action. An actor who never
fluffed his lines. Of course, his record was clean. One son

a solicitor. His second son a stockbroker in New York. Power to the family.

She drove from his constituency clinic and parked on the old disused pier. The tide was in, lapping dark against the wall. Some yachts and a large white cruiser belonging to her uncle were moored a short distance from the shore. Soon the pier would be converted into a marina but, for now, it was a lonely place with only an ocean to disturb her thoughts.

Sara came to Anaskeagh one last time. Catherine O'Donovan had seen her standing outside the farmhouse. Her camera hung from her neck. She had worn a long navy jumper, jeans and walking boots. When Catherine went out to invite her in she had disappeared.

"Perhaps she was a ghost," Catherine said. "She looked so insubstantial standing under the trees."

No ghost. Sara came to Anaskeagh after she returned from Africa. Her reasons for returning would always remain a mystery. Beth believed it had been a time of confrontation. Perhaps, also, she had sought healing in the shadow of Aislin's Roof . Whatever she sought she had not found and Beth was here in this place of restitution, ready to avenge her memory.

She had thought much about his death since her arrival. A sharp knife between his shoulders. A pillow pressed hard across his face while he slept. She had the strength and the will to do such things and kneel at peace beside his coffin. But they would bury him with full honours, read tributes over his grave, write obituaries in newspapers.

She wanted him to die slowly, loudly, aggressively. She wanted him to be the headline story, the inside page, the opinion column, the profile, the colour feature. She wanted journalists jogging his elbows, rooting in company records, researching, snooping, prying, faxing questions, demanding answers. She wanted flash bulbs chasing his car and cameras on the plinth of Dáil Eireann. She wanted a modern day execution.

Death by a thousand media knives.

*   *   *

New York was like a fist opening. Its noise overpowered Greg. It filled his line of vision. He welcomed the obscene heights of buildings, the anonymous crowds, the ceaseless roar of traffic. Between the towering skyscrapers he was able to breathe again. His tears or his laughter would fall unnoticed amongst the clamorous mass of creeds, cultures and colours that jostled past. How could anything he had done have significance in such surroundings? Human frailty or endeavour were equally irrelevant in a city that dominated the senses and diminished the ego. A fist had opened and he was free.

The only person willing to give him time was Eleanor Lloyd, a Limerick woman who worked as Stateside Review's chief advertising executive and had a soft spot for home-sick emigrants. They attended the opera together and dined in a small Greek restaurant close to the television station. She had divorced two husbands and settled on cats as the only tolerable live-in companions. Greg resisted a cat or a dog but he developed a relationship of sorts with an aquarium of sullen piranhas left behind by the previous tenant.

He knew the city from his student days. He had visited

it regularly when he worked on 'Elucidate'. A tourist on the trail of galleries and museums, the Empire State Building, the Guggenheim, the World Trade Centre, Central Park, seeking the idiosyncratic buzz of a city that prided itself on its aggressive indifference. On this occasion, he had no desire to gape at new sights. He could spend a life time on its streets and still never touch the core of this city. Instead, he developed a village mentality, staying close to his apartment in Greenwich Village, getting to know the nearby bars and shops and cafes.

Twenty years in New York had robbed Eleanor of the insatiable Irish lust for personal information. She asked no questions about his past. He felt no need to mention Eva and when he breathed Faye's name it was at night when he was alone. The pulse of the city beat silently outside his window. He never used to feel lonely in a city. On 'Stateside Review' there were opportunities to alleviate this state, beautiful women with anorexic shoulders and smiles that promised much. He resisted them, filled with a need to atone. Once a Catholic always a Catholic; punishment waited for those who sinned in the flesh. And when the punishment came it was a splinter, festering.

In his high rise apartment he watched the lights of New York City scar the skyline. The radio played classic hits, Freddy Mercury singing about champions with no time for losing. You lost out on that one, Freddy, he thought. But what a voice to leave behind. Such power. That was what it was all about. To leave something fine behind, music, words, a painting, a child … Something to mark the fact that he had lingered for a short while on the cusp of time.

CHAPTER FORTY-TWO

By the magic of moonlight Eva's cottage looked beautiful but she woke each morning to a heap of stones, protected by tarpaulin covers. It had become a blight on her horizon. Even the swans were hiding in the rushes, furious over the noise of drilling and hammering. She wondered if she was mad, chasing a dream amidst the clamour and humped earth with only Matt Morgan and his merry men for company?

She grew weary arguing with his crew of head-wreckers who called themselves carpenters, plumbers, plasterers. Tractors and diggers added to the din. If only this hullabaloo made a difference. It should be possible to bury her thoughts in the thump of a kanga hammer or the crash of falling masonry but sometimes there were phantom yearnings when she imagined the cry of a baby and her breasts tingled, as if milk was still flowing. The summer nights were mild. A full moon shone on the lake. The reeds stood tall and straight. The swans were sleeping, indifferent to her problems.

Her father arrived one afternoon and bullied her into coming back to Ashton for a week. Liz fussed and complained that she was too thin, malnourished and obsessed with murdering Matt Morgan. Eva obediently swallowed multi-vitamins and ate three solid meals a day, fretting and contacting Matt continuously on her mobile phone.

The early morning routine in Wind Fall had not changed. Guests rising for breakfast; then the slamming of car doors as they departed. Eva seldom entered the breakfast room, preferring the intimacy of the kitchen where she helped Liz prepare the bacon and slice freshly baked brown bread.

One morning, on her way to the river, she passed the wide window of the breakfast room. It was empty except for one guest who was speaking to her mother. The slope of Liz's shoulders and the man's serious expression as he turned to gaze at a christening photograph on the wall alerted her. They were talking about Faye. For an instant, she felt exposed, gossip fodder for a stranger. Her apprehension quickly died away. Liz was not a gossip. Her relationship with her guests was friendly but confined to light conversation about the weather and places of interest they should visit.

Later, by the river, she saw him again. At first she thought he was an angler and, having registered his presence, forgot about him. She was startled some time later when he spoke, apologising for disturbing her. He was staying at Wind Fall and wondered if she was Mrs Frawley's daughter?

Eva nodded, angry at having to make conversation, angrier still when he sat on the grass beside her. He laid an easel and sketch pad between them. His trousers were paint-stained. A briar had torn the pocket of his jacket, rust coloured threads hung loose. He gazed towards the river.

"It's such a peaceful place," he said. "It must have looked exactly the same a hundred years ago."

His voice had a hesitancy that irritated her, as if he was judging each word before he uttered it. Yet it was a strong voice, too loud in her head, too intrusive. He wondered if it was possible to paint such stillness. She glanced at his sketch pad. Scribbles, slashes. She did not want him painting her river. She did not want him sitting beside her, disturbing her solitude. His beard gave him a wild look, as if he should be climbing mountains or hacking forgotten trails in some far off outback. When she asked him to leave her alone he rose to his feet immediately. He was composed as he gathered his pad and easel.

"Mrs Frawley told me about your child," he said, his voice dropping low. "I wish I could find words to comfort you."

She flinched from his well-meaning sympathy and made no reply.

He nodded, acknowledging her desire to be left alone. He said goodbye and walked away. His car was missing from the driveway when she returned to Wind Fall.

* * *

Marjory was still in her dressing gown when Beth called to

see her after work. The air in the kitchen was musty, stale spilled milk and too many cigarettes.

"I was doing my shopping and decided to get a few things for you." She unpacked the groceries and stacked them into presses, resisting the temptation to open windows. "Why don't you make me a cup of tea while I put these away?"

Ignoring the suggestion, Marjory slumped in a chair and lit a cigarette. "How much do I owe you?"

"You don't owe me a penny. Can't I do something for you without it having a price?"

"Everything has a price, no matter how much you sweet talk your way around it." She gazed vaguely into the smoke and tapped her cigarette into an unwashed cup. Beth tried to control her annoyance. Her dislike for her mother often shocked her. She tried to assuage this guilt through regular visits and invitations to come to the bungalow. Marjory always refused. Since she sold her boutique she was drifting through each day, filling her kitchen sink with tea bags and cigarette butts. Worried over her mother's vagueness, Beth had checked the medicine cabinet on a previous visit and was shocked to see the amount of medication on the shelves.

"Why don't you come to dinner on Sunday?" she asked, making tea and sitting down opposite her.

"Conor and Jean have invited me to Cherry Vale," Marjory snapped. "I don't need your charity. I've managed well enough without it until now."

"The children want to know you better, Marjory. You should give them a chance."

"I saw that daughter of yours in town last week. She's a disgrace the way she dresses. Those rings on her face are disgusting." She shuddered. "I'm ashamed to be associated with her. As for that boy with her – I'd lock my doors when he's around, if I were you."

Beth opened her mouth to argue and closed it again. Nothing she said would make any difference. As she drove home, she wondered what her visits achieved. Marjory showed no joy in her company but, occasionally, Beth's presence gave her a chance to talk about Sara, to mourn her aloud and wander back in time to her daughter's shining childhood.

Lindsey was working in Woodstock for her summer holidays and seeing Tork Hansen again. No furtive meetings this time. She had brought him to Anaskeagh and presented him to her parents. His dreadlocks were as intimidating as ever but he was a tame sight compared to her provocative, pierced and tattooed daughter. No wonder Marjory was horrified.

Her own relationship with Lindsey was still abrasive, still prone to sudden rows but it had a deeper layer, an acceptance that Stewart must not discover the true facts about her last visit to Tom Oliver's apartment. They did not acknowledge this conspiracy to protect him. It remained an unspoken agreement – an acceptance that Beth would protect her children and keep them safe from night terrors.

Stewart admired the tattoos on Lindsey's shoulders: a ferocious eagle, a delicate rose, a fairy floating on gossamer wings; they multiplied alarmingly. "They're so extraordinarily detailed," he remarked after inspecting the latest one through a magnifying glass. "Like beautiful postage stamps."

"If I want to appreciate stamps I'll start my own collection," Beth retorted. "But I'd prefer to look at them on envelopes rather than on my daughter's body."

She often suspected there was a closet Hell's Angel throbbing beneath the calm exterior of her practical husband and was beginning to appreciate this hidden element of his personality, especially in the dark hours when he drew her into his arms. His old Harley Davidson was displayed in the reception area of TrendLines, a talking point when visitors came to the factory. Did everyone live their lives in tandem with hidden desires? she wondered. Safely compartmentalised, safely controlled.

"Don't you dare tell Peter Wallace I know anything," Lindsey warned her at every opportunity. "I hate him more than ever! What did you ever see in him? You must have been stoned out of your mind."

From the mouths of aggressive teenagers a truth could sometimes shine.

Stewart had been devastated by Lindsey's collapse and, later, by the realisation that she knew the truth about her natural father. In the weeks that followed, Beth had watched the bond between her husband and her daughter grow stronger. When Lindsey visited Anaskeagh they went for long walks along the cliff path behind the bungalow or climbed to the summit of Anaskeagh Head. Beth had no idea what they spoke about during their time together and they did not confide in her. She knew it would be Stewart, not she or Peter, who would bring their child through this crisis and felt no resentment at being on the outside of the close-knit relationship they had always shared.

Lindsey had refused offers from two art colleges and intended repeating her Leaving. If she achieved the necessary points next year she planned to study computer science and shrugged dismissively whenever Beth asked what had happened to her artistic ambitions. Painting had become a hobby, a convenient way to earn extra money in Nuala O'Neill's gallery. All those hills and the twisting roads rounding into breathtaking views of the Atlantic were just begging for a canvas, she declared. Even the rainy days suited her. Not everyone wanted azure skies on their walls. A rain drenched landscape could fetch a higher price because it was more atmospheric.

"Painting by numbers," she called her landscapes, deriding the pretty views she painted yet spending all her spare time working on them. Genetic roots sprouting.

*   *   *

"My dear boy. What a pleasure it is to see a familiar face." Tom Oliver rose to his feet when Greg entered Stateside Review's hospitality room. He grasped the journalist's shoulder, a vigorous wincing grip and smiled warmly. "I can relax now that I'm in the hands of a true professional."

The politician had arrived in New York the previous day, heading an Irish trade delegation. His interview would feature on the evening programme. Kieran Oliver, a small, colourless man with a startling dickey-bow, accompanied him. He offered Greg a lacklustre handshake, as if the ebullience of his father had drained him of any desire to compete.

As always, the politician was relaxed in front of the cameras. He spoke movingly about the curse of emigration and how Mother America had taken the Irish Diaspora into her welcoming arms. But a new day was dawning. He had a vision that would stem the haemorrhage of young blood from the land. In forgotten corners of Ireland he was involved in establishing creative centres of opportunity and employment. Greg admired his ability to flog the same hobby horse on every occasion and make it sound different each time.

The politician was a chameleon who blended into any environment, comfortable with his parochial roots, yet projecting an urbane image that embraced the problems of the nation. Greg had tried and failed on many occasions to penetrate the affable mask he wore. Rumours occasionally surfaced about his past. Questions about land deals had been asked but there had never been any evidence to carry a story. The documentary made for 'Elucidate' had been as boring as it was faultless, forgotten as soon as filming ended. Only Hatty Beckett – a diminutive, feisty redhead who sat high on a bar stool in the Anaskeagh Arms and ordered four glasses of rum and coke on Elucidate's tab – had been prepared to speak her mind.

"Transparency!" she snarled at Greg. "Now, that's a fine new word altogether. For what it's worth, Tom Oliver is about as transparent as the arse on an elephant – and I haven't the slightest problem putting it on the record."

On the corner of River Mall, a modern shopping centre stood in place of her famous chip shop. Hatty had been the stumbling block in its development, the only tenant who refused to move from the building. Her lease still had eight years to run and she refused her landlord's offer to buy it back. Visits from a health inspector began soon afterwards.

Rats were discovered in the storeroom and her business was closed down overnight.

"I know he was behind it," she insisted. "He was getting his kick-back from Ben Layden, the developer. That pair are as close as the hairs on a dog's coat. How soon can I go on the telly and say so?" She took a powder compact from her bag, inspected her face and lavishly applied crimson lipstick. It matched her hair perfectly. Hatty Beckett was determined not to grow old graciously.

Greg explained the problems she would encounter if she made such an accusation and the official files from the health inspector were used to discredit her story.

"Bugger that!" Hatty snorted. "The only rats in my chip shop were the two-legged variety and I'm only sorry I didn't have the guts to lay rat poison down for them." She glared around the lounge bar of the Anaskeagh Arms, daring anyone to defy her, then clicked her fingers for another rum and coke.

Hatty was fun but he had to let her go. No substance. Maybe she was telling the truth but truth without proof was a lost cause, too easy to manipulate and spin. He had seen it buried under soundbites and platitudes, losing its meaning under the loudest voice, the most forceful argument. He knew them all – the skilful abusers of word power, the media manipulators and even the media itself, all with their own hidden agendas.

"I must say that went extremely well." At the end of the interview Tom Oliver rubbed his hands together, daring Greg to look sceptical.

"As always, Deputy." Greg unclipped microphones and

escorted him back to the hospitality room where Kieran Oliver waited.

"How's Hatty Beckett?" Greg asked as they were about to enter. "Has she emigrated yet?"

"Hatty Beckett emigrate?" The politician paused at the door and smiled roguishly. "Now, that would be a sad day for Anaskeagh. Why do you ask?"

"She claimed you were behind a campaign to close her restaurant."

"Quite the little eccentric, isn't she?" His smile never wavered. "Her restaurant, as you so quaintly call it, was closed by the health authorities. As a result of this fortuitous action, the level of stomach viruses in our town went down overnight. The one problem with politics is that people blame you for everything that goes wrong in their lives and never think of saying thank you when things work out."

Before he left the television centre, Kieran Oliver proffered his limp handshake. "It was a pleasure meeting you, Greg. I hope you'll come to dinner soon. I'll be in touch shortly to arrange it."

CHAPTER FORTY-THREE

Three mornings a week, before the children awoke, Beth swam in a small cove close to the bungalow. Usually, she was the only person swimming at such an early hour but, occasionally, she met Conor Oliver jogging along the cliff path. One morning, when she emerged from the water, he had climbed down into the cove and was sitting on the rocks, watching her.

"Morning, Beth." He touched his forehead in a mock salute. "It's fit and well you're looking these days." He had his father's eyes, appraising. "Keep Saturday night free. We're having a party at Cherry Vale."

"A special occasion?" she asked.

"My father's birthday. Seventy years of living the high life and he's still as energetic as a man half his age. This will be an excellent opportunity for you and Stewart to meet the good people of Anaskeagh."

"You're very kind but—"

"No excuses, Beth." He wagged a warning finger at her.

"We've seen little enough of you and your family since you arrived."

"We've been so busy." She shrugged apologetically.

"We're all busy people. It's the way of the world today but this is a special occasion. I'm sure Stewart appreciates the importance of family connections, even if you don't." He had tied a sweat band across his forehead and it emphasised his large face and dark moustache. She had heard he was a formidable solicitor and had no reason to doubt it. His heavy thighs juddered, ready to take off on the final leg of his run. "Don't forget. Eight o'clock in Cherry Vale."

Stewart was heading towards the shower when she entered the bedroom. "What do you think you're doing, Mrs McKeever?" he demanded when she slipped up behind him and whipped the towel from his hips. "Trying to bring on a cardiac arrest. Wives have been burned at the stake for less." She laughed softly as he pushed the beach robe away and sank his face into her shoulder. "You do know that you're an exhausting woman?" he moaned, hurrying her onto the rumpled duvet where they had loved each other so often since her arrival in Anaskeagh. They made love urgently but quietly, aware that their children would leave home in horror if they realised what their parents did when they had a little time to spare.

"Just as well we read the four-minute management book." When he recovered his breath he grinned down at her. "Can we have a repeat performance tonight – with extra time for good behaviour added on?"

"If you ask nicely and don't work me too hard in the

factory you never know your luck." She luxuriated in their last few moments of freedom. "By the way, I met Conor Oliver in the cove. There's a big celebration in Cherry Vale on Saturday."

"We're not going." He nuzzled her neck, making no attempt to release her. "If it's not depraved sex then all I want at the weekends are my armchair and slippers."

She eased away from his embrace, keeping her tone light. "It's my uncle's birthday party. So, if you want to be a mover and shaker in this town it would be advisable to make an appearance. The powers-that-be from the ACII will be there. Perhaps we can bang a few heads together and get some action on those grants."

"Or give them a toe up the arse." Abruptly, he rose from the bed and wrapped the towel around his hips. It was time to waken the children and drive them to O'Donovan's farm. The brief interlude they had shared was over. Already, she could see the pressures of the factory settling on Stewart: delays and bureaucratic hold-ups, cancelled appointments with ACII officials, unanswered phone calls. The blocks he had set so firmly in place were beginning to shift. This time he headed towards the en suite and showered without interruption.

*　　*　　*

Eva had her first garden design contract if she wanted to accept it. It could be a lucrative contract, Judith Hansen said when she rang. The florist had purchased the building next door to Woodstock when it came on the market and was expanding into fresh organic fruit and vegetables. Tork was setting up a market garden to supply much of the produce and had entered a partnership with a businessman, who was prepared to finance him.

"He's renting land to Tork," said Judith. "It needs landscaping and cultivating. The owner wants to meet you. Are you interested?"

"Yes, I'm interested," Eva replied. It sounded a lucrative contract and she desperately needed money. A bad drainage problem and subsidence in the cottage foundations had taken their toll on her grandmother's legacy. Her bank manager displayed little sympathy when Eva mentioned cash flow problems. The future was uncertain. In truth, when she had the courage to think about it, her future was a mess.

*　　*　　*

Cherry Vale was decorated with congratulatory banners and balloons printed with the politician's name. His friends gathered in a loud circle, fleshy men who dined well and had a keen awareness of fine wines. Beth wandered outside to the garden, searching for a familiar face. Silver lights twinkled from trees. Night candles fluttered among the flower beds. The tennis court was still in place but the shed, where Sadie once languidly rested surrounded by her new born pups, had become a high domed glass conservatory and was serving as a bar for the occasion.

"Your uncle's looking mighty pleased with himself tonight." A statuesque woman in a backless dress and a dramatic silver choker around her neck joined her. Nuala O'Neill tilted her glass in the direction of the politician who had strolled into the garden, immediately attracting a crowd around him. His laughter reached them as he turned to stare in their direction. He bowed his head graciously when they smiled across at him.

"Politics has been good to him," replied Beth.

"He certainly doesn't look his age." Nuala watched as he moved on to the next group, shaking hands, kissing cheeks. "Lining your pockets at the nation's expense must be the best way to stay young and vigorous."

"Some say he's done an excellent job up to now," said Beth.

"Who says?"

"Those in the know."

"The Anaskeagh Mafia, you mean." They laughed quietly together, relaxed in each other's company. A spontaneous friendship had developed between them when they met in Nuala's gallery shortly after Beth's arrival in Anaskeagh. They shared the common bond of outsiders who were part of the community by birth but separated by experiences, and finding it difficult to reclaim their space.

"Have you spoken to Derry Mulhall yet?" Nuala asked, quietly.

"I called twice. He never answers."

"Keep trying. You'll be interested in what he has to say."

"Does he ever ask about his son?" Beth asked.

"He would – if I gave him the opportunity." Nuala smiled, grimly. "I don't." She quickly changed the subject as the politician walked towards them. "If you're talking to Lindsey tell her to call and see me when she's in town again. I've sold another one of her paintings."

"Lindsey is indeed a most talented young lady," Tom Oliver moved smoothly between them. "I've seen her work in your wonderful gallery, Nuala. I hope she appreciates the opportunity you're giving her." He smiled fondly at Beth. "If she manages to keep a steady head on her shoulders she'll be famous one of these days, mark my words."

Jean Oliver appeared at the patio door to announce that food was being served. In the main drawing room her husband exploded bottles of champagne and proposed a toast to his father. As the glasses were raised Marjory rose unsteadily from an armchair and clapped her hands. "For he's a jolly good fellow, for he's a jolly good fellow." Her reedy voice trembled off-key. The guests, embarrassed, began to sing along with her. When the song ended she clawed the air in confusion before she sank back down again, breathing heavily.

"Poor Marjory, the medication she's on doesn't mix with alcohol but she never listens." Jean spoke quietly to Beth. "She's an incredibly lonely woman. We hoped when your family moved here she would begin to relax but she's as wound up as ever." She paused, diplomatically. "Do you think you could persuade her to leave now, for her own sake?"

"Of course." Beth crossed the room to her mother and took her hand, suddenly moved by the ravaged expression on her face. "Marjory, if you're feeling tired I can drive you home."

"Why are you always trying to ruin things?" Marjory immediately became aggressive, drawing backwards and sitting ramrod straight on her chair. "I'm enjoying myself. Leave me alone."

"It's no trouble—" Beth stopped abruptly when the politician's arm circled her waist.

"I'll drive her home when she's ready to go," he

murmured in her ear. "I've always taken care of my own and I'm not going to stop now."

CHAPTER FORTY-FOUR

With advance warning, Eva had time to tidy the caravan and tie up her hair before her client arrived. She changed her jeans and took off her wellingtons. She applied perfume and eyeliner. Word travelled fast and one prospective customer begged another. First impressions were important.

She recognised him immediately. His beard still needed trimming. He had a firm dry handshake and held her hand for a moment longer than she thought was necessary. The same jacket, crumpled rust-coloured linen with a torn pocket. Judith said he was a widower, awkward without a woman to sew him into shape. She wondered what he had been doing in Ashton. Painting, probably. Aware that she had recognised him, he apologised for intruding on her privacy when she sat alone by the river. He understood about grief. He knew what it could do. The personal nature of his conversation surprised her. Business deals were not usually done in an atmosphere of yearning memories. Nor were they done in the middle of a bomb site.

She invited him into the caravan, thankful she had taken the precaution of tidying it. She was startled at how much at home he looked relaxing back against the cushions. Hard to imagine him behind a desk. He was too unkempt to inspire confidence yet he sat calmly in her caravan and discussed money in the matter-of-fact manner of an experienced businessman.

"When will it be convenient to visit Havenstone?" he asked.

"Havenstone?" she glanced enquiringly at him.

"My house. I want you to see the grounds first. Then we can discuss the possibilities."

She was suddenly nervous at the thought of her first major contract without her father's knowledgeable hand on her elbow. He saw her hesitation and misunderstood it, offering immediately to pay for the consultation.

"It's not that. I haven't worked since before ..." She paused, unable to continue.

He spoke gently for her. "Since Faye died."

The name of her child on this stranger's lips seemed natural. She took a deep breath and nodded, rigidly. Only afterwards did she wonder about the emotion in his voice.

"Monday," he said. "Come and see me on Monday."

Judith rang the following day. "Well, what do you think?"

"I have to see the grounds first."

"You don't sound too sure. Do you have a problem with him? He can be rather aloof but he's fine when you get to know him. He's been through a hard time since his wife died."

"When did she die?"

"Last year — a sad affair."

Something in Judith's tone quickened her interest. "She must have been quite young?"

"Too young to die," Judith agreed. "Afterwards, he was going to sell his house but he changed his mind and now Tork has persuaded him to lease his land."

The decision to withdraw his house came without warning. Carrie Davern was furious. She had new-age millionaires lined up and was counting her commission. Tough. Eva disliked the estate agent with her cold, speculative eyes and the ability to sell a nightmare under the guise of a dream.

Peter Wallace had intrigued her. Before he left her caravan he had glanced out the window and asked how she was managing to stay sane with the wrecking crew in action. He knew Matt Morgan by reputation.

"A temperamental man," he said. "Have you noticed?"

She nodded. The flood gates opened. She found herself telling this stranger about the rows and the delays and the hearing problems Matt suffered if she pointed out a flaw in his work. How she was afraid to bully him in case he downed tools and headed off on another job.

Peter Wallace asked to see the architectural plans. After studying them intently he went outside to look around. He talked to Matt, pointing to the walls and the bricks stacked on one side of the cottage. He tapped the plans, forcing the builder to look closely at them. His manner was high-handed, a born autocrat. She waited for Matt to stride off the site in a temper tantrum but, before she could intervene, he nodded sheepishly. She almost expected him to touch his forelock. Peter Wallace returned to the caravan, ducking his head as he entered. He offered his opinion. Matt had experienced some problems but he would soon have everything sorted out. She need have no further worries.

"I am perfectly capable of looking after my own business affairs," she snapped, angry that she had inadvertently revealed so much to a stranger.

"I wouldn't dream of suggesting otherwise but the bricks Matt intended using looked different to the ones specified on the plans." He stared evenly back at her. "An understandable mistake and easily rectified."

The thought of someone looking out for her interests made her legs tremble. She sat down, suddenly realising she was exhausted. After he drove away she marched over to Matt. "If you ever again try to pull one over on me you'll be off this job so fast you'll think there's a rocket up your arse," she shouted.

"Mother of God!" Matt was shocked. "That's no way for a lady to talk. Your mother should wash your mouth out with soap."

"I'm not joking, Matt. Don't you dare cut corners when you're working for me. I want the exact materials that are in the architect's plans. Understand? And I want this job finished on time. If you skive off and do any more nixers you can sing falsetto for your money."

He got nasty. He gestured towards the mud heaps. "If you insist on using threats instead of acting in a civilised manner we might as well call a halt to things right now. But I'll drag you through the courts for every penny you owe me."

"What about the Revenue Commissioners?" she

demanded, enjoying the startled look on his face. "How much do you owe them?"

"Don't bluff with me, lady." He was rising on his toes, ready to walk. "Everything I do is straight up."

"I'm not a lady, Mr Morgan. On more than one occasion I've been called a thundering bitch – and everything you do is not straight up. I have the evidence to prove it. Film. I followed you last week and two days the week before. I used my video camera to record exactly what you're doing when you're supposed to be working on my cottage. But that's between you and your friendly tax inspector. As long as you understand that you're working to a time contract and doing a job to the exact specifications in my plans, we should be able to get out of each other's hair as soon as possible."

"It was never going to be otherwise, lady." His voice was grimly resigned to working for a thundering bitch. "If you will allow me to resume my work I have a time contract to honour."

Back in the caravan she did not know whether to laugh or cry. He had bought her bluff. She was filled with elation. The first time since Faye's death that she felt alive again, without guilt, without kitten claws tearing her chest apart.

*   *   *

The grants package promised by the ACII finally came through. A sudden snipping of red tape. Power to the family. Tom Oliver called to the factory to assure Beth that everything was under control. He entered her office without knocking. He beamed at her, pleased that he was able to assist her husband. On the golf course he had met the owner of First Lady. Sam O'Grady had been effusive in his praise of TrendLines.

CHAPTER FORTY-FIVE

Derry Mulhall's cottage crouched on the edge of the Anaskeagh Business Centre. Apart from a spiral of smoke drifting listlessly from the chimney and the occasional sound of dogs barking, there was little sign of life within the peeling, mud-spattered walls. The front door was closed, the curtains drawn. Occasionally, Derry left his cottage and headed to the bar in the Anaskeagh Arms. On such occasions he talked too much. He was beaten up one night and left unconscious in a dark lane. He survived but not to tell the tale. After that, he drank more quietly, mainly in his stale kitchen in the company of dogs.

Beth approached the small cottage for the third time and knocked on the front door.

"You're wasting your time if you're trying to sell me something, Missus." Derry Mulhall glared suspiciously at her when he finally answered.

"I only want a few minutes of your time, Mr Mulhall," she replied. "I work in the business centre."

His eyes glittered. "That shower of fucking parasites. Get back where you came from – fucking blow-ins!"

"I'm originally from Anaskeagh. You used to know my father, Barry Tyrell."

"Be God, I did." For an instant his face softened then settled back into its belligerent lines. "And your mother too, a rare bitch of a woman, still is, from all accounts. You're Tom Oliver's niece, then?"

She nodded and stared across the field towards the business centre built on land once owned by the Mulhall family. She doubted if planning permission had ever been received for erecting her uncle's ramshackle factory but in those days no one objected, even when it closed down overnight, leaving the workers destitute. A forgotten building, no questions asked.

"We can't choose our relations, Mr Mulhall, although we can choose to disown them. You look like your son, Kevin. Nuala showed me his photograph. It was taken in Tokyo."

From inside his kitchen a dog barked. The farmer shouted over his shoulder and the animal fell silent. Beth imagined it cowering under a chair, out of reach of this surly man's boot. He moved from the shelter of his doorway and pushed his face forward. "He's not my fucking son and it's none of your fucking business, anyway. Don't you dare come here making accusations."

"I'm not making accusations. I'm here to talk about the sale of your land."

He pointed towards the gate, a sudden flush rising in his cheeks. "The gate's that way, Missus. Make sure you close it on your way out."

The dog began to bark again. A second dog joined in, a thinner, more feminine yelp.

"Who can you talk to any more, Mr Mulhall?" She stood firmly before him. "From what I hear you've been well and truly muffled."

"No one muffles Derry Mulhall. May their balls roast in hell for trying."

"I heard you were badly beaten up."

"Broken bones mend – what the fuck is he doing in Tokyo?"

"Designing skyscrapers," Beth replied. "What a pity you didn't realise your land would be rezoned so soon after you'd sold it. Imagine the profit you'd have made if you'd known the ACII were interested in building on it."

"What's your game, Missus?" he demanded. "If you're here to stir up trouble I've already told you where to find the gate."

"You were robbed, Mr Mulhall. Everyone knows that for a fact but no one is saying it out loud. I came here to see if there was some way of exposing the truth. But if you're not prepared to talk I won't take up any more of your time."

He threw back his strong red neck and laughed. "Jesus, Missus, but you're soft in the head if that's the way you're thinking. There's stories I could tell that would make your hair stand up straight but what's the sense in being dead. I'll be there soon enough and I'd prefer to do it with the help of the bottle rather than them shaggers in the Anaskeagh Mafia. What did you say your name is?"

"I didn't, but it's Beth McKeever."

"A quare sort of a niece you are – out here trying to make trouble for your uncle. You'd better come in seeing as how you've nosed your way into my business. But I'm not promising anything, mind."

The smoky kitchen caught against her breath. The dogs were cowering as she had suspected. A bowl of eggs and a half empty bottle of whiskey sat on the kitchen table. He offered her tea and a boiled egg. She accepted. The egg tasted like rubber. He poured whiskey into her cup and watched while she drank it neat. He told her his story.

"Talk to Kitty Grimes if you want proof," he said when she was leaving. "A more God-fearing woman never walked the streets of Anaskeagh and she knows what she heard from the mouth of that crook."

She left the photograph of his son on the table. He put it out of sight behind a clock. She did not ask for it back. He did not offer it.

Kitty Grimes worked as a machinist in TrendLines, a quiet nervous woman with a story to tell. Her husband had worked in Tom Oliver's furniture factory until its closure. Not a word to the workers, no warning, nothing. He died soon afterwards. Her mouth trembled when she mentioned his name. A quiet life snuffed out with the stress of it all, and who cared at the end of the day?

Little stories oozing quietly from the mouths of little people. Like Hatty Beckett, whose tongue was as sharp as ever. Until Beth arrived in Anaskeagh no one was listening.

CHAPTER FORTY-SIX

The reporter from 'Elucidate' was waiting when Beth parked her car at the old castle. Sheep grazed nearby and a flock of crows wheeled and dived over the empty fields. They picked their way through the long grass, heading towards the ruins of the castle. She disliked his lips, a pompous mouth that tightened angrily each time his fine woollen trousers snagged on briars. In the shelters of the walls she began to talk. Justin Boyd made no effort to hide his impatience.

"Let me get a grip on this," he said, interrupting her to check over his notes. "Your only sources are an alcoholic farmer and a chip shop owner whose business was forced to close because she broke hygiene regulations. That's one hell of a story to hand me."

"There is a story here and you can get to the bottom of it," Beth retorted. "I've seen what 'Elucidate' can do."

"But why should we invest time and money on the flimsy evidence you've just presented? If there are shady dealings afoot regarding land rezoning, and I stress – if –

there won't even be a postage stamp with Tom Oliver's signature on it. Will the farmer talk on the record?"

"Around here you don't make accusations about Tom Oliver too loudly," she admitted. "He can be a powerful enemy but I guarantee that once you scratch below the surface you'll be surprised at what people know and are prepared to reveal."

"I can't help wondering why you're so interested in destroying his reputation?" He regarded her suspiciously, touching his hair protectively when the wind lifted. It was obvious he had lost interest in the interview. Her carefully prepared scenario began to fall apart. She sounded too anxious, a vindictive woman with an axe to grind.

"He's a sleaze merchant, always has been, and he controls some of the officials in the ACII."

"So, what are you?" he asked. "The conscience of the nation?"

"No – I leave that honour to 'Elucidate'."

"It's a role we can only assume when we have information that is tangible." He flicked his note book closed. "'Elucidate' is inundated with stories and each one is carefully vetted before we make a decision. What I've got from you so far is pub gossip, innuendo. It's not enough, Mrs McKeever." He glanced pointedly at his watch. "Now, if you'll excuse me, I've a long drive back to Dublin."

"At least talk to Derry Mulhall."

"I'll see him before I leave. My gut instinct tells me this is a cul-de-sac but I'll discuss it with my producer and ring you when we've made a decision."

Justin Boyd finally returned her calls. Derry Mulhall had

been belligerent and drunk. A wild dog had shredded the leg of his trousers and the farmer had refused to call it to heel. The journalist's voice shook with anger. The file on Tom Oliver was whiter than white. There was no story. "The only problem I have with him is that he's a puffed-up ball of self-importance," he said. "But if that was a crime they could move Dáil Eireann to Mountjoy Jail."

"What about the Michael Hannon story?" she asked. "How did that start? I suppose the information was presented to you in its entirety and you had nothing to do except present us with the grand exposé."

"The Michael Hannon exposé had nothing to do with me. And the journalist responsible is otherwise engaged."

*   *   *

In the gatherings of film producers, actors, authors, musicians and visiting politicians, Greg was under no illusions that he had been invited to the Upper East Side of New York for his charm. Kieran Oliver was a collector of people. He dealt in stocks and shares and was finely tuned to the celebrity value of his guests. Greg bore him no ill will. The stockbroker served a handsome table and Greg was simply expected to make witty, insider political comments whenever the conversation demanded it.

When he was mugged one evening it added to his status. With zero tolerance, muggings in subways were becoming a rarity – but muggers still lurked in dark corners, still struck with sudden ferocity, and this was an insignificant event, witnessed only by buskers in ponchos, playing pan pipes. Greg thought he heard a bodhrán in the background but

that could have been his past life flashing before his eyes –
or the drumming of his heart.

His attacker wore an Adidas top, combat trousers and
trainers with thick-ridged soles. Within seconds, he had
pinned Greg efficiently against the tiled wall, the point of
a knife pricking the taut flesh under his chin. It was
impossible to understand what he was saying but his
message was clear enough. Greg removed his wallet, calfskin
leather, a gift from Eva, their first Christmas together. He
removed the money and held on to the wallet. The rasping
strains from the pan pipes floated towards them as the
mugger sprayed saliva over his face. He felt an itch, almost
an irritant in his throat and realised it was a warm trickle
of blood. His only emotion was one of incredulity that his
life could hang so easily in the balance of this young man's
crazed decision.

The musicians kept playing. Honey-skinned girls
giggled as they ran past. Passengers bought evening papers
and bagels. Trains continued to run on schedule. This, then,
was the meaning of indifference. The reality of invisibility.
The essence of diminishment.

"Count yourself lucky." The doctor in the casualty
department had seen too much to even pretend sympathy.
"I could be signing you over for an autopsy."

He woke at night, sweating, smelling the fetid breath of
his attacker, the tip of the knife against his skin. His baby's
existence had been snuffed out with the same whimsical
indifference. He could have raged against fate but what
good would it do? He became a journalist to find the
beginning of a story but the story kept fragmenting. There

was no logic to anything, just random events that defined people for the rest of their lives, leaving them with the eternal unanswerable question – if only … if only …

*   *   *

In the garden of Havenstone, the roots of old trees splayed like magnificent tendons across the grass. Roses climbed the walls, an abundance of white blossom forming an arch above the entrance to the house.

"Why do you want to change such a beautiful garden?" Eva asked. She was uneasy in this peaceful space, strangely reluctant to see it torn apart by diggers and landscaped to a new plan. Bees droned and hovered over lush borders of summer flowers, penstemons, phloxes, daisies, bergamots; spires of colour spilling a delicate fragrance into the air.

"That was never my intention," Peter Wallace replied. "The project I have in mind is at the back of the house."

She followed him around the side entrance into a terraced garden. White camellias blossomed in terracotta pots but the garden furniture looked neglected. Steps led down to a second level where an ornate fountain had become a repository for bird droppings and dead leaves. They reached a copse of slender trees which eventually led into a claustrophobic wilderness of briars, hawthorn and a shrivelled crab apple orchard. Rusting remains of metal frames and an old wall were almost obscured by thick layers of ivy.

An evening mist was falling. Midges swarmed around them, swirling on the smell of dead vegetation. When she slipped on rotting leaves he reached out to steady her, his gaze inscrutable in the flickering shadows.

"My father used to grow vines here," he said. "Some notion he had about making his own wine. This is the area Tork Hansen wants to cultivate."

They returned to the house which echoed with emptiness, the antique furniture sitting in dusty, airless rooms. The walls were bare. Lighter patches showed where paintings or photographs once hung. Eva wanted to fling open windows, fill the rooms with flowers, drown the fusty atmosphere with loud music. Marching bands might do the trick.

She promised to draw up plans, do her costings. Heavy machinery would be involved in the early stages and she would need to check access. For the first time since entering Havenstone, she felt motivated. In her mind she saw how it would look. Greenhouses and a walled kitchen garden. Trees heavy with fruit, vegetables all in a row, tubs of marjoram, rosemary, sage, dill, a bay leaf tree, vines clinging and climbing.

CHAPTER FORTY-SEVEN

Beth stared in amazement at the deep trenches and heavy machinery, at the heaps of mud, uprooted bushes, the crumbling outline of an old wall.

"Lindsey told me Tork had some scheme in mind but I'd no idea it involved so much work. Who's doing it for you?"

"A landscape designer I employed."

"He's good."

"She," Peter replied shortly and led her back to the house. He had phoned her at the weekend, wondering when she would be in Dublin on business, and suggested she call to Havenstone. He had cooked red snapper which he served with salsa and baked potatoes.

"I've offered Lindsey one of the rooms for a studio," he said when the meal was over and they were drinking coffee.

"So I heard. I'm sorry she was so rude."

He shook his head. "Her rudeness I can take. It's her indifference that hurts the most. She knows, doesn't she? We can't keep up this charade any longer."

She nodded, tired of lies and prevarication. "She knows but she won't accept it. She loves Stewart too much to let go of any part of their relationship."

"What can I do?" he asked, bleakly. "How can I reach her, knowing she hates me so much?"

"I don't know," she admitted. "In time, perhaps, she'll come to terms with everything but for the moment the only room she needs is in here." Beth touched her head with her index finger. "Stop trying so hard, Peter. If you give her the space she needs then maybe you'll both be able to form some kind of relationship in the future. Just don't try to shape it with preconceived ideas before it has a chance to develop. Nothing about Lindsey is easy. You'll never be able to take Stewart's place in her affections but there are other ways of reaching out to her."

*   *   *

Peter Wallace expressed surprise that the work had progressed so fast. He complimented Eva on what had been achieved, examining the walls she had uncovered, and listened intently when she discussed her plans with him. She was conscious of his scrutiny, a subtle, brooding awareness, difficult to pin down. Not a look that said he fancied her. Her instinct was never wrong in that department. No, it was something else, something too private for her to fathom but she sensed it and it made her nervous.

When he was not attending horticultural college, Tork Hansen worked by her side.

"Still swallowing flames?" she asked.

"Haven't you heard? Smoking is bad for your health."
He laughed and dug deep into the earth.

Occasionally, his girlfriend arrived with sandwiches and
flasks of the vilest, strongest coffee Eva had ever tasted. Her
fine dark eyebrows were decorated with tiny precisely
carved studs. They reminded Eva of bullets. A ring glistened
on her tongue when she opened her mouth. She never
stayed for long. If Peter appeared she took off with speed,
as if her appearance in the garden would anger him. She
offered to design a publicity leaflet for Eva's garden centre
and brought samples of her work to the caravan one night.
She suggested the name, Eva's Cottage Garden. It sounded
exactly right.

"We met before you started working in Havenstone,"
she said when she and Tork were leaving. She had a
penetrating stare that verged on rudeness. "In the village. I
thought you were a ghost – not that I believe in ghosts or
anything as crazy as that. But it's kind of weird. Every time
I see you I think of Sara."

Eva had no recollection of their meeting. "Sara?" she
asked, puzzled.

"She was married to my uncle. She's dead …" Her voice
trailed away. She climbed into the Woodstock van and Tork
accelerated away.

One evening, when she was leaving the garden, Peter
Wallace stretched out his hand as if he wanted to remove
something from her hair. For an instant, his hand remained
in a reaching position and she imagined his fingers in her
hair. A sharp, almost painful sensation flickered in her
stomach and she flinched, moved quickly aside, shocked at

her reaction. Later, alone in the caravan, she found twigs and leaves tangled in curls. She brushed them furiously to the floor.

The heavy work was finished and the contractors had departed. The landscaping was underway. Soon the greenhouses would be assembled, ventilated and electrified. They would have wooden frames that blended easily in their natural surroundings. Eva was bringing order to this wild place and the relief in the mornings when she left her own wilderness to drive to Havenstone was palpable.

October was a month of mist and light rain. Faye's birth month. A month that should have had a cake with one candle, balloons on the door. Eva drove to the cemetery and left flowers on her grave. She stood in a cemetery of angels, teddy bears and toy windmills blowing silently in the breeze. In the afternoon she spoke to Greg on the phone. He hung up when their silence grew too deep to break.

Peter Wallace had mentioned that he would be away for the day and she worked in his garden without resting. Tork, sensing her mood, kept his distance. Before leaving for Grahamstown she stopped off at the local supermarket to buy bread and milk. A baby lay in the cradle of a shopping trolley, pink and calm in a quilted sleeping bag. She raised her tiny pink fingers in a fist and let them fall again.

Eva stopped, unable to move past. She wanted to lift her in her arms and run to a silent place. She wanted her nipples to pucker under the suck of tiny gums. The back of her neck was cold with sweat as she moved away. Was this what she was destined to become? A demented baby thief, ripping babies from their prams and from the arms of their mothers?

She walked quickly from the supermarket and climbed into her van. Her legs trembled so much she was afraid to drive far. It was dark when she reached Havenstone. Peter had given her a key to the front door when she first accepted the contract. She turned it in the lock and entered the empty house. She sat by the long wooden kitchen table and stared at the surface, her eyes following the curving grain until it blurred. Then she placed her head against the wood, weeping.

She did not hear him enter. Her first awareness of his presence was the feel of his hands on her shoulders, a steady, comforting touch. She raised her head, covered her cheeks, appalled that he should discover her in such distress. Unable to speak, she ran from the kitchen, through the hall and down the front steps. She heard his footsteps behind her, his voice urgent, concerned. He caught her on the bottom step and forced her to a stand still. She did not resist when he led her back into the house. In the drawing room he poured a glass of brandy and stood over her while she drank it.

"Please don't apologise." Her silenced her attempts to explain her presence there. "I know today is your child's birthday."

"How do you know?" She was startled by his knowledge and when he mentioned Wind Fall she remembered the first time she had seen him in the breakfast room with Liz. She felt heat returning to her cheeks. Her breath steadied. She told him about the supermarket and the National Library – where her past was a headline on microfilm – and how she was unable to stop crying because she had climbed the headland and believed she was on the other side.

Once again she was confiding in this stranger who listened intently and did not make futile, sympathetic remarks. Nor did he hold her hand or stroke her hair, even though he was so close she only had to stretch out and touch him. When she was composed again he ignored her protests and drove her to Grahamstown in her van. The site looked desolate. The caravan was cold. He looked around the cluttered, untidy space then stared through the window at the darkness outside. He asked how work was progressing on her garden centre. Some planting for spring had been done but the cottage – she shrugged, too weary to talk about debts and her bank manager who refused overdrafts because it was a high risk project. She saw him· frown, tension gathering between his dark eyebrows, as if her problems were also pressing down on him. She ordered a taxi for him on her mobile phone and they drank coffee while he waited. Once again she apologised for intruding into Havenstone.

"I'm glad I came home and found you," he said. For an instant she thought he was going to take her in his arms. She stepped backwards, relieved when the lights of the approaching taxi swept over them. He signalled to the taxi driver to wait and turned back to her.

"If you're free some night I'd like to bring you out for a meal." He spoke carefully. "I want to discuss something with you. It's strictly business," he hastily added, seeing her startled expression. She was too weary to think of an excuse and nodded. Later, when the day with all its grief had faded, she would cancel. If he needed to discuss business, the garden in Havenstone was the appropriate place.

It rained that night. The wind grew in strength. The plastic coverings on plants fluttered loud as the wings of angry swans. In the small hours she rose from the bed and phoned Greg.

She wanted to talk to him about loneliness and empty nights. A woman answered. Her assertive drawl grew impatient at Eva's silence. In the background she heard rock music playing on a stereo. She hung up without speaking. The phone rang almost immediately. Peter Wallace was back in Havenstone but he was still worried about her. She assured him she was fine and returned to bed where she tossed sleepless for the rest of the night.

*   *   *

Eleanor Lloyd was hard-edged and tough. She entered Greg's office on the anniversary of Faye's birthday. All afternoon he had been anxious to talk again to Eva but her mobile remained switched off. Eleanor sat on the edge of his desk and did not ask him questions when he mentioned his daughter's name for the first time. That night she came to his apartment with her collection of Janis Joplin original vinyls and two king-sized steaks.

"No sense in suffering in silence, Enright," she said. "It's time to tell me why your heart is breaking."

It seemed strange to breathe private confessions into the ear of a woman he hardly knew. But she listened and did not pass judgement. Instead, she spoke of lost loves and lost opportunities. The phone rang when he was in the kitchen turning steaks.

"No one spoke," she said when he returned. "But I could

hear someone breathing. I think it might have been your wife."

He rang Eva's number but the line was engaged. Perhaps it was a crank call, said Eleanor. One of the many crazies that haunted the Big Apple.

*   *   *

The leaves began to fall, red-gold on the trees, rustling dry at the edge of the copse.

When Peter Wallace rang and informed Eva that he had made a reservation in Goodlarches she did not demur. She would wear black, a sleek dress with shoe-string straps, sheer black stockings that would tease and tantalise. They would dine by candlelight and drink a toast to the future. They would let the evening take care of itself.

CHAPTER FORTY-EIGHT

Goodlarches was silent with the weight of money and diners in their twilight years. Elderly wives in floral silk suits flanked by serious husbands, silver-haired devils behaving themselves for a change. No prices on the menu. Greg would immediately have demanded to know why. Probably, he would have done an 'Elucidate' special on the scam of the celebrity chef.

Peter Wallace had shaved off his beard. He looked younger without it, more exposed, firm full lips, a strong chin. He ordered their meal with authority, chose the wine after a brief glance at the menu. A sophisticated man, used to dining out in restaurants without prices. They were tense throughout the meal, unsure of the roles they should play. Their voices sounded too loud when they spoke. As soon as the meal ended he flashed his credit card and they left the restaurant.

He suggested a night cap in Havenstone. Eva accepted. He poured brandy into goblets, handed one to her and proposed a toast to the success of her garden centre. She raised her own glass and they drank together. He seemed calm but she sensed his uneasiness, shared it, and when he leaned towards her, she thought he was going to touch her. She tensed her knees, acutely conscious that she had sunk deeply into soft cushions and her black dress was sliding up along her thighs. The thoughts she had harboured of making love to this middle-aged man mortified her. She wanted to pull her dress over her knees but that would have made her embarrassment obvious. Suddenly, the room seemed hot or perhaps it was her own heat rising in her cheeks. She heard a clock ticking somewhere nearby and wondered about the woman who had once shared this house with him.

"Are you having financial problems with the centre?" He asked the direct question without preamble and she nodded agreement. There was little sense denying it any longer. He had paid for her work in Haven-stone. The money sank without a ripple. He did not seem surprised when she outlined the problems she had encountered. He believed her idea for situating a garden centre in Grahamstown was excellent. But she was under capitalised. He wanted to invest money in it.

The suddenness of his offer took her breath away. He spoke carefully, as if he understood the thoughts going through her mind. There would be no strings, emotional or financial.

"Why?" Her question was blunt and he answered calmly. His offer had certain stipulations. He wanted a share in her company. It would be a silent partnership and she would be completely free to make her own decisions.

"I have the money," he stated, "you have the expertise. When your business is established I expect to make a return on my investment."

"Why should it matter to you whether or not my business succeeds?" She repeated her question, keeping her tone as businesslike as his. He hesitated before replying, as if he too sensed the heat in the atmosphere.

"When Sara died …" He stumbled over his wife's name and fell silent for an instant. "When she died I went to pieces. I drank too much and made stupid business decisions I now regret."

"You must have loved her very much." It seemed the right thing to say but she knew it was an empty comment. Love. He shrugged the word aside. He had wanted to destroy everything in this house that reminded him of their life together. What he had not realised was that in destroying her memory he had almost destroyed himself.

He stood up and walked to the window, pulling the curtains closed on the night. He had money to invest. Tork Hansen had been his first investment. He was prepared to offer Eva the same opportunity.

The night was over. They shook hands. He stood at the entrance to Havenstone, watching her until the taxi rounded the bend in the driveway and turned towards Grahamstown.

*   *   *

Greg asked questions about her new business partner. A man who was willing to invest a small fortune to help her business stay afloat – or rooted to the earth. Either way, she was in the black again.

His wife was breathless and impatient with his suspicions. "He is an entrepreneur," she said. "Elderly."

If this was supposed to reassure him it failed. An entrepreneur who took her out to dinner. A business meeting that ended in his house with brandy and dubious business propositions.

"What kind of discussion was that supposed to be?" he demanded. "Where was it conducted – in the boardroom or the bedroom?"

"Stop behaving like a ridiculous fool," her laughter snapped down the line. "I need the money and I accepted. It's strictly business."

"There's nothing left for me to say, then."

"What makes you think you have the right to say anything?"

"I'm still your husband."

"That wasn't the impression I got the last time I rang your apartment."

"I can't remember the last time you rang. I'm always the one who rings you – for all the attention—"

"On the night of Faye's birthday ... what should have been her birthday, I rang and had the pleasure of hanging up on your latest girlfriend."

"I haven't a clue what you're talking about."

"Forget it then." She was preparing to put down the phone.

"No, wait. You're talking about Eleanor. For Christ's sake, Eva, that was Eleanor Lloyd. She's a good friend, and quite ancient."

"Ancient?" His wife laughed again, an unpleasant sound. "Then she must be the same as Peter Wallace, my business partner. It's such a relief that neither of us has anything to worry about."

Peter Wallace was a name that rang bells. Alarm bells but also memory bells. Greg had heard it before but he could not put a face on him. The imaginary face he drew was wizened, decrepit, octogenarian.

"I miss you, Eva," he said. "There's no one else in my life ... no one but you."

He heard her sharp intake of breath then silence. When she spoke again her tone had softened. "When you come home for Christmas we'll talk."

He was suddenly aroused by the sound of her voice, picturing her tall rangy body and tumbled hair lying beside him, the soft contours of her breasts, the muscular strength of her arms. She was such a contradiction, blowing hot and cold, yielding in love yet unbending when it came to forgiveness.

"Will the cottage be ready?" he asked.

"Yes."

"Can I stay with you?"

" I'd like that."

"Eva ... do you love me still?" he asked.

"I'm confused and I'm angry. But love doesn't die easily."

Her words were hesitant. They gave him comfort.

CHAPTER FORTY-NINE

Eva drove on the finished section of the motorway – a long grey slash with flashing signs, bypassing narrow main streets that had been crumbling under the force of juggernauts and traffic jams. It seemed as if the whole county had turned into a massive building site. She was part of this new vision. In Grahamstown, houses were being occupied, mock-Tudor fronts mushrooming fast among old bungalows.

The thatcher had finished her roof. A roof put a stamp of permanence on a house. It was an undeniable fact, a shelter from the world. Her cottage walls stood sturdy and strong, a sun splash of yellow on the front door.

Matt Morgan declared a ceasefire. He collected mushrooms in a nearby field and brought them to the caravan. She fried them in butter and garlic then called him in to share them. They talked about joists and thatch and the number of angels that could dance on the head of a nail.

*   *   *

On 'Stateside Review' it was also a time of change. Overnight, a new producer was appointed. Desks were emptied. Falling ratings; the cardinal sin. 'Stateside Review' was going for a softer touch, dumbing down and focusing on the human side of the political image. Greg remained in his usual position by the window. It offered him a view of trains running across the skyline and ant figures hurrying beneath grey spires.

"I am becoming a purveyor of pap," he said to Eleanor, who briskly ordered him from her office. She had a new sales target to reach.

"From now on, Enright, you can forget about slush funds and misappropriated documents," she warned. "If you want to save the world join Greenpeace. If you want to hold this job keep your head down and your chin in. Viewers have complained about its aggressive slant."

He returned to his apartment where his voracious shoal of piranha was prepared to offer him more sympathy. They, at least, would eat the hand that fed them – an acknowledgement of sorts that he still existed.

*   *   *

Eva's Cottage Garden officially opened in November. With her new partner's investment securely lodged in her bank account, she was able to hire an assistant to help her in the centre. Jean Wilson belonged to the Grahamstown Horticultural Society. Her delphiniums won first prize at the annual Festival of Flowers. She would bring business to the centre, spread the word where it mattered.

Sometimes, when she was on her knees, her hands deep in soil, Eva forgot about Faye for a short while. There were terrifying moments when her child's face was not so clear in her mind. Then she took out her photographs, devouring them. Her father was right. Gardening was therapeutic, thoughts sinking into the earth and finding rest. This, she believed, was what healing meant. Short bursts of amnesia. Time was a thief that eventually took everything, even memories.

*   *   *

The season of goodwill was a short break in the Big Apple where the population faltered momentarily in its pursuit of the big buck. Unlike Ireland where the nation glutted for a week. Who was right? Who was wrong? What did it matter? Greg was not coming home for Christmas.

'Stateside Review' had planned a Festive Special which he would present. In the hostels of the greatest democracy in the world he would walk among the homeless who had found shelter at the inn. They would fill their bellies with turkey and cranberry sauce. Cameras would be aimed at their grateful faces. New York vagrants were a polite breed who wished their benefactors a good day. When they talked about their broken lives they would cast a dutiful but brief shadow over the Christmas celebrations. There would be many politicians present.

He reminded his producer that a flight home at Christmas had been built into his contract.

"Whatd'ya expect us to do? Line up the bums a week beforehand and feed them turkey so you can have a holiday?" His new producer was a man who did not mince his words. "Get fucking real, Enright."

"Feeding the homeless on Christmas Day?" Eva

congratulated him on his altruism when he rang to discuss the change of plan. "How noble of you, Greg."

"It has nothing to do with generosity," he replied, annoyed by her dismissive tone. "I know what my contract says and I can fight this on a point of principle. But they'll find an excuse to shaft me when I return. Things are very uncertain at the moment. Falling ratings. I can't take the chance."

Eva did not appreciate the significance of falling ratings. She laughed at his suggestion that she employ someone else to take her place at the garden centre and fly to New York.

"Like your producer said, get real, Greg! I won't close until late on Christmas Eve. You know it's impossible."

"Nothing's impossible, if you make the effort."

"You make the effort then – or have you other plans?"

"I told you! I'm filming on Christmas Day."

"Then we're hardly going to have time to pull crackers together, are we?"

"I suppose you'll have time to pull crackers with your business partner," he snapped back.

She hung up on him. He was unable to believe how quickly words turned into arguments whenever they spoke. So silly to believe a marriage could be saved in a festive atmosphere of holly and mistletoe.

*   *   *

Would Eleanor Lloyd give him his Christmas present wrapped in glittering paper or were her gifts bestowed in the sultry darkness of the bedroom? He said she was an advertising executive with class. An assertive drawl disguised the remnants of a Limerick accent. She kept cats and accompanied him to the opera. Opera buddies. It sounded comfortingly maternal. Eva did not believe him. The face of Eleanor Lloyd was vibrant and young, as sensuous as the dawn on a Portuguese mountain.

CHAPTER FIFTY

Christmas week was hectic. Most of the time Eva was out on the road making deliveries while Jean shifted poinsettia and chrysanthemums, holly wreathes and Christmas cherries. When the last customer left on Christmas Eve, they locked the gates of the centre and drank a toast. They were exhausted and giddy, unable to wind down now that the rush was over. The centre resembled a scene from the blitz but the cash register had keyed in profits. Her business partner would be pleased.

Earlier, he had called to say goodbye. He was driving to the country to stay with relations.

"I wanted you to have this." He handed her a parcel wrapped in gold foil paper. When she opened it she saw a painting of Murtagh's River.

"It's beautiful." She was suddenly embarrassed at not having a gift to give him in return.

He brushed aside her apology. "It's the first thing I've

painted in years that gave me pleasure. I wanted to share it with you."

She walked with him towards his car which was parked outside the cottage.

"I'll see you in the New Year," he said and suddenly leaned forward to kiss her cheek. Inside the car she saw the glowering face of Lindsey McKeever and an elderly woman, who smiled back at Eva as he drove away to celebrate a family Christmas.

*   *   *

Connie was tired and crumpled after the long journey. It was her first visit to Anaskeagh. Until then, she had resisted all Beth's invitations. Anaskeagh was Barry's life before they met and she had always displayed a quiet deference towards his wife's wish that their paths never cross. She only agreed to come when she heard that Marjory was spending Christmas in New York. Peter escorted her into the house, carrying her suitcase, leaving Lindsey to trail behind. Trouble was brewing, observed Beth. It was obvious from his grim silence and the bee sting pout on Lindsey's bottom lip.

"They were arguing the whole way down," Connie confided when Beth led her into the bedroom she would occupy for the holiday. "She's a bold brat when she makes up her mind to torment a body. My head's weary with the pair of them." She moved to the window and gazed out over the darkening headland. "Barry talked so much about Anaskeagh. I'm glad I've had a chance to see it at last." She smiled, turning to face Beth. "Would you look at the cut of you? A real glamour puss, if I ever saw one." She crossed the room and hugged her daughter-in-law. "I'm glad to see you looking so well, pet. It's been a rough time for all of you and you deserve some happiness. Don't worry about Lindsey. She's a prickly little miss but there's a good heart in her. I'd be lost without her these days."

*   *   *

It was late when Eva reached Wind Fall. At midnight mass she dozed off, unmoved by the singing and the wafting clouds of incense drifting over the congregation. Yet, when she went to bed, she was unable to sleep. The painting of Murtagh's River was propped against the wall. A strange abstract image, as if the river flowed through a shrouded landscape where nothing had a recognisable shape; sound and movement suspended. Their first meeting place.

He intruded in her thoughts too often, his direct gaze always watching her. When he first came to her caravan and by the river, even when she sat mourning Faye, he had watched her. She remembered the close, almost claustrophobic feeling in the copse. His strong grasp on her waist when she slipped. He had kissed her cheek outside the garden centre and she had had a sudden image of their mouths opening in a deep searing kiss. The thought had shocked her equally as much as the jolting excitement that ran through her. He too had seemed infused with the same desire and when she pulled away she was aware of an almost physical wrench separating them.

Her relations came in the morning, the Frawleys and the Loughreys, hearty voices noisily greeting each other, hugging Eva too tightly. Maria arrived, radiant, accompanied by the first two-legged love of her life. Desmond Thorpe was a rugged man with good shoulders and a strong pair of hands for handling high-spirited fillies.

"Magnificent in jodhpurs." Maria confided to her cousin. Her eyes were glorious blobs.

"Spare me the lurid details," Eva warned. "And run as fast as you can in the opposite direction."

Her friend placed two fingers in her ears and said, "I'm joyously deaf. Shut up." She skirted around the subject of Greg's absence before asking outright if their marriage was over.

"Was it ever on?" Eva replied. "We had nothing in common – *nothing*. When it came to making choices between his career and his marriage there was no competition. Do we have to talk about him today? I'd much rather hear about Desmond. Tell me everything. I mean *everything*."

Maria moaned happily. "Where do I begin …"

Dinner was boisterous. They wore party hats and read silly riddles from Christmas crackers. It was their first Christmas without Brigid Loughrey and everyone was determined to be merry. This time last year Faye was a bundle of love passed from one set of arms to the next. They toasted absent friends and Liz cried quietly into a paper tissue printed with holly.

Greg rang from New York. He was sharing a meal with some Irish friends. When his phone call ended Eva told her mother she was returning to the cottage. Liz protested, shocked at her decision.

"I have to go." Eva had no excuse to offer her. The words became a mantra. "I have to go."

Liz followed her to the bedroom. "What about your marriage?" she demanded. "You hit the first wall and that's it, is it? Is that all your husband means to you?" She fired questions, her face flushed, sternly challenging. Did Eva think her marriage to Steve was easy in those early years? Their dreams falling apart month after month. "It's not that easy to cope with sperm bottle experiments, no matter what you may think to the contrary," she cried.

Eva winced back from her anger. She sank to the edge of the bed and placed her hands over her face, shamed. "I'll never forgive myself for that remark, Liz. All I can do is ask you to forgive me."

Her mother's shoulders slumped, weary suddenly from the intensity of emotion in the room. "Go if you must," she said. "But remember this, Eva, grief is a lonelier journey if you insist on walking it alone."

*   *   *

'Stateside Review' filmed the unwashed, the unloved, the forgotten. Smooth-faced congressmen with tans shook them by the hand and turned their good profiles to the camera. Greg returned to his apartment to shower away the smell of over-cooked turkey and took a cab to Kieran Oliver's house.

The politician was present at the Christmas feast, his complexion gleaming with good cheer and fine malt. His sister sank deep into the cushions of an armchair and sipped sherry. Marjory Tyrell had the vague look of someone who would forget names as soon as the introductions were over. A cigarette dangled dangerously from her fingers. The hostess cast desperate looks in her direction and nudged ashtrays under her hands. The guests recreated an Irish Christmas, becoming noisily jolly and singing nostalgic ballads. They argued about politics and religion. Tom Oliver made a rousing speech about Ireland's finest asset. He raised his glass in Greg's direction and inclined his head graciously towards Ireland's youth – her Diaspora, long may they spawn the world. Greg felt a hundred years old. He wondered how soon it would be appropriate to leave.

His wife was sleeping alone on this festive night. Last Christmas, in her parent's house when everyone was in bed, and Faye was contentedly sleeping close by them, they made love in front of the fire. The room flickered with flame and passion. Such pleasure, deep yet soaring, lifting them, sinking them into each other's being. How could it fade so quickly?

He saw her image that night in Kieran Oliver's house, a photograph on top of a display cabinet. A young laughing woman, her hair falling over her eyes.

Marjory Tyrell followed his gaze. "My child," she sighed. "My poor lamb."

*   *   *

The spirit of Christmas did not improve Lindsey's mood. She deliberately stepped out of Peter's way every time he walked past. His gift to her was ignored and remained unopened under the tree. On this occasion, the presents he gave his nieces and nephews had been chosen with care: a book on Celtic music traditions for Robert, a magician's set for Paul, and Gail's present – a toy dolphin that could swim and leap in the bath – created such interest that she insisted on Peter filling the bath and showing her how it worked.

When he returned and saw Lindsey's present still under the tree he made no comment. Nor did he respond when she refused to sit near him during Christmas dinner and remained calm when she contradicted him every time he spoke during the meal. Connie ordered her to behave, using a tone of voice that would have invoked instant rebellion if Beth had tried it, and she subsided for a short while. But her resentment cast a pall over the festivities. Stewart was the lash she used. Never had her love for him been displayed so openly and she seemed elated by the tension she created.

"Have you any idea how much you're upsetting everyone, especially your father?" Beth spoke sharply to her daughter when they were alone.

"Which one are you talking about?" Lindsey snapped back. "The one with my heart or my DNA?"

Nuala O'Neill drove to the bungalow on the afternoon of St Stephen's Day and announced that she had sold three of Lindsey's paintings before Christmas. This innocent remark proved to be a spark that struck the tinderbox and afterwards, Beth could only wonder how the row had not erupted sooner.

"I'd love to see your work, Lindsey." Peter was unable to hide his pleasure as Nuala discussed the paintings she has sold. A tangible link was being established. Creative spirits mingling. Beth watched the storm clouds gather as he continued to question Lindsey about her techniques, the materials she used, and why she had changed her mind about going to art college when she had such a natural talent.

Lindsey, tired of monosyllabic replies, rose to her feet.

"Why don't you mind your own fucking business and stop poking your nose into mine. I don't need your pathetic opinions on what I paint. It has nothing to do with you and never will – understand?" She turned to Stewart and smiled brilliantly. "I need some exercise, Dad. How about coming for a walk with me? I'll get my jacket." She stalked from the room, leaving a stunned silence behind.

Nuala looked bewildered. "Was it something I said? I've never seen Lindsey behave that way before."

"Count yourself lucky," sighed Stewart, rising to accompany his wayward child on a walk along the blustery cliff.

Nuala left shortly afterwards. Connie retired for a nap. She was pale, her eyes red-rimmed, looking old and vulnerable in a way that worried Beth. But Connie insisted she was simply tired, too much rich food. She closed her eyes and waved Beth from the bedroom. Robert went off to meet some friends on Turnabout Bridge, a meeting place for teenagers. He was creating a new musical wave, he told Peter. Celtic rock rage was a protest against manufactured boy bands and would soon take the country by storm.

"Sounds like Horselips on speed." Peter laughed. "How do you intend promoting this new wave?"

"I've formed a band," replied Robert. "We're called Hot Vomit. Packs a punch, don't you think?"

"Right in the gut," agreed his uncle. "I'd love to hear you some time. Perhaps when I'm senile and totally deaf."

"I'm returning to Oldport," he said when he was left alone with Beth. "I'm sorry to have been the cause of so much sorrow."

She did not try to change his mind. He offered to come back at the end of the week to bring Connie home. She told him there was no need. She had an important meeting in Dublin early in the new year. On his way out, they passed the open door of their daughter's bedroom. Paint tubs and brushes were heaped untidily on the floor. His eyes rested hungrily on an easel which held a half-finished canvas. She wondered briefly what kind of parents they would have made. It was an abstract thought, fleeting. Once it filled her world.

He was gone when Lindsey returned. She pretended not to notice.

CHAPTER FIFTY-ONE

Eva cooked an evening meal. She spent time preparing it, fresh herbs and an expensive white wine poured generously into a sauce which bubbled gently when she added chicken and sun-dried tomatoes. She placed it on the coffee table and watched it congeal. Despite her hunger she had no desire to eat.

It was cold in her bedroom. She stood in front of the long chervil mirror and pulled a nightdress over her head. It reached to her feet, a sleek ivory robe which emphasised her pallor. She touched her face, cupped it with both hands, and stared into the mirror. She looked like a ghost, haunting the night hours, she thought, shivering. Grief needed a companion. She returned to the living-room where the fire still burned brightly and the aroma of her untouched meal made her realise how little she had eaten that day. She was about to pick up the phone when the front doorbell rang. Her body quivered with shock, her need for Greg so immediate that she believed he was standing outside the door. The thought died just as quickly and when the bell rang again, a prolonged impetuous summons, she figured it was a motorist lost in the labyrinth of narrow country roads surrounding Grahamstown. She draped a jacket over her shoulders and opened the door.

Peter Wallace had started to walk back down the driveway. He turned when he heard her surprised voice and apologised for intruding so unexpectedly. He had noticed the light when he was driving past. She wanted to remind him that she was now bypassed by a motorway but it would have added a personal element into their conversation.

He followed her into the living room and sat down beside the coffee table. She whisked the dishes past his troubled gaze and out to the kitchen. He too had found the spirit of Christmas too tedious to endure and had returned early to Dublin. He refused her offer of a drink or coffee and they sat in an uneasy silence before the fire. Eva added a log and watched the sparks splutter, conscious that he was watching her every movement.

"Your husband interviewed me once." He spoke suddenly.

"Are the scars still showing?" she asked, keeping her tone deliberately light.

He smiled, not amused, and fell silent again. He looked out of place in her small room, his long legs stretched too close to the flames, his shoulders too broad for chintzy armchairs. She found it impossible to imagine him in a factory or an office. Her mind was set with him beside a river bank. She would hang his painting on the wall when he left. It would always remind her of Faye.

"You should be with him tonight." His words startled

her. "You should be in his arms, talking of love. Why are you sitting alone? I want to understand – how can he love you and let you go?"

"What do you know about love?" she demanded. His questions were so attuned to her own thoughts that she wanted to lash out at him. "How can you talk to me about my marriage when you banish your wife from every room in your house?"

She rose to her feet. "I think you'd better leave now before we say things we'll regret later." He too stood up, facing her, standing too close.

"I came here to talk to you – to tell you things you need to know." He paused, his gaze sinking into her eyes, holding each other captive in a tense, unwavering stare.

"Why do you keep looking at me?" she cried. "You watch me constantly … all the time I feel your eyes on me."

"All the time." He echoed her words. "Always …"

In that instant there was a shift in desire, so sudden that when she swayed towards him she knew before she reached him how it was going to end. She did not resist when he kissed her, their lips pulsing as she drew him in deeper, the tingling shock of their tongues touching, probing, their mouths crushed in that first wounding kiss. The jacket slipped from her shoulders and she heard him moan as he pulled away, almost forcing her from him, and when she gasped, shocked by his abrupt withdrawal, she saw such passion in his face that she closed her eyes and cried out his name, her arms urgently pulling him close again. Her hands were on him and his on her, touching her breasts, sliding the nightdress upwards, the fine silk shimmering as he smoothly slid it over her hips, his fingers on her bare flesh, opening her to his touch as she too sought and held him, unable to believe she was seeking such relief; sunk in shame and pleasure and escape.

He loosened her hair from its clasp until it hung to her shoulders, showering over them. The savage intensity of their passion amazed her, so demanding, infinite, free. She did not want to move from this place, or to slow the intensity of their lovemaking, knowing that anything else, a movement towards her bedroom, delicate foreplay, teasing words of anticipation, would bring her back to her senses. She was lifted in his arms. Her legs encircled him. The power of his desire moulded her into him. She felt the thrusting strength of him entering, heard their breath shuddering as they moved together.

She did not reason why she was in his arms. She only knew that her body had taken control, battering her through the numbness that had overwhelmed her for so long, and when they came together, it was an aching release, as if they had spent a lifetime knowing each other's desire. She cried into his shoulder, clinging to the pleasure of the moment, wanting to surge forever on its crest, his voice calling her name – Eva … Eva … Eva …

It was over as suddenly as it started. His arms supported her when she collapsed against his chest. He sank back to the sofa, pulling her with him, breathing fast, their clothes still tangled around them, half on, half off, and they huddled together, unable to talk, to understand, to make sense of the wildness that had consumed them.

For a while she slept. When she was conscious again he was watching her and they slid once more into their lovemaking. This time it was slower, more deliberate, staring down into his eyes as she sank into him, their bodies unable to rest until they had driven each other to the edge of oblivion – and even then, she suspected, they would never be satisfied.

He left in the morning. She ached with exhaustion, still feeling his touch on her skin, suffused in the heat he left behind. In the shower she switched on the cold water and gasped as it spilled over her breasts. He had touched them with reverence, his lips gently arousing the area where Faye has once suckled so voraciously, as if he was trying to imprint another memory on them. Gradually, she calmed down but she was unable to think beyond him.

She opened the garden centre, relieved that her sales assistant was still on her Christmas break. Business was brisk, last minute gifts, bouquets and plants, purchased on the way to parties and festive dinners. She had little memory of the day, the customers, the mundane chores that killed time until the night.

They had not planned a further meeting and she decided to go to bed early. He phoned as she was about to lie down. He said he was sorry. He had abused her trust. He never intended it to happen. She clamped her lips together and held tightly to the receiver.

"I love you desperately," he said. "But we can't see each other again, not like that – not like that." His voice shook, a raw gasp, as if he too was remembering the sounds of their passion.

"Stop it!" She groped blindly for the duvet and pulled it over her. "Don't dare patronise me. How can you patronise me after what we've just shared?"

"No, no! Listen to me, Eva. I don't want to hurt you. But I know I will."

She hung up on him, his pathetic excuses. She tried to sleep. She heard his car outside. His footsteps on the gravel. She went to the door. Wordlessly, he took her in his arms and carried her to her bedroom. Sated with pleasure, they finally slept.

CHAPTER FIFTY-TWO

Eva was caught in the waiting stillness, wondering. Why did it happen? What chemistry merged and melted them? She tried to understand this passion, to experience some relief from it. She drove too fast, turned corners too sharply. Once, when the van rocked on a bend, she pulled into the side of the road and tried to compose herself. Was this a nervous breakdown? Was she exhibiting symptoms of exhilaration? Did she love him? The answer no longer mattered. She loved Greg and he went away. She loved Faye and she died. Love had no substance.

She went to the cemetery on the anniversary of Faye's death. Peter phoned her that evening, aware of the day and its importance, and asked if she would like him to come to the cottage. When she said she would prefer to be alone, he accepted her decision but he stayed on the phone, and they talked about her childhood, quiet recollections that calmed her. Greg rang later, annoyed that the line had been busy for so long. She tried to concentrate on what he was saying but, afterwards, she was unable to remember their conversation.

*   *   *

Greg's ex-producer from 'Elucidate' flew into New York to attend a conference on racism within the media.

"A tricky subject at the best of times," said Sue Lovett when the speeches were over and she was relaxing with Greg in her hotel foyer. She informed him that his destiny in life was to be a big fish in a small pond. In New York he was a flounder, floundering out of his depth.

"Come home," she said.

"What's at home?" Greg asked.

Ireland was a time bomb, ticking with the excesses of the past. Politicians trying to shake off the touch of golden handshakes. Captains of industry scrutinising their tax returns and discreet off-shore accounts. Brutal sacred secrets finally spoken aloud through the media confessional. Tom Oliver's name was mentioned, the hint of a land scandal. It came to nothing in the end, as all enquiries did when they concerned him. Justin Boyd had dropped the story. No proof.

"If his source was a rum swilling redhead, I'm not surprised," Greg said.

"His niece," Sue Lovett replied.

He was surprised. "Bad blood, obviously."

She nodded. "She went over Justin's head and contacted me directly."

"And—?"

"She impressed me. The story could be worth looking at again. Are you interested?"

"Not particularly. In case you've forgotten, I have a job here."

"I've watched 'Stateside Review'," Sue said. "Interesting stuff. Why aren't you surrounded by dancers with sequins in their belly buttons?"

"It's not that bad!"

"You interviewed a congressman last night about the welfare of domestic pets."

"New Yorkers keep strange pets in their apartments," he replied. "Iguanas and snakes—"

"He supports execution by lethal injection." She impatiently interrupted him. "What's happened to you, Greg?"

"Nothing. Apart from clearing out the "we-make-a-difference" clap-trap from my head. What difference did I ever make? Michael Hannon? There's talk of his party rehabilitating him back into the fold now that he's purged his contempt for family values. His wife is still holding his hand and his girlfriend has become a celebrity on game shows."

"While your marriage has broken up – and your child is dead. Is that the way you're thinking?"

"I'm not thinking at all, Sue. I'm surviving. That's what you do in this city."

"Or disappear into a programme called 'Stateside Review'."

"My friend Eleanor calls it candy floss. Her advertising revenue has never been higher since the format changed."

"I believe you." She stood up and shook his hand. She had arranged to have dinner with some friends and he was due back at the office. "You have a job waiting if you decide to come home."

"I thought Justin Boyd was more than adequately filling my shoes."

"Justin's a boy scout not a muck raker." She frowned. "I need you on the programme, Greg. But I've no intention of begging. Tom Oliver's niece said the story would never have died if you'd been handling it. Do you want her number?"

"For what purpose?"

"Oh, you know." She shrugged and opened her brief case. Briskly, she handed him a business card. "Just in case your producer decides to bring on the belly dancers."

In his office he thought about Tom Oliver and how, on Christmas night, he drank malt whiskey and delivered a lusty rendering of 'A Nation Once Again'. A true blue armchair patriot who would take credit for the building of a dog kennel. Justin had dismissed the woman's evidence. Stories, rumours, pub gossip. Yet, each had its own momentum. He had seen the rumour mill in action, the media frenzy once the hint of a scandal was floated and discovered to have substance. The hidden voices coming out of the woodwork when they knew there was someone who would listen. He felt an almost forgotten clench of excitement as he lifted his phone and asked to speak to Beth McKeever.

*   *   *

Spring brought the garden centre to life. In the mornings it was mostly older women and men who wandered among the plants and shrubs. At weekends young couples arrived, baby slings and go-cars, planning gardens, buying trees and shrubs that would grow with their children.

In the evenings, while she waited for her lover to arrive, she walked by the lake, through a meadow of bluebells, primroses, wild daffodils, cowslips, forget-me-nots fluttering in green shady hollows.

They made love in his bedroom. It reminded Eva of an old man's room, dark walls and walnut furniture, a solid bed with a carved wooden headboard. It once belonged to his father, he told her. A silent man with fine silver hair who grew grapes in the garden she had restored. His mother was a strong woman, dominant. He brought his parents alive with a few words but he would not talk about his wife. Eva shivered when she passed the room where Sara Wallace once slept. He kept it locked.

She tried to sense her presence in the old house. There were no photographs, no clothes, no odds and ends to suggest she ever existed. She imagined her shadow wandering lost in those empty rooms where all that remained were the colours and textures she had created around her. Eva did not want to think about her but somehow, surreptitiously, she was becoming part of her thoughts. Why did she die? Had her husband's passion been repugnant to her? Was there ever any passion between them? What did she know about Peter Wallace: lonely only child, one-time factory owner, failed artist, childless widower?

She watched him painting. Sometimes she saw parts of herself, a curl of blonde hair in a green circle, her fingers reaching out from a flame or perhaps it was a sun blast, a nuclear explosion. Like the painting of Murtagh's River, nothing had a recognisable shape yet there was such vigour in the colours, in his bold sweeping strokes. She did not understand what she saw but it moved her, this excitement he created.

Her passion strayed far beyond the pleasure she had shared with Greg and the other young men she knew briefly and carelessly in her student days. It was madness, this desire. It had to burn out. But not yet ... not yet.

CHAPTER FIFTY-THREE

Greg had forgotten the moist wind, the hint of rain, the buffeting, restless clouds. He had forgotten the patchwork green that rose to meet him as the plane flew low over the Irish coast. But, when he walked into the arrivals hall of Dublin Airport and saw Eva waiting, he felt the fist closing again. He looked into her eyes and knew that nothing had changed.

Back in the fold of 'Elucidate' he found it difficult to believe he had ever been away. The sounds were the same, hot house gossip, speculation, the excited buzz of facts confirmed and packaged for an evening's viewing. No one mentioned the word failure, but he wondered what the team said behind his back. Eva claimed he had lacked the hairstyle to make the grade on 'Stateside Review'. His face needed air brushing to blend in with the dross he was expected to deliver. Her opinion had as much credibility as the analytical discussions he had with his colleagues about the sociological/cultural differences within the global media. His decision to come home had nothing to do with the politics of 'Stateside Review' or hairstyles or the indignity of having his work reduced to a few bland comments, impact without input. He was home because he had been lonely. In the capital of the world he had been wretchedly, grindingly lonely.

He took back his apartment which had been rented to a friend, a forty-year-old engineer with the hygienic habits of a student on the razz. By the time he finished sponging, mopping and bleaching, it was as organised as it had ever been in his pre-Eva days. The household plants gleamed. The exotic fish still swam with stately grace in their aquarium, friendly and darting, unlike the sullen killer shoal he left behind in New York. He sat watching them at play, wondering if they had noticed his departure or grieved for his friendly hand to feed them. He knew the answer to that one. Why clutter your mind with incidental emotions when you only have to concentrate on swimming in a straight line. If he started envying fish he was halfway to a long stay at the nearest funny farm.

*   *   *

Her husband was back in the interrogator's chair. Once again his sardonic smile withered the rhetoric of politicians and businessmen who tried to defend the indefensible. A class act to watch and Eva did watch him. She was still fascinated by this hard-faced man who wept with joy when their child was born and wept so bitterly into her shoulder when her brief life ended.

In his apartment they sat stiffly opposite each other. He spoke about their relationship. They were both ego-driven individuals who rushed into marriage without considering their needs. They had an unplanned baby. Faye broke their hearts. He was unfaithful to Eva but it could have been absolved if they had stayed still in the welter of grief that surrounded them and considered what they meant to each other. Instead, they ran in different directions and now, quiet at last, they had a chance to salvage something from their experiences.

She envied his ability to lay his thoughts in such logical order. Hers were incoherent. She wondered what he would say if she told him about Peter Wallace. Would he reason with such calm assurance if he knew about these nights, the lust and thrust of passion?

She told him there was no going back. For an instant he was silent. Then he offered her something they both needed. Friendship in exchange for pain. No demands. No expectations. It would be a new experience for both of them. Could friendship rise from dead love? It was something they wanted to believe. This time, when he spoke about Eleanor Lloyd, Eva believed him. Deceit had a different face and words were spoken with guileless ease, not in reassuring tones of disbelief.

Later, they met Maria and Desmond in a jazz club. Desmond was not so one-dimensional after all. When he was not urging horses over water jumps, he played a mean tune on the saxophone. The jazz club was dense with smoke and earnest musicians who beckoned him forward for an impromptu session. Maria sidled close to her cousin and yelled into her ear, demanding the latest information. Was Eva's marriage on or off or in a state of abeyance?

Eva told her they were friends.

"No such word!" Maria rolled her eyes back in her head. "Never heard of it before." She sparkled at Desmond and stamped her feet for more. Eva clapped her hands above her head until he played an encore, wondering when the night would end. This was passing time, a choreography of movement that would bring her nearer to real time and the wanton pleasure of Havenstone.

CHAPTER FIFTY-FOUR

Whenever Beth returned to Dublin on business, the city traffic seemed worse than ever, congested trails of frustrated drivers gridlocked no matter how they twisted and turned. Greg Enright was waiting for her in the hotel foyer. He ordered coffee and they sized each other up.

"I can't be associated with this story," she warned him. "My husband's future is tied up with the business centre. But I'll help behind the scenes in every way I can."

In the flesh he was less intimidating than on television, kinder eyes and an attentive manner that immediately reassured her. Beth thought it was a pity he did not smile more often. He listened carefully to everything she had to say. Under his careful questioning Derry Mulhall's rambling story began to take shape. She told him about Kitty Grimes and her fear of exposure.

"Don't worry, I'll handle her gently," he said.

She mentioned Hatty Beckett and saw him smile before he shook his head, almost regretfully. His gut instinct was to start the investigation with the business centre. He would focus on its development and start digging the dirt from there. They shook hands before they left the hotel, quiet conspirators.

*   *   *

"Good morning, Greg." The politician answered the door in person. "I hope you've been receiving a true Anaskeagh welcome."

"Thank you, Deputy Oliver. I've no complaints so far."

"How long will we have the pleasure of your company in our little town?"

"Until my story is fully investigated."

"An investigation!" Tom Oliver raised his eyebrows and smiled. "That sounds very serious. Are you suggesting we have secrets to hide in Anaskeagh?"

"Secrets?" Greg shrugged. "How can we tell if there are secrets. Unless, of course, people are prepared to reveal them. I hope you will do us the honour of being interviewed."

"My pleasure, Greg. When are you thinking of arranging it?"

"We'll be filming in the business centre. I believe you were actively involved in locating it in Anaskeagh. I thought it would provide an interesting location for your interview."

"An excellent idea." Tom Oliver clasped his hand in farewell. "I'm delighted to be of assistance. But please remember, I've a very busy schedule and need advance warning."

The Anaskeagh Business Centre was a compact semi-circle

of white buildings that looked as if they had been dropped from outer space into the green countryside. The road was twisting and narrow, pot-holed in places. Not exactly the ideal infrastructure for small industry but the ACII in its wisdom had deemed it a perfect location. According to Beth McKeever, the original location was Clasheen, a small town located about twenty miles away. The road bypassing Clasheen was wide and smooth, linking directly to the main Dublin Road, but suddenly, without warning, Anaskeagh was chosen.

The meeting with the business people was held in Stewart McKeever's office. They were enthusiastic and excited, anxious to milk the publicity their companies would receive from the television exposure. Greg felt embarrassed, as he often did on such occasions, knowing that most of the filming would be edited out by the time the programme appeared. But, when the shit hit the fan, as he hoped it would, the Anaskeagh Business Centre would receive more nationwide publicity than any of the group of people facing him could possibly realise. Beth McKeever did not attend the meeting. A busy woman, she had a factory to run.

Derry Mulhall had the bulbous nose of an alcoholic and a high whining voice that stumbled over facts until they sounded like lies. His story was explosive but if Greg ever managed to get him in front of a television camera, the sympathy vote would be lost as soon as he opened his mouth.

Eight years previously Derry had been approached by Conor Oliver. The solicitor was acting as principal on behalf of a consortium who intended buying Derry's farmland for agricultural purposes. Anxious to make a quick sale, Derry had been beaten down easily on the price he demanded. Soon afterwards, the land was rezoned from agricultural to industrial use and sold for a prime price to the ACII, who built the business centre.

Derry was in no doubt about the true identity of the purchaser. Tom Oliver, lining his pockets as usual, wily old fox. The farmer glowered, unable to hide a skulking admiration for underhand dealings.

Greg detested his self-pitying whine yet he believed him. Just as he believed Kitty Grimes, even though she shuddered away from his questions. She was a nervous, elderly woman who had never stepped out of line in her life. Her thin face flushed anxiously. She was worried about her children. They had good jobs in Anaskeagh. If she spoke out of turn it could damage them.

She had been a cleaner in the solicitor's office. Arriving early for work one evening, she overheard an argument between father and son taking place behind closed doors. The politician was shouting about delays in a land transaction. She realised they were talking about Derry's land and passed the information on to the farmer. Soon afterwards, Derry was beaten up for talking too loudly about corruption in high places and Kitty had remained tight-lipped ever since.

Greg assured her that no pressure would be put on her to go public with her story. He soothed and charmed and listened. Eventually, she allowed him in.

*   *   *

Twilight was settling on Anaskeagh Head when Beth parked her car on the old pier and walked along the stony, uneven surface. A white cruiser had come to a stop some distance from the shore. She watched a group of men on board busily anchoring and securing the vessel. Seagulls screeched and swirled above them, anxious to partake in the results of a successful fishing trip. Four men climbed down the ladder and into a small dinghy which cut swiftly through the tide. As they mounted the stone steps at the side of the pier she saw her uncle. He looked ruddy and relaxed from his day's fishing. He was flanked by two friends and his son.

"Evening, Beth," he said, smiling broadly as he embraced her. Her face was pressed against the stiff fabric of his life jacket. His arms were hard and purposeful. "Meet my favourite niece." He introduced her to his companions, Ben Layden, and Jack Mackey, an accountant. They nodded politely, anxious to be on their way.

When their cars disappeared from view she returned to her own car and watched the sun sink beyond the peaks. Greg Enright had a narrow watchful face. His hair was dark with a smattering of grey. Too young to be going grey but there was nothing youthful about him. He would take her uncle apart and then she would finally be able to breathe freely again.

*   *   *

It was dark when Greg drove from Anaskeagh. He had his story. Already, he could sense the shape of it but he knew he had to move slowly and carefully. He was used to secret meetings, deliberate leaks, anonymous tip-offs. The motives people had for trusting him with their secrets were as varied as their methods chosen to impart them. To settle a grudge, to scupper a reputation, to discredit and disgrace, to seek revenge. Seldom was the motive one of morality, although it was usually cited as such. Beth McKeever had not pretended she was spilling the beans for the benefit of mankind. The first thing he had noticed were her eyes. Vengeful. She could control her emotions in a dead-pan recital of facts but her eyes could not disguise her hatred. He sensed another story behind the trail she had laid before him. It would come to the surface eventually. When the time was right it would settle firmly within his grasp.

CHAPTER FIFTY-FIVE

Bit by bit the layers peeled away. One night Peter spoke about Lindsey McKeever. Afterwards, Eva was surprised she had not guessed. His broad forehead. His penetrating stare. On the rare occasions when Lindsey smiled, it was his smile Eva now saw. The same impetuous mouth and aggressive energy. He found it difficult to talk about Lindsey's mother. Beth McKeever left for England while he – unaware and engrossed in his new love – never paused to wonder why. But what of Sara? Eva asked. Did she know? He shook his head. Not then, but later, many years later she realised the truth and it consumed her. He fell silent, unwilling or unable to continue, and she probed deeper, shocked to discover that Sara Wallace trampled on her sister's love and claimed it as her own. What kind of relationship did the two sisters have, Eva wondered, that one could wound the other so deeply?

Lindsey refused to acknowledge him. Peter had no rights. No rites of passage leading to fatherhood. We do not own our children, Eva thought. We do not own anyone but ourselves. She had never thought about her natural father. He remained an icon in a fairy story, a blonde prince with a sturdy shield and bravery in his heart. She did not stare into the faces of strange men, hoping for a sudden revelation. Instead, she became a watcher of women. On the streets of Anaskeagh she had stared, sifting them into age groups. Young, she must have been young. A teenage mother, terrified.

Eva returned to Anaskeagh again, a magnet pulling her backwards into the past. The O'Donovan farmhouse was plain, pink-washed, two-storeys high. In the narrow lane leading to the house a herd of cattle approached, ponderously moving before an elderly woman, their heavy milk-filled udders swaying. She recognised Catherine O'Donovan, who carried a switch, using it to swipe at straying animals who blundered too far to the left or right. One of the cows lifted its tail and splattered the road. The odorous dung steamed in the air and caught unpleasantly in Eva's throat. Catherine smiled, politely saluting her as a stranger. She enquired if Eva was lost. Eva guessed the widow had been too grief-stricken at her husband's funeral to have noticed her.

"I'm hill walking," she replied and listened politely as Catherine advised her to be careful. The mist could fall unexpectedly and confuse a stranger who was not used to the lie of the land. Eva thanked her and hesitated, falling silent when a car approached, the wheels easing into the edge of the hedgerow as the cattle passed. The driver, a younger woman, turned to speak to two children in the back seat who were trying to open the door. When the cattle had moved on into the farmyard, the children leaped out from the back seat and attached themselves to Catherine. She lifted the little girl in her arms and handed her the switch, then bent her head to talk to the driver through the open window.

Eva nodded goodbye and walked on. She had reached the end of the lane when the car stopped and the driver leaned out the window to offer her a lift.

"My car is parked in the beach car park," Eva said, hesitating. "I was going to cut across the headland and climb down to the strand."

"That will take forever. I'm heading into town. I can drop you off on the way." Sheila O'Donovan had pale-blue eyes and a darting gaze. As she drove towards the beach she talked about her family and her job as a child-minder, pausing long enough to enquire about Eva's business in Anaskeagh. Her chattering voice grew wary when the Anaskeagh baby was mentioned.

"It's research," Eva said. "A thesis I'm doing on the culture in Seventies Ireland. This was an important story at the time."

"I wouldn't talk to loudly about abandoned babies in Anaskeagh," Sheila warned. "People still have hard memories about the lies that were written in the papers. Blamed it all on us. Even though no one had a blessed clue who the mother was." She tried to stay silent on the subject but her resentment spilled over, the suspicions of that time, the interrogation her fiancé had been subjected to by the Gardaí.

"Mud sticks," she muttered. She broke off her

engagement for a while. But common sense prevailed and in the end she accepted his innocence. "Bernard is a good man," she said. "The best. Why should he and his brother have been singled out because the baby was left on their doorstep?"

The other brother went to Australia, unable to cope with all the innuendoes and suspicion. Eva asked if anyone knew the identity of the mother. "Plenty of names were bandied about, including my own, but no one really knew," Sheila replied. "Now, no one wants to know."

Peter fell silent when Eva told him where she had been. "What is it?" she asked. "Why are you so upset?"

"Why can't you let it go?" he demanded. "Your childhood was precious and secure. Why do you want to stir up things you know nothing about?"

"I thought you understood. Why don't you want me to find out about my birth?"

She saw fear on his face, naked for an instant before he drew her close. "The present is what matters," he said. "Now and the future. Let the past to rest in peace."

"I can't," she cried. "I have to find out."

"What if it becomes more important than what we have now? What will you do then ... what will I do?"

*   *   *

In a pub in Temple Bar, Greg was among the young people who gathered to hear Loughrey's Crew. Afterwards, when the crowd had dispersed and the musicians were loading their equipment into their van, he spoke to Annie Loughrey about his wife.

"Do you know if she's seeing someone else," he asked. "She usually confides in you."

Annie rang her fingers over the strings of her fiddle, as if checking its perfect pitch, and said she knew nothing about her niece's personal life. "It's difficult to communicate with her these days. As far as Eva's concerned, you betrayed her at the most vulnerable time in her life. But, I believe she still loves you, despite everything she—"

"Loved," he interrupted. "Past tense, Annie. If what I hear in her voice is love, than I guess I've been listening to the wrong songs."

He had seen Eva in the city one night. She had passed by without noticing him and turned into the entrance at Goodlarches. He followed her inside and watched as a tall, dark-haired man rose from a table to greet her, an older man, disturbingly handsome still, who took her hand with the familiarity of a lover and guided her into the seat opposite him.

The shock of having his suspicions confirmed had sent blood rushing to his head. He had offered friendship to his wife in the vain hope that it could lead them back to love. But friendship, he realised, was impossible. Did he want to hang around and pick up the pieces? In his life, where everything had a place and a purpose, all he desired was peace of mind and the acceptance that his marriage was over.

*   *   *

Swans would never again swim on Base Road. The narrow pot-holed lane fringing the estuary shore had disappeared, replaced by the half-completed slip road which would be banked by flyovers and roundabouts. Luxury apartments would soon rise from the site of Della Designs and Woodstock was a handsomely fronted specialist store. When Beth returned to Oldport she found it difficult to remember the bends and gateways, the old houses, the ridged fields of cabbages and potatoes, the burgeoning hedgerows, heavy with summer hawthorn and autumn berries.

Peter looked younger, as if years have fallen away from him. His skin was fresh, no angry blotches, his eyes alive. She recognised the old restlessness from his student days, the same sweeping contagious energy. He had started painting seriously. He told her he was hoping to mount his first exhibition. They went upstairs to the studio, reclaimed again and alive with colour, chaotic as it used to be in his student days, the sharp, breath-catching chemical smells instantly familiar.

She walked with him to the back of the old house and entered the market garden, standing still for an instant to absorb the transformation. The old village had been encapsulated into this walled enclosure where the scent of herbs, the rows of vegetables, the fruit trees and meandering cobbled paths created a peaceful haven far removed from the traffic and the unceasing roar of progress.

Later, when she called to Connie's house and met Lindsey, she understood the reason for his enthusiasm.

"Her name is Eva," Lindsey announced. "And he's absolutely crazy about her. *Imagine* falling in love at his age."

"He's not due for the old folk's home yet." Beth laughed. "Falling in love is not solely the prerogative of the young, you know. Is the feeling reciprocated?"

"I'm not sure." Lindsey frowned and shook her head, as if puzzled by the complexities of human emotions. "She spends a lot of time at Havenstone and he cooks her fabulous meals, so she's either in love with him or is a compulsive over-eater."

"What's she like?" Beth asked, remembering times when Peter had cooked for her, showing off his culinary skills, both of them heavy-headed with excitement and anticipation for the hours that would follow. Such recollections had become fleeting impressions, as if they belonged to the memory of someone else.

Lindsey was frowning, a puzzled expression on her face. "I like Eva a lot – but I don't know if it's because she reminds me of Sara."

"Sara?"

"It's kind of weird. Sometimes I think it's my imagination and then she moves her head in a certain way or smiles and it's as if I'm looking at Sara. I thought she was a ghost when I saw her first. I hope Peter's in love with her for the right reasons."

Beth was startled by her daughter's comment but before she could reply Connie arrived home from the village. She was carrying grocery bags and seemed frailer than she had been at Christmas, but cheerful as she fussed over Beth and enquired about her grandchildren.

"You have to visit us again," Beth said. "No more excuses."

"Maybe I'll come for Easter," said Connie when Beth was leaving. "If you're sure it won't be upsetting for your mother."

"Don't worry about Marjory," Beth was unable to keep

the bitterness from her voice. "She hasn't visited us once since we moved." She hugged her mother-in-law. "Your grandchildren miss you – and so do I. That's all that matters."

Lindsey phoned a week later, sounding worried. "Will you talk to Granny Mac about going to the doctor?" she said. "She won't listen to anything I say."

"What's wrong with her?"

"I'm not sure ... but I think she's sick. I woke up one night and heard her throwing up in the bathroom. And she's gone very quiet ... like she's in pain but not pretending."

Beth immediately rang Dr Andrews and drove to Dublin the following morning. Connie was in bed, cheerful and resolute. Dr Andrews had assured her there was no need to worry – and the tests he recommended were just precautions.

The realisation that Connie was dying stunned her family but she calmly accepted the prognosis. Every weekend Stewart drove to Oldport and they talked quietly about the past, a time Beth had not shared, when Stewart was a small boy watching from Pier's Point for the sight of his fisherman father coming home.

When Marina heard her mother's cancer was terminal she phoned from London to announce she was returning to Oldport to nurse her.

"It's only a little growth but it'll magnify if I have to endure Marina for long." Connie was dismayed. "Please, Beth, ring and tell her there's nothing to worry about."

But Marina was adamant. All her glittery life she had neglected her mot-her but she was fired with determination which, Lindsey insisted, had little to do with Granny Mac's illness and everything to do with Peter Wallace.

"I won't be able to move for her make-up and wigs," she moaned. "And I'll have to listen to her stories about that *stupid* rock star and the tabloids chasing her."

*   *   *

Marina McKeever arrived unexpectedly at Havenstone one evening. From the drawing-room Eva heard her high-pitched laughter and Peter's surprised voice at the front door inviting her in.

"Darling, how utterly inconsiderate of me to call tonight. I'd no idea you had company." Marina stopped abruptly when she entered, unable to hide her surprise. "Introduce me, please," she commanded, turning archly to Peter. When he made the introductions she held out a cool hand and tipped Eva's fingers, immediately turning her attention back to him. She handed him a carrier bag containing a bottle of wine.

"Be a darling and pour me some wine. I've had a wretched day. Who'd have believed I'd end up emulating Florence Nightingale?" She took off her jacket and draped it across his other arm then sank gracefully into an armchair. The sinuous ease with which she moved was in marked contrast to her shrill laughter.

As Peter uncorked the wine he seemed relaxed but Eva sensed his annoyance at the sudden intrusion of this woman into their evening. Marina pouted gratefully when he handed her a glass. He held the bottle towards Eva, who shook her head. He also refrained from pouring a glass for himself and placed the bottle on the mantelpiece.

"Darling, I'm hoping you'll be able to help me in a small matter concerning my sanity." The older woman laughed, tilting her head back to expose her throat. "It's about Lindsey. I haven't room to breathe with her rubbish. And you know me? I need my space uncluttered. She needs somewhere to stay. Why don't you offer her a room here?" She glanced at Eva and smiled. "That's if you have the space, darling. I wouldn't dream of cramping your style."

"I already have asked her," Peter's tone was curt. "I won't repeat what she said. I'm sure you're aware that my relationship with Lindsey is far from cordial."

"Oh dear – she is *such* a histrionic little bitch. How Connie copes with her is beyond comprehension. But in the present situation it's impossible for her to stay with us. You're the obvious choice, Peter." She tapped a long blue nail against her glass, watching him as he moved to the window, his face caught in a sudden spasm of grief. He seemed submerged under her suggestive voice and the heavy scent of her perfume.

"Whatever else I may be, I'm far from Lindsey's choice." He spoke with his back turned to them. "I'll ask her again, if you wish. But I already know her answer."

"I'm sure you'll be able to persuade her. You always had a way with words." She languidly pushed her hair from her eyes and smiled at Eva. "Oldport was a dump when I was growing up. A tomb – except for Peter, of course." Her voice lilted suggestively over past indiscretions. "He was the only asset, as far as the girls were concerned, weren't you, darling?" Her impetuous voice forced him to turn around. "Then Sara came along and the rest, as they say, is history, or does history begin to repeat itself?" She held out her empty glass. "One more for the road and I'll be on my way. I've intruded enough already."

Eva was embarrassed by her behaviour. Marina McKeever would always be a woman who challenged other women, forcing them to either compete or retreat before her coy domination. "You haven't intruded, Marina. I just called to discuss some unfinished work in the garden. I didn't intend staying so late."

She walked quickly towards the door, anxious to escape the woman's aimless chatter. She had met Connie McKeever one evening on Main Strand Street. Frail and old, trembling on her granddaughter's arm, the old woman had asked questions about the garden at Havenstone, remembering how it used to be – luscious vines and a spreading crab apple orchard, a plum tree that cast its fruit on the ground and white pear blossom in the spring. When they were parting she called her "Sara", lifting her hand to her mouth in apology when she realised her mistake.

Peter rang the garden centre to break the news of the old woman's death. He had spent the night in the hospice with her family and they were returning to Havenstone where they would stay until after the funeral. Remembering the speculative gaze of Marina McKeever, Eva had no desire to meet his relations or to be the subject of their curiosity, and was relieved when he did not suggest seeing her.

The following day she drove to Woodstock with emergency flower supplies. Judith was busy with wreaths for the funeral. The old woman was well respected in the village.

Annie Loughrey stood among the mourners at the

graveside. She rang Eva on the evening of the funeral, demanding freshly percolated coffee before heading off to a gig in the city. She was giddy from too much wine and session memories, old friends from Celtic Reign reunited around Connie McKeever's graveside.

"Of course, I was just a tot in my Celtic Reign days, not an old crone like now," she said when she arrived at the garden centre. She was accompanied by the singer from Loughrey's Crew, a young man with a shaved head, who protested vigorously over her use of the word "crone", and was ordered off to look at the swans.

Eva had stopped keeping track of her aunt's companions, who got younger as Annie grew older. "Sexually, we're both in our prime," she explained when Eva demanded to know when she was going to stop behaving so outrageously with school boys. A slight exaggeration. They had usually received the key of the house when Annie invited them in. Her good humour quickly disappeared as she surveyed her niece.

"How are you enjoying life since you decided to become a hermit?" she asked.

"Busy, busy," Eva replied.

"Don't annoy me, Eva. I'm too long in the tooth to listen to balderdash." Annie had a fine snap to her voice when she was annoyed. "You should never be too busy to visit your family. Liz said you look as skinny as a bag of bones and she's right. There's only one thing makes a woman that way and it's not happiness." Annie's eyes narrowed. "So, tell me. Is he *also* married?"

Eva shook her head. "Annie, nothing you say will make

any difference. I've got someone who loves me, who cares. You've no idea how much he cares."

"And what about Greg? Have you thought about his feelings in all of this?"

"It's got nothing to do with him."

Impatiently, her aunt slapped her words aside. "Fine sentiments. I hope they don't bite you back. Who is he?"

"No one you know." Eva wondered if they had rubbed shoulders at the funeral. Perhaps they had spoken in the graveyard or in the Oldport Grand, where Annie had gathered old musicians around her to reminisce about times past and smoky ballad sessions in the Fiddler's Nest.

CHAPTER FIFTY-SIX

The Anaskeagh Business Centre had turned into a forest of cables and cameras. On the production floor of TrendLines, the excitement heightened among the machinists as a burly cameraman moved among them, positioning his equipment. The journalist stood calmly, waiting. His hair had been cut since Beth last saw him. It spiked aggressively in front, sharpening his features, and the glasses he wore while checking his notes added to the severity of his image. Since he entered the centre he had not spoken or made eye contact with her.

She moved to the entrance of the factory, accompanied by a young woman with a clip board, who checked her watch when the politician arrived. Tom Oliver was on first name terms with the machine operators, asking after the health of their children, making jokes, familiar local banter. He chatted knowledgeably to the 'Elucidate' crew as he was wired for sound. Noise and action surrounded him when filming began. Computerised cutting machines sliced through layers of fabric. Sewing machines clattered as the women, self-conscious in fresh hair styles and make-up, ran fabric through their fingers. Some, unable to resist, waved into the camera. Then the machines were silenced and the interview began.

Greg Enright was courteous and relaxed. He listened carefully as the politician described how he had spent his political career working unstintingly to create rural employment – not just for his constituents but for small forgotten parishes throughout the rural community. His own furniture factory had been a shining example but he had been forced to close down because of cheap imports flooding the market. He deftly evaded a question about lack of planning permission. Such a trivial consideration when he was putting bread on the table of his workers. But these were modern times, a new era. The Anaskeagh Business Centre was a shining example of his commitment to his community.

"Was that the reason why the location was changed from Clasheen to Anaskeagh?" asked the journalist. "Surely Clasheen, with its superior road infrastructure, would have been much more suitable for such a venture?"

Tom Oliver did not appear surprised at the sudden change of questioning. He smoothly offered statistics and solid reasons why Anaskeagh had been the better choice.

"It was an ACII board decision. Unanimous." The politician stared steadfastly into the camera then turned and made a slight bow towards the staff. "I'm sure any of these lovely ladies will be happy to explain why Anaskeagh is the perfect location. This is a small town, Mr Enright. Employment opportunities mean the difference between emigration or building a prosperous future in one's own community."

The journalist repeated the question. His tone was measured but Beth sensed his determination to stay with the same question until he received a satisfactory answer.

"Deputy Oliver, can you explain why Mr Derry Mulhall's land was rezoned for industrial use so soon after it was purchased?"

"The decision to rezone was unanimously passed at county council level." Tom Oliver once again appealed to the women, spreading his hands outwards, as if to indicate his bewilderment. "I was not present when the decision was made so, I'm afraid, I can't assist you any further. In my role as a public representative I've staked my reputation …"

An actor in perfect control of his lines, Beth thought, as familiar words tripped from her uncle's lips. He smiled into the camera. No tell-tale flush on his face. No flustered hand movements. He shook his head gravely when Greg Enright asked him if he knew the identity of the consortium who had purchased the land from Derry Mulhall then sold it on to the ACII. His shoulders gave an involuntary heave when Kitty Grimes muttered something, creating a low ripple of laughter among the women. Beth sensed something rising from them, a palpable wave of antipathy.

He knows he's in trouble, she thought, unsure as to whether it was exhilaration or terror that made her heart thud. She walked away, no longer able to listen to the unrelenting questions. In her office she pressed her face into her hands. When Stewart entered she tried to look composed but he was too agitated to notice her distress.

"What the hell was all that about?" he demanded. "I

thought 'Elucidate' was doing a story on the business centre. This stuff is way off beam. What the fuck is Greg Enright suggesting?"

"Tom is well able to handle himself."

"He was getting a bit rattled at the end of the interview." Stewart sounded thoughtful. "Mark my words, Beth, there's a hidden agenda behind all this."

"Yes, I suspect there is," she replied. "We'll just have to wait and see. I suspect there'll be a lot of talking done in the pubs tonight."

Conor Oliver had the same jovial smile as his father and offered the same firm handshake. "Could we please get to the point of this meeting, Mr Enright? I have an extremely busy day ahead of me and fail to see how I can assist you in the making of this documentary."

"Eight years ago, you acted as solicitor for a consortium who purchased Derry Mulhall's land," said Greg. "Obviously, we're not suggesting any impropriety on their part but 'Elucidate' needs confirmation of certain facts. I've compiled a list of questions and would appreciate you passing them on to your clients."

The solicitor moved to the water cooler and poured a drink into a plastic container. He sipped, thoughtfully. "You must be aware that all business conducted on behalf of my clients is strictly confidential. If 'Elucidate' is inferring that incorrect procedures were carried out, I must warn you that such accusations will be answered through the full rigour of the libel laws. Do we understand each other."

"Perfectly, Mr Oliver. But, as an investigative journalist, I have a responsibility to explore any allegations connected to this story. Your father has gone on record and denied any connection with this consortium yet certain allegations have been made that he was the sole purchaser of the land in question."

The solicitor sat down behind his desk. "I know you have a reputation as a serious journalist, Mr Enright. My father holds you in high esteem. If you want to keep your reputation intact I suggest you leave my office immediately."

Greg leaned forward and placed a sheet of paper on the desk. "I will be in touch with you tomorrow. If you wish to make a statement on behalf of your client – or clients – 'Elucidate' will be happy to accommodate you."

Conor Oliver lifted the sheet of paper and tore it in two. He folded his hands over the torn sheet and smiled. "Allegations do not bother my father, Mr Enright. He has enemies who will gladly try to damage his reputation if journalists are gullible enough to listen to them. If you will excuse me, sir." He rose to his feet and opened the office door. "You've taken up enough of my time. Any further queries must be made through your company's legal representative."

*   *   *

The phone was ringing when Beth entered the bungalow. At first, it was difficult to make out what her mother was saying. Marjory's sentences were incoherent as she angrily demanded to see her daughter immediately.

Beth drove into Anaskeagh and braked outside her house. Despite the brightness of the evening the curtains were drawn. Marjory answered the door in her dressing gown and walked rapidly ahead into the dining room. The television was on with the volume lowered.

"I heard about the interview in your factory," she snapped, sitting down and staring at the silent screen. "That awful man shouting insults at Tom. The nerve of him."

"He wasn't shouting. He was asking questions. Anyway, it's got nothing to do with me."

"Hasn't it? I know the way your conniving mind works. Making trouble for your uncle. God knows why, considering there'd be few enough airs and graces about you and your husband if it wasn't for his generosity."

"Generosity!" Despite her decision to remain calm, Beth felt her temper rising. "We're employing thirty people in our factory and we've never looked for or received any favours from that crook."

Her mother pressed the remote control and switched off the television. She was suddenly alert. "A crook, you call him. Is that what I heard you say?"

"I'm only repeating the rumours that are rife in this town."

"No one had much to say until you arrived, Madam. You needn't look so innocent with your smarmy smiles and your charity, thinking you can make up for years of neglect by shoving a few tins into my presses." Her voice shook with anger. "That man can ask all the questions he likes but he'd need to be up early in the morning to put one over on my brother." She slipped lower in her chair. Her jutting bottom lip and hooded eyes reminded Beth of a lizard, wrinkled and burned out. "Even when you were a little girl there was badness in you – and you're doing it again. I know about the questions you've been asking around the town.

You hate Tom so much you'd bring disgrace on this family to destroy him."

"Why do I hate him?" Beth shouted so suddenly her mother's thin frame jerked with shock.

"It's your father in you. He was always jealous because he had neither the brains nor the drive to be like Tom. All he ever did with his life was play music and run around with whores."

Beth was weary of her mother's unrelenting bitterness. "Connie McKeever is dead. Can't you let her rest in peace? Why do you always avoid my question? How much longer will you go on denying—"

"My tablets," Marjory gasped. She pressed her hand against her chest and pointed towards a small brown bottle on top of the television. "You're distracting me so much I've forgotten to take my heart tablets. Give them to me." Quickly, she gulped two tablets down with a drink of water. "The doctor says I need plenty of rest and I'm not to be getting upset about things." She raised her shoulders so high her face seemed to shrink between the thin blades.

"What's wrong with your heart?"

"He said I'm not to be worrying so much but how can I stop when you're always going on at me?"

Beth imagined gripping this embittered old woman by her shoulders and shaking her until her head lolled to one side and she stopped breathing. Horrified by her thoughts, she was gentle as she led her mother to the bedroom. She fixed the duvet around her, noticing cigarette burns on the cover. She asked questions about the doctor's diagnosis. Marjory answered vaguely, nodding sleepily as she sank deeply into the pillow and closed her eyes. Beth tidied the room, gathering up the discarded underwear and tights, the stained coffee cups.

"Why did she say such a thing … such a terrible thing to say to me?" Her voice was languorous, drifting. "My Sara … how could she hurt me so?"

"What do you mean?" Beth stopped at the door and looked back at her mother. But Marjory appeared to be sleeping, her mouth slack and slightly open, a tear trickling into the furrows on her cheek.

*   *   *

Gossip in the pubs, in the shops and on the streets. Beth McKeever was right. They were coming out from the woodwork, rolling back the years. Slights and oversights, grievances, humiliations. Greg walked through the centre of Anaskeagh and stopped outside the politician's headquarters. Only one light shone from the upstairs window. Tom Oliver lived in a humble enough abode considering the amount of money he had salted away over the years, probably off-shore, coded, untraceable.

The 'Elucidate' crew had returned to Dublin, leaving him and the cameraman, Chas Woods, to wrap up. The filming at the Anaskeagh Business Centre had been completed. Brushed up and made over, Derry Mulhall looked quite presentable as he displayed the documents he had signed on conclusion of his land deal. Kitty Grimes was nervous but she told her story in simple words. Hatty Beckett sulked in her coffee bar because Greg refused to interview her. A builder who had been promised work on the Clasheen site came forward and went on record, claiming that he had been forced to seek employment abroad even since he complained aloud about the change of location. The builder had based his future prosperity on the proposed centre, maybe he even greased a few palms to get the promise but it came to nothing in the end. Like Derry, he had discovered it was a bad mistake to make such an accusation out loud and now spent most of his time separated from his family and working on the building sites in Germany.

"It's a crazy state of affairs when the whole country is crying out for construction workers." He paused for breath and said, "I know for a fact that every contractor who got work on the Anaskeagh centre paid a percentage to Tom Oliver."

"Will any of them go on record and admit it?" Greg asked.

"They might." The builder smiled grimly. "But why would they spit on their bread and butter when they don't know if you can put jam in its place? If you want answers there's only one person who can give them to you – and I wouldn't be putting any money on your chances of getting an honest word out of his mouth."

Greg was hearing little stories, cruel stories that he wanted to tell, but most of them were insubstantial, easily deflected. The real truth was still beyond his reach. He needed more facts and figures, documents. Something that would directly implicate Tom Oliver before blood could begin to flow.

He shivered, suddenly afraid the story would fall apart. Since Faye's death he had felt his confidence draining away. The ending of his marriage and the mugging in New York had increased his sense of insecurity. As if life had taken him by the collar and shaken him into the reality that nothing lasts – nothing.

Annie Loughrey had confirmed his suspicions. The musician still evaded his questions. Instead, she gave him advice in her own inimitable way. "Eva in the grip of a fever," she said "You screwed up once, Greg. If you want to save your marriage don't do it a second time. Just be there when she falls – because that's exactly what's going to happen to her."

Anaskeagh was far removed from the glass towers of the Big Apple. Here, lights twinkled lower to the ground. Narrow lanes and small houses bunched together, fronted by the elegant River Mall and the brash shopping centre with its cinemas and swimming pool. And, in the distance, the headland loomed, a bloated shadow falling silent as a shroud over the secrets of Anaskeagh.

*   *   *

Marina McKeever drove into the garden centre and parked on the gravelled car park at the side of the cottage. Eva was locking up at the end of the day and invited her into the kitchen for coffee, knowing that whatever reason Marina had for visiting, she was not seeking advice on flowers. Instead, the older woman suggested a walk by the lake. She had heard there were swans living in the reeds.

They sat on the garden bench and stared at the still water. Her voice droned aimlessly, remembering a glittering career in an industry that no longer had any use for her. Just like Oldport, a changed village, friends married and even those who were widowed had nothing to offer. Since her mother's death she was drifting, regretful of lost opportunities. She sighed as she made this confession and Eva wondered how long it would take before she got the point of her visit. She offered her condolences, trying to find appropriate words to fill the sudden silence.

"Your mother was a lovely woman. I met her shortly before she died."

"She told me. You reminded her of Sara Wallace."

Eva was shocked by the blunt admission. "Do I look like her?"

"Superficially, yes. I knew her briefly when she lived in London. We were never friends – too much history. Her father and Connie lived together." Her high energised voice faltered as she stared at the swans gliding by with the same lofty indifference she must once have displayed on the catwalk. "My father's bones were hardly recovered from the sea before she took up with Barry Tyrell. I never forgave her. Even now – I can't."

Eva was surprised to discover that the frail old woman had had a past. Co-habiting with a married man in the dark Irish Sixties when the rest of the world was dizzy on Pill power and free love. What a small world, she thought. Such tangled, broken boughs on the tree of life. Swallows dived and skimmed over the water. The wind suddenly picked up. Marina pulled her jacket tighter around her.

"You and Peter …" Her perfect face tautened. "Spring and autumn lovers. Not always the wisest combination."

"You disapprove?"

"What's disapproval got to do with anything? You're a big girl now." She told Eva about the London trips, how he occasionally spent nights in her apartment. "It didn't set the sky alight for either of us. He was sleeping between cold sheets by then, seeking comfort."

"Weren't they happy together?"

"Happy? Who's happy, for Christ's sake?"

"They were married a long time. Surely that has to mean something."

"What does it mean? You can be a long time on heroin but that doesn't mean you love your addiction. Does he ever speak about her?"

"Why should he? Their past has nothing to do with me."

"He's not the right man for you, Eva."

"And he is for you?" Eva asked.

The look Marina gave her was neither bitter or jealous. "Not for me either. But for different reasons. He knows who I am. Does he know who you are?"

The question hung between them in the silent dusk, unanswered.

CHAPTER FIFTY-SEVEN

Sara Wallace, ghostly wife. Eva wanted to picture this woman who once knew his body as intimately as she did. She wondered if she was jealous of a dead woman and shied from the thought. The dead did not inspire jealousy – unless they consumed the living – and, sometimes, when he loved her, Eva wondered whom he saw lying beneath him. Was she his fantasy, his undying love?

Peter was out when she called unexpectedly to Havenstone one evening. Apart from the anniversary of Faye's birthday, Eva had never entered the house when he was not present. She stood in the drawing-room and pictured his wife staring from the same window down at the familiar sight of the village before slowly climbing the wooden staircase to her bedroom. Did Sara Wallace know, as she closed the door behind her, that she would never open it again? Eva shuddered at the image and hurried from the room. She wanted to leave this house with its haunting past but she longed to know more about this mysterious woman. She climbed the stairs and hesitated outside the bedroom door. The feeling that she was moving through an invisible veil was so strong she had to force herself to turn the key and enter. Such a weird eerie space, white walls decorated with mirrors. So sterile and narcissistic; so devoid of warmth. Her reflection was replicated, scared and tentative, as she approached the bed and rested her hand upon it.

Later, she asked him to tell her about Sara, to give her a shape. She wanted to see a photograph. He shook his head, refusing to listen.

"You must have something!" Eva cried. "A life time together. Why did you hate her so much? Tell me about her?"

He groaned and pressed his lips across her mouth. She forced him away. "Marina told me I looked like her – do I? Answer me?"

"No! Don't listen to her, to anyone. The past no longer exists. The love we have, that's all that counts." He touched her finger tips. "Can't you feel it?" he demanded. "Electricity. We charge each other."

She told him she had trespassed in his dead wife's room. Now she felt as if part of her had been left inside it. He rocked her in his arms, accusing her of crazy superstitions.

She refused to be comforted. "I want to make love in her room." The words were out, a thought hardly realised. "Did you hear what I said, Peter? I want to love you in her room – on her bed. She is haunting me. I want to banish her."

*   *   *

The large manilla envelope had been left for him at reception. Greg's name was written on the front but inside there was nothing to indicate who sent the photocopied newspaper clippings or the unsigned note.

This may provide you with useful background
material for your documentary. Tom Oliver will
be happy to talk to you.

An old story. He was six years of age when it hit the headlines. Same story in each clipping, different angles. Tom Oliver had made a public appeal to the mother to come forward and be comforted by her own people. His photograph was large, his expression concerned.

He rang his producer to tell her about the clippings.

"The Anaskeagh baby. Of course!" Sue Lovett sounded surprised. "I knew there was something about the town but I couldn't bring it to mind. It created one hell of a fuss at the time. Single motherhood was becoming the big issue rather than the big sin. What happened in Anaskeagh highlighted what the women's movement was saying. But I don't know where it fits into the plot today."

"Nor do I, yet. But my instincts tell me it's important. As it stands we could run it as background information. Small town moves from shadow of scandal, that sort of angle. I wonder why Beth McKeever sent those clippings to me?"

"Did she send them?"

"The note wasn't signed but I'd take an oath on it. I have a feeling she's hand feeding me."

"Then eat," his producer advised him. "Like you, I have a gut feeling about this story and we're only at the nibbling stage."

"Sue, does the name Peter Wallace mean anything to you?"

"Not offhand. Why?"

"It's nothing important. I'll talk to you tomorrow."

*   *   *

The politician made no attempt to rise when Beth entered his clinic. "What is it this time?" he demanded, wearily. "I've had a busy evening and I hardly imagine you've come to enquire about my health."

"It must make you proud to be so indispensable, Tom."

He smiled and waved her to a seat. "I do the job I've been elected to do."

"You do it well, Tom." She continued to stand before him. "That was an impressive interview you gave at the factory. I was quite impressed by the way you stood up to Greg Enright's insinuations. He should listen to the truth instead of malicious rumours."

He sighed, heavily. "The media are part and parcel of a politician's life. We tolerate them, just as we must tolerate earwigs or bad breath. But that doesn't mean we have to give them credence. It's late in the evening, Beth. If your reason for coming here is to discuss Greg Enright then I suggest we save this conversation for another time when I'm not so tired."

"He's looking for background material on Anaskeagh. It seems he did some research about the baby, the one that was abandoned on the headland. He asked if I could steer him in the direction of someone who was in a position to talk knowledgeably about it. I hope I wasn't acting out of turn by mentioning your name?"

She heard his deep intake of breath, saw the quick, uncontrollable flush of his cheeks. His fingers trembled as he opened a file and stared down at the contents. When he looked up again his eyes reminded her of a dead fish. Frozen on a slab and still staring. He glanced down again at the file and turned a page.

"I've just interviewed a young deserted wife whose husband left her with four children under the age of six. I hope to move her into a council house on Fatima Estate next week. That is the reality of the here and now. What you are talking about is history which no one in this town has the slightest interest in revisiting. They won't take kindly to outsiders coming in and stirring things up."

"It's just some background information. As you were a county councillor at the time, it seemed appropriate to pass on your name." She turned towards the door. "I wanted to let you know he'll be in touch so that you have time to refresh your memory."

*   *   *

In a bedroom of mirrors they made love. Eva heard him moan when he came, grasping her hair, his hands tangled so deep in the tresses her eyes stung with pain. He laid her back against the high white pillows. She gave herself up to his mouth, his hands, the rhythm of his body.

One night he opened the wardrobe and removed a dress, a delicate fabric with the gleam of dark wine. It fitted her, a second skin moulding her body. In the dining room candles burned on the polished table. He laid food before her. White roses sat in a silver dish. The curtains were open. The lights of Oldport wavered below, diamonds spilling into the black night. He lifted her in his arms. He bruised her throat with kisses. She rejoiced in his touch, in his drowning pleasure.

What was happening to her? How could she tell this to Maria ... to Liz ... to Annie. Impossible. This was dark secret passion. She was a whore, a virgin, a bride. Without shame. She would do anything for him. He would do the same for her. They were reflections of each other's deepest desires. Reflections trapped in a white room. Their hearts beat time together, counting down the hours.

CHAPTER FIFTY-EIGHT

The builder from Clasheen was the first to ring. He was taking a plane to Berlin where there was work waiting on a building site. He refused permission for his interview to be used on 'Elucidate'. He gave no reasons and hung up on Greg's questions.

Derry Mulhall sounded drunk when he came on the line, belligerent, threatening. He shouted above the noise of barking dogs. He had been conned into saying those things. If the interview was not pulled immediately he was going straight to his solicitor. A gently apologetic Kitty Grimes rang soon afterwards. Her children were horrified that she had allowed herself to be exploited by the media who would use her and then move out of her life, leaving her to pick up the pieces.

His producer listened as Greg outlined his disintegrating story. "The man is as guilty as sin and I can't find a shred of evidence that will stand up against him." He tried to control his frustration. "But I'm not giving up. I'm on to something and I'm determined to see it through."

"You may not have the opportunity, Greg." Sue replied. "Conor Oliver is threatening to apply for an injunction if you continue harassing his father."

"Harassing? Don't make me laugh. That old fox doesn't know the meaning of the word."

"You've been ordered back to Dublin. We've arranged a meeting with our legal team and we need you at it."

"Abandoning the sinking ship?" Beth McKeever rang as he was packing to leave.

"I'm going back to Dublin for a meeting with my producer," he snapped. "There's no reason to stay here unless you have more trustworthy sources at your disposal."

"You give up easily."

"*Easily.* Conor Oliver has documentation that proves beyond doubt that his father was not involved in the purchase of the farmer's land. Information from the Tax Revenue Department also shows that everything in his life is above board. He claims a systematic attempt by 'Elucidate' to damage his father's reputation is underway and we have not come up with a shred of evidence to refute this accusation – except from your friends who are now falling over backwards to deny everything."

"Which of us do you believe?"

"At this point it doesn't matter. The fact that I've no proof is all that matters."

"What about the Anaskeagh baby?"

"Yes, Mrs McKeever?" He pressed the phone against his ear. "What exactly are you saying to me?"

"I'm telling you to ask the right questions."

"Ask who?"

"You're the journalist. Do your job!" she said and hung up.

"Damn you, Beth McKeever." He stood for an instant with the receiver in his hand, staring into the mouthpiece as if he expected her voice to return, providing answers to a story that had been hovering out of reach since the first time they met.

The group of men parked their cars on Anaskeagh Pier. They removed fishing tackle and chatted quietly as they pulled peaked hats over their heads and belted their life jackets. A balmy early summer evening, the sea calm, gently rocking the large white cruiser moored off-shore. Tom Oliver was late arriving. He strode towards the men and uttered a brief apology for keeping them waiting.

"This is it, Chas." Greg spoke tersely to the cameraman. They emerged from behind the corner of the high pier wall. The cameraman stepped backwards as his camera swept over the group of men. Greg moved close to the politician and held the microphone towards him.

"Deputy Oliver, we're doing a story on the Anaskeagh baby. I have a primary source who maintains you are familiar with the events leading up to the tragedy."

The politician was shocked to a standstill by their appearance. He turned away from the camera, shouting. "Jesus Christ! As well as harassing me you're breaking the law. Are you aware that there is an injunction about to be served on your programme?" He breathed heavily as he tried to move past Greg and reach the steps.

"The Anaskeagh tragedy is a different story," Greg kept step with him. "It's a human interest story. I repeat, we have a primary source who is willing to go on record to tell her story. As you were a county councillor at the time you were obviously involved in the investigation that followed and—"

"This is outrageous!" Tom Oliver lashed out his hand at the microphone. "That unfortunate tragedy had nothing to do with me. Like everyone else in Anaskeagh, my only interest was in helping the mother – but, as she never came forward, there was nothing more any of us could do."

One of the men pushed against Greg. "You're upsetting Deputy Oliver." He shouted and shoved again. Greg staggered, almost losing his balance. Sweat trickled under his arms. He was too close to the edge of the pier. Another man tackled Chas, blocking the camera with his hand and attempting to push it to one side. As the cameraman tried to keep his balance he fell, hitting his head against the wall. His camera crashed on the stony surface. Casually, as if he was kicking a fish back into the water, his attacker nudged it over the side then dragged Chas to the edge.

"Can you see it?" he roared. "Do you want to go down and look for it?"

Chas's head was forced downwards. He made a choking sound, wheezing as the craggy surface of the pier pressed into his neck. Greg recognised the attacker as Ben Layden, the property developer who owned the shopping centre in Anaskeagh.

"Fucking media!" Another man jabbed his chest as he struggled to reach the cameraman. "You think you've nothing better to do than come down here hassling people."

"Gentlemen, please." The politician's words immediately eased the threatening atmosphere. Ben Layden loosened his grip on the cameraman who moaned loudly, too breathless to rise to his feet.

"My camera – he fucking kicked my camera into the sea." Chas was almost incoherent with rage as he struggled upright. He flung himself towards the burly man who had attacked him but Greg held him back, frightened by the intimidating stance of the men. Pillars of Anaskeagh society, the politician's men, each with their own reasons for keeping their dealings with Tom Oliver under wraps.

"A most unfortunate accident." The politician stared down into the rippling water.

"Accident! You call that a fucking accident?" Chas roared.

"That's exactly what I call it, young man. And these four men are witnesses." He faced Greg, unflustered. "Just remember this, Mr Enright. You and your colleague have attempted to besmirch my reputation with innuendo and allegations. This incident has added to the seriousness of your situation. I suggest you leave here quietly and allow us to begin our fishing trip. I wish you a safe journey home. The next time we meet it will be in a court of law."

*   *   *

Beth stared in amazement when the door of her office opened and her mother entered. Lipstick smudged her upper lip, a garish slash on her face.

"Marjory ... what's wrong?" Beth moved swiftly towards her. "How did you get here?"

"I drove, of course." She looked ill and exhausted as she

slumped into a chair and waved her daughter away. "What have you been saying to that television reporter fellow? Ben Layden's wife told me he was down on the pier asking questions about that baby ... the one who was abandoned on the headland. What's that got to do with Tom? Tell me that? What's it got to do with any of us?"

"How should I know?"

"He says he knows the identity of the baby's mother. How can he know that? How *can* he?"

"Marjory, it's got nothing to do with me. I wasn't living here at the time."

The anger that had forced the elderly women to the factory suddenly evaporated. Her eyes lost focus as she gazed at her daughter. She fumbled towards her handbag but it slipped from her fingers.

"Do you need your tablets?" Beth moved from behind her desk and lifted the handbag. Marjory snatched it from her and clasped it to her chest. "No wonder May Oliver hated you." Her mouth quivered. "She never had a good word to say about you. She hated you till the day she died."

"She had good reason to do so."

"Not like Sara, my lamb. She loved Sara."

"I'll drive you home, Marjory."

"Leave me alone ... always making trouble with your stories. Why did she say those things to me? Why?" Her hands fluttered upwards then fell limply to her lap. She began to sob. "She had no right to say those things about her uncle. He was so good to her ... he loved her so much."

Beth stared at her mother's bent head. "Sara told you, didn't she?" she spoke softly. "Before she died she told you ... and you denied her."

"You filled her head with your crazy nonsense, that's what you did."

"How could you refuse to listen to her? You cherished her. How could you deny her when she came to you?"

"Those things … it was all so long ago. She adored Tom. He was so good to her … sending her to boarding school and always watching out for her. He would have done the same for you too – but, oh no, you had to go your own road, always making trouble … accusations." Her voice trailed away as she clutched the desk and struggled to her feet. "Take me home. I'm not to be upset, that's what the doctor said. Take me home, Beth. I have to sleep."

* * *

Greg was checking out of the Anaskeagh Arms when his producer rang. She came straight to the point. "They're screaming assault, intimidation and defamation of character."

"That's rich coming from the Anaskeagh Mafia. You're lucky you're not bearing two drowned bodies back to Dublin."

"It might be an easier option for us to handle," Sue snapped back. "I can't believe a journalist with your experience would undertake such an inept door-stepping interview without the proper support systems in place. The end result was the destruction of a valuable camera but that's another matter which will be dealt with in the fullness of time." Her voice carried to Chas who grimaced and formed a noose with his hands. "'Elucidate' is successful only because we have always based our investigative features on a solid bank of evidence. I want the two of you in my office as soon as you get back to Dublin. And the sooner the better. The controller of programmes has raised serious questions about your future."

On the outskirts of Anaskeagh Greg's mobile phone rang. The voice on the other end of the line was elderly, quavering. He waved his hand towards Chas, ordering him to pull the car into the side of the road. At first he could not understand what the caller was saying then realised she was giving him directions to a small estate of town houses.

A stained-glass lantern lit the front porch. She opened the door and beckoned him inside. "You – stay outside!" She gestured towards Chas who retreated from her fierce expression with a muttered oath. She opened the door wider to admit Greg and closed it sharply behind him.

Mutton dressed as lamb was his first thought. A leathery tanned complexion, gold neck chains, knuckle duster rings on her wrinkled fingers. When she drew deeply on a cigarette he remembered her. Last time they met she was slumped in an armchair in Kieran Oliver's brownstone house in the rarefied atmosphere of New York's Upper East Side.

He followed her into a small room with a velvet three-piece suite and a sideboard gleaming with Waterford glass. Marjory Tyrell did not ask him to sit down. From a drawer at the base of the cabinet she lifted out a thick folder of documents. "Land deals," she said. "My late sister-in-law, May Oliver, believed they would be useful one day. A silly woman who never understood the virtue of silence."

He removed the documents from their folder and examined them. Old documents from the Eighties. The politician had trusted his wife in the days before his son took over his affairs. "You do realise the implications of handing this information to me," he told her. "They will destroy your brother's political reputation. They could lead to his imprisonment."

"Oh yes. I understand." She pressed her hands against the folder. Her nails turned white from the pressure as she forced the papers towards him. "There will be a scandal. But the truth is important, don't you agree, Mr Enright?"

"You've had these documents in your possession for some time, Mrs Tyrell. Why have you decided to release them now?"

She stood up and waved her hand towards the door. "My reasons are my own business. You have the story you came to investigate, Mr Enright. There's nothing more for you here. Now please leave my house. I seldom welcome visitors."

CHAPTER FIFTY-NINE

Eva believed their passion was strong enough to vanquish Sara Wallace but she still walked by their side, a ghost made stronger by her invisibility. The nights they spent in her white bedroom had the substance of dreams, still vivid enough to shiver through Eva's thoughts but unreal, the actions of strangers. She would never again enter that space.

In his studio loud music played, thunderous notes beating with life. Outside, on the landing, a tight spiral staircase with wrought iron banisters twisted upwards towards a small closed door. She left him painting and climbed the winding stairs. For an instant, as she stood in the dim slanted attic where glutinous cobwebs hung in corners and the remnants of times past gathered dust, she almost expected to find his wife mad and raving in the shadows.

In a wooden chest with a curved lid she found books on wine, old yellowing recipes, histories of vineyards and a diary kept by Bradley Wallace on his wine-making

successes. In boxes, she rifled through religious pamphlets
and prayer books, accordion files of business documents,
newspaper features on Della Wallace, who had been a role
model for journalists in the early wave of the feminist
movement. How dated it all seemed, Eva thought, reaching
towards a thick leather-bound scrap book.

The pages were filled with information about Sara
Wallace. Over the years, Peter had collected everything,
every column inch of newspaper space, reviews, features,
photographs, catalogues from her exhibitions, a
miscellaneous collection that charted the photographer's
success. Eva found photographic prints and transparencies,
files of them stacked together, as if they had been dumped
and then forgotten.

With her camera Sara Wallace had created another
world. The boy sleeping in the shelter of a cardboard box
could have been a dog, or a heap of discarded rags. Fat
women in miniskirts stood on street corners. Wasted young
girls lingered on the canal banks. Neon glitter; the Liffey
reflecting.

She was leaving when she noticed a canvas turned to the
wall. She carried it to the light and stared at the slanting
formation of rocks. They reminded her of a sacrificial altar,
a shaft of moonlight between the supporting boulders. Just
looking at the randomly scattered boulders, the craggy
peaks and stunted wind-blown tree in the background made
her nervous.

A large sketch pad lay beside the canvas. She flicked
through the pages, examining each sketch. These were no
abstract images swirling with life. One woman's face had

been drawn in all of them; a tense beautiful face. She stared at her own reflection and yet she knew it was not her, the features too mature. Eva was not beautiful. Her mouth was wide, her forehead too high. She lacked the delicacy that he had drawn into this wounded face. Yet she saw herself, her expression framed in mirrors, angry, aroused, laughing, crying. She was able to trace the chronology of these drawings. Two faces battled for supremacy. In the final page Sara Wallace was a ghostly image, ephemeral, submissive. Eva was the stronger. The younger. The victor. Superimposed. A mirror framed in red stones held her face. The same mirror that had held her reflection on those searing nights when she had stared from its depths. She felt as if she was choking; as if her soul had been taken without permission.

When she returned to his studio she demanded to know whom he had been drawing. He tried to calm her down, dismayed by her fury.

"It was an experiment that failed," he explained. He wanted a theme of reflections and the mirrors in his wife's bedroom had inspired him. Listening to him Eva felt breathless, as if his hands were on her throat. Possessing her.

"Leave me alone," she shouted. "You're strangling me ... it's too much ... too much!" She ran to the white bedroom and tore the mirror from the wall, smashing it to pieces on the floor.

His hands shook as he picked up the shards. He promised to destroy them all. He gathered her close, not possessively, not even passionately. As if the words she had screamed had sobered them for a short, resting time.

*   *   *

'Elucidate' devoted its entire programme to Tom Oliver. Kickbacks, insider information, the familiar story of power and corruption. A close-up of his constituency clinic flashed on the screen, journalists hovering, already on the scent, microphones poised. A closed door opened to reveal the stocky figure of his son, who read a prepared statement.

Conor Oliver spoke slowly, with sincerity. Since his father entered politics he had served his constituents unstintingly. Phone calls of support and endorsement had been flooding into the clinic all day. The politician would be happy to address these allegations frankly but he was not available for comment until he had completed a thorough investigation of his files and diaries. He had nothing to hide. The allegations dealt with issues pertaining to the Eighties, a different era when his father was working tirelessly at a local level to stem the tide of emigration from an impoverished state in the throes of recession and emigration. How could a man of his advanced years be expected to remember every meeting he attended, every decision that had been made in council chambers? Every file relating to his endeavours would be thoroughly examined and these appalling allegations laid to rest.

Journalists jostled forward, barking questions. The Eighties was the tip of the iceberg. What about the recent allegations? The business centre, for instance? The farmer's land deal? Conflicts of interest were everywhere. Conor fled before the hail of questions and 'Elucidate' returned to the studio for a panel discussion on corruption. Another tribunal in the shaping – hype, speculation, leaks. Greg would receive an award for courageous investigative journalism. Service to a nation of junkies holding out its arm for the mainline story.

*   *   *

Sr Jess O'Donovan rang Eva's Cottage Garden. She left a message on the answering machine. She hoped Eva would agree to meet her soon. There was something she needed to discuss with her. A story she had to tell.

CHAPTER SIXTY

The nun spoke hesitantly, as if feeling her way through unfamiliar territory. She seemed nervous yet Eva, looking into the resolute brown eyes, knew that this woman would not flinch from the truth. They drank tea together, polite strangers who should have been making polite conversation.

Eva was right. A teenage mother, terrified. Her child's mind closed down to her baby's existence so that Eva became a growth without shape, without meaning. Something to be destroyed and left beneath a rock. Her sister ran through the night to the lights of a farmhouse and saved Eva's life. Jess O'Donovan did not use those words but Eva heard them, nonetheless.

An aunt made the child-mother strong again. She stopped the bleeding and gave her tablets to banish bad dreams. No one must know she was unclean. She was a shining star. A good girl. She was told to carry her shameful secret to her grave. Otherwise, she would destroy the good name of her family forever. And so she remained a shining star.

Twenty-seven years later, in an African village, she confided her secret, and returned home ready to confront the past. But fear destroyed her and she chose death instead.

At first Eva did not understand.

"Your mother is dead," Jess said. "Sara is at peace." She made it sound like a prayer.

"Sara?"

"Sara Wallace was her name."

Eva wondered how she could breathe so calmly. When she looked down at her hands, clasped tightly in the nun's strong grip, she realised they were shaking. Jess O'Donovan's words were far away, somewhere above her head, soaring away from her. Tears glistened in the nun's eyes. "I'm so sorry, my dear, so sorry. I never realised he had contacted you until I met Marina McKeever when she was visiting her brother's family in Anaskeagh. I knew her many years ago when we were young women. She has no idea of your identity but she suspected Peter's love for you was based on some mistaken resemblance to his wife. It's important that you know the truth before this relationship can continue."

He had traced her to Ashton. He knew – that day when she sat by the river bank mourning Faye ... he knew. When he held her, dominating her with his passion, he knew. When he spoke of love, searching her heart for the same passionate response, he knew.

Soon afterwards Jess O'Donovan left. They embraced each other and said they must meet again. Eva sensed the nun's uneasiness, the worry that she had made a wrong decision. She assured Jess she was fine. She needed to know. Why expend energy on a dead search?

*   *   *

In Cherry Vale, the politician sought refuge from journalists. Behind the pampas grass and the cherry blossom tress there was a place to hide for a short while from phones that continued to ring and loud abrasive questions. A few diligent reporters still remained outside the gates but others had retreated for the night, bunkering down in the bar of the Anaskeagh Arms, swapping anecdotes and filling Hatty Beckett with rum and coke.

Lights shone behind the drawn curtains. At the top of the steps Conor waited for her. He looked drained from the media onslaught, the tension lines around his mouth deepening with suspicion as he watched her approach. "Why can't you wait until tomorrow to see my father, Beth? He's exhausted."

"I won't keep him long, Conor. As I said on the phone, we have something private to discuss."

The solicitor's eyes narrowed suspiciously as he moved into the hall. "Why not discuss it with me first? If I find out you have anything to do with the information leaked to 'Elucidate' your days in Anaskeagh are numbered."

"Don't you dare threaten me." She faced him squarely. "Your father's reputation is ruined but I had no hand, act or part in his destruction."

"Then tell me why you want to meet him?" He stopped outside a door and rapped loudly. "I insist on being present at this meeting."

"Certainly. I have no secrets to hide from anyone."

The door opened suddenly. Her uncle wore pyjamas under his dressing gown, a dull plaid pattern and matching slippers. "Leave us alone," he barked at his son. "Beth's visit will be short and private. She has worries about TrendLines that I can sort out for her."

After his son's departure, he attempted to lock the door. The key fell between them with a clang. He pushed her aside when she bent to pick it up. "I can manage, I can manage."

"Locking the door won't keep the past from being exposed." She watched him as he sank into a chair. "As I've already told Conor, I had nothing to do with the information leaked to the media. You have many enemies, Tom. One of them has effectively axed your political career."

"If you've come to gloat then you may as well leave right now." He stared coldly back at her. She could feel his fury coming towards her in waves. "By next week the media scum outside the gates will be scratching elsewhere. What's the worst that can happen? I resign and get on with my life. You don't seriously believe a few harmless land deals are going to bring the country to a halt. My reputation will stand the test of time. People won't forget what I've done for this town."

"I agree with you, Tom. A land scam is not a bad class of a scandal. It's in the cute hoor category and people can understand. But this story won't go away. When people know the real truth about you—"

"And what would that be?" he interrupted. "What new games are you playing now?"

"I came here tonight to talk about my childhood. I want you to know how it was … your touch always on my skin, your shadow walking behind me. And how, when I was no longer around to abuse, you took my sister's innocence, Sara's sweet lovely innocence, and destroyed her."

"I'm weary, Beth." He rubbed his hand across his forehead. "This farce has gone on long enough. If you don't leave this room immediately I'll have you thrown out."

"You told her about Lindsey." She continued speaking, drowning out his words. "How did you know? Even my secrets – nothing was safe from you."

"Your sister said she wanted to confront the past – and I gave it to her on a plate. What did she expect, coming here with her ridiculous accusations? Did she honestly expect me to sit and allow my reputation to be ruined by the ravings of a crazed woman?"

"And Lindsey? You built up her trust, knowing I would never have allowed you within breathing distance of any of my children."

He slapped his hand hard on the desk. "Your daughter also wanted the truth. If you're trying to destroy me you're playing a dangerous game. Stop and think wisely before you say anything else."

"I'm not going to destroy you, Tom. All I intend to do is tell the truth."

"And what truth would that be, Beth?"

"The truth about the Anaskeagh baby."

He stood up and moved swiftly towards her. For a moment she thought he was going to strike her and forced herself to stand firm. He stopped in front of her. "Bitch … I'm warning you for the last time – don't dare play games with me."

"When I tell the *real* truth those journalists outside your gates will seem like a Sunday morning prayer gathering. Remember the last time? The questions? The suspicions? How long did it take to die away?"

"Are you listening to me?" He blew out his breath in a violent gasp and gripped her wrists, gripping them so tightly that she winced with pain. Close to him she could smell his fear. She saw it in his eyes, locked memories.

"Let me remind you of the real truth, Beth. I've always had your welfare at heart, and Sara also, always in my thoughts, the pair of you. Do you think Peter Wallace would have stayed in business if I hadn't supported him financially? My money brought you and your family back from England and gave your husband an opportunity to make something of himself. Look at the business he's created here. Do you think he could have done that without my help? We're a small community, suspicious of outsiders. I smoothed the way, cut through the red tape. I even persuaded the chain store to take him on – and now – just when he has it all together, you want to ruin him. What kind of vindictive wife are you? I could lift the phone to Sam O'Grady this minute and he'll pull the plug on your pathetic factory so fast you won't have time to blink. And that's exactly what I intend to do if you dare threaten me again with your foul insinuations."

She waited until he finished, then, as if she had not heard him, she spoke softly. "Who remembers her now, I wonder? The Anaskeagh baby? *Our* baby born in the shadow of Aislin's Roof. That's where it happened, Tom. A hard cradle rocked our daughter into life."

The strength left his body. He staggered back to the chair and sank into it. When he tried to speak his voice faltered and died. He stared back at her, speechless.

"*Our* daughter," she repeated.

"You are evil incarnate." His face was swollen with anger.

"Filth. You carried it within you even as a child … the soul of evil."

"No, Tom. I carried innocence and you trampled it under your feet. And Sara too …" Her voice broke. "May God forgive you. I know I never will."

"What do you know about God?" He pulled in his breath in a shuddering gasp. "When did you ever raise your hands in prayer. Get out of my sight, this instant."

For the first time she saw him as an old man. Not elderly or stately but old with liver warts on his hands, his lips drawn across his teeth, too white and perfect for an old man's face. "She finally found the courage to face you and you destroyed her again." She stared coldly down at him. "But I'm made from sterner clay. You won't dominate me so easily. I believed I was a victim but I'm not, Tom. I'm a survivor who stayed silent for too long – but not any more."

"Jesus Christ! You're every bit as crazy as your sister. Are you trying to kill your mother?" He still laboured to control her. "Have you any idea how ill she is? She could die any minute, too much stress and her heart will give out—"

"I'm going to bring journalists to Aislin's Roof." Her voice was relentless. "I'll show them the earth where our daughter laid her head. I'll show them the rocks that sheltered us and the path I walked on my way to O'Donovan's farm. I'm going to smear your name over every newspaper in the land – and when you're in jail you'll find out how many supporters you have."

He pressed his hands to his eyes, as if to banish her from sight. Or to stem tears of shame, of regret. She would never know. As she walked towards the door the words he spoke were barely audible. "Liar … bitch. You're not the mother."

She turned the key and turned to stare at him for the last time.

"But I could have been, Tom," she said. "That's the one and only truth we both share."

*   *   *

Tom Oliver's death was a public affair, coast guards, helicopters, divers, uniting in their efforts to find his body. When his cruiser was located it was drifting, empty. The journalists speculated, suicide or death by drowning. Soon they would move on to the next story and Anaskeagh would be at peace again. A small town minding its own business.

"No news yet." Marjory was calm when she put down the phone.

"Will you come back to the bungalow with me?" Beth asked

"I'd prefer to wait here."

"You should be with your family at this time."

"My family is dead."

"I'll stay with you tonight," said Beth. "I don't want you to be alone."

"They hounded him to his death. All those questions …"

"He wasn't able to answer them, Marjory."

"Sometimes there are no answers."

The two women gazed at each other. Marjory's mouth puckered and tightened, as if she was forcing back words she needed to say. She swayed, defenceless against the sobs that racked her thin frame. Beth put her arms around her. She held her mother's brittle body and, when Marjory tried to pull away, she still clasped her firmly, securely, until the old woman's movements stilled and they cried together.

The body of Tom Oliver, when it was washed from its watery grave, would end their story, and, perhaps, it would begin another one where forgiveness was not demanded but gently passed from one to the other in silence. Life's problems were not always resolved. Sometimes, they were just contained until it was time to deliver them into the void.

CHAPTER SIXTY-ONE

The garden centre was closed for the night. Greg parked his car in the empty gravel car park and knocked on the cottage door. Annie Loughrey had spoken of a fever and he understood what she meant when his wife opened the front door. He was shocked by her appearance, her lank hair and the dull pain in her eyes.

"What's happened to you, Eva?" He followed her inside. "Why haven't you answered my phone calls?"

"I can't talk about it." She turned away from him. "I have to work this out for myself."

"Can't or won't," he asked. "Why can't you trust me to understand?"

"Not this! I'll never be able to talk to anyone about it. I don't want to. Ever—"

"Let me stay with you tonight," he said. "Just for tonight, Eva. The apartment … it's a difficult place to be on my own."

"Are you blaming yourself for that politician's death?" she asked.

"Who else is there to blame?" he replied

They slept together fitfully in her bed. Friends. It had been easy. Her grief separated them, killed any desire that might have flared when their bodies touched. Peter Wallace came in the early morning. When Greg opened the front door the two men made no attempt to hide the hostility that flared between them. To rattle antlers, to butt and charge and roar victorious would have been a simple way of dealing with the situation. Infinitely preferable to engaging in conversation with this stranger whom his wife refused to meet.

This middle-aged man with his haggard face and unkempt hair bore little resemblance to the suave person Greg had seen greeting Eva in Goodlarches. Nor did he look like a smooth business man who invested money in struggling garden centres. He was a man who could not sleep, an artist whose painting of Murtagh's River hung in his wife's cottage.

"I've got to see her." Peter Wallace was insistent. "Tell her I'm not leaving until she gives me a chance to explain."

"If it's business it can wait for another day," said Greg. "If it's something else – it can wait forever."

"For Christ's sake! What are you? Her bodyguard? This is between Eva and me. You may think you're helping her but you haven't a clue. It's essential that I talk to her – just once. Then I'll be out of your lives for ever."

"That's not long enough," he replied but she came from behind him and said, "He's right, Greg. We have to talk."

He watched them walk towards the lake. They faced each other. Angry gesticulations. Greg wondered if she would raise her hand and strike him, willed her to lash out and, when she did so, he saw Peter Wallace flinch and grasp her shoulders. As her head moved back in submission, Greg knew he had to leave.

There was nothing left to hold him here. In this fertile garden, they had once loved against a crumbling stone wall and conceived their child. The swans raking the air with their wings. Unrecognisable now. Everything gone, everything.

*   *   *

Peter was leaving, moving to Tuscany, a dream at last realised. He stared bleakly at the water, watching the early morning mist lift above the lake. In a small medieval hamlet he would live quietly among hills and vineyards. A 'For Sale' sign had been erected outside Havenstone and the land at the rear of the house sold to Judith Hansen.

His daughter had stayed silent when he said there would always be a welcome waiting for her – but when he offered his address she had accepted it. He hoped some day Lindsey would come and they could become friends or, maybe in time, he shrugged, they could find a different way to know each other.

Now, he had come to Eva demanding relief, a chance to unburden. She had refused to answer his letters, his phone calls, and she felt his determination, his passion undiminished as he forced her to listen, to understand what had happened between them.

His sister-in-law had revealed Sara's story to him before

she moved to Anaskeagh. Afterwards, unable to rest, he had contacted Jess O'Donovan and tried to draw further information from her. Jess had been guarded in her replies but she mentioned a small Wicklow village set in a valley and a garden centre where Eva had worked until her marriage. He searched and found Ashton.

In Wind Fall, Liz was happy to talk about her daughter. He saw photographs on the wall of the breakfast room, school photographs, a graduation, a wedding, a young mother with a baby in her arms. Eva's life was secure and he had no desire to intrude any further. But something, a restlessness, a need to know more about her, made him return. He had found her sitting by the river. Her grief was raw enough to touch, to understand.

"I wanted to help you," he said. "You have to believe me. That was all I wanted in the beginning. To play a small part in your life. I'd be giving something back to Sara, making some kind of restitution for the pain we'd caused each other throughout our marriage. But … I didn't realise I was already in love with you." His eyes darkened with yearning. "I won't make excuses for what happened between us. You brought me back to life and I think … I know I did the same to you. It was incredible—"

"But did you once stop to think of the pain you'd cause if I found out?" she demanded. Passion had turned to ash. Only her anger burned, searing him. "Or was that part of the thrill? The ultimate hit. Who did you think I was? Your dead wife?"

The colour drained from his face. He moved closer to her. "I won't let you distort our love. You can't destroy what we shared—"

"Shared! When have you ever shared anything?" She was not prepared to offer him mercy. "How dare you come here demanding my understanding – my forgiveness – when you've destroyed me with your obsessions." Her hand flamed against his cheek when she struck him and he held her, his face ravaged as he tried to prevent her walking away.

"Do you want to cut into my flesh, Eva?" he asked, his lips almost touching hers. "Will that help? Will it?"

"Nothing that gives you relief will help me. You deceived me from the beginning, just as you deceived yourself. You were in love with a ghost ... or some ideal woman you created. But not with me ... you were never in love with me!" She believed he understood, even when he shook his head in vehement denial.

"I love you, Eva, only you. You have to believe me. You have no idea ... please let me explain."

"I never want to set eyes on you again." She forced herself from him, afraid she would collapse before she reached the cottage, knowing that if she believed him it would draw her back again into his consuming love. She walked away from the jagged sound of his grief – and from a truth that no longer mattered. Cobwebs glistened in the rising sun, slinging links between the dark reeds, a fragile chain that swayed and broke when the swans stirred in their nest.

Above the fireplace in her cottage the painting of the river had disappeared. Another one hung on the same spot. Grainy rocks bathed in moonlight. The brush strokes gave the impression of boulders flung upwards in some violent eruption before coming to rest in an uneasy alignment. His farewell gift.

*   *   *

It nagged Greg continually, this sense of recognition. The answer came to him the following afternoon. A straightforward and boring interview about a factory strike. Another recollection clicked into place. Peter Wallace had been married to a photographer. He had interviewed her during the Oldport motorway protests. An exhibition of photographs, swans swimming down the centre of a road. She died soon afterwards. Her book launch had been a posthumous affair.

He replayed the interview in the 'Elucidate' library. A tall blonde woman, bloodless, her personality oddly at variance with the energy of her photography. She suddenly reminded him of Eva. He freeze framed her image. The same high flat cheek bones dominating their faces, the same lost eyes.

Jean Wilson suggested he wait in the cottage. It would not be long before Eva returned. She was designing a water feature for a client and had phoned to say she was on her way.

"How is she?" he asked.

"As busy as ever." Jean replied.

"That's not what I meant."

"It's not my business to pass personal comments, Mr Enright."

"I care about her, Jean. I can't help worrying about her."

The sales assistant unlocked the door of the cottage and

stood back for him to enter. "If you're that worried stay with her and block your ears when she says she doesn't need you. You're not the only one who worries."

"Birthing stones," Eva said. He was standing in front of the painting when she entered.

"What do you mean?" he asked.

"Isn't that what it suggests? Primitive creation?"

"It's more like the aftermath of an earthquake."

"Same difference." Her voice was expressionless. "He's going to Italy. A one way ticket. Why are you here?"

"We need to talk."

"What about?"

"Us. Divorce. Marriage. Whatever." He wanted to shake some life into her, rouse her to anger, anything to banish the emptiness in her expression.

"If you want a divorce I won't stand in your way."

"I'm not talking about me. Do you want to be free to marry this man you love? If that's it then say so for Christ's sake. Go to Italy with him because I can't stand the way we're living any longer."

"I don't love him." She drummed her fists off her thighs, her hands moving fast over the rough denim.

"You must tell me what's wrong." He held her still, trying vainly to calm her distress.

"You wouldn't understand. I can't understand it myself."

"I love you, Eva. Nothing else matters. Can you hear what I'm saying to you?"

She stood beside him and stared up at the painting. "I don't know who I am?" she whispered. "I'm lost ... I can't find my way back."

He took the book from his briefcase and laid it on the table. She stared at the title, *Silent Songs from an African Village*. The author's photograph was on the back cover.

"Is that the reason?" he asked. "Did Peter Wallace try to make you his wife?"

She sat down on a chair and looked at the photograph than pushed the book from her, a child's gesture of rejection, shuddering when she heard the thud of the hardback cover hitting the floor.

"Tell me!" he demanded. He forced her to look at him, helplessly reaching towards the woman he had known and loved.

"My mother." Her voice trembled on the edge of hysteria. For an instant he thought he had misheard. "My murdering dead mother."

She reached down and picked up the book, tore the dust jacket from the cover and crumpled it into a tight ball. "It was my mother he loved all the time." Still clutching the cover she began to sob. "Can't you understand why I don't want to talk about it? Can't you … can't you … can't you?"

When she grew calm again she smoothed the crumpled dust jacket and stared at the image of a woman she would never know. She told Greg her story. The big story. The ultimate scoop. The one story he would never tell.

*   *   *

They climbed together towards the summit of Anaskeagh Head. Below them, kittiwakes swooped and turned, skittish birds fanning out above the murmuring caves. A cormorant shrieked, nosediving into the waves then swooping upwards, wings outstretched, its body etched like a cross against the firmament. Waves crashed upwards. Eva watched them break over the rocks until all that remained of the ferment was the sting of salt on her lips. They continued climbing, dipping and rising with the lie of the path.

She was tireless in her search. On the way down they found it. Aislin's Roof. The ground beneath the boulders was mossy and dank. Eva moved forward. Large putty-coloured fungi mulched beneath her feet. The rank smell of dead vegetation seeped upwards, a curiously private smell that belonged to private places. From her mother's womb she had been forced into this odorous, brooding landscape. She imagined a child staggering into the reaches of wild ferns, knowing she would never escape the clutches of that dark, dreadful night.

Eva pulled grass with her fingers. The rough blades cut deep into her hands. She called her mother's name – Sara … Sara … Sara. She began to cry. It was Faye's cry that rose from her lips, a whimpering, bewildered, new born cry that understood only the spill of light on bare flesh, the flow of wind through the trees, the crashing tide, the song of birds, the earth beneath. And pain. A splintering red light filling her head. The cry rose and fell and faded. She touched her forehead. Her hair felt limp and damp. No blood.

Rising to her feet, Eva moved forward from the shade of Aislin's Roof. The sun shone above the headland, a molten pulse beating against the waves. Her legs trembled as she was forced to a standstill at the edge of a steep rocky shelf. No safe footholds to steady her. Nothing but a sheer slice of granite between her and the drop below. Greg moved ahead, lowering his body until he was secure on the flat plateau of rock. Then he held out a hand to his wife and guided her downwards to safety.

Duncan Osbourne was not just Eva's solicitor. He was one of her father's closest friends and she had known him since she was a child. In his office, which always reminded her of an elegant Georgian drawing room, she sank carefully into a fragile chair. He smiled across his desk at her.

"You look lovelier then ever, Eva."

"Thank you, Duncan."

"From what Steve tells me you're running the garden centre with great success. Your dear departed grandmother would be most pleased."

"Yes, everything has worked out quite well."

"Good … good. And dear Greg is in good health, I hope? Did I read somewhere recently that he's now writing a book? How very interesting. I shall look forward to an autographed copy. Tell him he's sadly missed on 'Elucidate'."

"I will of course, Duncan." The mercy of small talk was a stalwart bridge.

"Well, Eva, let us get down to the business in hand." Her solicitor's smile was replaced by a businesslike expression.

"It's obvious that your relationship with Mr Wallace is extremely contentious – but he is most insistent that I carry out his orders. I sincerely hope you will not continue to give me a difficult time over this matter."

"I've already told you how I feel, Duncan. Mr Wallace and I do not owe each other anything. This question of recompense is demeaning and I refuse to have anything to do with it."

"Eva … Eva." Duncan tapped the tips of his fingers together and sighed the sigh of one who has battled valiantly but in vain on a bloodied field. "At your request, he reluctantly severed your business partnership before he left for Italy. But, as I've already tried to explain, this is not a business investment he wishes to make. Sara Wallace was your birth mother and you are the rightful inheritor of her estate. Your insistence on refusing this bequest surprises me as much as it distresses Mr Wallace – so I hope you will accept his alternative offer. He has instructed me to bequeath his late wife's estate to your future children and, in the eventuality of there being no natural heir to the estate, the bequest will be donated to a charity of his choice."

Duncan glanced down at the documents on his desk and handed the top one to her. "You can read the details of his proposal in your own time and notify me as to your intentions. I'm anxious to bring this matter to a satisfactory conclusion. To be frank with you, Eva, dealing with clients like you may be an invigorating experience – but refusing to claim an unexpected legacy does upset the natural order of things in a solicitor's life. Is there anything you wish to ask me before we conclude our business?"

"What if I refuse to accept this bequest."

Duncan's eyes rested discreetly on her stomach before he rose to escort her from his office. "Somehow, Eva, I don't think that eventuality will arise."

*   *   *

A late afternoon hush hung over the cottage, disturbed occasionally by the arrival of a car or the voices of customers strolling through the garden centre. A year had passed since their journey to the headland. The months that followed had been painful as they slowly, tentatively, rebuilt their marriage.

The child sleeping in a carry-cot stirred. His eyelids fluttered, as if a deep sweet dream had been disturbed. Greg leaned down to rest his finger on the boy's cheek. He stroked the wispy blonde hair and listened to the even sound of his breathing, wondering how it was possible to endure the terror and the joy that existed in equal measure when he thought about the responsibility that rested upon himself and Eva for the future of this tiny infant.

He returned to his computer and turned his attention to the task in hand. His book was almost finished, with only the final edit and checking of footnotes to be completed. Eva was right. Corruption could be just as effectively exposed in the company of swans and hanging baskets of begonias.

*   *   *

The quiet side road was untouched by the building development taking place in the nearby village and the cottage garden was in full bloom when Beth parked her car at the entrance to the garden centre. She entered a domed interior where wooden stands overflowed with bedding plants and heathers. A middle-aged woman directed her outside. The land had been partitioned into avenues of shrubs and rose bushes and, beyond the neatly arranged displays, sloped gradually towards a lake.

A young woman walked towards her. Her hair tossed lightly in the breeze, an outdoor face, tanned and lightly sprinkled with freckles.

"Can I help you?" she asked, smiling.

Beth gazed into her eyes, so achingly familiar – into the vibrant gaze of what might have been – what should have been. She raised her hand to her lips to stifle an involuntary cry, then allowed the memory of Sara to rest peacefully among the scented flowers.

"We met once before." She spoke softly, tremulously. "You won't remember me, Eva … it was a long, long time ago."

ACKNOWLEDGEMENTS

For those who shared the days of uncertainty and encouraged me to write the two words – The End – with conviction I'd like to extend my sincerest thanks. In particular, my husband, Sean, whose support never wavered, and my family, Tony, Ciara and Michelle, who always had time to listen. To my extended family and friends, those who write and understand the compulsion – and those who know the right moment to ring and remind me that there is much more to life than a computer – a special thank you.

I'd like to extend my appreciation to Sean McCann, who had a strong influence on my decision to become a writer, and to my agent, Faith O'Grady, for her encouragement. Thanks also to Deirdre Considine, Mary Coffey, Cara Walsh, Michael McDonagh and Ronnie Norton, for responding so willingly with advice.

To the team from New Island who made the publishing process seem so painless, especially my publisher, Edwin Higel, marketing manager, Joseph Hoban, and Suzanne Barnes – thank you for your commitment. Finally, I find myself in the rather unique position of thanking my editor and daughter, Ciara Considine, for her professional and incisive editing of my work. For both of us this was an unusual experience, which she handled with care and sensitivity.